BETRAYED BY DESIRE

Damien stared into her eyes, trying to decide if she was frightened enough to heed him. He saw wariness, and a generous measure of contempt, but nothing akin to the naked fear he had witnessed earlier. Apricot light was streaming through the carriage window and spilling across her pale skin, revealing a coral cast on her cheeks and lips. It was strange, but the natural blush of her lips in the soft morning light seemed far more appealing than the artfully applied stain she had worn the night before as Celia Reed. Her breath was shallow, and he was vaguely aware of the scent of jasmine and roses. He let go of her chin to lightly caress the warm silk of her cheek.

"If I ever hear of you spying again, Josephine, I will take great pleasure in punishing you personally. Do you understand?"

A flicker of fear ignited in her eyes. Damien was not sure if it was kindled by his threat or his touch, but he drew perverse satisfaction from it.... His tongue grazed languidly over her and she gasped in shock. He responded by boldly invading her mouth, kissing her deeply, robbing her of breath and thought and even the ability to protest....

Also by Karyn Monk:

SURRENDER TO A STRANGER

The Rebel and the Redcoat

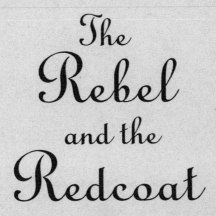

Karyn Monk

BANTAM BOOKS

New York   Toronto   London   Sydney   Auckland

THE REBEL AND THE REDCOAT
A Bantam Fanfare Book/May 1996

ISBN 0-553-57421-3
Published simultaneously in the United States and Canada

Bantam Books are published by Bantam Books, a division of Bantam
Doubleday Dell Publishing Group, Inc. Its trademark, consisting of the words
"Bantam Books" and the portrayal of a rooster, is Registered in U.S. Patent
and Trademark Office and in other countries. Marca Registrada. Bantam
Books, 1540 Broadway, New York, New York 10036.

PRINTED IN THE UNITED STATES OF AMERICA
RAD   0 9 8 7 6 5 4 3 2 1

To my dearest Philip
who fills my life with light.

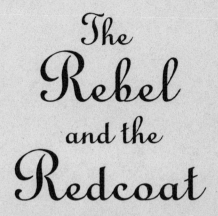

The
Rebel
and the
Redcoat

storm the house, and Jo knew she would never have time to reload before they reached her. That they would brutally kill her was certain. What was less certain was whether they would find Anne and the children. She bit down hard on her cheek as a sickening mixture of raw fear and cold determination flooded through her. Blood, warm and sharp tasting, seeped onto her tongue.

She scanned the yard, wondering which of the four would be in range first. If they did not kill her immediately, she must do everything in her power to distract them from the house. Her greatest terror was that after killing her, the savages would set fire to the buildings. Instead of being slaughtered, Anne and the children would slowly burn to death. She forced the ghastly image from her mind, fearing it would snap the taut thread of control she was so carefully maintaining. No, they would not burn the house, she assured herself. All she had to do was kill one, and the rest would run away like the vile, cowardly animals they were. She readjusted her cramped grip on the musket and inhaled another breath of blisteringly hot air.

Dear Lord, she pleaded silently, *please spare Anne and the children.*

Damien scanned the fields of unripe corn, vainly searching for anything that looked ready to eat. There was nothing but acre upon acre of young, leafy stalks bearing thin green ears. He cursed. He knew he would have no choice but to confiscate the produce of the farm's kitchen garden. It was dangerous to try to accomplish that alone, especially since it seemed likely the farm was owned by rebel sympathizers. But the two soldiers who had started out with him this morning on this foraging expedition had fallen ill with dysentery, and he had been forced to order them back to camp. His friend Gil had been most reluctant to leave him alone, but ill as he was he was useless to Damien anyway, so he had finally relented.

Damien's jaw tightened as he stared at the sea of green corn. The lack of decent food had reduced nearly one third of his men to illness. That, combined with the malaria and the ungodly heat of this wretched colony, had left his legion severely debilitated. He swore silently. He could not lead sick men into battle. His gaze moved to the little white farmhouse sitting quietly at the edge of the field. There was a cow grazing idly beside it. Fresh meat would do his men good. They could make a thick stew, and give his sick soldiers broth to help them regain their strength. Perhaps the farm would even have some chickens. He nudged Glory forward, grimly encouraged by that possibility. Loyalist or rebel, he would take whatever he could from this farm. The needs of his men were far more important than the needs of a few simple colonists.

He rode back into the woods, quietly circling toward the farmhouse through a dense veil of trees. Suddenly there was a flash of movement in the yard. He reined in Glory and tried to spot what had caught his attention.

The cow continued to graze lazily, looking hot and bored. Damien frowned and slowly urged Glory closer. Perhaps it had been a dog—which would be unfortunate, since a dog would announce his arrival long before he was actually at the door.

Just as he was about to move into the open, something streaked from a tree over to a barrel near the barn. Damien halted Glory and loaded his musket. All was quiet and still again. He waited patiently, his blood surging through his veins. Sure enough, after a moment there was another flash of movement in the yard. This time he understood what he was seeing. He counted four Indians slowly approaching the quiet little farmhouse, preparing to unleash their particularly brutal form of warfare on the unsuspecting colonists inside. The thought filled him with a mixture of fury and revulsion.

For a moment he was uncertain what to do. The Indian tribes in the colonies were largely allies of the British. Although he loathed their methods, they had been incredibly effective in terrorizing the countryside of both the northern and southern colonies, substantially reducing the number of rebels who would otherwise have made war on British soldiers. But many tribes were using this war as an opportunity to massacre white colonists no matter whether they were Patriots or Loyalists.

As he swiftly considered his options, the Indian hiding behind the barrel decided the time for stealth was past. He let out a high-pitched cry and began to race toward the house, furiously swinging his tomahawk. The brave was beyond the range of his weapon, but perhaps he could create a diversion. He leveled his musket, taking aim. Suddenly a shot from the house tore through the air, striking the attacking Indian in the chest. The savage's war cry diminished into a pathetic whimper as he collapsed onto the ground.

A deafening cacophony of bloodthirsty screams erupted from the remaining three braves as they ran to the house and stormed inside. Damien leapt off his horse and sprinted into the yard, throwing himself down behind an old wagon. Seconds later one of the Indians emerged from the house, dragging a struggling young woman behind him.

She was fighting her captor with all her might, shrieking as she clawed at his naked skin. Her fury would have been impressive had she not been so hopelessly outmatched. The Indian quickly grew impatient with her futile show of strength. He raised his arm and smashed the back of his fist against her face. The girl cried out as she fell to the ground. For a few seconds she lay motionless. The Indian towered over her, contemplating what next to do with her. Then he reached down and grabbed her by her hair, roughly shaking it loose from its pins. A thick length of blond silk spilled across her back.

Damien watched in horrified fascination as the brave leisurely dragged his fingers through the lustrous mass. Its glorious flaxen color reminded Damien of a wheat field drenched in sunlight. Evidently the Indian appreciated its uncommon beauty. He began to twist the sunlit silk around his dark fist, binding the girl to him by her hair. Then he jerked her up from the ground, forcing her to her knees in front of him. He slowly unwound the coil of her hair until it stretched into a taut skein that caught the white-hot glare of the afternoon sun, turning it into a shimmering banner of gold. The brave let out a cry of elation as he raised his tomahawk with a thickly muscled arm.

For a moment everything was still. Damien stared down the barrel of his musket at the dark, muscular warrior, at the banner of gold he held, and finally, at the ashen face of the girl who knelt helplessly before him. She did not cry, or scream, or beg for mercy. In fact, her expression seemed calm, almost tranquil. It was as if she accepted what was about to happen to her, despite the terror that must have been flooding through her.

In that frozen second, he knew he had never before seen such extraordinary beauty and raw courage.

The warrior let out a scream as the blade of his tomahawk carved a silvery arc in the sunlight, slicing down toward the girl. Damien squeezed the trigger. A shot ripped through the air, and a burst of scarlet bloomed on the Indian's bronzed chest, his cry of victory reduced to a startled, gurgling gasp. Blood poured from his mouth in a crimson stream. He looked around in confusion, vainly trying to understand where the shot had come from. His tomahawk fell from his grip. Then he dropped heavily to the ground, pulling the girl down with him, his fist still clenching the thick twist of gold that in another second would have been his.

The sound of the shot brought the remaining two braves running out of the house, dragging a frantically struggling boy. One of the Indians was carrying a musket. He looked in shock at his friend lying on the ground, then scanned the surrounding area. His keen glance fell on the wagon. Then his eyes met Damien's.

Damien threw down his empty musket and reached for the loaded pistol in his belt. The Indian was already racing toward him, screaming with wild fury, taking aim with the musket. The weapon exploded. Damien rolled, but it was a second too late. The musket ball tore into his side, ripping him open.

The pain was excruciating. Hot blood soaked through his shirt and into the heavy scarlet wool of his jacket, pulsing rapidly over his fingers as he attempted to put pressure on the wound. The Indian saw his predicament and smiled. He threw down his empty musket and reached for the sharp hunting knife sheathed at his thigh.

In that instant Jo rose from the ground and grabbed the tomahawk dropped by the brave who had tried to scalp her. The Indian holding Samuel shouted a warning, but Jo had already reached the brave. She lifted the tomahawk high above her head and let out a terrible scream of rage. Then she swung the blade down with every shred of her being, burying it deep into the muscle and bone of his supple, naked back.

The Indian turned and stared at her in astonishment. Yet he did not fall. She took a few steps back from him, suddenly appalled by what she had done. The mortally injured brave staggered toward her, moaning softly, speaking to her in a language she did not understand. Blood began to run down his legs. He groaned and clumsily sank to his knees in the dirt. His dark eyes gave her one final, questioning look before he sighed and fell forward onto his face.

The remaining Indian instantly released his hold on Samuel. Her brother used this opportunity to attack him with a frenzy of kicks and punches. With a fist to his jaw, the brave sent him crashing into the wall of the farmhouse. Then he moved toward Jo, his face twisted with rage, a knife gleaming in his hand.

Jo backed away. She turned to run, but tripped over the body of the man she had just killed and went sprawling onto the ground.

Damien fought to stay conscious. It would be so much easier to simply close his eyes and let the sickening blackness take over, but if he did that, the girl would die. Slowly, using both hands, he lifted his heavy pistol and trained it on the advancing Indian.

Take this, you goddamn bastard.

Damien fired.

Jo had been lying, paralyzed with terror, on the ground, waiting for the knife to carve into her back. Despite her determination not to show her fear, a sob escaped her lips. She was going to die. When the Indian fell on her, crushing her with his weight, she screamed, a scream born of utter despair. She had failed. Now Anne and Lucy and Samuel would die. The warrior jerked a few times, then was still. Jo lay frozen beneath him, uncertain what had happened.

Damien dropped his pistol and collapsed against the ground, cursing with every breath he took. He realized his wound was severe, and that he was losing a tremendous amount of blood. He rolled onto his back and vainly tried to stanch the flow with his hands. In a moment or two he would be so weak he would be past the point of caring whether or not he bled to death. It was strange, he mused grimly, but somehow when he had come to the colonies he had not imagined his death would be at the hands of an Indian as he tried to save a simple farm girl.

"Are you hurt, Jo?" demanded Samuel anxiously. He moved to where she lay buried beneath the dead warrior.

"I don't think so," she managed, her voice thin and trembling. "Help me get him off."

Samuel grabbed one of the Indian's arms and pulled. Jo pushed until the dead man's body moved enough for her to scramble out from underneath it. The minute she was free she rushed to the injured man who had saved her life.

Her throat constricted as she stared down at him. She took in the scarlet color of his torn jacket, the white waistcoat stained ruby with blood, and the filthy white of his breeches. "Oh, dear Lord," she gasped. "You're a *redcoat!*"

Damien forced his eyes open to look at the woman who had cost him his life. Her eyes were the color of the sky, as clear and brilliant a shade of blue as he had ever seen. Her sunlit hair tumbled wildly over her shoulders, forming a golden veil of silk around her. *It was worth it*, he decided absently as pain clouded his mind.

She did not move closer, but continued to stare at him, her expression both wary and fearful. He frowned, wondering why she was afraid. And then her words pierced through the dark haze.

Christ, he thought as blackness drowned his senses.

A bloody Patriot.

Chapter 2

*I*s he going to die?" demanded Samuel.

"I don't know," Jo replied uneasily. "Help me get him into the barn."

The soldier had slipped into a state of semiconsciousness, but somehow Jo and Samuel managed to get him on his feet. Together the two of them half dragged, half stumbled with him into the barn, with Jo bearing most of the burden of his weight. The soldier swore vehemently as they moved him. He cursed them with terrible words Jo had never heard before, but she knew it was because of the pain and so she tried her best to ignore it. They moved him to a thick mound of straw and lowered him onto it as carefully as they could. Jo knelt beside him. She removed his heavy sword and cast it aside before starting to peel away the blood-soaked wool of his jacket.

"Samuel, go into the house and tell Anne and Lucy it is safe to come out," she instructed quickly. She set to work on the shiny gold buttons of the soldier's waistcoat. "Tell Anne to bring a needle and thread, clean bandages, hot water and a blanket out to the barn immediately."

Samuel stared blankly at the injured soldier, who had resumed cursing fiercely as Jo pulled at the bloodied fabric of his waistcoat.

"Tell Anne to also bring a jug of whiskey," snapped Jo, not wanting her brother to hear any more of the soldier's profanity. "Hurry!"

Samuel ran for the door.

Jo bit her lip with dismay as she opened the soldier's waistcoat and saw the warm red pool pulsing rapidly over his torn shirt. She inhaled deeply to calm herself, then reached up to unfasten the buttons.

Damien's hand snaked around her wrist with bruising force, making her cry out in surprise.

"What, exactly, are you planning to do to me?" he demanded harshly.

Jo held her breath as she stared at him. His gray eyes were clouded with pain, but there was a dark intensity to them that was openly threatening. She knew he was nearly incapacitated by his wound, and the blood that continued to pulse out of him as he lay there was making him terribly weak. Yet even in this helpless condition there was a dangerous quality to him. His grip on her was strong and relentless, and the gaze he held her with was intimidating.

"I am going to tend to your wound," she told him, trying to keep her voice even.

He looked at her with faintly amused skepticism. "Why?"

"Because if I don't, you will die," she informed him brusquely. She tried to wrench her aching wrist free.

He responded by tightening his grip on her and pulling her down even closer to him. "And why should my death displease you?" he demanded softly.

His pain was extreme, she could feel it in the bone-crushing strength of his fingers and in his uneven, labored breathing. She searched the gray ice of his eyes, trying to understand why he would want to punish the one who sought to help him. And there, beneath the wariness and the clouds of pain, she saw a piercing glint of fear. Suddenly she understood his need to frighten her. If she did not help him, he would die.

This man was not used to someone having that kind of power over him.

She hesitated before answering. She sensed he would know if she lied, and she had to gain his trust if he was to allow her to help him. "Your death wouldn't displease me overmuch," she admitted. The implications of her nursing a British soldier were terrifying. If he were discovered, she would be arrested and tried for treason. The shame she would bring on her family, who were all vehement Patriots, could never be washed away, not in a hundred years. If he died now, she could simply bury him in the fields and no one would ever know he had been here.

But this redcoat had risked his life so she could live. If not for him, her mangled body would now be lying bleeding in the yard, and Anne and the children would be screaming in helpless terror as they burned to death inside the farmhouse. This man had saved them all. She could not abandon him to his injuries, regardless of the uniform he wore.

"But you were wounded while saving my life," she continued in a matter-of-fact voice that completely belied her struggle with her decision. "Therefore, I would like to make an effort to save you."

He continued to stare at her warily, obviously unconvinced. "So you can turn me over to the tender care of your rebel army?" he spat, his voice dripping with sarcasm.

Jo stiffened at the fury of his accusation. She had not thought about what she would do with him if he recovered. There was no question it was her duty to turn him over to the authorities. She considered this a moment, and then shrugged her shoulders.

"I had not really thought about it. Perhaps I will do a poor job of it, and you will not live."

Damien frowned, wondering if she thought that possibility was somehow reassuring. He searched her sky-blue eyes, which seemed so young and open and guileless. When had he ever looked into eyes like that before? A wave of pain surged through him, overwhelming in its brutal intensity.

He inhaled quickly and clenched down hard on his jaw, struggling to gain control of it. After a moment he expelled the breath he had been holding. He opened his eyes to see the girl watching him, her face pale and drawn. Evidently she was not unaffected by his pain. Then he felt the delicate bones of her wrist twist within his savage grip. Perhaps it was her own pain that caused her to wince.

He did not know if he could trust her. Yet it would appear he had little choice. It was either submit to the tender mercies of this rebel farm girl, or lie on the filthy floor of this barn and bleed to death. Neither choice was particularly appealing, but he supposed the first was somewhat preferable to the latter. He reached out and wrapped his other bloodstained hand around her other wrist, then pulled her down so close he could feel her shallow, frightened breathing puff lightly against his cheek.

"I will have your word that you will not turn me over to the rebels," he stated softly.

She looked at him in disbelief. "You are hardly in a position to bargain, redcoat," she informed him flatly.

He smiled, vaguely wondering why she did not struggle to free herself from his intimate embrace. "True," he admitted. "But if you cannot give me your word that you will not turn me over, then I will not allow you to tend to my wound."

She stared at him in shock. "But you will die!"

Her heart was beating so rapidly he could almost feel it throb against his chest. He knew it was the loss of blood that was making him focus on such ridiculously insignificant things. He relaxed his hold on her and sighed, feeling all at once incredibly weary. "I would rather die on the floor of this barn and get it over with, than sit rotting in one of your squalid Yankee prisons," he informed her bitterly.

Silence stretched between them as Damien waited for her answer. He had released his hold on her, but she continued to hover over him, her eyes filled with uncertainty, her breath blowing softly against his cheek as she wrestled with her decision. After a moment he closed his eyes, past giving a damn whether she tended to him or not. The pain was starting to ease, and somehow he sensed that was not a good thing.

"Very well."

He opened his eyes, uncertain he had heard her correctly. "Very well, what?" he demanded.

"You have my word, redcoat," she announced reluctantly. "I will not turn you in."

Damien regarded her with skepticism. She could be lying to him. He had to be sure. "Swear it," he persisted. "Before God."

Jo cast him a scornful look. What did a redcoat know about God? "I have already given you my word, redcoat—"

"Swear it," repeated Damien harshly, "or leave me. You choose."

Jo scowled. "Fine. I swear to you before God that I will not turn you in."

They stared at each other in silence a moment, each acknowledging the gravity of her oath. Then Jo straightened and set to work unfastening the buttons of his shirt.

She stripped away the last layer of blood-soaked fabric that covered him, revealing a deep, pulsing wound on the left side of his abdomen. The torn flesh surrounding where the musket ball had entered was charred black, and bright red blood gurgled from the hole. She quickly wadded up the front of his shirt and pressed it firmly against him. Then she gently shifted him onto his side, praying feverishly that the ball had exited through his back. A black hole in the bloodied fabric of his jacket confirmed it had, and she uttered a quick prayer of thanks. If the ball had remained buried within him, she would never have been able to remove it, and he would certainly have died.

Very carefully, she eased him out of his jacket and waistcoat. The wadded front of his shirt was now drenched with blood, so she pressed the clean part of his waistcoat to the wound and gently stripped the shirt over his shoulder and down his arm. As she pulled the fabric across his back, a gasp of shock escaped her lips.

"What is it?" he snapped.

"These scars——" she managed, aghast. Dozens of white lines crisscrossed his body in a thick web, stretching a pale, horrible pattern across the bronzed skin of his back.

"Your concern for me is touching, madam," he grated out stiffly. "But I would ask that you focus on my new wounds, and not concern yourself with the old ones."

His irritation pulled her attention back to her task. She swallowed her revulsion as she pressed the wadded cloth of his jacket firmly against the wound at his back, applying pressure to both sides of him in an effort to control the bleeding.

"Jo—are you hurt?" called Anne breathlessly as she rushed into the barn.

Damien looked up to see a tall, red-haired woman staring at him, her expression horrified. In one hand she carried a basket, in the other, an earthen jug. Beside her stood the boy who had tried to fight the Indians, holding a steaming kettle and a blanket. Next to him was a little blond girl, who clutched a metal basin protectively against her chest.

"It's all right, Annie," said Jo calmly. "He isn't going to hurt us. Bring me the bandages."

Anne did not move. "But Jo," she stammered, "you cannot mean to help this man! He is *a British soldier!*" She made it sound as if this were something unspeakably evil.

Jo looked down at the redcoat, who was watching her. His gray eyes met hers calmly. There was no challenge there, only resignation. Anne was right. The man she was helping was a British soldier. Nobody needed to tell Jo what evil, sadistic butchers the redcoats were. After all, they had murdered her father. At any moment they could slaughter her brothers in battle, or burn her and Anne and the children off the farm. If she let this one die, that was simply one less vicious, thieving murderer she and her family had to worry about.

She bit her lip and stared hard into his eyes, trying to discern if there was evil lurking there. She saw nothing but the steady, pain-shrouded gaze of a man who was virtually past caring whether he lived or died. She pressed more firmly against his wounds. "He saved my life, Annie," she stated quietly. Hot scarlet blood soaked through the wadded cloth and wet her fingers. "He saved *all* our lives," she continued fiercely. She turned to look at her brother's wife. "We owe it to him to help him."

"If I help you save him, I am helping a man who may someday try to kill Benjamin," Anne pointed out. "Or Abraham, or Elias. You cannot ask such a thing of me." She slowly placed the basket and jug on the ground. "I'm sorry," she whispered, casting a quick, guilty look at Damien. "May God forgive me." She turned abruptly and hurried out of the barn.

Jo swallowed. The redcoat's wounds were severe, and she had been counting on Anne to help her with him. "Lucy," she called firmly, "please fetch that basket and jug for me."

Her little sister immediately picked up the requested items and brought them to her, depositing them onto the ground along with the basin she held.

"Thank you." She looked over at her scowling brother. "Samuel, you may put the kettle and blanket down over here," she instructed, "and then you both may go."

Samuel walked over and threw the blanket down beside her. "I ain't leaving you alone with no lobsterback," he declared.

"Don't say 'ain't,'" ordered Jo. She quickly exchanged the blood-soaked waistcoat and jacket for clean rags, which she wadded up and pressed hard against the soldier's wounds. "If you wish to stay, then you must help. If you don't want to help, then leave."

Samuel hesitated, clearly torn. "But Jo, he's a redcoat. We shouldn't help him. He's the enemy."

Jo looked down at the soldier, whose icy gray eyes still watched her. "Today he is not the enemy," she countered, her gaze holding his. "Today he is the man who saved our lives." She emptied some water from the kettle into the basin and began to carefully clean his wounds. The redcoat winced, but remained silent.

"What was he doing here in the first place?" demanded Samuel. He looked down at the soldier with open contempt. "He was about to raid our farm, to steal everything we have and burn us out. Why, the woods are probably crawling with his lobsterback friends, just waiting to make their move. They could attack us at any moment, and he would just stand by and let them kill us!"

Damien felt the girl's hands hesitate. It was obvious she had not considered the possibility that there could be more British soldiers in the area.

"Are there other soldiers with you?" she demanded sharply, her blue eyes searching his.

"No," lied Damien without the slightest hesitation. Any information he revealed could easily be passed on to the local militia and jeopardize the safety of his men. "I got separated from my regiment over a week ago. I am alone."

The girl studied him uncertainly. "What were you doing here?"

"I was going to take from you," admitted Damien. "Food. Nothing more. But I was not going to harm you."

"As if stealing our food isn't harming us!" sneered Samuel.

Suddenly a terrifying possibility occurred to Jo. "The men from your regiment are undoubtedly looking for you," she speculated. "If they find you here, they will raid the house and kill us all."

"No," stated Damien quietly. "They would not touch you."

Jo gave a bitter laugh as she continued to clean his wound. "You must think I'm just an ignorant farm girl, to believe such a lie."

"They would not touch you," repeated Damien firmly, "because I would not permit it."

Jo looked at him in confusion. "You are just one man," she argued. "You could not stop them."

"Yes I could," he assured her. "I would issue an order, and my men would obey it." His voice was deadly calm. "Or they would suffer the consequences."

The harsh conviction with which he spoke the words told Jo the consequences he spoke of were not trifling ones. She thought of the scars on his back, and found herself wondering what terrible thing he had done to earn such a brutal lashing.

"I don't trust him," declared Samuel.

Despite the fact that the boy was profoundly irritating, Damien could not help but respect his caution. He was absolutely right not to trust him. No one could be trusted in the middle of a war. Evidently the boy had learned this critical lesson early. It was obvious there was no man on this farm at the moment. This youth of twelve or thirteen had a very big role to fill.

"Then go out and move his horse in here," ordered Jo, growing impatient. "Once you have done that, you can go to the back field and start to dig a grave to bury those Indians in. I'll be along as soon as I can to help you."

"But Jo—"

"I have given you an order, Samuel!"

The boy stared at his sister in surprise. He cast a look of hatred at Damien before turning and leaving the barn.

Lucy stepped forward. "I'll help you, Jo," she offered.

"There is going to be a lot of blood," Jo said to her little sister. Lucy was only eight, and Jo did not want to expose her to any more horrors than she had already seen today.

Lucy shrugged her shoulders.

Jo nodded. Another pair of hands would be of tremendous assistance. "Empty this basin out in the yard, then bring it back in here and pour clean water in it," she instructed.

Lucy did as she was told.

Jo lifted the heavy earthen whiskey jug and brought it to the soldier's lips. "Take a big swig, redcoat," she ordered. "I'm going to start stitching in a minute. This will help take your mind off it."

Damien gratefully obliged her, although somehow he doubted a few little stitches could possibly worsen the agony he was already enduring. He took a long, hearty swallow. When the girl started to pull the jug away, he reached up and held it at his mouth, drinking down the strong liquid fire until it leaked down his face and a hot stream burned all the way to his chest. The girl let him have as much as he wanted, then placed the jug on the ground and set to work threading her needle.

His pain slightly subdued, Damien watched her as she worked. Her pale blond eyebrows knit together in concentration as she deftly slipped the needle into his skin. A dark purple bruise was starting to appear on her cheek where the Indian had struck her, and he felt a stab of fury. He was glad he had killed the bastard. Whichever side those Indians had been on, it was shameless and cowardly to make war on women and children.

The girl carefully pulled the thread across the opening of the wound, then pierced the needle through the other side. Her little sister knelt beside her, obediently following her commands to rinse out a cloth and use it to mop up the blood trickling from the wound so it wouldn't interfere with her work. The girl's stitching was quick and sure, her touch firm yet gentle. Damien could not help but think she was far more skilled than most of the British army surgeons he had encountered after battle.

As she worked the boy returned, leading Damien's horse. He removed Glory's saddle and bridle and then shut him in a stall.

"What do you want me to do with the lobsterback's weapons?" Samuel asked Jo. "He left a musket and a pistol lying in the yard."

"You can bring them here," commanded Damien tautly as he struggled through another wave of pain.

"No," interjected Jo. "Take them into the house, along with his sword." She indicated the deadly silver blade gleaming against the straw. "I'll find a place for them when I get there."

"I want them with me," Damien growled.

Jo calmly continued to lace his wound closed. "I'm sure you do," she agreed, pulling the dark thread tight. "But I am not so stupid as to have an armed, whiskey-drenched redcoat lying in my barn."

Damien wanted to argue with her further, but the pain and the whiskey had slowed his tongue, and besides, the boy had already left to do her bidding. He decided to let the issue of his weapons die, for the moment.

"That should hold this one," she said finally. She dabbed at his closed wound with a clean, dry cloth. Then she wiped her face with the back of her hand, leaving a streak of Damien's blood on the hot skin of her forehead. "I need you to move onto your side, redcoat." Despite the brusqueness of her tone, she was infinitely gentle as she helped him shift onto the blanket she spread out for him over the coarse straw.

Damien flinched as he felt her cloth press into the wound in his back. He searched for something to take his mind off the pain. "What is your name?" he grated out.

She looked down at him in surprise. Why would a redcoat care what her name was? She hesitated a moment. She supposed there was no harm in telling him. After all, Samuel and Lucy had already used it freely around him. Obviously he had been too preoccupied with pain to notice. "It's Jo."

Damien frowned. He had heard her family call her that, but he didn't like it. She was far too beautiful and feminine to have such a short, ugly name. "That is a man's name," he said disapprovingly.

Jo shrugged as she continued to clean the wound on his back. "That's my name, redcoat. If you don't like it, you can call me Miss Armstrong."

"Jo is short for Josephine," chirped Lucy. "But Jo doesn't like anyone calling her that."

Damien felt the needle jab deeply into the flesh of his back, as if in reaction to this revelation. "Really?" he ground out, manfully stifling the curse that nearly exploded from his lips.

"Don't even think about calling me that, redcoat," said Jo warningly. She pulled the thread taut and stabbed her needle into the other side of his wound.

"I believe I would prefer it if you called me Damien," he declared through clenched teeth.

Jo considered this a moment as she worked. Calling a British soldier by his first name seemed too intimate, somehow. This man may have saved her life, but that did not change the fact that he was her enemy. "I don't believe *I* would prefer it, redcoat," she countered flatly.

Silence reigned between them after that. When Jo had the wound stitched to her satisfaction, she washed it a final time with clean water, then carefully wrapped his torso with bandages. Lucy was sent off to the house carrying the empty kettle and basin. Once again Jo lifted the whiskey jug to his lips and let him drink from it. He closed his eyes as he drank, and did not open them when she finally moved the jug away. His brow was deeply creased with pain and exhaustion. Jo bit her lip as she studied him. The only thing she could do for the moment was let him sleep. She arranged the blanket loosely around him, not wanting him to be too warm. He appeared to be resting relatively comfortably. Satisfied that he would sleep for a few hours, she scooped up his blood-soaked clothing and went to leave.

"Where are you taking my uniform?" demanded Damien thickly.

Jo looked down at the detestable scarlet and white cloth in her arms. "I am going to burn it," she informed him coolly. She knew she was going to enjoy that small ceremony immensely.

"No." He struggled to raise himself onto his elbows, causing white-hot streaks of pain to shoot through him. "Bring it back."

"It is stained and torn beyond repair, redcoat. Besides, I don't want you wearing it while you are staying in my barn. I will find something else for you to wear."

He shook his head. "I have to have it. If I am caught, and I am not wearing my uniform, I will be executed as a spy."

Jo hesitated. What he was saying was true. Any soldier captured out of uniform was immediately accused of spying.

The punishment was death. Despite her hatred of the redcoats, she had not taken the trouble of sewing this one back together just to see him hanged. "Very well," she relented. "I won't burn it. But it is soaked with blood. I will wash it before I bring it back to you."

He grunted his acceptance and collapsed against his bed of straw.

Jo moved toward the door.

"Josephine—"

She whirled around in irritation, ready to tell him not to call her that.

His eyes were closed and his head had fallen limply against his shoulder. The deep creases of pain across his brow seemed to have eased, and he did not appear to breathe.

In that instant she thought he had died, and she was flooded with anguish.

Please, God, please don't let him die.

"Yes?" she whispered, her throat tight.

There was silence for a moment. And then his lips moved ever so slightly.

"Thank you."

The words were so soft she barely heard them. Her heartbeat slowly steadied. He was not dead. She stood there and watched him sleep for a few moments, assuring herself that she did not need to stay, that his chest would continue to rise and fall even if she left him. And yet she remained where she was, frozen, fearing if she left him even for a moment, he might quietly slip away from her.

At last she turned and hurried from the barn, not understanding why a redcoat's death should matter so much to her.

Burying the Indians was no small task. Nightfall was spreading a dark, cool cloak across the little farm by the time she and Samuel finally trudged wearily into the house. Jo was hot, filthy, and exhausted. She wanted nothing more than to bathe and collapse in a deep sleep on her bed. But before she could retire for the night, she would have to look in on the redcoat. If he was awake, he might be ready to take a little food. As for her, she did not think she would be able to eat for days. The ordeal of moving and burying the Indians had twisted her stomach into tight knots of revulsion. She felt certain that if she took a single bite of food, she would be violently ill.

Samuel went straight to his room to wash, and Jo went into the kitchen to fetch a pitcher of water to take to her room. Anne was sitting at the kitchen table, carefully stitching a tiny white gown for the baby she was expecting. Her strawberry-tinted hair spilled in soft waves over her shoulders, and her head was bent as she concentrated on her task. Peach and gold light from the oil lamp on the table cast a warm glow over her as she worked. The quiet maternal picture she created cheered Jo, briefly making her forget the violence and bloodshed they had faced that day. Brutality, fear, and death were all around them. And yet, in the midst of this terrible war, Anne was creating a new life. That simple yet miraculous act filled Jo with determination and hope.

"I want to talk to you, Jo," Anne said seriously, breaking the tranquil mood she had briefly woven over her.

Jo sighed. "It is late, Anne." She knew her sister-in-law wanted to argue about the redcoat, and Jo was far too exhausted to discuss it now. "We can talk tomorrow."

"We could all be dead by tomorrow!" Anne stabbed the baby gown with her needle. "There is a British soldier lying in our barn, and he could get up and murder us all as we sleep!"

"That isn't going to happen," Jo assured her. "First of all, I don't believe he wants to hurt us. And even if he did, he's as helpless as a newborn kitten."

"His very presence is a danger to us," countered Anne, her voice taut with fear. "His regiment is undoubtedly looking for him. If they find him here, they will not just take him peacefully and go. They will raid the farm and kill us."

"He has promised me they won't." Even as she said it Jo realized how ludicrous that was. Why on earth should she trust the word of a redcoat? Especially one who was severely wounded and would undoubtedly say anything to get her to help him?

Anne shook her head. "You cannot mean to keep him here, Jo. You must turn him over to the rebel forces immediately."

A heavy swirl of guilt rose up within her. Of course Anne was right. It was her duty to her country to turn him over. And she had no right to endanger the safety of her family. But she had given the redcoat her sworn oath before God, and she could not break it. After all, he had nearly died trying to save her. She owed him that much, at least.

"I can't do that, Annie," she said quietly. "I swore to him I would not, and I intend to keep my word. Anything else wouldn't be right."

"Right?" repeated Anne incredulously. "Is it right what the redcoats have done to us? Jo, they came here to make war upon us. Right now they could be fighting Benjamin, or Abraham, or Elias. They killed your father, Jo, or have you forgotten?"

Jo's head began to throb. All she wanted was to lie against the cool sheets of her bed and close her aching eyes. A few hours of sleep, in which she could forget about this dreadful war, and the glassy, vacant stare of the Indians as they looked up at her, waiting for the first shovelful of dirt to rain down on their dark, blood-smeared bodies. In sleep she could block out the threat of the injured redcoat lying in her barn, who had risked himself to save her life, and now deserved no less from her. Sleep would let her escape. Just for a few hours.

"I haven't forgotten. Do you think I don't know that I may be healing him so he can go out and kill my brothers?" she demanded, her voice trembling.

She turned away from Anne and stared out the window at the dark silhouette of the barn, where the redcoat lay, wounded, exhausted, and helpless. "But he saved our lives today, Annie," she continued softly. "He saved you, and the baby, and Samuel, and Lucy, just as much as he saved me.

If not for him, we all would have been hacked to pieces by those Indians." She paused to let the enormity of his actions sink in. In truth, she could not understand why he had done it. British soldiers were all a bunch of evil, thieving cutthroats, who never did anything unless they thought they could gain from it. Weren't they?

"Now the man who saved us is in my barn, and he needs my help," she whispered. "And I intend to give him that help." Her resolve grew firmer. "You don't have to agree with me," she informed her stonily. "You don't have to assist me. You don't even have to go *near* him if you don't want to. But as the head of this family I have made my decision, and I expect you to go along with it." She turned to face her sister-in-law. "We will *not* turn him over."

She lifted a pitcher of water off a shelf and left the kitchen, feeling hopelessly weary. She was sorry she had spoken so harshly to Anne. She was sorry there was a war on. And she was especially sorry that God had seen fit to send an evil, butchering redcoat to her rescue today, forcing her to choose between her duty to her country, and her own morality.

Damien dreamed he was on fire. He was lying in a field slowly being engulfed by an orange and white blaze, while the agonizing screams and blood and gore of battle raged around him. The tremendous heat burned his clothes and seared his flesh, shooting pain through every charred nerve in his body. No one on the field stopped to look at him or offer him help. They were either too absorbed with the demands of the battle, or too afraid to challenge the magnificent power of the fire as it swept over him in a brilliant curtain of deadly flames. The pain was unbearable. He opened his mouth to scream. All that came out was a weak, parched cry that died halfway up his throat, lost somewhere in the heat and the dryness, and the dismal fact that nobody gave a damn if he burned to death or not.

"Shhh—" soothed a voice, soft and feminine.

Something cool and wet came to rest against his forehead, dousing the flames that burned there. It lifted away after a moment and he moaned a weak protest. Then it came down again on his searing hot cheek, cool and wet and wonderful. Slowly it slid to his other cheek, across his chin, down his throat. Then it lifted away once more and he was filled with helpless frustration. He heard the faint sound of water splashing in a metal basin, a musical, calming sound, filled with promise. And then the coolness was back, dabbing gently at the heat raging in him, fighting the fire with a steady, confident, liquid touch, which made him think perhaps he was not going to burn to death after all. He lay there and accepted this sweet relief, vaguely wondering why someone would bother tending to him. He knew he did not deserve any respite from his suffering. Perhaps God had decided to be merciful with him today, although Damien could not fathom why that should be. The coolness deserted him again. This time Damien did not protest, so certain had he become in those few brief moments that the relief being offered to him was not fleeting.

The coolness slid down his neck to his chest, gently swabbing at his aching, heated flesh. It drifted over his shoulder and down one arm, and then the other, deliciously soothing. He felt water splashing over his hand, running through his hot, stiff fingers like a winter stream. He sighed with pleasure. The cloth gently scrubbed at his hand, paying careful attention to each blood-caked, throbbing finger. Then the water was sluicing over his hand once more, cooling the heat and making him feel clean and whole. The cloth moved to his other hand, scrubbing at it with gentle, measured persistence before it was showered with cool water.

The flames devouring his flesh began to weaken.

Music, so soft it barely reached his ears, began to accompany these soothing ministrations. A velvety whisper, caught somewhere between humming and singing, filled his swirling consciousness with a breathy, uneven tune. It started and stopped at irregular intervals, alternately filling him with pleasure and loss as the quiet notes filtered languidly through the air. The sweet, fragile song had no accompaniment, other than the tinny splash of the water in the metal basin, and the muffled sweep of the cloth as it slowly skimmed across his skin. He sensed the music was not meant for him to hear, and somehow that made his appreciation of it even greater. Something was spilled onto the floor; there was the sound of fresh water pouring into the basin, and then the cloth was on his forehead once again, sodden with liquid coolness that ran in little streams down his scalp and into his hair. The sensation was intensely pleasurable.

He slept for a while. He did not know if it was for hours or minutes, but when he began to waken he felt a hand upon his brow. The fingers that stroked him were soft and soothing, their touch as light and tender as an angel's. He could not imagine who would be touching him so. He lay there and pretended to sleep some more, afraid if he opened his eyes the stroking would stop and she would disappear into the mists of a hallucination. Finally the caresses ceased. He heard the splash of water being wrung from a cloth, of objects being gathered together, and he realized she was leaving. Filled with a desperate sense of loss, he opened his eyes.

The girl named Jo was sitting on the straw beside him, collecting a basin, a kettle, and some damp rags. Not an angel, he realized with disappointment, just a flesh-and-blood rebel farm girl, who would not be overly disappointed if he died. He tried to speak to her, but the only sound he could make was a dry croak. She turned and looked at him, her brow creased with exhaustion. For the briefest of instants he thought he saw a flash of relief cross her face. Before he could be sure, the expression was gone.

"Don't try to talk," she ordered.

She poured some water into a cup, then placed her hand under his neck and raised his head to drink from it. The liquid flooded the papery dryness of his mouth, then flowed in a cool stream down the burning heat of his throat. When he had had enough, she took a cloth and

Chapter 1

South Carolina

June 1780

The polished wood of the musket felt smooth and cool against the hot, damp skin of her hands. She adjusted her grip on the clumsy weapon as a thin stream of sweat slowly trickled down her back and soaked into the coarse cotton of her dress. Her heart was pounding so hard against her chest she thought a rib would crack. She forced herself to shove her fear aside and focus on the four Indians creeping silently toward the house. She had sighted them moments earlier and quickly ordered Anne and the children into the cold cellar beneath the kitchen floor. She took a long, deep breath as she watched the savages stealthily continue their approach. They moved warily, searching for the slightest movement from the house.

They did not know she had seen them.

As soon as one of them was within range, she would take careful aim and shoot. She prayed her shot would strike one of them dead, and asked God to forgive her if she did kill one of them. Then maybe the others would flee. It was a desperate, unlikely hope, but it was the only hope she had so she clung to it fiercely. If they did not flee, they would gently blotted at the water that had leaked onto his face. He studied her as she did so, taking in the tangled disarray of her golden hair, the deep purple bruise that stained her cheek where she had been struck, and the exhaustion that filled her blue eyes. He frowned in confusion and looked around, trying to understand what time it was. The barn was dark, despite the pale glow of the lantern hanging on a beam above them. The door to the yard was closed, but he could see faint slivers of silvery light filtering through the chinks between the boards.

"What time is it?" he demanded hoarsely.

"Nearly dawn."

He closed his eyes as he absorbed this. Nearly dawn. He had slept all night. And he was still exhausted. His entire body was feverish, aching, and stiff. He was so weak he did not think he could even stand if he had to. But he felt reasonably certain of one thing. He was not going to die. And for that small, unworthy miracle, he was indebted to this golden-haired rebel. He opened his eyes again to look at her.

"Thank you."

She stared at him in silence a moment, her expression caught between surprise and confusion. And then the crease in her brow faded and her face grew nonchalant. "You gave me quite a scare, redcoat," she announced bluntly. She began to shake out the rags in her basin and neatly fold them. "For a while there I thought all my fancy stitching was going to be for nothing."

"I am lucky to have fallen into the hands of one so skilled with a needle," he observed. "It is fortunate you aren't given to swooning at the sight of blood."

"I've stitched up my brothers often enough."

Damien tried to imagine the kinds of injuries her brothers might sustain while working a farm. Although he knew life on a small, struggling homestead such as this was often hazardous, somehow he did not think her brothers regularly came home with deep, gaping musket-shot wounds.

"Are you hungry?"

Damien shook his head.

"You should eat something," she said. "You need to build up your strength." She glanced over at a tray sitting on the floor. "I brought some soup for you last night, but it's cold now. I could take it back to the house and warm it up."

"I am not hungry."

She stared at him in silence a moment, uncertain what to do next.

When she had looked in on him last night, she had told herself it would just be for a few minutes to make sure he wasn't dead, and to leave him some food. But she had found him moaning and trembling violently against his bed of straw. The sheen of sweat glistening on his wounded body told her he was burning with fever. And despite her determination not to care, she found she could not leave him. She stayed by his side and tended him through the night, knowing there was little she could do for him except try to ease his discomfort. He would either conquer his injuries, or they would conquer him. He was a strong, muscular man, in the full prime of his youth, and it seemed to her his death would have been a terrible waste.

Even if he was a redcoat.

During those long, quiet hours spent by his side, as she bathed his strong, aching body and cooled his burning brow, she found herself wondering about him. About who he was, and how he had come to be in South Carolina, so far from his home in England. About why he had become a soldier, when there were so many more honorable ways to make one's place in the world. About how many homes he had destroyed, and how many decent men and women he had viciously butchered during this war, all for the sake of Britain's desire to tyrannize a people who wanted to rule themselves. Many times during the night she had asked herself if it was right to heal a man who would simply go on to kill, either one of her brothers, or somebody else's brothers. By saving his life, how many Patriots was she condemning to death? she wondered, her heart sick with guilt. Yet she could not let him die. And because of her sworn oath to him, she

could not turn him over to the rebels. But if he lived and
was not turned in, he posed a deadly menace to the lives
of others. She had no idea if she had done the right thing
by saving him.

"I better go back to the house," she said, suddenly anxious to put some distance between them. "Everybody will
be waking soon and wondering what happened to me."

Damien regarded her with amusement. "You mean they'll
think that after saving you yesterday, I then decided to murder you as you nursed me?"

Her cheeks flushed with embarrassment. She had not
meant to insult him. "You have to understand," she began
awkwardly, "with all the terrible stories we have heard about
the redcoats—"

He weakly lifted his hand to stop her. "Don't apologize."

For all he knew, most of those terrible stories were true.
There was a war going on, and war by its very nature was
a calculated exercise in brutality. That was a given in battle.
But beyond the killing fields of battle were the atrocities
committed against the men, women, and children who were
not part of any army. Damien knew that even the British
army, which was the most highly disciplined army in the
world, had men in it who enjoyed terrorizing and plundering. Their vile behavior had been a particular problem in
the southern colonies, where many Loyalist soldiers and
freed black slaves took savage pleasure in attacking rebel
homes, whether mansion or hovel. This girl's fear of the
British army was by no means unfounded.

The realization filled him with fury and disgust.

She was getting ready to leave again, and for some incomprehensible reason he did not want her to go. He knew
this was selfish. What right did he have to expect her to
stay with him now that he was awake? Nevertheless, a sensation of loss enveloped him as he watched her collect her
things.

"I'll be along later today to look in on you," Jo informed
him. "Until then, you should try to get some sleep."

He studied the lines of exhaustion on her face. "So
should you."

Jo regarded him with confusion, uncertain how to respond. The redcoat returned her stare calmly. The bandages she had wrapped around him were stained with blood, but it did not appear to be fresh. She was confident his bleeding had stopped. Nevertheless, his wounds were severe. If putrefaction set in, he could still die. But she and her family would live.

Because of him.

Suddenly she needed to understand why he had done it. Her image of the redcoats did not include them risking their lives to save rebel Americans, especially when they were under attack by Indian allies.

"Why?" she asked. "Why did you save me?"

Damien hesitated before he answered. His mind drifted back to the moment he first saw her, angry and beautiful and afraid, yet magnificently courageous as she knelt beneath the brilliant glare of the Carolina sky and waited to be savagely mutilated. In that moment he had not known if she was rebel or Loyalist. And he had not cared. He could not have let them kill her, regardless of whether she was his enemy or his ally. The politics of war had no bearing on his need to keep her safe. And even now, knowing she was his enemy, he would risk his life again for her in an instant. His brain was too clouded with whiskey and pain to understand why. Still, he could not allow her to believe he would not harm her if he had to. At the moment his life lay in her hands, and that was dangerous.

"I thought you were a Loyalist," he lied. "Therefore it was my duty to try to protect you."

She contemplated this a moment. And then she shook her head. "South Carolina is heavily rebel," she pointed out. "And the Indians are mostly allies of the British. When you saw them attacking us, you had no reason to think this was a Loyalist farm."

Damien closed his eyes and shrugged his shoulders. "I made a mistake," he drawled with weary indifference.

She stared at him a long moment, uncertain whether he spoke the truth or not. And then she spun around and rushed out of the barn. Dawn was streaking the sky with ribbons of peach and silver, but she could find no beauty in it.

She was too horrified by the realization that if the man she had nursed all night had known she was a rebel, he would have simply stood by and allowed the Indians to slaughter her.

Chapter 3

Jo left the redcoat to sleep for most of the day.

With her three older brothers off fighting, there was always a tremendous amount of work to be done on the farm, and today was no exception. Since many of the men in the surrounding area had left their families to join either the Carolina militia or Washington's Continental Army, the local women had banded together to help each other with the major tasks of planting and harvesting. Work parties of women and a few strong boys and old men were organized to move from farm to farm plowing fields, planting corn and wheat, and then harvesting the crops when they were ready. Everyone who was able helped, and everyone benefited. Jo had volunteered to be part of this temporary work detail, and thus far their enormous task had been accomplished with amazing success. Although most of the livestock in the area had been taken during raids by the British army, the surrounding fields were green and gold with young corn and wheat. If the crops survived to harvest time, and then could be stored somewhere safe, there would be food for winter. Of course, with regiments of British soldiers constantly roaming the countryside, plundering and burning in a determined effort to crush the spirit of rebel families, the future of the crops was far from certain. If they did survive to maturity, the next challenge would be to gather them before the British army had the opportunity to harvest it for themselves.

It was late afternoon by the time Jo finally found a moment to look in on the redcoat. She carried with her a tray bearing cheese, cornbread, some boiled eggs, and a jug of cool water. It was her intention to make sure he was all right, and then, if he seemed strong enough to feed himself, to leave the tray with him. There was still much work to be done, and she had no desire to waste her time in the company of a murdering lobsterback.

It was cooler in the barn than it was outside, although there was no breeze. Jo had left the doors and windows closed, thinking this would keep the redcoat better hidden if they suddenly received unexpected visitors. As she stepped out of the hot glare of the afternoon sun, it took her eyes a moment to adjust to the soft, dusty gray light inside. The barn smelled sweet and dry and earthy, a familiar mixture of horse and leather and straw. The redcoat's horse watched her with interest as she entered. Despite her determination to dislike everything belonging to him, from his scarlet and white uniform to his expensive European saddle, she could not help but notice his horse was a truly magnificent animal.

Her father and brothers had each taken a horse with them when they went off to join the war, leaving Jo with only an old gray mare named Belle who was almost as slow as she was stubborn. By contrast, the redcoat's horse was a glorious beast, with a gleaming coat the red-brown color of a pecan shell, and a snowy white star splashed across his noble forehead. Jo was sorry the animal had to stay cooped up in a stall all day, but she did not think she could risk letting him outside to graze. If anyone saw him, there would be questions about where he had come from. The horse tossed his head and eyed her mournfully, as if sensing her thoughts. Jo reached out and gave him a soft pat on his nose. The animal responded by nudging himself firmly against her hand, trying to befriend her. Jo snatched her hand away and took a step back from the stall.

"I don't think so, redcoat horse," she said coldly. "I won't be making friends with an animal that is used in battle against my countrymen."

The horse stretched his long, powerful neck farther toward her, and finding her out of reach, he snorted and stamped his foot in frustration. Jo sighed. She supposed it wasn't the horse's fault he belonged to a redcoat. She reached out and stroked his velvety nose again.

"Maybe tonight I'll come back and take you out for a while," she whispered. "Would you like that?"

The horse regarded her with gentle brown eyes and bent his head even lower. Jo ran her hand lightly up over the star on his forehead, and gave him a quick scratch behind the ears. When the horse had finally had enough, she turned to look at the redcoat.

He lay sound asleep on his thick bed of straw, one arm flung casually behind his head for a pillow. His black hair was damp and tousled across his brow, and glistening beads of sweat shone on his sun-bronzed skin. Wondering if he still battled a fever, Jo placed her tray on the ground, knelt beside him and tentatively laid her hand against his forehead. He seemed hot to her, but not overly so. She splashed some water from the jug onto a cloth and bathed his face. His sleep was deep, for he did not stir. Jo brushed his dark hair off his face with her fingers. Then she squeezed her cloth over his brow, letting the cool water trickle into his scalp. The redcoat let out a faint sigh of pleasure.

He was not an unattractive man, Jo decided as her cloth moved along the chiseled line of his jaw. His hair and eyebrows were as black as night, and the dark stubble painting shadows on his cheeks gave him a faintly sinister look. That was appropriate, she mused, given the evil nature of the army he belonged to. His forehead was marked with deep lines of anger, which again reflected the kind of mean temperament required of a man who chose to plunder and burn and slaughter as a profession. It was not what she would

call a pleasant face, for it was far too hard and angular to
be described as such. However, he had a harsh attractiveness
to him, and a lean, rugged quality quite unlike the florid-
cheeked, white-wigged image she had formed in her mind of
the typical British soldier.

Once his face was cooled to her satisfaction, she moved
down the thick column of his neck, then onto his chest.
Her wet cloth moved in slow, even circles over his warm,
sun-darkened skin, lingering on the ridges of firm muscle
that stretched across his body. It was obvious he was a man
of considerable strength. Despite her determination not to
notice, she found herself distracted by his impressive phy-
sique. His shoulders were massive and strong, his chest was
sculpted into solid contours of hard muscle, and his skin
felt smooth and velvety warm. Flushed with curiosity, she
let her fingers brush lightly over the dark tuft of hair growing in the shallow valley that separated one wall of chest
muscle from the other. His nipples were two dark, flat medallions against a sea of copper-colored skin. She swabbed
them with her cool, wet cloth, and watched in fascination as
they sprang to life, tightening beneath her touch. She darted
a nervous glance at the redcoat's face, fearing she might have
wakened him. His eyes remained closed and his breathing
stayed deep and even. Apparently he was oblivious to her
ministrations. Encouraged by the fact that he was obviously
a heavy sleeper, she continued her forbidden exploration of
him.

She followed his ribs to the hard, flat plane of his stomach, which quickly disappeared beneath the thick layers of
bandages she had wrapped around him last night. She knew
he would have scars where she had stitched him, but hopefully his wounds would heal nicely and the mark would not
be great. She thought of the terrible scars that tangled
across his back in ugly white branches, and her stomach
clenched with anger. A few more scars probably meant
nothing to him, she reflected. It was criminal to punish a
man so brutally. She knew the British army was infamous
for disciplining its soldiers with the lash. This common
form of punishment had given rise to the insulting nick-

names of "lobsterback" and "bloody back." Once again she found herself wondering what terrible crime this man had committed to have earned himself such a vicious punishment. She skimmed her hand across the expanse of his chest, as if that small, intimate gesture could somehow ease the hideous pain he had endured.

"Good afternoon, Miss Armstrong."

She gasped and yanked her hand away. Her cheeks flaming with embarrassment, she slowly raised her eyes to his.

Damien regarded her with amusement. "Am I healing to your satisfaction?"

"I—I think so," she stammered.

"I am relieved to hear it."

"I brought you something to eat," she blurted out defensively, as if this were a perfectly reasonable explanation of why she had been laying her hands all over him.

He resisted the urge to smile. "Thank you."

Awkward silence stretched between them. Feeling like a naughty child who has been caught doing something she shouldn't, Jo lowered her eyes and stared miserably at the folds in her skirt, wishing she could lose herself in them.

"May I have some?" he finally asked.

She looked up at him in bewilderment. "Some what?"

"Some food." He nodded toward the abandoned tray.

"Oh!" Suddenly remembering why she had come to the barn in the first place, she reached over and lifted the tray. "Can you feed yourself?" She desperately hoped he could. That way she could leave without humiliating herself any further.

Damien hesitated. If she simply gave him the tray and left, he would have to stay here alone in the dark until she came back to fetch it. The thought did not appeal to him. It was bad enough lying on the floor of a rebel's barn feeling weaker than a newborn infant. But now that he was awake and relatively lucid, he did not relish the idea of only having Glory for company for the next few hours. Besides, perhaps this rebel farm girl could provide him with information that might be of use once he returned to his regiment.

He winced dramatically and pretended to stifle a curse as he attempted to sit up. "I don't think so," he groaned, collapsing against the straw.

Jo bit her lip. She disliked the idea of having to spend time with him now that he was awake. "I can only stay a few minutes," she said reluctantly. She uncovered the plate of cornbread. "I still have a lot of work to do."

"Are there only the four of you here?" he asked casually.

"Yes." She broke off a piece of cornbread and placed it in his mouth. "I have three other brothers besides Samuel, but they're off fighting. Anne and I are running the farm until they come home."

He noted the firm conviction in her voice as she spoke. No doubt she feared for her brothers' safety, but her tone was utterly confident, as if their return was certain and inevitable.

"Where is your father?" he asked. Surely there was some man helping them run things here. He recalled that the fields surrounding the house were almost all planted. He did not see how two young women could possibly manage a farm of this size in the middle of a war on their own.

Her sky-blue eyes grew dark and cool. "Killed by your kind, redcoat," she grated out bitterly. "At the Battle of Brooklyn Heights in seventy-six." Her voice was taut with pain and pride.

"I'm sorry." The words came out instantly, as good manners dictated. Yet amazingly, he actually did feel sorry. It was obvious the loss of her father had hurt this girl deeply, and he was not unaffected by her pain.

"No you're not," she countered. She threw him a scornful look. "Why should you be? After all, you redcoats won the battle. A thousand Americans were killed that day, and a thousand more were taken prisoner. I'm sure when you heard the news, you were overjoyed."

Damien shrugged. "Actually, when I heard the news, I didn't give a damn one way or the other. I had not yet joined the British army, and the rebellion in the colonies was of no interest to me."

Jo stared at him, appalled. "Your country was at war. How could that be of no interest to you?"

"My country is always at war," he remarked indifferently. He opened his mouth to receive another chunk of cornbread.

Frowning, she dropped the bread in his mouth. She could not begin to comprehend his cavalier attitude. "If you didn't care, then why did you join the British army?"

He pondered this a moment as he chewed. "I suppose because at the time, running away to join the celebrated British army seemed as good a thing to do as any," he said finally.

His answer was utterly outrageous. "Are you saying you are fighting this war because you have nothing better to do?" She was disliking him more by the minute.

"No," he replied. "I am fighting this war because it is my duty as a British soldier." He slowly chewed another piece of bread and then swallowed. "But I joined the army because I had few other options available to me."

She shook her head in disgust. Her brothers were risking their lives for their country, because they believed in their hearts it was right to do so. They were fighting for their rights, for their land, and for their future. This redcoat was fighting because he had chosen war as a profession. While she understood about loyalty to one's country and having to answer its call, she could find nothing even remotely honorable in his actions.

"So," she began, her voice dripping contempt, "you came to America to make war on us, not out of the need to protect your family and your rights, or even because you believe in your country's cause, but simply because you have chosen war as your profession." She gave him a look of unmitigated scorn. "That makes you, in essence, a professional murderer."

"A fascinating twist of logic," commented Damien. "Except that all men who join armies receive some form of pay, so that would make anyone who calls himself a soldier a professional murderer, regardless of his reasons for joining."

"It is not the same," argued Jo. "My brothers are fighting

for freedom. They are fighting for our rights, and for our future here."

"How very inspiring," remarked Damien, his tone blatantly condescending. "It's too bad their government doesn't quite see it that way."

"The British Parliament is not our government, redcoat," Jo informed him icily. "We are an independent country with our own government. The sooner you and your lobsterback friends accept that, the sooner this killing can stop and we can all get back to living normal lives."

Her eyes were sparkling with challenge, and her voice shook slightly as she spoke. Despite the ridiculous naïveté of her convictions, Damien found he could not help but admire her passion.

Since he had first arrived in the colonies in the summer of seventy-seven, he had never ceased to be amazed at the tenacity of the rebels. At first he had believed the British forces would be able to crush this absurd little colonial uprising quickly. After all, it was the finest army in the world against a disorganized group of untrained, unarmed, undisciplined colonists—hardly a daunting opponent. And yet, battle after battle, year after year, despite losses and hardship and lack of decent weapons and supplies, the rebels had shown an extraordinary ability to keep fighting. Listening now to this simple farm girl speak with such heartfelt emotion about her brothers and their reasons for fighting made him feel slightly humbled. His own reasons for going into battle were not nearly so commendable. Quite simply, he had needed to distance himself from his shambles of a life in England. Joining the army had seemed the perfect opportunity to escape his failures. It was hardly a grand gesture of selfless, heroic idealism. But then, he had never pretended to be either selfless or heroic. The shattered past he left behind in England was testimony to that.

The girl was looking at him with disdain, which was irritating. Suddenly he was weary of this talk of war.

"Tell me, what made your family settle here?" he asked, changing the subject. He could not fathom why anyone would choose to live in this unforgiving, godforsaken place.

South Carolina was untamed, isolated, and hotter than the fires of hell. He had seen some of the grand plantation homes of the wealthy, who formed a kind of untitled aristocracy here. That sort of life he could understand. But to come to this southern colony to scratch out a miserable existence of endless drudgery on a struggling farm was beyond his comprehension.

Jo eyed him suspiciously. Why would a redcoat care how her family came to be here? she wondered. Try as she might, she could detect no sarcasm or malice in his expression. Instead his gray eyes seemed to reflect genuine puzzlement. She could almost feel sorry for him. Could he not just look around and see why anyone in his right mind would feel blessed to live in South Carolina? Her father had come all the way from England, and he had told her that South Carolina was the most beautiful place in the world. Jo had never been anywhere else, but she was certain he spoke the truth.

"Have you ever been to a place called London, redcoat?" she asked testily.

Despite the effort it took, Damien resisted the urge to smile. "A few times."

"Then you know what a filthy, crowded, noisy, ugly, ungodly den of thieves it is," she pronounced authoritatively.

Damien looked at her in astonishment. "You have been to London?"

"Of course not!" she snapped. "But my father was born and raised there, and he told me all about it."

"I see," remarked Damien. "Is that where your father came from?"

"That's right." Remembering she was there to feed him, Jo offered him a bite of boiled egg, which he accepted. "My father was born in London as John Reed," she began proudly. "His father was a bookseller, who saw to it that all his children learned to read and write and respect their Bible. My father began to work in the bookshop when he was twelve, and a few years later, his younger sister, Clarice, began to work there as well.

"There was a man who used to come into the shop every

week. He was a fine gentleman, with fancy clothes and an expensive black carriage that waited for him while he looked for books. He was always very nice and well mannered. He would chat with Clarice as she wrapped his books in paper and tied them together with string. Not many rich people came into my grandfather's bookshop, and I suppose Clarice thought he was about the finest gentleman she had ever met."

A thread of bitterness began to color her voice.

"One evening, when Clarice was leaving the store to go home, she saw the gentleman's carriage waiting in the street. It was raining hard that night, and the gentleman offered to give her a ride. At first she said no, but the gentleman was insistent. The carriage looked so pretty, and the gentleman seemed so nice, and it really was raining hard, and after all, this man was known to her father, so what harm could there be in his taking her home? So Clarice finally agreed and climbed in."

Jo suddenly became preoccupied with arranging a cloth over the uneaten cornbread. She did not know why she had started telling this story to a stranger. Worse yet, a redcoat. Except that maybe it would make him understand what an evil place he came from.

"What happened to her?" asked Damien quietly. He was certain he already knew the answer.

"That man did—terrible things to her," Jo managed awkwardly. "And when he was finished, he dropped her off in front of her home, and told her not to tell anyone. But her clothes were torn and her face was bruised, and my father, who was eighteen, saw her as she came in and made her tell him what had happened. Well, he wanted to go straight to the man's house and kill him there and then, but my grandfather stopped him. He said it was up to the law to handle it. He promised my father there were laws in England that protected women from men like that. And so my father and my grandfather reported this terrible attack on Clarice to the authorities. But instead of going to arrest this man, they informed my father that the man he was accusing was a titled gentleman who was well-known. They asked my father what kind of a young girl would get into a carriage alone with a man?" Her voice began to tremble with anger. "And they made it seem as if it were all her fault. As if somehow she got no more than she deserved." She stopped, unable to comprehend their indifference.

"What did your father do then?" Damien sure as hell knew what he would have done.

"When my father realized the law was not going to help them, he decided to take matters into his own hands. And so he went to this man's house and confronted him with his terrible crime, fully expecting him to deny it. And do you know what this man did?" she demanded furiously.

Damien shook his head.

"He smiled, and told my father no real harm had been done. He said that his sister was a pretty little thing, and should have no trouble finding herself a husband. And then he offered him money, saying 'this should be enough to buy her a new dress.'"

Jo fixed her gaze on the pale stream of dust floating in the barn. "My father went into a rage and attacked the man," she said finally. "There was a violent struggle. The man fell and hit his head. And my father was arrested and charged with murder. He could have been hanged. But the judge who tried him sentenced him to life as an indentured servant in the colonies instead." She paused and looked thoughtfully at the redcoat. "I like to think he did it as an act of mercy, because of my father's youth."

More likely because he believed life as a slave in the colonies was a punishment far worse than death, thought Damien, but he did not tell her that. "But your father didn't serve his entire sentence," he surmised.

Jo shook her head. "He was sent to work on a farm in Virginia. That's where he met my mother. She was an orphan, and had traded her passage to the colonies in exchange for seven years' service. She worked in the house, and my father worked in the fields, along with the other indentured servants and some slaves. He stayed there three years, enduring all kinds of abuse. And then one day he and my mother ran away. My father changed his name to Armstrong, and they got married. They worked here and there, saving everything they earned, until finally they ended up on this farm in South Carolina. And that's how we came to be here, redcoat," she announced, her voice filled with pride. "And all you need do is look around to see it is the finest place in all the world."

Her eyes were sparkling with challenge, as if she were daring him to argue with her. But in that moment, Damien did not think he could have formed a convincing argument. After all, here was a place where a convicted murderer and a young girl who faced God only knew what sort of life on the streets of London could marry, buy a farm, and raise a family. They might not have become rich, but they had built a life that was honorable and self-sufficient. It was not a life that would have ever suited Damien, but even he could appreciate the simple, honest dignity of it. And he could well understand that it was worth fighting for.

He found himself suddenly curious about the legacy of this man called John Armstrong. "You say you have three older brothers?"

Jo nodded. "Benjamin is the oldest. He is married to Anne. Then there's Abraham and Elias. All three are part of Washington's Continental Army. Elias is in the cavalry," she added proudly. "He is two years younger than me, but he can handle a horse better than any man I know."

"And your mother?"

"She took sick and died a few months after Lucy was born."

Her tone was void of any emotion, but a brief shadow darkened her eyes, telling him her mother's death had hurt her terribly. And left her with the heavy burden of three younger siblings, who undoubtedly had looked to her to fill her mother's place.

"I'm sorry," he said quietly.

Instead of rejecting his sympathy, as she had with her father, she simply nodded. After all, the British had nothing to do with her mother's death. "That was over eight years ago." She stared at the dust motes dancing in a slender ray of sunlight. "But sometimes," she continued softly, "I wake

up in the morning, and for a few seconds, before I am entirely awake, I think she is still alive. My father too. And for
those few brief seconds, I am really, truly happy."

Damien watched her in silence. Light from the hot afternoon sun was filtering through the cracks between the
boards, painting her in alternate shadows of gray and gold.
Her honey-colored hair had been pinned up, but much of
it had slipped from its pins and fallen in soft curls onto her
neck and shoulders. For the first time he noticed the shabbiness of her day dress. It might once have been a bright
color, but the fabric was so worn and faded it was impossible to tell what that color had been. The afternoon heat
had forced her to undo the buttons that otherwise would
have closed over the delicate bones beneath her neck, revealing a soft expanse of sun-kissed skin. The coarse, damp fabric clung to her tightly, hugging the soft curves of her body
in a way that somehow rivaled the most revealing ball gown
Damien had ever seen. She would never have been considered a great beauty in London he decided; not against the
perfectly coiffed, pale-skinned, amply fleshed women with
whom he was used to keeping company. But somehow, in
the hazy afternoon light of this shadowed barn, she managed to set a standard of beauty different from any he had
ever known. A beauty made strong and lean by outdoor
work, with silky hair and glowing skin that was used to the
warmth of the sun upon it. He noticed a faint spray of
freckles across her nose and on her cheeks, and he found
himself utterly captivated by them.

"But I don't suppose you would know anything about
that," she declared scornfully, breaking the spell she had inadvertently cast over him. "Any man who would join an
army because he had nothing better to do, can't know very
much about love, whether it's for a place or a person."

Her contempt washed over him like an icy wave of water.
The girl who now glared at him was at odds with the enchanting image of quiet beauty she had seemed only a moment earlier. And her barb stung him more than she
realized. Damien felt himself recoil. She was a rebel, he re-

minded himself, which made her his enemy. He must not allow himself to forget that. Not even for a moment.

"Thank you for the food, Miss Armstrong," he ground out stiffly. He settled back against the straw and closed his eyes, dismissing her.

Suddenly Jo was sorry she had spoken to him so sharply. He was obviously tired. He had almost died for her, she reminded herself guiltily. He'd said it was because he had thought she was a Loyalist, but she was not entirely convinced of that. And ultimately, his reasons didn't really matter. If not for him, she and her family would be dead.

"I am sorry," she apologized awkwardly. "Sometimes I say things without thinking."

Damien said nothing.

"My father used to say it was a terrible flaw," she admitted. "He said I would have to constantly work on it my whole life."

Silence.

Not knowing what else to say, she hesitantly offered, "If you like, I will leave this food with you. You may get hungry later."

He did not respond.

She stood and brushed the straw from her skirts. In a few hours she would need to change his bandages, but she would not mention that now. She turned and headed toward the door.

"Josephine."

She stopped. She never allowed anyone to call her by that name and thought that had been clear to him. But somehow the way he said it was strangely soothing, almost tender, which was puzzling. Slowly she turned to find him watching her.

"It is not such a terrible flaw," he assured her quietly.

His eyes held her a moment. In that instant she thought she saw a shadow of pain darken his features, a haunting anguish that seemed to go deeper than mere physical wounds. And then, just as quickly it was gone.

"I am tired," he muttered, closing his lids. "Forgive me."

She had been dismissed, but she did not leave. She stayed

at the door and watched him a while, sensing the exact moment when he drifted away from consciousness. Even in his sleep he frowned, she realized with surprise. She wondered if his lines came from meanness and anger, or just an exhaustion that never abated, even in slumber.

Finally, remembering she still had work to do, she turned and left him to sleep, secure in the knowledge that for the moment at least, he was safe.

She heard them coming before she saw them.

It was early morning of the following day, and Jo and Anne were in the kitchen washing the breakfast dishes. Samuel and Lucy had been sent outside to work in the garden. The instant Jo heard the muffled clop of hooves and the jangle of harness, anxiety surged through her. Her first thought was that a regiment of lobsterbacks had arrived, searching for their missing soldier. She had to lead them to him before they started to terrorize the children and rip the house apart. Swallowing, she wiped her dripping hands on her apron and hurried out into the yard, ordering Anne to stay inside.

When she saw the scraggly, rough-looking group of rebels dismounting from their horses, her anxiety blossomed into pure, cold fear.

There were five of them in all, wearing ragged blue coats and breeches heavily soiled with slime and filth. It was obvious they had recently been in battle, for three of them were injured. One huge bear of a man had a bloodstained kerchief wrapped around his forehead. Another had his arm bound in a dirty, tattered sling, and the third had his thigh wrapped in foul-looking rags and was using his musket as a makeshift crutch.

There was an older soldier in the front who appeared to be the leader of this bedraggled group—a tall, heavyset man with graying hair and pale blue eyes that seemed grave, but not unkind. His face was generously etched with lines, betraying his age to be well past forty. He dismounted from a magnificent pearl and slate dappled horse, and on seeing Jo, he stepped forward and removed his hat. He carried himself with solemn dignity, the bearing of a man who has seen more in life than he wanted, and found some of it hideous.

"Good morning, ma'am. I am Captain Jackson Lee. I am looking for the head of the Armstrong family."

A flicker of dread ignited in the pit of Jo's stomach. "Captain Lee," she returned stiffly. "I am Jo Armstrong. I am in charge of my family while my brothers are away fighting in the rebel army."

Her voice sounded strangely hollow to her ears. She desperately tried to think of all the reasons why a detachment of Patriot soldiers might need to speak with her. Perhaps they wanted to warn her about British raids taking place in the area. Perhaps they wanted to know if she had seen any redcoats pass her farm, or if she had experienced any trouble. Or maybe they simply wanted to ask her for food. Or blankets. Or medical assistance. There were lots of possibilities, she assured herself. Lots of reasons besides being here to search for the redcoat.

Or to tell her one of her brothers had been killed.

She bit down hard on her lip to stop it from trembling.

"Looks like you've had a little trouble here," called out the huge soldier with the bandage around his head. He pointed a thick, grimy finger at the dark brown stains splattered across the dry earth in the yard. Then he raised his eyes questioningly to Jo. "This here looks like blood."

"It is blood," Jo said. "We had some Indian trouble here the other day." The other four soldiers were starting to wander around the yard, examining the bloodstains, following the various dark trails they made. She knew she must not let them follow the trail that led into the barn. "We managed to kill a couple of them," she continued, "and the others ran off. Since we haven't had any rain, the blood has not yet washed away." Her tone was dismissive, as if the incident were over and done, and therefore of no consequence.

Samuel and Lucy suddenly appeared from around the side of the house. They stared at the rebel soldiers, their eyes wide with both wariness and fascination.

"It's all right, Samuel and Lucy," called Jo, trying to sound calm. "Go on into the house."

Samuel gave her an openly rebellious look. It was clear he felt his place was out here with her. "But Jo—"

"I said take your sister into the house, Samuel," Jo said curtly.

Samuel grabbed Lucy's hand and scowled at Jo as he stalked past her and went into the house.

The soldier with the injured thigh spat contemptuously on the bloodied ground. "See any lobsterbacks with these Indians?" he asked. He was a tall, scrawny man with greasy brown hair and suspicious eyes.

She hesitated for a fraction of a second. "No. Just Indians." Her stomach knotted. Now there was no going back. If they discovered the redcoat in her barn, they would know she had lied. The punishment for treason was hanging. She tried to push that thought from her mind.

"Was anybody hurt?" asked Captain Lee with concern.

Jo shook her head. It was obvious he did not mean the Indians.

Apparently satisfied with her explanation, the soldiers abandoned their interest in the bloodstains. Captain Lee moved toward her.

"Miss Armstrong," he said, his voice low and serious, "may I have a word with you in private?"

Her heart began to beat with trepidation. *Stay calm.*

"Certainly, Captain Lee." She did not want to leave the other four soldiers out in the yard. They might decide to have a look around and find the redcoat in the barn. "You men must be thirsty. Why don't you all step inside and have a cool glass of water?"

"That's very kind of you, Miss Armstrong," interjected Captain Lee before any of his men could answer. "But my men will remain outside. If it's not too much trouble, I'm sure they would appreciate a cool drink out here."

Jo managed a stiff smile. "Of course, Captain."

Please, Lord, don't let them go into the barn.

She turned and went into the house, with Captain Lee following behind her.

"Anne, this is Captain Jackson Lee," said Jo as they came upon Anne in the hallway. "Captain Lee, this is my brother's wife, Mrs. Benjamin Armstrong."

"Ma'am," said Captain Lee, politely tilting his head.

Jo turned to Anne and forced herself to smile. "Captain Lee's men are in need of some refreshment. Would you take some water out to them?" She stared at her intently. *And don't mention anything about the redcoat.*

Anne gave Jo a look of reluctant comprehension. "Certainly."

Her tone was amiable, but Jo could hear the tenseness in it. She knew Anne must be as terrified as she was. If the soldiers discovered the redcoat in the barn, they would all be accused of treason. And there was no reason to think these rough men would bother to have them tried by an official army court. There was a war on, and in a war, the rules of common decency did not apply. Those men outside in their ragged blue uniforms had suffered enough to harbor the most virulent hatred of redcoats and Loyalists. Anyone caught helping them should not expect any mercy.

"Why don't we sit in the parlor, Captain Lee?" suggested Jo as she opened the parlor doors. The room was oppressively hot and stuffy. She closed the doors behind the captain, then seated herself on the sofa and indicated a chair for him. "Now then," she began, her voice artificially bright, "what is it you wish to speak about?"

Captain Lee's expression was grim. "Miss Armstrong, I am afraid I have some bad news."

Fear streaked up her spine. She would not ask him what he meant. As long as she did not ask, as long as he did not continue, she did not have to know whatever it was he wanted to tell her. It was ridiculous, of course. She could not suspend this moment forever. But she knew whatever he was going to tell her concerned one of her brothers, and she did not think she could bear it. And so she simply sat there and stared at him blankly, as if he had been speaking to her in a foreign language she could not understand. For one brief, frozen moment she remained there, trapped between not knowing and knowing. It was terrible, but not as terrible as learning the irrevocable truth.

Captain Lee looked at her, his brow creased with concern. "Miss Armstrong?"

She reached out and gripped the arm of the sofa with one hand. The fabric was worn and felt vaguely slippery beneath her fingertips. She swallowed down the fear rising from her chest. "Forgive me, Captain Lee," she apologized tautly. "Please continue."

Captain Lee cleared his throat. "Miss Armstrong, it is my unfortunate duty to inform you that your brother Elias is dead." He spoke the words with gruff apology, his weary blue eyes filled with regret.

The clock in the parlor ticked loudly, slowly counting off the seconds as she struggled to absorb what he was telling her. Elias. This man was saying Elias was dead. A thin stream of sweat trickled down her spine. The room was hot, but suddenly she felt chilled. Handsome, charming, funny Elias, who at eighteen was two years younger than she, and just becoming a man. He had trailed around after her his entire life. They had been close not only in age, but also in spirit. Not just brother and sister, but best friends. She had not wanted him to join the army, but at eighteen, he could not be stopped. He wanted to serve his country, like his father and older brothers. She had fought terribly with him before he left. She told him she needed him here, to help her run the farm and care for Anne and the children. The Armstrong family had sent enough men into battle, she assured him bitterly. But Elias was resolute. He told him his country needed him more than the farm did. It was his duty as an American. And then he had gone, brimming with excitement and the idealistic determination of youth.

Assuring her she had nothing to fear. Promising her he would return.

He had lied.

"Miss Armstrong?"

She raised her eyes to Captain Lee. He was watching her closely, his expression troubled. He was expecting her to say something. Or maybe he was expecting her to cry. She thought she should cry, but somehow the tears would not come. Perhaps it was the shock. Or perhaps it was because somewhere in her heart she could not bring herself to believe he was really dead. If she started to cry, it would mean she had accepted that Elias was gone, and she wasn't ready. Not yet.

The clock continued to mark off the seconds. She knew she should say something. She supposed she should ask "How did it happen?" so Captain Lee could tell her some story of Elias's incredible bravery before he died. But she did not want to know. She did not want to hear all the horrible details, which would weave together in her mind and form a ghastly picture of Elias's last terrible moments. She knew the image would haunt her forever, and she had to protect herself from that. She was strong, but there were limits to her fortitude. And if this Captain Lee told her a story of British brutality, it would make her hate the redcoats even more than she already did, and as traitorous as it seemed, she did not want that. Because at this moment there was a redcoat lying in her barn who had saved her life.

Whatever atrocities he may have committed, she did not want to hate him for Elias's death.

"Miss Armstrong ... can I get you something?"

Numbly, she shook her head. What could he possibly bring her? she wondered bitterly. He couldn't bring Elias back. And he couldn't bring this war to an end. Those were the only two things that could make her world right again.

"He was a brave soldier, your brother," offered Captain Lee awkwardly. It was obvious he was disconcerted by her silence.

"Did you know Elias well?" she murmured. It seemed the appropriate thing to say. But she had to speak softly, or she would end up screaming.

"He fought in my cavalry regiment, under Colonel William Washington," Captain Lee explained. "We lost a lot of men at Monck's Corner, either killed or taken prisoner by Bloody Tarleton and his goddamn British Legion." His voice seethed with fury. He cast her an apologetic glance. "Forgive me for swearing, Miss Armstrong."

Despite the anguish swirling within her, Jo wanted to laugh at his gallant sense of propriety. Swearing was such an insignificant offense, compared to the atrocities of war. Compared to her brother's death.

"We call him the Butcher," remarked Captain Lee, as if he felt this was something she should know. Clearly he preferred to fill the silence with conversation. "Lieutenant Colonel Tarleton and his legion of Loyalists. They don't like to take prisoners, so they butcher as many men as they can." He paused. "Even after the men have surrendered," he ground out harshly.

She knew he was going to tell her something about Elias's death. Something horrible that had to do with this evil man Tarleton. *Please don't tell me. I don't want to know.* It seemed a pitiful, cowardly request. She could not bring herself to say it aloud.

"After Monck's Corner, a group of us joined up with Colonel Abraham Buford and his Virginia Continentals," Captain Lee continued. "They had been heading toward Charles Town, to help the American forces there. But Charles Town fell before Colonel Buford's force arrived. So we headed north. We camped at Waxhaws Creek, near the North Carolina border."

She had to stop him. She did not think she could bear hearing the details. But at the same time, something within her wanted to know. Wanted to know what those butchering redcoats had done to her Elias. And so she said nothing. She just sat there and gripped the arm of the sofa, as if it were a branch that was keeping her from drowning.

"Tarleton and his legion came after us," Captain Lee went on. "We fought them as fiercely as we could, but it quickly became clear we could not win against these vicious Tories. Since there was no point in sacrificing faithful men to a battle that could not be won, Colonel Buford sent forth an ensign waving a white flag of truce." His weathered face twisted with fury, deepening the lines. "And he was immediately shot down."

Jo looked at him in horror. To shoot the bearer of a white flag was a despicable, cowardly act, but worse than that, it signaled you had no intention of accepting a surrender. But the whole point of battle was to get the other side to surrender. Wasn't it?

"It was a massacre after that," stated Captain Lee, his voice low and bitter. "Tarleton's men slaughtered every man they came upon, even as our men threw down their arms and vainly tried to surrender. When we realized what was happening, some of us managed to get away. The rest the redcoats cut down with their swords and bayonets, hacking and stabbing at the wounded men who lay on the ground and begged for quarter. No one was spared." He looked at her with a mixture of rage and sympathy. "Including your brother."

Jo closed her eyes. Her mind was instantly flooded with images of men being hacked to pieces, their butchered bodies gushing fountains of scarlet blood, their deafening screams of agony tearing through the hot, still summer air. Brave, fine, helpless men, begging for mercy and being answered with the brutal thrust of a bayonet. The heavy stench of smoke, and blood, and death.

The air in the parlor became suffocating. A wave of nausea crashed over her, choking the breath out of her body. Elias was dead. Her beloved younger brother was dead. She inhaled sharply and snapped her eyes open, desperately trying to maintain control. But it was too late. A ragged moan escaped her lips.

From somewhere down the hall, Anne was calling her name. The doors to the parlor flew open with a bang, and Anne, Samuel, and Lucy rushed in.

"What is it?" demanded Anne, her voice trembling. "What has happened?"

Jo lifted her head and struggled to swallow the cries filling her throat. She shouldn't tell Anne in front of the children. She knew that. But it was too late. They all realized one of the Armstrong men was dead. She could see it in each of their stricken faces. The only question was, which one? It wasn't fair to keep Anne from the truth. She had every right to know it wasn't her husband.

"It's Elias," she managed brokenly. "Those evil redcoats have killed Elias."

They stared at her a moment in stunned silence. And then Lucy burst into tears and raced down the hall. Anne rushed out after her, calling her name. Jo raised her eyes to Samuel, who remained standing in the doorway. His lower lip began to quiver and he bit down on it brutally. His hands balled into tight fists, and his face contorted with pain and rage.

"Redcoat bastards!" he spat. His blue eyes seethed with hatred. "Do you see what they do, Jo? Do you see?"

Jo knew what he wanted to do. He wanted to reveal the redcoat in the barn, as a way of punishing the redcoats for Elias's death. First they had killed his father, and now his brother. She could well understand his feelings. At this moment, she too hated that redcoat in the barn. It didn't matter if he had been involved in the slaughter at Waxhaws or not. The uniform he wore condemned him. And yet, somewhere deep in her heart she knew that was wrong.

"No, Samuel," she ordered, adamantly shaking her head. "No." Samuel did not understand the consequences if he told the rebels they were tending a British soldier in their barn. He would be condemning Jo and Anne as traitors. He would be condemning them to death.

"I hate them!" he cried furiously. Tears began to spill from his eyes, wetting his smooth, freckle-spattered cheeks. "I hate all of them!" It seemed to be a plea for her to understand what he was about to do.

"Samuel, please," begged Jo, desperately trying to dissuade him in front of Captain Lee without revealing anything.

"Not just the one who killed Father, or the one who killed Elias," he continued, his strained voice cracking with emotion. *"All of them!"*

She rose to her feet and went to put her arms around him, her heart torn in two by his terrible pain.

He shoved her away and glared at her as if she were somehow responsible for Elias's death.

Captain Lee rose from his chair. "Miss Armstrong, if there is anything I can do—"

"I'll see them all dead!" shouted Samuel wildly. "All of them!" His voice had become a terrible, anguished scream. *"Including the one in the barn!"*

Captain Lee stared at him in shock.

Her chest tight with panic, Jo whirled around to face the rebel officer. "Captain Lee," she began desperately, "my brother is very distraught and—"

"The barn!" bellowed Captain Lee, his powerful voice reverberating off the walls of the room. He cast Jo a look of fury, then raced out of the room and down the hall. *"Search the goddamn barn!"*

Damien watched the soldiers lying around the yard through a crack between the boards of the barn. They were all stretched out on the shaded ground beneath a huge tree, looking hot, tired, and utterly bored. He had been watching them from the moment they rode up to the house. Initially he assumed they had come for him. It seemed Miss Armstrong had sent word to the rebels of his presence, despite her promise to him that she would not. Rage had flooded through him in that moment. But when he saw her standing on the verandah talking with their captain, her face pale and taut with anxiety, he was no longer so sure she had invited the rebels here. The soldiers had seen the blood on the ground and started to wander about. He was certain they would see the stains that led straight to the barn. But then Miss Armstrong said something, and the soldiers immediately lost interest. The captain followed her inside, while the remaining men found places to lie on the ground. The other girl, Anne, brought them water, which they drank. Then she returned to the house, and the men lay down to rest. A couple of them looked as if they might even be sleeping.

He leaned heavily against the wall, clutching his bandaged side and breathing deeply. A nauseating wave of dizziness swept over him, forcing him to close his eyes. He cursed. His wounds were throbbing viciously from the strain of his movements. If he moved too much, the stitches would not hold. Still, he could not go back and lie down. If these rebel soldiers suddenly decided to look for him, they sure as hell would not find him sprawled out, half naked and helpless on a mound of straw. He briefly scanned the barn for his weapons, but of course the girl had taken them away from him. Not that he was fool enough to believe he could fight five armed soldiers anyway, especially in his weakened condition. If the rebels headed toward the barn, his only chance would be to get on Glory and ride like hellfire out those doors.

The odds of his escaping were so pathetically ridiculous he refused to think about them.

The front door of the house swung open and the captain came racing out onto the verandah. He appeared extremely agitated as he spoke to his men. Damien could not hear what he was saying. Within seconds it did not matter. The men on the ground sprang from their reclining positions, including the injured ones, and quickly began to move toward the barn, loading their muskets as they went. Their expressions were filled with predaceous excitement and wary anticipation.

"Damn deceiving bitch!" swore Damien furiously. He moved awkwardly across the barn to the stall where Glory stood watching him. He breathed deeply as he entered the stall and swiftly slipped the bridle over his horse's head. He was forced to lean his forehead against Glory's neck for a few seconds, fighting the dizziness and pain that was making him weak and clumsy. There was no time for his saddle. He grunted loudly as he hoisted himself up onto Glory's back; it felt as if the movement had torn his side wide open.

The rebels were trying to be quiet as they approached the barn, obviously thinking they would catch him unawares. Damien bent low over Glory's shoulders and nudged him over to the doors leading out to the yard. Speed and surprise. These were the only two things he had left. To thunder out those doors and ride Glory right over whoever was foolish enough to get in his way. Adrenaline began to pump through his body as he waited for the right moment.

Jo stood alone on the verandah, watching as the rebel soldiers moved cautiously toward the barn. Her heart was pounding so hard she thought it would burst through her chest. Despite her anguish over Elias's death, she wanted to scream a warning to the redcoat. It was absolutely crazy, of course. She knew he didn't have a chance against five armed soldiers. Even so, she wanted him to at least know they were coming. But if she warned him, it would only make things worse for her and her family, and now she had to think of them first. She had put them in enough danger as it was. She did not want to contemplate what the soldiers were going to do with her once they had captured the redcoat. Hopefully she could convince them that she was fully responsible, and they would leave Anne and the children alone.

Captain Lee and three of the soldiers were loading and raising the muskets as they moved. The one with the wounded arm positioned himself at the barn door, preparing to swing it open. The others formed a line in front of it.

"All right, you worthless, gutless lobsterback," called Captain Lee harshly. "Come out slowly, with your hands high." He nodded to the soldier at the door to open it.

The heavy wooden door swung open. Jo squinted her eyes, trying to shut out the bright glare of the sun and see into the darkness of the barn.

For the briefest of seconds everything was still.

Suddenly the redcoat came crashing out of the barn on his magnificent horse, bent low over the animal's neck, with one hand gripping the reins and the other clutching his wounded side. The rebels went flying backward like startled geese, swearing and shouting in surprise as they tried to avoid being trampled to death by those thundering hooves. The redcoat surged past them, his horse throwing up clouds of bloodstained dust as he flew by.

Go, thought Jo desperately, confused by the conflicting emotions churning within her. Get as far away from here as you can.

Captain Lee quickly recovered from his shock, lifted his musket, and fired. The shot missed.

"His horse, goddamn it," roared Captain Lee furiously as

he struggled to reload his weapon. "Aim for his goddamn horse!"

The soldiers obediently lifted their muskets and fired. A second later the redcoat's horse let out a terrible cry of pain. The animal hesitated a moment, its beautiful neck arched in agony. It bravely tried to take a few more steps.

Then it whimpered and crashed heavily onto the ground, taking the redcoat down with him.

"I got him!" bellowed the huge bear soldier triumphantly. He let out a whoop of pleasure. "Did you see that?"

"Noooo!!" screamed Jo, her heart bursting with anguish. She gathered her skirts in her hands and tore across the yard toward the redcoat and his fallen horse. The rebels followed slowly behind her, casually reloading their muskets as they walked.

Damien moved off Glory's back and placed his hands on the animal's sides, urgently trying to see where he had been injured. A black hole in Glory's side was gurgling blood like a scarlet spring. The musket ball was buried somewhere deep within him.

"Jesus Christ, Glory, I'm sorry," said Damien to the hopelessly injured beast.

Glory snorted and vainly tried to get up, as if he knew it was imperative that they get away.

"No, stay," soothed Damien, moving closer to Glory's head. He began to stroke his neck. "It's all right," he said quietly. "You're a good boy. Just stay."

Jo reached them before the rebels did. "Oh God," she blurted out helplessly as she saw the blood leaking from the horse. She lifted her eyes to Damien's. "Are you hurt?" Her voice was raw and desperate.

The look of scathing contempt he cast her made her blood run cold. "I am just fine, Miss Armstrong," he replied sarcastically. His gray eyes were burning with rage. "Thank you for asking."

"Please," she began urgently, "I never—"

"Well, well," interrupted Captain Lee in a darkly satisfied voice as he moved closer to them. "Looks like we've caught a genuine bloodyback here, judging from that nasty mess on his back."

Damien stiffened at the reference to his scars, but said nothing. He ignored the rebels and continued to stroke Glory's neck.

"Get up, you worthless lobsterback dog," ordered the bear soldier, "or I'll shoot you like I did your horse!"

With a snarl of rage Damien leapt to his feet and smashed his fist twice into the face of the startled rebel. The huge soldier let out a howl of surprise. The other three soldiers immediately went to his aid, viciously clubbing Damien with their fists and muskets until blood was leaking from his mouth and he was staggering beneath their blows.

"Stop it!" Jo screamed, appalled by their brutality. "You'll kill him!"

Captain Lee turned and regarded her thoughtfully for a moment. His grave blue eyes had grown hard.

The rebel soldiers continued to ruthlessly beat Damien, who was weak but still struggling. Captain Lee looked on, apparently untroubled by the savagery of his men. It was only when Damien collapsed to the ground and the soldiers continued to kick him and strike him with the butts of their muskets, that he finally called out "Enough!"

The bearlike soldier gave him one last kick to his ribs before he broke away.

"Tie his wrists," ordered Captain Lee.

Two of the rebels grabbed Damien by his shoulders and hauled him roughly to his feet. They wrenched his arms behind his back and bound his wrists. His mouth was filled with blood. He slowly lifted his gaze to the captain. Then he spat a red stream contemptuously onto the ground.

"My compliments to your rebel training," he drawled. "Your men seem to have developed a real fondness for their work."

"What is your name and rank, soldier?" demanded Captain Lee, ignoring his sarcasm.

"I am Lieutenant Colonel Damien Powell." Damien enjoyed the look of surprise on Captain Lee's face. It was obvious he had not realized he was dealing with an officer, and one with a notorious reputation at that.

"So, you are the infamous Colonel Powell," stated Captain Lee. The corners of his mouth lifted in a hostile smile, indicating he was pleased with the significance of his catch. "Well, Colonel, you are now my prisoner."

"Thank you for clarifying the situation."

Glory raised his head and let out a whimper of pain. Using his last shreds of strength, he made another pathetic attempt to stand.

"Easy, boy," called Damien. Ignoring the rebel soldiers, he began to move toward his fallen horse.

The bear soldier started to stop him, but Captain Lee raised his hand in restraint.

Drowning in despair, Jo watched as Damien awkwardly knelt beside his magnificent horse. The sun beat down on its cinnamon-colored coat, making it glisten like burnished copper. Unable to lay his hands on the animal to calm him as he had done before, Damien leaned his bloodied face over him and spoke quietly into his ear. Jo could not hear what he said. Glory snorted and lowered his head onto the ground, breathing in shallow, rapid pants. Pink froth began to foam around his mouth.

Damien lifted his gaze to the rebel soldiers. "Would one of you put him out of his misery?" His voice was strained and bitter.

The soldiers looked at each other uncertainly a moment. "I ain't wastin' good powder and shot on some dyin' Brit horse," sneered the bear soldier. He spat on the ground. "Let him suffer."

"How many times has that horse helped you kill one of us?" demanded the tall, scrawny rebel with the festering thigh. "Don't see why we should show it mercy. You redcoats showed none to us at Waxhaws." He planted his musket defiantly on the ground and leaned heavily against it.

Damien cast them a look of disgust. He wished to God he had his pistol so he could shoot poor Glory himself.

Jo stared incredulously at the rebel soldiers. Then she marched over to the soldier with the injured thigh and snatched his musket-crutch out from under him, causing him to swear furiously as he struggled to regain his balance.

"Give me my goddamn musket!" he snarled.

Jo glared at him, her eyes glittering with contempt. Then she moved to Damien and his horse. None of the other soldiers tried to stop her. She did not know why, and she did not care.

The horse lifted his head as she approached, staring at her with huge, pain-drenched eyes. Innocent eyes, which did not understand war, or emotions like anger and hatred. Or blame. Jo raised the musket and took careful aim at his head. The animal whimpered. Damien said something to him, but Jo could not hear beyond the roaring in her ears.

It seemed that death was all around her. Blood, and death, and suffering. She wanted it to stop. She bit down hard on her trembling lip, and took a deep breath.

"I'm sorry," she whispered brokenly. Her finger squeezed the trigger.

The musket exploded, blasting a hole into Glory's magnificent head. He lurched in reaction, then lay still. Blood began to pulse from the hole.

She threw the musket onto the ground as if it had scalded her. Slowly she turned to Damien. "I'm sorry," she managed, feeling sick and helpless and guilty. "I'm so sorry."

He raised his blood-smeared face to her. His bared chest and back were covered in cuts and dirt, and blood was starting to seep through the layers of his now filthy bandages. His gray eyes were ice-cold, and filled with loathing. "I'm sure you are," he grated out.

"Take Colonel Powell back to camp," ordered Captain Lee. "I'll deal with him when I return."

Jo watched in misery as the bearlike soldier jerked Damien to his feet and tied a length of rope to his bound wrists. The other soldiers retrieved their horses and brought them over. Then they mounted, leaving Damien on the ground. The bear soldier tied the end of the rope to his saddle and hoisted himself up.

"You cannot expect him to walk," gasped Jo. She turned

and looked at Captain Lee. "His injuries are too grave—you will kill him!"

"Given the number of American soldiers he and his regiment have killed, I am afraid that possibility does not trouble me," he said tautly. "You should be more concerned about what is to happen to you than to this piece of red-coat scum."

"But what good is he to you if he is dead?" Jo demanded, ignoring his threat. "He is a lieutenant colonel—he must have important information that could help you." With that statement perhaps she could convince them she had always meant to turn him over, and give them a reason not to kill him at the same time.

Pure, black rage exploded within Damien. How could he have been so blind to her? he wondered bitterly. How could he have allowed himself to believe she would honor her oath not to turn him over? He had been a fool to think he could trust her.

"Treacherous rebel bitch!" he spat.

Jo stepped back as if he had struck her. His dark eyes were burning with fury. He had risked himself to save her and her family. Now he believed she had betrayed him. She wanted to tell him she had tried to protect him. But Captain Lee and the others were watching, and she was afraid. Afraid of what they would do to her and her family if she admitted that she had wanted the redcoat to simply heal and go away. To ride off on his beautiful horse, back to wherever he came from on that terrible afternoon when she had knelt beneath the blazing Carolina sky and waited for her life to end. The afternoon when he had unexpectedly ridden into her life, and risked everything so she could live.

"Bennett," began Captain Lee, speaking to the bear soldier, "I will be staying here to question Miss Armstrong and her family. Make sure the prisoner is kept alive long enough for me to interrogate him when I return to camp."

Bennett scowled, obviously displeased with his orders. "Yes, Captain."

"Until we meet again, Miss Armstrong," drawled

Damien. "Perhaps one day I will be able to repay your kind hospitality."

Jo could feel his hatred.

"Move out!" ordered Captain Lee sharply.

The horses began to walk, and Damien staggered after them. Jo watched as the soldiers slowly led him around the lifeless body of his horse, her heart constricting in pain. Her father was dead. Elias was dead. And a redcoat named Lieutenant Colonel Damien Powell would soon be dead, because he had been foolish enough to risk his life for a family that turned out to be his enemies.

As the soldiers moved out of the yard, Captain Lee turned to her. "And now, Miss Armstrong, I am afraid it is my duty to place you under arrest for aiding and concealing a dangerous enemy of the United States of America," he informed her coldly. "Whether or not I arrest your sister-in-law as well and have you both executed for treason will depend on you." He tilted his head toward the house.

Jo slowly turned and began to walk toward the house, with Captain Lee following closely behind her.

$\mathcal{Y}$ou don't know how it pains me, Miss Armstrong, to see the way you and your family have so thoroughly dishonored your father's and brother's memory," said Captain Lee grimly as he contemplated his whiskey.

"I always meant to turn him over."

It was a complete lie of course, but the truth would instantly condemn her and Anne as traitors. She knew her protest of innocence was cowardly. After all, she had betrayed her country. The honorable thing to do would be to admit her crime and stand trial for it. But if she were arrested, Lucy and Samuel and Anne would be left alone in a violent, war-torn countryside. Even worse, Anne might be arrested as well. However guilty Jo might be of treason, she could not allow that to happen. Anne and the children could not be punished for what had been her decision alone.

Captain Lee settled back in his chair and studied her, his expression hard. "Then why didn't you tell me Colonel Powell was in your barn the minute we arrived?"

"I was afraid." That part at least was true. "The children

were outside, and I feared they might get hurt if a struggle suddenly erupted between your men and the redcoat."

"Don't play me for a fool, Miss Armstrong," he warned brusquely. "You had more than enough opportunity to inform me you had a redcoat in your barn after the children were inside. As I recall, you and I came and sat in this very room. At that point there was no danger of either my men or Colonel Powell hearing what you had to tell me. Yet you said nothing."

"You were telling me my brother was dead!" burst out Jo, her heart flooding with fresh anguish. "Of course I forgot about having a redcoat lying in my barn—surely you can understand that?"

He studied her over the rim of his glass. "Perhaps," he allowed. "But what of your sister-in-law? What kept her from speaking up?"

"Anne was expecting me to tell you," explained Jo. "I am head of this household in my brothers' absence. Anne cannot be held accountable for my actions."

Captain Lee tilted his head back and drained his glass. "I can hold each and every damn one of you accountable, if I so choose," he informed her harshly, banging his glass down on the table. He rose from his chair and began to prowl restlessly about the room.

"Colonel Powell has made quite a reputation for himself here, not unlike that of his good friend Tarleton." His voice was bitter. "He leads a band of men called the Scarlet Legion. These redcoats have slaughtered hundreds of Patriots, both on and off the battlefield." He paused and narrowed his gaze on her. "Men like your father and brother, Miss Armstrong." He began to pace the room again. "He is responsible for the capture of at least three wagon trains carrying much-needed food and supplies for our soldiers, leaving them severely weakened before battle. He is known to order attacks on soldiers when they are most vulnerable, seeking them out in the middle of the night, then brutally hacking them to pieces as they sleep. He and his Scarlet Legion have terrorized the countryside, viciously attacking helpless, peaceful homes where they murder the men before raping and torturing the women. Whatever they can't steal they burn, including the crops. That way, if anyone miraculously manages to survive one of their attacks, they will starve to death instead."

Jo shook her head, trying to imagine the redcoat she had cared for committing such atrocities.

He moved to stand behind her. "In a recent raid on a plantation home, a beautiful young woman like yourself was found brutally murdered in her bed." His voice was soft and deadly cold. "Her unborn child had been cut from her womb. Written on the wall above, in her own blood, were the words: 'Thou shalt never give birth to a rebel.'" He leaned down until his mouth hovered just inches from her ear and hissed, "Not exactly the kind of man who deserves to be nursed and hidden from his enemies, is he?"

"I wasn't trying to hide him," insisted Jo. She closed her eyes, appalled by Captain Lee's words. She thought of Colonel Powell lying bleeding and helpless in her barn. She had known from the beginning that his uniform made him ruthless. She had felt it in the crush of his grip as he held her against him and made her swear before God not to turn him over. The soldier she had tended was a man of relentless determination. She had accepted that.

But she had never imagined him to be the hideous monster Captain Lee was describing.

"As a military officer, I have to go by what I see," he continued, moving away from her. "I see an infamous British colonel, all bandaged and lying as comfortable as you please in a barn. Not tied or locked up, with no one guarding him, and with easy access to his horse." He paused to splash more whiskey into his glass. "Now, I come along, and no one bothers to tell me of this dangerous prisoner, even though there is plenty of opportunity to do so." He fixed his cool gaze on her. "Just what am I supposed to think, Miss Armstrong?"

"He was not tied or guarded because his wounds were severe—he could not have escaped even if he wanted to," Jo protested.

"He was doing a remarkable job of escaping before my men shot his horse out from under him."

"But I did not think he would be able to escape," Jo countered stubbornly. "And I would have told you about him, if you hadn't shocked me first with the news of Elias's death."

Captain Lee regarded her for a long moment, weighing her explanation. Then he drained his glass and soberly shook his head. "I'm afraid, Miss Armstrong, you will have to explain that to an army court." He sounded genuinely disturbed by the thought.

Panic, fresh and dark, began to surge through her. "You mean to arrest me?"

He nodded. "And your sister-in-law as well. I cannot be sure that she was not part of your deception."

"But you can't!" burst out Jo, horrified. "What about Samuel and Lucy? Who will look after them?"

Captain Lee shrugged his shoulders. "Perhaps you could leave them with your neighbors," he suggested. "If not, the children can accompany you to your trial until other arrangements can be made for them."

It was a nightmare, what he was describing. Samuel and Lucy accompany her to a trial where she would be sentenced to death? And what of Anne? If she were arrested, the shock of such a terrible ordeal might cause her to lose her baby. "My sister-in-law is expecting a child," she said, her voice tight with fear. "You cannot arrest her."

He sighed and shook his head. "It is unfortunate," he admitted, "but it does not excuse her treasonous acts. Perhaps the court will be merciful in her case. Sometimes women who are with child behave irrationally. However, I cannot allow her condition to prevent me from carrying out my duty."

Jo gave him an imploring look. "I will go with you, Captain Lee," she promised. "I will tell the court what happened, and they can punish me however they see fit. But I beg you, do not arrest Anne. She is innocent in all this. Let her stay here and take care of the children. Please."

He studied her a moment, contemplating her request. Jo

struggled to appear calm, while on the inside she wanted to scream. Her entire world was shattering, and there was nothing she could do to stop it.

"There is a possibility," he began at last, "I might be willing to reconsider this entire, unfortunate situation. But it would mean you would have to prove to me beyond a doubt of your loyalty to the Patriot cause."

A spark of hope lit within her. "How?"

He poured more whiskey into his glass. Then he went to the window and stared pensively at the trees and fields beyond. "It just so happens," he mused quietly, "I am in serious need of a spy." He took a hearty mouthful of his drink. "And you, Miss Armstrong, might be just what I am looking for."

She wasn't sure she had heard him correctly. "A spy?"

"I am looking for a woman of a particular strength and courage," he continued. "A woman who is shrewd and determined, and not given to hysteria and tears. A woman who is able to weave a convincing lie. To perform, if you get my meaning."

Jo started to protest, but he raised his hand to silence her. "I am not, of course, suggesting that you have been lying to me," he qualified, his tone faintly acerbic. "However, I have seen how you handle yourself in a situation of extreme emotional pain and stress. I have watched you relieve a soldier of his weapon and fire it." He paused and slowly surveyed her up and down, his appraisal strangely void of both lust and menace. Jo felt as if she were a farm animal he was contemplating buying. "It is clear you are a woman of considerable resources," he concluded.

Jo was not sure which resources he was referring to, but she felt reasonably certain he did not only mean her ability to stand her ground. "Just what, exactly, would I have to do?" she asked warily.

"The surrender of Charles Town last month was a disastrous blow to us." His voice was low and bitter. "General Lincoln held out against the redcoats for as long as he could, until it became obvious the bastards intended to blow the city up street by street. Almost the entire southern rebel army was forced to surrender." He shook his head in anger. "Nearly five thousand men were captured, and all their weapons and ammunition. Now the redcoats are using Charles Town as the base for their operations in the south. General Cornwallis and his lobsterback officers have moved into the finest homes in the city, after arresting the men who own them and tossing their families into the street.

"They are rewarding themselves by throwing parties and balls," he continued with contempt. "Naturally they want women there, so they invite residents of Charles Town whom they believe to be Loyalist, and who have taken the oath of loyalty to the king. But," he qualified, "they have no real way of knowing if those who claim to be Tory really are."

Unease rippled through Jo as she realized what Captain Lee was asking of her. "Are you saying you want me to go to Charles Town and spy at these parties?" she asked, incredulous.

He nodded. "It is the perfect opportunity for a spy. Men at parties drink and laugh, and tend to forget themselves, especially around a beautiful woman. You could befriend some of the officers, and earn their trust. Then you could casually turn the conversation to the subject of the war. Any information they reveal, however small or seemingly insignificant, could help us. And at this moment," he finished bluntly, "we need all the damn help we can get."

It was impossible, what he was suggesting. "But I don't know anything about balls or parties," she protested. "I've never been to the city. I don't even know how to dance."

"That would all be taken care of. We would find someone to teach you, and give you time to learn before you went out into society."

"I have nothing to wear." Her tone was a mixture of helplessness and mounting panic. "And I hardly think they would let me into a ball wearing a gown like this." She gestured to her faded work dress.

Captain Lee did not appear to be concerned. "Our contact in Charles Town would see that you had a suitable wardrobe. She would also make certain you were taught the social graces you needed before you attended your first affair. Then she would watch over you, and see to it that you were introduced to the British officers. You would not be out there alone," he pointed out, attempting to reassure her.

Jo bit her lip as she considered this. What Captain Lee was proposing was extremely dangerous. Yet, in a strange, exhilarating way, it was enormously tempting as well. After all, she hated the British army. They had murdered her father and viciously butchered her brother. The idea of striking back at them was sweet indeed, and as a spy, she might be able to deal them a significant blow. Why should her brothers be the only ones to fight this war? If she had been a man, she would have taken up arms and joined General Washington's army as proudly as Benjamin and Abraham had, and woe to the miserable redcoats who came within range of her musket.

But the idea of going to a strange city and spying on British officers was terrifying. She had no idea if she could learn to dance and pretend to be a Loyalist lady of society. Even if she could, how would she ever be able to conceal her hatred of the redcoats? How could she attend parties, and laugh and talk and let them dance with her, when all she wanted to do was spit in their faces? And if she were caught, she would immediately be executed for spying. She could expect no mercy from her redcoat enemies.

"I can't do it," she stammered, her stomach knotting with fear.

Captain Lee's blue eyes narrowed. He left the window and seated himself in the chair opposite her. "Think carefully before you make your decision," he advised, the suggestion mild yet threatening. "You have been caught harboring a highly dangerous senior British officer, whom you carefully nursed and attempted to hide. This man is responsible for the slaughter of hundreds of American men. Decent, patriotic, honorable men like your father and brother. I could easily arrest your entire family and charge them all with treason. Instead, I am offering you an alternative. If you perform your mission successfully, it will convince me that your failure to turn Colonel Powell over to me immediately was merely an unfortunate oversight, and not worthy of criminal charges.'"

Jo shifted uneasily on the sofa.

"Think of the shame it will bring upon your family, to know you have performed such a highly treasonous deed." He leaned toward her, making her feel trapped. "How will your other brothers, who still fight in the Continental Army, feel when they hear this terrible news?"

Her brothers would be ashamed of her. There was no doubt about that. Horrified, appalled, and utterly ashamed.

"This is a way for you to absolve yourself and your sister-in-law of this most unhappy incident," Captain Lee said, his tone eminently reasonable. "Don't you feel you owe this to her? And what of her unborn child? Don't you owe it to your brother to do everything in your power to save that child?"

Anne's baby. How could she let anything happen to either Anne or her baby? Jo wondered desperately. Perhaps what Captain Lee was proposing wasn't so terrible. All she had to do was spy on the redcoats occupying Charles Town and send back reports. In return, Anne would be safe. She would be able to stay here and look after Samuel and Lucy. And the dreadful dishonor Jo had brought to the Armstrong name would be erased. When she returned home, they could pretend it never happened.

"What if something went wrong?" she asked. "What would I be expected to do?"

"Should something go wrong, and you find yourself in danger, your contact would help you leave Charles Town immediately." You would return here to your farm, and I would contact you as soon as I was able. But if for some reason you left Charles Town and failed to return here, Miss Armstrong," he added warningly, "I would be forced to conclude that you had betrayed us yet again. If you did so, I would have your sister-in-law arrested."

She was afraid of what he was asking her to do. But she was even more afraid to refuse. Refusal meant her and Anne's arrest, and a hideous mark of shame that would dishonor her family for generations. Her father's and brother's sacrifices would be buried beneath her treasonous conduct. And if she were discovered, what could the redcoats possibly do to her that was worse than being hung by her own countrymen as a traitor?

She took a deep, shaky breath, trying to push from her mind the ghastly image of the young woman with her baby cut out.

"Very well, Captain Lee," she said. "Tell me what I have to do."

Damien leaned back against the tree he was tied to and regarded the bear soldier through a fog of pain and exhaustion.

"Hungry, redcoat?" asked Bennett with a sneer. He slowly bit into a hard, unripe apple, grimaced slightly, and began to chew. "Bet you lobsterbacks are used to eatin' fancy meals. Stealin' food from us rebels so you can fill your redcoat bellies before you kill us. Ain't that right, redcoat?"

Damien shifted his position and said nothing. He was extremely hungry, but he knew this Bennett would never share his food. Being fully aware of the unpleasant intestinal results of eating such unripe fare, he had no desire to partake anyway.

"Where's your Scarlet Legion, Colonel Powell? An important British officer like you, you'd think these woods would be crawlin' with redcoats just dyin' to set you free." He spat a tough piece of apple skin onto the ground. "Wouldn't you?"

Damien shook his head. "I got separated from my regiment weeks ago. They could be anywhere by now."

Bennett considered this as he picked at his stained teeth with a filthy fingernail. "Is that so?" He sucked a wayward bit of apple through a gap in his teeth and smiled. "Then I guess your sorry redcoat ass belongs to me now."

Damien closed his eyes, uninterested in responding. He knew this soldier was stupid and brutish, and he had no desire to waste his waning strength arguing with him.

He was numb with exhaustion. The rebel soldiers had dragged him behind their horses all day in the blistering heat, never once stopping to rest. Darkness had fallen by the time they finally reached this camp, joining with perhaps another seventy or so men. He had been taunted and jeered as he staggered into their midst. On learning he was the notorious Colonel Powell, the rebels surged forward, spitting at him and trying to get in a few blows. But the soldiers who had brought him here made certain no one touched him.

Evidently Captain Lee's order that he be kept alive and coherent until his return was to be taken seriously.

The wound in his side had finally stopped bleeding. He was grateful Miss Armstrong's stitching was more reliable than her sworn oath. The wound had opened slightly, but most of the stitches had held. If he could just keep infection at bay, he would survive. He thought perhaps he had cracked a rib during his fight with the rebels, but his whole body was aching so profusely he could not be sure.

One of Captain Lee's junior officers had attempted to question him, perhaps thinking to impress his captain with vital information when he returned. The sergeant barked questions at him again and again, threatening him with beatings and starvation in a rebel prison if he did not cooperate. Damien knew the man was trying to take advantage of his severely weakened state, hoping it would cause him to accidentally reveal some important military information. It was exactly what he would have done had the situation been reversed. But his years in the British army had left Damien nothing if not disciplined. Nothing they could do to him would make him reveal information that might compromise his side. Nothing.

The sergeant had ordered him searched. Since all he wore were his breeches and boots, this was merely a formality. The young man seemed disappointed that there were no grounds for him to charge Damien with spying. He carried no incriminating documents on him, and although he was half naked, what he did wear could hardly be considered a disguise. Once his interrogation was finished, the sergeant irritably assured Damien that when Captain Lee was through with him, he would wish he had merely been executed.

The thought was not reassuring.

"Hey, redcoat, what'd you do to earn that whippin' on your back?" demanded Bennett suddenly.

Damien slowly opened his eyes.

"Made an awful mess of you, whatever it was," the rebel commented, his voice taunting.

Ignore him. He is trying to provoke you. Don't be led into it.

"Yes, sir, a mess like that would take a whole lot of lashes. A whole lot."

Two hundred, thought Damien bitterly. Two hundred lashes, to punish him for forgetting his place in the British army hierarchy. Two hundred lashes, to teach him a lesson he had needed to learn, and would never forget. Never, ever react impulsively, unless you are willing to accept the consequences. Especially when you are dealing with someone who has power over you. However insignificant or unjust that power may seem. It had been a lesson in control and discipline, and he had learned it well.

Lash by excruciating lash.

"Must be awful to be whipped like a dog," continued Bennett with mock sympathy. "Must make a man feel lower than a snake."

"You're wrong," remarked Damien quietly.

Bennett snorted with laughter. "I suppose you're tryin' to tell me you liked it?"

"I didn't say that."

"Then what the hell are you sayin?"

Damien sighed and closed his eyes, fighting dizziness. "I am saying that nothing any man does to me can make me feel 'lower than a snake,' as you so aptly put it."

The rebel frowned in confusion. "Is that so?" he grated sarcastically. "And just why the hell not?"

He didn't respond.

"Answer me, you goddamn redcoat!" snapped the soldier impatiently.

But Damien didn't respond. He closed his eyes and began to snore, pretending he had fallen asleep.

Bennett cursed and flung the remains of his mangled apple core at him. Then he pulled himself to his feet and stalked away.

Because, thought Damien, his mind once again starting to burn with fever, *only I can make myself feel that low.*

The wind blew cool and sweet across the hills, rippling through the tall grasses that painted the land in alternate shades of pale green and lemon and gold. Damien inhaled deeply, drawing the cool, fragrant air into his lungs. The wind caressed his cheeks and blew his hair about his shoulders as he studied the enormous dove-gray estate that rose from an emerald sea of velvety lawns in the distance. How splendid Waverley looked, set against the slate-colored sky with its dark, smoky clouds threatening to burst any moment and drown them all in a deluge of silvery cold rain. How he loved to look upon it, and pretend he was still a boy and that this was still his home. Warm and safe, and filled with his mother's gentle laughter, and the soft touch of her cool fingers against his brow as she vainly tried to discipline a wayward lock of hair.

He took a step and was at the front door, which of course made no sense at all, but it was his dream and he could do whatever the hell he liked in it. His brother's butler tried to stop him from entering. He shoved the man aside and went in, determined to find Victoria. He raced up the enormous staircase two steps at a time, crazed by the muffled sound of her weeping. He flung her bedroom door open and stood there, dripping wet, wild with fury.

And aching with a desperate, hopeful need, the kind that will not accept that some things are simply not possible.

Victoria was seated at her dressing table, wrapped in layer upon filmy layer of rose-colored silk. Her hair was unbound and flowing in a cloak of chestnut curls down her back. She slowly lifted her ashen face to the mirror and he saw a plum-colored stain spreading beneath her eye, shimmering with crystal tears. A terrible rage exploded within him, stripping him of his ability to think. He would kill him; he would find his brother and smash his fist into his smug, self-satisfied, arrogant face until no feature was left recognizable. Then he would wrap his hands around his throat and slowly choke the life out of him.

And he would enjoy it.

"No!" pleaded Victoria, her voice as soft and helpless as the bleating of a lamb. But nothing could have stopped him in that moment. So tremendous was his fury, so deep and cutting and torturous was his love for her, that nothing could have kept him from punishing the man who took such savage pleasure in tormenting her.

He was in Frederick's study, all carved mahogany and polished oak, dark and oiled and vaguely musty. The smoky scent of burning firewood and dust-laden books, out of reach and never read. And there sat Frederick, shorter than he, heavier, with thinning hair and liver-colored lips, staring at him with supercilious disdain. The eldest son. The Earl of Strathmore. The man who became obsessed with stealing Victoria away from him, and then, once he had her, proceeded to punish her endlessly for having once loved Damien. Damien hated his brother for taking away what should have been his. And hated him even more for treating what he loved with such contemptuous cruelty. But no more. Today he would take Victoria far away, and Frederick would never be able to hurt her again.

He was shouting at him, telling him what he thought of a man who would beat and terrorize a woman. And Frederick was laughing and reminding him that she was his wife, and he could do whatever he wanted to her. A terrible rage exploded within Damien, pure, blazing, uncontrollable. His hands were around Frederick's throat.

His brother's eyes were bulging with fear.

Victoria floated in, pink and soft and gentle as an angel, her loose, rose-colored gown wafting about her as if she were traveling on a gust of wind. "Please stop, Damien," she whispered. He did, releasing his iron grip on his brother so he could reach out and gently caress the silk of her purple-stained cheek. She was small and beautiful and delicate, and he wanted to wrap his arms around her and take her away to a place where he could love her and keep her safe. He bent down to kiss her. And then Frederick was coming toward them, a heavy brass poker raised high above his head. "Goddamn whore!" he snarled. The poker began to fall.

"No!" roared Damien, roughly hurling Victoria out of the way.

Damien twisted and turned in an effort to waken, but the dream tightened its relentless grip on him and forced him to continue.

Victoria lay on the carpet before the heavy marble-topped sideboard she had fallen against, moaning softly. Suddenly her eyes flew open and she screamed. Blood and fluid from the fragile life within her began to leak onto the rose silk of her gown, and she writhed in agony. Horrified, Damien lifted her into his arms and carried her up to her room as she wept. A doctor dressed in black closed her door and went downstairs to speak with Frederick. Damien slipped silently into her room where she lay against cool, white sheets, her hair damp, her face drawn and pale. He reached out to gently take her hand.

"You killed him!" she shrieked, the words cleaving his heart in two. "I hate you, I hate you, I hate you!" Her face began to change, and suddenly it wasn't Victoria anymore, but that treacherous golden-haired farm girl, spewing her hatred at him as if he alone were responsible for the war and all the death and devastation it had brought. "Murderer!" she cried. She clawed at his arms and chest and face. *"Murderer!"*

"No!" he protested roughly, thrashing around as he tried to stop her from tearing at him. "No!"

"Jesus Christ, Damien, take it easy!"

The voice cut through the thick, swirling torment of the dream. He stopped struggling and opened his eyes.

A British soldier was leaning over him, slicing loose the rope that bound him to the tree. He thought his mind must be playing tricks on him.

"Gil?" he murmured in disbelief.

Gil smiled. "Nice to see you alive, Colonel Powell."

Damien struggled through the mists of his fever and looked around. Two rebel soldiers lay motionless, sprawled facedown on the ground. No other soldiers were in sight. "What the hell is happening?" he demanded, still feverish but suddenly alert.

"We have been looking for you for three days," explained Gil as he sawed at the rope tying Damien's wrists. "While searching for you, we found this rebel camp, and the next thing we knew, you showed up. There are only a dozen of us, so we couldn't attack. I ordered the men to create a distraction about a mile west of here, firing off their muskets as fast as possible so it would seem as if there were more of them. Sure enough, all the rebels went to see what was happening, leaving only two soldiers to guard you. I took care of them." His knife sliced through the rope at Damien's ankles. "I must say, you look like absolute bloody hell, my friend. Let's get out of here." He grabbed Damien's arm and helped him to his feet.

Savage pain tore through Damien. He ground his teeth together, ordering himself to ignore it.

"Jesus Christ, can you walk?" demanded Gil.

Damien clutched at his wounded side and leaned heavily against his friend. "Yes. Let's go."

Together the two of them began to move as fast as Damien's injuries would allow toward Gil's horse.

"Only one mount?" asked Damien.

"Sorry. Where's Glory?"

"Dead."

Gil inhaled sharply. "Jesus, Damien, I'm sorry."

Damien nodded. Only Gil knew how fond Damien had been of his horse.

"Colonel Powell, I am insulted that you wish to leave us so soon," interrupted a low, harsh voice from the shadows.

Gil's hand flew toward his pistol.

"I wouldn't do that if I were you," warned Captain Lee. He stepped forward. "My musket is pointed directly at Colonel Powell's back. You have two seconds to drop your weapon or I'll fire."

Damien swore softly. Realizing he had no choice, Gil dropped his pistol onto the ground.

"I believe I would like your sword and knife as well."

Gil hesitated and looked at Damien. Damien nodded. The heavy blades joined the pistol.

"Excellent," Captain Lee said with satisfaction. "It is a relief to know the British army is not entirely made up of fools."

"A pity the same cannot be said for the American army," returned Damien dryly.

"Oh, I don't know," mused Captain Lee. "You may have lured my men away with your little diversion, but at least I had the sense to double back and check on my illustrious prisoner. And now I have not one, but two redcoats under arrest. Turn around."

Gil and Damien slowly turned to face him.

"Now, Colonel Powell, you will tie your redcoat friend to that tree where he found you."

Gil helped Damien stumble back over to the tree. Gil lowered himself onto the ground, and Damien took a piece of rope and secured him to the trunk.

"Very good. Now you move to that tree over there and sit down."

Damien slowly moved to the tree. Captain Lee retrieved a piece of rope from his saddle and walked over to him.

"A pity to be caught again when you thought you were so close to escape," he reflected, his musket pointed at his chest.

"I am still close to escape," Damien assured him.

"Is that so? How interesting." Captain Lee crouched before him and held out the rope. "Give me your hands, Colonel."

Damien's hands instantly shot upward, flinging a blinding cloud of dirt into the rebel's eyes.

Captain Lee swore violently as he raised his fists to his grit-filled eyes. Damien grabbed his musket out from under him and pointed it directly at his head.

"Forgive me, Captain Lee," he apologized tersely. "Delightful as your colonial hospitality is, my friend and I find we simply cannot stay any longer." He lifted his gaze to Gil, who had already shed the rope Damien had loosely secured around him. "Tie him up."

"You'll never get away," Captain Lee assured him furiously as Gil began to bind his hands behind his back. "The woods are crawling with American soldiers just dying to put a great big hole in you, Powell. You would be better off to stay here and sit out the rest of the war in prison. At least that way you'll stay alive."

"I am deeply touched by your concern for me," returned Damien, his tone sardonic. "You will forgive me if I do not take you up on your most generous offer."

"You redcoats are fools if you think you can win this war," Captain Lee snarled as Gil finished tying him to the tree. "Do you know why?"

Damien's gaze fell upon Captain Lee's enormous pearl and gray charger. "I hope you won't mind if I take your horse," he said, ignoring the question. "Unfortunately, I find myself without a mount."

"You bloodybacks can't win, because we will never give up," declared Captain Lee vehemently. "Never."

"I shall be certain to bring that piece of news to the attention of General Clinton." With difficulty, Damien pulled himself up onto Captain Lee's horse, grunting against the pain the effort cost him. "Until then, Captain Lee, I am afraid I must bid you good-bye. Tell your friend Bennett I will miss his charming company."

Captain Lee glared at him, his eyes burning. "I'll see you dead, you murdering redcoat bastard. You and every last one of your vile Scarlet Legion."

"Forgive me," apologized Gil as he withdrew a kerchief from his waistcoat and stuffed it into Captain Lee's mouth. "We can't afford to have you alerting your soldiers that we are gone." He quickly mounted his own horse and looked at Damien.

"Let's go," Damien ordered brusquely.

He dug his heels into his mount and thundered out of the rebel camp, clutching at his side. The pain was overwhelming. He held his breath and bit down violently. When that didn't help, he tried to concentrate on how good it felt to be free again.

But as his bandage grew warm and wet against his fingers, and the pain became excruciating, he focused his thoughts entirely on what he would do to that lying rebel bitch if he ever saw her again.

Chapter 5

Charles Town, South Carolina

July 1780

Thick lavender mist swirled over the pearly streets and shimmering rooftops of the magnificent city of Charles Town, shrouding mansions and slave quarters alike in a cooling cloak of sea-scented vapor.

It wafted around the glorious steeple of St. Michael's church, that beloved structure which had played a joyful symphony of bells each and every hour since 1764. For years the graceful white tower had stretched one hundred and eighty feet above the sun-washed city beneath it, patiently marking the passage of time, and serving as a welcoming beacon for rich merchant ships searching the Carolina coast for Charles Town. The once-gleaming spire was now stained an ominous black. When the British General Sir Henry Clinton arrived with the British navy in February and began a long, terrifying siege of the city, the people of Charles Town quickly realized their glorious church was a perfect target for thundering cannon. With typical practicality, they bathed it in black. Despite the destruction the forty-two-day siege had wreaked on them, the steeple of St. Michael's, miraculously, still stretched high above the resilient city below.

Jo placed her hands on the cool wrought-iron railing of the little balcony off her room and drank in a long draft of sea-drenched air. The rain had doused the terrible heat that had plagued the city these past few days, and left a wet shimmer on the houses and sidewalks. The salt tang of the harbor was still new to her, and tonight it mingled with other aromatic scents. She inhaled the summery perfumes wafting from the thousands of flowers blooming in Charles Town's gardens; wonderful fragrances from yellow jessamine and oleander, sweet bay and honeysuckle, jasmine and roses. In the countryside, she reflected, plants were grown to eat. If you wanted to look at flowers, you only needed to lift your gaze to the meadows or take a walk in the woods. But in the city, people were not burdened with having to grow their own food. Great quantities of fresh produce, meat, and fish were brought in from the countryside and the sea, to be sold at the market and on the wharves. While each home did maintain a small kitchen garden, nearly everyone devoted most of the land in the front and back of their house to the cultivation of magnificent plants and flowers. Encompassed by two shimmering rivers and an ocean, and bursting with lush greenery and color, Charles Town was, by any standard, exceptionally beautiful. Although she longed to return home to the wide open spaces of the countryside, Jo found herself reluctantly adjusting to the grandeur and bustle of this elegant town.

She had been here nearly four weeks. Captain Lee had arranged her travel to the city, where she was immediately put into the hands of a Mrs. Henry Tucker. Mrs. Tucker, or Aunt Hazel as Jo was to call her, was a silver-haired matron with a generous bosom and an even more generous backside. She was a prominent member of Charles Town society, the widow of a prosperous rice planter who died shortly before the outbreak of the revolution. A portrait in the parlor revealed she had once been a great beauty. Her face was now sagging, partly from age and partly from its ample fleshiness, but Aunt Hazel still conducted herself regally.

At first Jo thought this elderly, well-padded woman, who often smelled suspiciously of rose water and gin, a most unlikely connection for a spy. She soon discovered Hazel Tucker harbored a hatred for the redcoats that nearly rivaled her own. Although during the early years of the war Aunt Hazel had declared herself to be a loyal British subject, the death of her only son at Monck's Corner in April had shattered that allegiance. Hazel would in fact have preferred to spy on the British herself if she could. Unfortunately, her fondness for gin and her inability to hear anything below a bellow made that desire, however noble, somewhat impractical.

In the guise of Miss Celia Reed, Hazel Tucker's niece from the countryside, Jo found society's doors thrown wide open to her. It was her job at the opulent parties and balls to move amongst the British officers who were laughing and talking and sipping champagne, and draw them into seemingly harmless conversations about the war. From these discussions she was to glean whatever information she could about the movement and state of their troops, the needs of their posts, and the routes of their supply trains. She was to report regularly on everything she heard, regardless of how insignificant her observations seemed. The method for passing on this information was never the same twice. In the three weeks since she had been introduced to Charles Town society, Jo had managed to deliver two messages. She did not know whether the information she relayed was of value.

In preparation for her new role, Aunt Hazel had put her through a training program as rigorous as that demanded by a general of a soldier in any army. Within five minutes of their meeting, Jo was loudly informed that she knew neither how to stand nor sit nor walk, to say nothing of her farm girl table manners and her utter ineptitude in the fundamentals of gracious conversation. Jo was outraged. Oblivious to her insult, Aunt Hazel continued to rail about ordering gowns and arranging for dancing lessons, and what on earth were they going to do with all that hair? Jo quickly realized the woman did not mean to be offensive, she was simply making a swift and thorough list of her apparently disas-

trous shortcomings, and organizing a battle plan to overcome them. It helped to realize that Aunt Hazel was not
yelling at her in anger. The elderly woman was simply unable to hear herself, or anyone else for that matter, at anything below a resounding battle cry.

Aunt Hazel announced she would begin by teaching Jo
how to stand. Jo insisted she already knew how to stand
perfectly well, but Aunt Hazel was not to be argued with.
In polite society, she explained, everything one did had to
be performed with an audience in mind. A beautiful young
woman like Jo must learn to use her body to its best advantage, charming her spectators with each seemingly inconse-
quential movement. A casual tilt of the head, a delicate
flutter of her fan, a slow, graceful walk across a room, each
of these actions should be executed with unhurried grace.
Haste, warned Aunt Hazel sternly, was the sign of a servant
or rustic, and had no place in the salons of Charles Town
society.

And so Jo learned how to stand.

She assumed she would dispose of this lesson quickly.
She soon discovered that there was more to standing, and
especially standing still, than she had thought. One had to
achieve an elegant carriage, with the head held high, the
back perfectly straight, the shoulders pressed back, and the
arms falling gracefully at the sides. Easy enough for perhaps
a moment or two, but Aunt Hazel insisted Jo must be able
to stand without fidgeting for no less than fifteen minutes,
a task that seemed impossible. For hours she stood in the
drawing room with her back pressed firmly against the wall,
her hands clasped lightly before her, and her jaw clenched
with effort as Aunt Hazel lectured her on every ridiculous
ordinance of polite society, from holding a wine glass to
dropping her fan.

Once Jo had finally mastered the art of standing to Hazel's satisfaction, she was generously rewarded.

"Now," announced Hazel magnanimously, "you may
progress to sitting."

This, Jo had thought, would be easier. That was before
she learned that ladies in polite society were forbidden to

sit with any degree of comfort. One had to maintain the same perfectly erect yet seemingly relaxed carriage of standing. Certainly your back was never permitted to touch the chair. This was impossible anyway, because the enormous hoops of Jo's new gowns prevented her from actually sitting. At best she was able to perch on the edge of the seat, and pray she didn't slide off the slippery silk upholstery and land unceremoniously on her backside.

Once she had perfected her sitting, she was permitted to graduate to walking.

Although Jo thought she had been walking just fine for some nineteen years, it turned out she was mistaken. In walking, Aunt Hazel lectured, the body must express a light, floating quality, as if one were sailing across the floor. "Your pace must always be moderate," she instructed loudly, "neither too quick nor too slow, to give your spectators an opportunity to appreciate your grace and discipline." Strapped into a stiffly boned corset, encumbered by the awkward hoops of her bell-shaped skirts, and tripping over her new, ridiculously impractical high-heeled shoes, Jo slowly tread up and down the length of Aunt Hazel's drawing room with two heavy books balanced on her head, until she felt she would scream from the idiocy of it all.

Next came dancing lessons.

Jo vehemently protested that she had no desire to dance with redcoats. Aunt Hazel explained that an officer was at his most unguarded when he was dancing, because his mind was occupied with the rhythm of his feet and the beauty in his arms. It was her patriotic duty, Hazel told her, to dance with her oppressors.

And so Jo learned to dance.

Her tutor was a short, balding man, whose generous girth prevented him from holding her too close, which suited Jo just fine. She liked him well enough, because he was exceptionally good-natured about the countless times she mashed his feet with her treacherous new shoes. Partly because she was anxious to please him, and partly because she was eager to get out there and start gathering information that would compromise the British, Jo practiced her dancing alone for hour upon hour in the evening. After seven exhausting days, she found she could sweep into a waltz or perform a stately minuet with the requisite ease.

Table manners, elegant grammar, polite conversation, the art of flirtation, and how to use one's fan to captivate and charm—all were covered with militant thoroughness. At the same time Jo was outfitted with a lavish wardrobe which grandly proclaimed her new station as the beautiful, unmarried daughter of a wealthy plantation owner. She had never seen such luxurious fabrics, and could hardly believe there were people who dressed like this all the time. It seemed immoral to spend money on such finery, when there were people like her family in the countryside struggling to put food on their table. She tried to keep in mind that she was not dressing this way by choice, and this extravagance was a weapon in her fight against the British.

"Celia, dear, are you ready?"

Jo turned to see Aunt Hazel standing in the doorway of her room, awkwardly trying to fasten a sapphire bracelet to her wrist. After a moment the glittering band dropped to the floor.

"Let me do that for you," Jo said. She swept into the room, her voluminous skirts barely making a sound as she glided across the polished floor. Keeping her back ramrod straight, she bent her knees to retrieve the bracelet, the boning of her bodice digging mercilessly into her waist.

"Thank you, my dear," said Aunt Hazel loudly as Jo fastened the bracelet around her wrist. "You look lovely tonight. Pretty enough to turn the heads of every British officer there."

"Thank you," Jo replied. "I'll just be a moment."

Hazel's sagging face puckered into a frown. "Not going?" she demanded incredulously. "Why ever not?"

Jo shook her head and put her mouth closer to Hazel's ear. "I said, I'll just be a moment."

"Fiddlesticks," declared Aunt Hazel impatiently. "Of course you are. I shall expect you downstairs in two minutes." As she moved toward the staircase, her black silk gown rustling loudly, she murmured, "Not going, indeed."

Jo smiled. Over the past weeks, she had grown fond of her eccentric guardian. Hazel Tucker was a strong, independent woman, who despite her age and physical limitations was doing what she could to help the Patriot cause. Fostering a rebel spy was no small contribution. Jo hoped she could uncover enough vital information to make all the risks worthwhile. Captain Lee had made it clear that Jo must pass along sufficient information to inflict tangible damage on the British army. Only then would he be satisfied that she was not a traitor to her country, and allow her to go home. The need to return to Samuel and Lucy and Anne, who would be struggling to run the farm without her, filled her with cool determination as she went to her dresser to retrieve her fan.

She paused to give herself a final evaluation in the mahogany-framed looking glass. Her gown was of cream and gold striped silk, intricately stitched with delicate sprays of flowers bursting from satiny green stems. Four layers of frothy lace cascaded from the elbow-length sleeves, and more lace trimmed the edge of the overskirt and fluttered in rows across the exposed underskirt, which puffed around her like a voluminous silken cloud. The rigid stomacher was elaborately trimmed with sprays of seed pearls and twining ribbons of gold brocade. The boned bodice was tightly fitted and cut extremely low, revealing a pale expanse of bosom which was just within a hairbreadth of what was considered an acceptable amount of exposure.

Aunt Hazel's servant Letty had swept Jo's hair up into an artful arrangement of curls and then liberally dusted it with powder, reducing the gold shine to a dull gray, which was considered far more attractive than natural color. A bouquet of tiny cream and yellow roses had been pinned throughout this tall creation, which would slowly release their delicate fragrance with every flirtatious tilt of her head. A skillful application of cosmetics had paled the unfashionable sunwashed glow of her skin. The familiar scattering of freckles across her nose and cheeks lay hidden beneath a dusting of fine white powder, her eyebrows had been lengthened and darkened, and her cheeks and lips were stained scarlet. A glittering necklace of deep green emeralds circled her neck, and her ears shimmered with the silver sparks of heavy diamond clusters. The overall effect was one of elegant sophistication, making her appear far older and more experienced than her twenty years.

Although she had been dressing in this elaborate, provocative fashion since her introduction to Charles Town society nearly three weeks ago, Jo was still startled each time she caught her reflection in a mirror. The richly adorned woman who stared back at her with her beautifully coiffed hair, her immaculately manicured hands, and that indecent swell of exposed bosom, was a complete stranger. She did not look as though she could last a minute planting corn under a blazing sun. She certainly did not appear capable of loading and firing a musket, or burying a hatchet into the back of an attacking Indian. Or stitching up and caring for a gravely wounded redcoat. An image of Colonel Powell flashed into her mind, standing beaten and bleeding beside the body of his dead horse, his eyes burning with hatred.

A chill swept over her.

The memory of Colonel Powell had haunted her these past weeks. He came to her at night, his dark eyes accusing. Sometimes her mind reenacted the terrible beating the rebel soldiers gave him, her heart constricting with each savage blow. Other nights he would lie before her, his beautiful body raging with fever, and she would relive the hours she had stayed at his side and swabbed him with cool water, begging God to not let him die. Every night since he had been taken away by the rebels, broken and bleeding and consumed with hatred for her, she had pleaded with God to let him live. She knew he despised her. And if his ghastly reputation were true, he was an evil, ruthless murderer, who took pleasure in butchering helpless women and children. But he had also risked everything to help her and her family. One thing was certain. If Colonel Powell somehow managed to survive, and they ever crossed paths again, he would take pleasure in punishing her for her supposed betrayal. If he lived. A possibility which, given the severity of his wounds and the brutal treatment he was certain to receive in the care of Captain Lee and his men, seemed remote.

The thought filled her with guilt.

Please, God, don't let him die.

The woman in the glass looked tired and desolate. Not at all like a spoiled young lady who thought no further ahead than the next British officers' party. Tonight, I am not Jo Armstrong, she reminded herself coldly. Tonight I am the pampered and privileged Miss Celia Reed, ardent Tory and outrageous flirt. And if by being Celia Reed I can help defeat these loathsome redcoats, then I will perform this role gladly. Not because I have been forced to do so by Captain Lee. I do this for my father. For Elias. For my whole family. And for the future of my beloved country. I will *not* stand by and let these redcoats destroy us.

"Celia, are you coming, or do I have to send Cain up to get you?" bellowed Aunt Hazel.

Jo forced herself to soften the grim line of her scarlet-stained lips into a smile. With an accomplished snap of her fan she turned away from the stranger in the looking glass, determined to make this night a victory for the American cause, and to bring her one step closer to going home.

The ballroom was sweet with the scent of myrtleberry wax that wafted from the hundreds of flickering candles slowly melting in the crystal chandeliers. The peach-colored light spilled warmly onto the swirling crush of dancers below. Garlands of fragrant blossoms festooned the room, and tall emerald-leafed trees bearing lemons, oranges, and massive puffs of pink and white flowers were arranged in silver tubs, transforming the ballroom into a magnificent tropical garden. The silk and satin gowns of the women added to the illusion, for they were of every floral shade imaginable, from teal blue, to brilliant yellow, to the liveliest and most vibrant of pinks.

The sole deviation to this garden theme were the dress uniforms of the British officers, in whose honor the ball was being thrown. Neither the garlands, nor the trees, nor even the elaborate gowns of the women could compete with the overwhelming sea of scarlet and white and gold. Beyond the boundaries of Charles Town, the war between the rebels and the British raged on. Yet in this decadent and colorful oasis, the victors were laughing and dancing and drinking champagne with the vanquished.

It was, Damien reflected, bizarre, to say the least.

He did not want to be here. He had come to Charles Town at General Cornwallis's request, to discuss the difficult situation in the Carolinas. General Clinton had placed the southern command of the British army in the hands of General Cornwallis—then had returned to New York, taking most of his army with him. That left General Cornwallis with less than four thousand regular troops to fight the rebels in North and South Carolina, maintain order in Georgia and Florida, and move north and take Virginia. This agenda could only be achieved by securing sufficient numbers of Loyalist men to swell their ranks.

But the actual number of Loyalists, or Tories, was not nearly what they had expected. Certainly there were some Loyalist regiments. The most notorious was the British Legion, fighting under the brutal command of Lieutenant Colonel Banastre Tarleton. Instead of signing up with the British army, small bands of Loyalists were forming independently and going on personal rampages, settling scores with rebels who had harassed them for years before the British arrived. The whole countryside was in a chaotic state of rebellion and terror. General Cornwallis's task was to root out and disarm the rebels, supply his own troops, and at the same time establish a system of authority and order. If one confined one's gaze to the extravagant illusion playing out in this ballroom, where well-fed officers wore immaculate uniforms and civilians laughed and happily toasted their king, one would think the war had already been won.

"Colonel Powell, what an unexpected pleasure."

Damien turned to see Captain Laurence Sterns standing before him. Laurence had served for several months in Damien's legion in the north. He quickly showed himself to be intelligent, courageous, and a natural leader, and Damien had no choice but to recommend him for promotion. It was a loss for Damien, but the British army needed good, experienced officers.

"Captain Sterns, don't tell me General Cornwallis has assigned you to fight the enemy in the ballrooms of Charles Town."

Laurence laughed. "I am afraid he has, temporarily. A number of us are here to help establish British authority. Charles Town is a crucial supply center, so we must get the town running smoothly again. Despite what you see here tonight, not everyone in this city is happy that we are here."

"Given the fight they put up to keep us out, I suspect there are far more in the city who despise our presence than welcome it," Damien remarked.

Before coming here this evening, he had given himself a brief tour of Charles Town. For the most part, it was a prosperous, orderly town, filled with pretty houses and stately mansions built in the Georgian style of architecture. But a number of streets lay in blackened ruins, devastated by the bombardment of British cannon and the subsequent fires. For forty-two endless days the inhabitants of Charles Town had lived under attack. Once the British had them completely ringed in, they were unable to get supplies into the city. By the time General Lincoln finally surrendered, both the inhabitants and Lincoln's rebel army were starving.

"The local Tories were pleased enough to see us capture the city," qualified Laurence. "Then there are those former Patriots who have accepted the fact that Britain is going to win this war. They have decided to take General Clinton's oath of loyalty to the king and ally themselves with us."

"Of course General Clinton declared that anyone who did not take the oath would not be permitted to return to their business," Damien said, continuing to watch the crush of dancers.

"That is true," agreed Laurence. "What of it?"

Damien shrugged his shoulders. "He will hardly root out the rebels that way. My guess is, anyone who wants to eat or feed their family will go down and take the oath. Then they will simply continue their rebel activities in secret."

"You may be right," allowed Laurence. "With Lincoln's

surrender, we took over five thousand men prisoner. The militia were permitted to go home if they swore not to take up arms again. Already we have had reports of many of them joining other militia groups."

"And the regular Continentals remain here."

Laurence nodded. "General Clinton did not feel they could be released, or they would just march back to General Washington. Some have been exchanged for British prisoners, and some are paroled on islands around Charles Town. The rest, unfortunately, we had to imprison."

Damien frowned. He had heard about the appalling conditions in which the American Continental soldiers were being kept. Most of them were being held on prison ships in the harbor. The ships were overcrowded, inadequately supplied, and hotter than the fires of hell, and the American soldiers were dying like flies. Of course this had not been General Cornwallis's intent. The British army was having a hard enough time supplying its own troops. Nevertheless, it was a shocking way to treat one's enemy.

Laurence accepted two glasses of wine from a Negro servant bearing a silver tray. He offered one glass to Damien, then lifted his in a toast. "To the lovely ladies of Charles Town," he proposed. "Without whom this ball would not be nearly so enjoyable."

Damien sipped his wine and gazed disinterestedly around the crowded room. The ladies of Charles Town were attractive enough, he supposed. A bit too primped and powdered for his liking. They were all strapped into a heavy armor of corsets and hoops, with their thickly powdered hair arranged high on their heads and their cheeks and lips stained pink with artificial color. It was strange, he mused, but this evening he found himself indifferent to the prospect of selecting one to seduce. Normally after a few weeks in the field he was anxious to find an attractive woman with whom he could indulge in a night of mutual pleasure. He had certainly done so often enough when he was stationed in New York. But tonight the extravagantly gowned ladies in this ballroom did not appeal to him. Frowning, he took another swallow of wine. Perhaps he was tired.

"How long are you here for, sir?" asked Laurence.

"A few days," Damien replied. "I'm here to meet with General Cornwallis, but he has not yet arranged a time. I understand his duties keep him fairly busy."

"Then I must introduce you to some of the city's fairer sights," Laurence suggested. "After all, we don't want you to be lonely during your stay."

Damien shook his head. "Thank you for your concern, Captain, but that won't be necessary."

"But the room before you is full of exotic flowers just waiting to be plucked," protested Laurence poetically. "And since I have been here long enough to make the acquaintance of many of Charles Town's loveliest ladies, I can lead you to the choicest blossoms."

Damien surveyed the women who were dancing. Perhaps Captain Sterns was right. Since he was obliged to stay a few days in this town, why not enjoy himself? Feminine company would be a welcome diversion from the war, and might ease the black mood that had descended upon him since his interlude with that rebel bitch.

Rage flamed within him. She had sworn before God that she would not turn him over. She had stitched him and bathed him and watched over him, pretending to care that he lived. And then she had contacted the rebels and coldly watched as they killed his horse and beat him until he could barely stand. He had nearly given his life to save her and her family. He had foolishly believed he could trust her.

And she had repaid him by turning him over to his enemies to die.

"Miss Annabelle Jackson is a remarkably pretty girl, the daughter of one of Charles Town's leading Tories," Laurence was saying enthusiastically. "Then there is Miss Melanie Westlake, a delightful young woman whose father is a prominent local silver merchant. She likes to complain about how dreary life is in the colonies, and drop hints that she would love nothing more than to marry and move to England."

"I am not looking for a wife," Damien pointed out dryly. In his experience, sheltered daughters of prominent fathers expected marriage after a few unsatisfying kisses. "Isn't there anyone here who is a little more, shall we say, sophisticated?"

"Of course there is," Laurence assured him. "Charles Town has in its grasp a most charming young woman by the name of Miss Celia Reed. She arrived a few weeks ago from her father's plantation in the countryside, and is now residing with her aunt, Mrs. Hazel Tucker, who acts as her chaperone. The only problem is that Miss Reed is constantly surrounded by a flock of officers, all shamelessly competing for her attentions. I must confess," he said, laughing, "even I have been known to join them."

Damien frowned. Reed. Where had he heard that name recently?

"Miss Reed is exceptionally beautiful and vivacious. I am certain you would enjoy her company. Would you like me to introduce you to her?"

Damien hesitated. He supposed it might be amusing to see if Miss Celia Reed lived up to her reputation.

"Very well, Captain Sterns." He drained his wine glass. "Lead me to the charming and vivacious Miss Celia Reed."

Jo tilted her head back and laughed, a delicate, silvery sound she knew the officers gathered before her found enchanting. The gesture had the added advantage of causing her to stretch the pale column of her throat and thrust her bosom forward slightly, which was certain to grasp their attention. After a few seconds she lifted her fan and began to flutter it coyly over her exposed neckline, pretending Major Ferguson's marginally witty comment had succeeded in making her flush.

"Why, Major Ferguson, you are the most wicked man!" she exclaimed with a carefully contrived mixture of delight and shock.

Nigel Ferguson's pale lips curled with pleasure. "Perhaps, Miss Reed, I need a woman of your remarkable grace and charm to reform me," he returned, his brown eyes burning with invitation.

Jo regarded him over the edge of her fan, trying to look

as if she had never met anyone quite so dashing. "Perhaps you do," she purred. She let the implication of that statement hang between them for a few seconds. Then she swept her gaze over the other men. "But then, perhaps all you dear, handsome officers require some reformation!"

Her covey of British admirers began to laugh. Jo plied her fan and smiled coquettishly. She knew she was playing her role well this evening.

These eight redcoats had attended to her for well over an hour. At a ball where so many ladies competed for the attentions of an officer of His Majesty's army, this was no small achievement. Aunt Hazel's lessons had not been in vain, she reflected scornfully.

Learning to stand had been invaluable.

She surveyed her captivated audience, and her eyes came to rest once more on Major Nigel Ferguson. He was a tall, imposing figure of a man, who wore his hair fashionably powdered and curled. He was striking rather than handsome, with a long nose that dipped into a sudden, pronounced angle, reminding Jo of a bird's beak. His cheeks were flat, his lips two pale slivers which were prone to clamping together disapprovingly. Though not ugly, his face had a disturbing quality that seemed to support his reputation as a cunning and callous officer. A few casual questions had revealed that Major Ferguson was posted to Charles Town only temporarily, where he was assisting General Cornwallis with the establishment of the new British administration. A man in his position was undoubtedly privy to all kinds of information, Jo reasoned. She had therefore selected Major Ferguson as her principal quarry for the evening.

"Dear Miss Reed, I believe we have kept you standing in this corner far too long this evening. Would you care to dance?" asked a young man hopefully.

She turned to him and forced a practiced smile. Captain Robert Williams regarded her with adoring blue eyes.

"Why, Captain Williams, you flatter me with your charming invitation," she cooed prettily. "But I am afraid I find it far too warm this evening to start spinning on that crowded dance floor." She did not want to stray too far from Major Ferguson. At the first opportunity she would discreetly get him to take her out into the garden, but she could not do so with all these officers surrounding her. She waved her fan rapidly, causing wisps of her hair to dance across her bare shoulders. "Why don't you fetch us all a lovely tray of champagne?" she suggested brightly.

Young Captain Williams beamed. "It would be my great pleasure, Miss Reed." He gave her a small bow and hurried off, only to return moments later with a Negro servant bearing a silver tray of champagne-filled glasses.

"A toast," said Nigel Ferguson as he handed Jo a glass. "To His Royal Highness, King George the Third. Long may he reign."

The officers dutifully lifted their glasses before drinking. Jo did the same, but not before silently amending her toast. She hoped that the English king would not live long at all, but drop dead to the floor this very evening.

"And now, another toast," proposed Nigel. "To the enchanting Miss Celia Reed," he drawled. "The most magnificent flower in all of Charles Town."

"Here, here," called out another officer. The men happily lifted their glasses and drank.

"Why, Major Ferguson, you overwhelm me with your extravagant compliment," Jo said, once more fluttering her fan over her bosom. "But since you British officers are known to be so gallant, permit me to make a toast to you." She raised her glass. "To the brave and valiant soldiers of the British army," she began, barely able to hold back a note of sarcasm. "Perfect gentlemen, every one." She took a bitter swallow of champagne, then smiled brilliantly, as if she had never known such a perfectly splendid evening.

Damien threaded his way through the warm crush of men and women poised on the edge of the dance floor, following Captain Sterns. A silvery peal of laughter wafted through the air, piercing the drone of music and conversation. It came from the corner they were approaching, where a crescent of scarlet and white uniforms hid someone from view. Damien was not really in the mood to join a crowd of fawning officers competing for the attention of some silly flirt. He suddenly felt bored and tired, and longed for nothing more than the quiet of his room and a decent night's sleep in a real bed. He was about to turn to Laurence and excuse himself when one of the officers stepped aside for a moment, allowing him a glimpse of Miss Celia Reed.

She was exquisite. Though her face was half hidden by her fan, he could see her skin was as luminous as the whitest of silks, her features fine and delicately etched. Her lush body might have been poured into the low-cut gown she wore. The sparkle of emeralds and diamonds against her creamy skin indicated a woman of considerable fortune, but even without them she would have been magnificent. She was listening to one of the younger officers as he awkwardly recited a story, hanging on his every word as if nothing in her life had compared to this moment. Damien found himself on the verge of a smile.

When the story was completed, she tilted her head back and laughed, a sparkling sound that floated in golden ripples around her and brought smiles to the lips of her admirers. Then she lowered her fan over her bosom, revealing her face in its entirety.

He experienced a stab of confusion.

There was something oddly familiar about her. A moment later, the scarlet curtain closed around her once more.

"Good evening, Miss Reed," Laurence said, joining the officers. "You are radiant this evening."

"How splendid to see you again, Captain Sterns," said Jo, extending her hand so the young man could press a kiss against it. "I feared you were not in attendance this evening." She made it sound as if the possibility had been deeply troubling to her.

"Not even the war could keep me from an opportunity to see you," Laurence assured her, bending low over her wrist. "Permit me to introduce one of the most distinguished officers in the British army." He took a step back, making room for his friend. "Miss Celia Reed, may I present Lieutenant Colonel Damien Powell, the illustrious commander of the Scarlet Legion."

Shock sliced through Jo, freezing her breath in her chest.

Colonel Powell was alive. He was here. And in the next second, he would have her arrested.

Somehow she managed to force a smile as Damien calmly stepped forward. His enormous stature seemed to dwarf the other officers, including Nigel Ferguson, who until this moment had seemed impressively tall. She instantly raised her fan to the crest of her cheeks and graciously extended her arm, clinging to the hope that the dramatic changes in her appearance would be enough to conceal her identity from him.

Damien bowed and pressed a kiss against the delicate hand resting lightly against his fingers. As soon as he lifted his lips the hand was withdrawn, rather hastily he thought, but perhaps he was being ridiculous.

"Miss Reed, I am enchanted to make your acquaintance," he said. She must have found the room warm, for she was making use of her fan, allowing him to see her face only intermittently. She really was the most glorious creature, he reflected, with her elegantly chiseled cheeks and that scarlet bow of a mouth, and those crystal-blue eyes that were shyly regarding him over the gilded edge of her fan. They were the color of the sky, as clear and brilliant a shade of blue as he had ever seen. He could only recall seeing eyes like that once before.

He frowned.

"It is a pleasure to meet you, Colonel Powell," Jo returned, keeping her tone light and musical, the way Aunt Hazel had trained her.

He was not dead. As she slowly absorbed this fact, her shock and fear mingled with an incomprehensible sense of relief. Colonel Powell had somehow, miraculously, survived. And escaped. And now here he was, towering over her in his tightly fitted scarlet and white uniform, his black hair neatly tied back, the fact that it was unpowdered further distinguishing him from every other man.

"Tell me, Colonel," she said coyly, "what momentous feats have you performed to earn such an eminent reputation?"

She was not certain, but she did not think he had recognized her. She reminded herself that in this moment she bore little resemblance to plain Jo Armstrong, with her faded work dresses and her sun-browned skin. She must continue to play the part of Celia Reed, and pray that the flash of confusion she had seen in Colonel Powell's eyes was nothing but a momentary puzzlement. Because if he realized who she was, he would undoubtedly take great pleasure in exposing her as a rebel spy, and having her arrested and hanged.

"You must have countless fascinating stories to share with us," she prodded gaily.

"I am afraid my reputation is greatly exaggerated." His expression was deceptively casual as he continued to study her. He found himself distracted by her elegantly arranged hair, the artfully applied cosmetics, the glitter of her expensive jewels. Then there was that gown, which had been designed to attract a man's gaze to the soft swell of her breasts. He could not recall ever meeting Celia Reed. Nevertheless, there was something disturbingly familiar about her.

He knew her, and somehow he sensed that she knew it.

"Come now, Colonel Powell, you are being overly modest," protested Laurence. "Tell Miss Reed about the time you tricked that group of rebels into thinking they were capturing a dozen of your soldiers, and then you and your men appeared and made prisoners of the lot of them."

"There is nothing to tell, really," Damien assured Miss Reed pleasantly. Her expression seemed an open mixture of curiosity and amusement, as if she were eager to be entertained by his tale. But there was something else behind it, a shadow of something that he could not quite identify.

"My men and I were patrolling the area northwest of Charles Town, shortly after the city had fallen," he began. "We sighted a band of rebels marching south, evidently thinking to reinforce General Lincoln's troops. They had not yet heard that the city had rightfully been restored to British authority."

He thought he detected a flicker of darkness in her eyes. Before he could be certain, it was gone.

"Since the rebels outnumbered us," he continued, "I decided it was better to lead them into a situation in which they believed they had the advantage, before revealing the balance of my men. Fortunately, my strategy worked."

"Colonel Powell captured over a hundred rebels that day!" young Captain Williams exclaimed. "Over a hundred rebels captured, and some dozen or so killed, and he only had twenty-seven members of his Scarlet Legion with him!"

There it was again. Another flash of emotion in Miss Reed's eyes, only this time it lingered a second longer. Stunned disbelief surged through him. Because this time Damien recognized it as pure, unmitigated hatred.

And he knew with piercing clarity that he was standing before Miss Josephine Armstrong.

"How utterly clever of you!" Jo burst out prettily, as if he had just regaled her with some wonderfully amusing tale, instead of a story in which her countrymen had been brutally murdered. Just as Elias had been.

"Indeed," remarked Nigel Ferguson, his tone arid.

Still reeling with shock, Damien pulled his gaze away from Josephine to regard Major Ferguson, whom he had not noticed until now. "Good evening, Nigel," he said, affecting considerably more calm than he felt. How the hell had that rebel farm girl transformed herself into this dazzlingly sophisticated woman? And what in the name of God was she doing here? "Enjoying your interlude in Charles Town?"

Nigel's pale lips pressed into a thin line. "It suits me well enough," he remarked brusquely. "For now."

Damien managed a barely civil nod. "I am pleased to hear it. Perhaps General Cornwallis will require your services here for some time to come."

Nigel's expression grew dark. "Don't count on it, Colonel Powell." His tone was faintly menacing. "Please excuse me, Miss Reed." He gave Jo a small bow before walking away.

Damien turned his attention back to Josephine. Her elaborate disguise had distracted him, but this was the woman who had saved him only to betray him. She had tormented his thoughts these past weeks, until he could barely waken without being suffused with rage. He had promised himself he would find her before the war was over. He had sworn he would make her pay for her betrayal. But he had never imagined he would discover her in the midst of a crowded ballroom, holding court before an assembly of captivated British officers with the skill of a royal courtesan.

Somehow she had transformed herself from a simple, unaffected farm girl into this stunningly elegant woman. A woman who wore sumptuous, immodestly cut gowns, and laughed and flirted shamelessly as she sipped champagne with men she loathed. She could only be here as a spy, he realized. One word from him, and she would instantly be surrounded by a dozen soldiers who would place her under arrest and haul her away to prison, where she would be tried and executed.

The idea was not nearly as satisfying as it should have been.

Perhaps such a revenge was too swift, he reflected. Maybe it would be more gratifying after he toyed with her a while longer. "Miss Reed," he drawled pleasantly, "would you honor me with a dance?" He extended his hand in invitation.

"Why certainly, Colonel Powell," she breathed sweetly. "I would be delighted."

Her heart was pounding hard against her chest as she laid her hand upon his outstretched palm. His fingers closed over hers, warm and strong and firm. Feeling as if she were being led to her execution, she accompanied him onto the dance floor.

With his hand against the small of her back, Damien pulled her to him as close as the hoops of her cream and gold gown would allow. She began to move in his arms with fluid grace, as if she had been born to glide around a ballroom floor. He studied her in silence, contemplating the moment he first saw her, weeks ago. Their circumstances had been much different. He had been staring at her down the barrel of his musket as she knelt beneath the hot glare

of the sun, bravely waiting for an Indian warrior to brutally
end her life. Her clothes, her hair, her speech, her entire de-
meanor bore no resemblance to what she was flaunting tonight. But somehow, the essence of her had been the same.
Her lavish disguise could not hide that from him.

"Tell me, Miss Reed, how are you enjoying your stay in
Charles Town?" he asked conversationally.

She lifted her gaze and regarded him with sunny playfulness. "Why, I absolutely adore Charles Town, Colonel
Powell," she assured him gaily. "It is so much more stimu-
lating than the countryside."

Damien thought back to the day her family had nearly
been massacred by Indians. Somehow he did not think it
was a lack of stimulation that had driven her to spy in this
occupied city. "It is peculiar," he remarked, his expression
pensive as he guided her around the floor, "but I could almost swear we have met before."

Panic flooded through her. She masked it by tilting her
head back and laughing lightly, offering him what she knew
was a distracting view of her décolletage.

"Forgive me, Colonel," she apologized airily, "but you
have no idea how often gentlemen say that to me."

Damien smiled. "I suppose it is not the most singular of
expressions," he agreed, amused by her attempt to divert his
attention. "I take it you have not been in Charles Town
long."

"Only a few weeks," she replied vaguely. Her brow
creased into a delicate frown. "Do you suppose we might
have met at some other function?"

Her acting was commendable, especially given the fear
that must have been coursing through her at this moment.
But of course, Damien had witnessed her exceptional acting
ability before. "Not likely," he remarked. "I only arrived this
morning."

"Really? Where have you been?" she asked, smoothly
changing the subject.

"My men and I have been maintaining order in the countryside."

If that is what you call terrorizing and murdering rebel men, women, and children, Jo thought bitterly. "How exciting," she declared. "And where is your esteemed Scarlet Legion while you dance the night away in Charles Town?"

Damien found himself smiling again. Despite the precariousness of her situation, she was taking advantage of this opportunity to try to extract information from him. She was not lacking in determination, this rebel farm girl.

"My men are posted to the British garrison at Ninety-Six," he replied. "I will be returning there when my business in Charles Town is finished." The lie was more instinctive than conscious. He never revealed the true whereabouts of his legion, except to his superiors. Keeping its movements confidential gave the Scarlet Legion the advantage of surprise when it chose to strike, and kept the rebel network from laying traps for it. If Miss Armstrong thought she had learned something of significance, she was mistaken. Not that she would have the opportunity to relay it to her contacts. He fully intended to have her arrested as soon as this dance was finished, as his duty demanded.

Another couple whirled close to them on the dance floor, forcing her to lean into him. The scent of jasmine and roses filled his nose. Suddenly he became achingly aware of how soft and small and delicate she felt, trapped in his arms. She raised her eyes to his and smiled, her enormous summer-sky eyes faintly shadowed with a mixture of hatred and fear. She had every right to be afraid, Damien thought. In another moment, he would expose her for what she was and toss her to her enemies.

He felt a stab of self-loathing.

She was a spy, he reminded himself furiously. She hated the British army. She had made that abundantly clear from the moment she first saw him. That was why she broke her word and turned him over to a rough band of rebels who had no interest in treating their prisoner honorably. His thoughts flashed to the American rebels dying on the sweltering British prison ships. Perhaps, in war, there was no such thing as treating your enemy with honor, he reflected bitterly. Regardless, the woman he held in his arms was his enemy. And a spy. As an officer of the British army, it was his duty to turn her over immediately. And given her betrayal of him, he should find the act enormously satisfying.

Why, then, did he hesitate?

It was not so peculiar, he assured himself. After all, if she were a spy, it was unlikely she was operating in Charles Town alone. The British army suspected there was an extensive network of Patriot spies operating in this city, of which his little rebel farm girl was only one link. Perhaps if he allowed her to go, she would lead him to an entire nest of rebels. Their subsequent capture would be a great deal more crucial to the operations of the British army than the simple arrest of one Miss Josephine Armstrong, he reasoned. Once he had broken this Patriot spy ring, he could still have her arrested.

His decision was only rational. He would not arrest her now. Instead he would use her to lead him to the other American spies operating out of Charles Town.

After that, he would have her arrested.

The music finally came to an end, and Jo began to fan herself with exaggerated breathlessness. "Thank you, Colonel Powell. You are a splendid dance partner."

"I fear I am sadly out of practice." He offered his arm to escort her back to her corner. Once he had deposited her amongst her admirers, he would pretend to take his leave of her, so she would think her masquerade had been a success. Then he would watch her closely to see whom she spoke to and danced with. It was possible her contact was someone in this very room. He laid his hand over hers. "Perhaps later you would honor me with another—"

"Forgive me, Colonel, but I believe you have monopolized Miss Reed's attentions long enough," interrupted Nigel Ferguson. "Miss Reed, may I have the honor of the next dance?"

Jo felt Damien stiffen. She sensed the hostility between the two officers and wondered about its source. But she was thankful that Major Ferguson had offered her a perfect escape from Colonel Powell.

"I would be delighted, Major."

Damien felt a disconcerting possessiveness surge through

him. *Get hold of yourself.* He forced himself to smile and released his grasp on her.

"I shall leave you then, Miss Reed." He gave a small bow.
"It was a pleasure to meet you. I hope you enjoy the remainder of your stay in Charles Town."

"Thank you, Colonel Powell," she returned, fluttering
her fan at her throat. "You are most kind."

"My apologies for leaving you with him so long," said
Nigel after Colonel Powell had taken his leave. "When I returned to find you again, Captain Williams told me Powell
had asked you to dance. I tried to locate you as quickly as
I could, but the room is crowded."

"How very gallant of you to be concerned," cooed Jo,
waving her fan and trying to sound like a woman who had
need of being rescued. In fact, she was feeling rather weak
with relief. She had managed to fool Colonel Powell. This
time. She would make sure to avoid him until he returned
to his legion at Ninety-Six.

"If you are too warm in here, perhaps you would enjoy
a walk in the garden," Nigel suggested.

She looked up at him as if the idea were positively brilliant. "Why, Major Ferguson," she purred, "I do believe you
have the power to read my mind."

The mansion had been built on the fertile bank of the
Ashley River, which stretched like a silver ribbon at the foot
of the extensive grounds, glistening in the moonlight. A
cool breeze rustled the thousands of plants blooming in the
intricately designed garden. The air was sweet with the delicate bouquet of magnolia and yellow jessamine, oleander
and coral honeysuckle, intermingled with the pungence of
lemon and lime. The enormous formal garden was laid out
to showcase a glorious array of thickly blooming trees,
bushes, creeping vines, and clumps of fragrant flowers. Immaculately trimmed boxwood swirled in a graceful pattern,
creating a series of smaller gardens within the larger, and
growing high and dense in some areas to enclose secret
niches with dark emerald walls. It was a world apart from
the wild, tangled beauty of the countryside, Jo thought, but

it was beautiful in its own right. Somehow she felt more at ease out here, with the river breeze blowing softly against her face and glittering stars studding the ebony darkness above her, than she had in that hot, crowded ballroom.

Especially now that she was away from the threat of Colonel Powell.

"Miss Reed, your beauty puts every blossom in this garden to shame," Nigel declared.

Jo lowered her eyelashes. "Why, Major Ferguson, you say the most perfectly charming things."

"I speak only the truth. I am hopelessly captivated by your overwhelming loveliness."

He leaned into her, trying to capture a kiss. The delicate fragrance of the garden was suddenly obliterated by the sickly sweet odor of whiskey. The man is drunk, Jo realized in surprise. She turned her head modestly and took a step away from him, shrouding her revulsion in an air of virtuous restraint.

"I do so want to get to know you better, Major Ferguson," she demurred. "Come, let us walk some more and you can tell me about yourself."

He gave a small sigh and obediently trudged after her, evidently undaunted by her little play for time.

"How are you enjoying being posted to Charles Town?" she began. She remembered his hostility toward Damien. It was obvious Nigel Ferguson was not pleased to be here. A disgruntled officer might be more apt to reveal things inadvertently.

"It suits me well enough for the moment," he allowed brusquely. "But in a month of so, I will have to get back to my men," he continued, puffing up with importance. "I am only here because General Cornwallis required my expertise in bringing order to Charles Town."

"Really?" exclaimed Jo, trying to sound impressed. "Then you must be involved in the day-to-day activities of governing the city," she prodded.

"I practically run this town," he boasted.

She felt a genuine swell of excitement. "How fascinating. Such a responsibility must be extremely challenging."

"It is. Especially since the citizens of Charles Town have to be made to understand that *we* are in charge now." His brown eyes narrowed. "There are those within the city who only feign loyalty to the Crown, while secretly continuing their rebel activities. This rebel scum has to be rooted out and destroyed."

"A noble task." Jo was careful to keep her tone void of sarcasm. "But surely you are not speaking about anyone I might know," she added incredulously, hoping he would reveal the name of someone considered suspect.

"Have no fear, Miss Reed. Whoever is foolish enough to remain in Charles Town to fan the flames of rebellion will not escape capture for long, I assure you. When it comes to rebels, I have a special sense."

"How remarkable!" She wondered how Major Ferguson would react if he realized he was currently trying to seduce a rebel. "I assume, Major, that a man of your many abilities does not spend all his time searching for rebels," she persisted teasingly, trying to learn more about his responsibilities.

Nigel clasped his hands behind his back and affected an air of authority. It was obvious he enjoyed talking about himself. "I also assist in the placement of officers in suitable homes." He was referring to the British officers' practice of appropriating the finest mansions in Charles Town for their own residences. "And I organize the movement of supplies from Charles Town to our various garrisons in the southern colonies. Then there is the task of coordinating soldiers to clean up the streets of this town, which—"

"That must be terribly difficult," interrupted Jo, her heart beating a little faster at the mention of supplies.

Nigel looked at her in confusion. "What?"

"Moving supplies," she replied lightly as she reached down to pick a flower.

He nodded with satisfaction, evidently pleased that she could appreciate the complexity of his duties. "Keeping our troops fed, clothed, and armed in these colonies is no small task," he assured her pompously.

"I would imagine not. Especially since the weapons and uniforms aren't manufactured here," she added offhandedly.

"The ineptitude of the fools responsible for shipping our supplies to us from England is mind-boggling," he complained, his words lazily strung together. "Now that our forces are concentrating at Camden, I am up to my ears in daily requests that simply cannot be met."

Jo's pulse began to race. If the British troops were concentrating at Camden, it could only mean they were preparing for an attack. But an army had to be supplied before it could march. The American soldiers were desperate for food, clothing, and weapons. If she knew when the next train of British supplies was moving from Charles Town to Camden, perhaps the rebels could organize an assault and capture the entire shipment. Such a feat would not only deliver a serious blow to the British troops, it would also furnish vital supplies to the rebels. Decent food, weapons, and boots would help them win further engagements against the redcoats.

"But I am certain a man as clever as you has no trouble overcoming such a challenge," she said admiringly.

Nigel looked arrogantly pleased. "Of course not. Here, let us rest a moment."

They had wandered down to the end of the garden, and now found themselves stopped by the Ashley River. Huge live oak trees grew along its bank, heavily draped in dark gray veils of Spanish moss. An intricately carved wooden bench had been placed beneath one of these trees. Nigel helped Jo to sit before collapsing heavily onto the bench beside her.

Jo sighed and became engrossed in the task of adjusting the neckline of her gown. "I would dearly love to see you at work," she declared wistfully, drawing his attention to the swell of her bosom as the petals of her flower brushed against the pale skin. "I imagine with your exacting standards, you are there to personally supervise the loading of the supply trains before they leave."

"I am," he replied, his gaze fastened on her breasts.

She looked up at him, her eyes sparkling with eagerness.

"That must be so exciting. Would it be possible for my aunt and me to visit you the next time you are organizing a shipment? We wouldn't be in the way at all."

"Of course. A supply train for Camden is being prepared on Saturday, at the southern end of the wharves. I would be honored if you and your aunt would visit me there."

Saturday. Today was Thursday. Actually, it was early Friday morning, Jo realized, feeling a prick of alarm. If the rebels were to have any chance of arranging an ambush as the supplies moved north to Camden, she had to get this information to them immediately.

"That would be wonderful," she exclaimed. "I shall be sure to speak to my aunt about it as soon as we return. And now, I believe I have taken you away from your duties long enough, Major. Perhaps we had best go back to the party." She began to rise.

Nigel grabbed her wrist and pulled her back. "Not yet," he said hoarsely. He slid his arm around her shoulders, drawing her close.

"Why, Major Ferguson, this is most inappropriate," protested Jo. His whiskey-saturated breath blew hot against her face. She concealed her disgust in a cloak of ladylike outrage. "Let go of me at once, sir!"

"Let's stop playing games, shall we, Celia?" he suggested thickly. He clasped the back of her neck and pressed a rough kiss against her mouth. Jo slapped her hands against his chest and tried to shove him away, but Nigel was too strong for her.

"We both know what kind of a woman you really are, don't we?" he drawled. He traced his finger down her throat.

His voice was soft, but there was a strange, menacing quality to it. The dark pleasure glimmering in his eyes suggested Nigel Ferguson was a man who actually enjoyed a woman's resistance. Sensing that by fighting him she would only arouse him further, Jo decided to change tactics. She slowly reached up and wrapped her hand around his, just as it neared the swell of her bosom. Instead of wrenching it away, she pressed it firmly against her, taking control of his touch. Nigel's eyes widened with surprise, and perhaps a hint of disappointment. Watching him intently, Jo moved his hand back up the length of her neck, then brought it to her cheek.

"You may be right, Nigel," she murmured, her voice low and flooded with heat. "But this is not the time. I told my aunt I would be ready to leave with her at midnight, and it is well after that now. She is certain to have someone looking for me this very moment." She drew her brows together, as if a new thought had occurred to her. "Unless, of course, it was your plan for us to be caught in a situation that will clearly compromise my honor." Her grip on his hand increased as her gaze became openly hopeful.

Nigel swiftly withdrew his hand. Jo could see she had captured his attention. After all, she was not some helpless servant girl who could be violated and discarded. In her role as Celia Reed, she was a gentle lady of society. If Nigel Ferguson was discovered doing anything that might stain her reputation, he would be forced to marry her. Immediately. Which Jo suspected was not precisely what he had in mind.

"Of course you are right," he agreed, his ardor quickly cooling at the notion of a forced marriage. "We must find another, more intimate situation. Until then, shall we return to the party?" He stood and offered her his arm.

Damien watched in amazement as Josephine calmly accepted Nigel's arm and began to walk with him back up the path leading to the mansion. For a moment he had been certain he was going to have to intervene on her behalf, revealing the fact that he was following her in the process. He was well acquainted with Nigel's loathsome methods when it came to women. Despite the fury Damien harbored toward Josephine Armstrong, he was not about to stand by and watch her be raped. But somehow she had managed to get Ferguson under control. He did not believe for a moment she had actually enjoyed the bastard's touch—she hated the redcoats too much for that. She had endured his advances for the sake of gaining information from him.

Damien wondered whether Ferguson had stupidly revealed something important.

He waited until they had disappeared into the ballroom. Then he slipped back into the mansion through a different set of doors. His eyes scanned the packed room, searching for her. She was nowhere in sight. He quickly worked his way around the dance floor, trying to catch a glimpse of her cream and gold gown amidst the myriad of colorful silks and satins swirling to the music. Then he searched the corners of the room, to see if she had resumed holding court for her admirers.

She was gone.

He raced to the front of the mansion and burst out the doors, just in time to see a flash of cream and gold disappear into a carriage. The Negro driver shut the door and climbed up onto his seat. Damien began to run down the long line of waiting carriages toward his horse as Josephine's carriage disappeared down the gravel driveway. Finally reaching Liberty, he hoisted himself into the saddle and set off after her.

Her sudden departure was likely prompted by the fact that she had learned something important. Whatever information she had, it would be of no help to the rebel cause. Because as soon as she led him to her contacts, he was going to arrest the whole goddamn lot of them.

And he would enjoy it.

Chapter 6

*D*amien stood patiently in the darkness, waiting.

He had trailed Josephine's carriage to this elegant, whitewashed mansion on King Street. An elderly woman of considerable dignity had emerged from the vehicle first. Damien presumed this was Mrs. Hazel Tucker, the woman posing as Celia Reed's wealthy aunt. Josephine quickly followed, her diamond and emerald jewelry shimmering in the pale glow of the lamps burning at the front gate of the house. She daintily accepted the assistance of the driver as she stepped down, looking very much like a gently bred lady who required masculine aid to disembark. The memory of her burying a tomahawk deep into the back of an Indian flashed into Damien's mind. Miss Armstrong's little show of delicacy was most impressive, he reflected with arid amusement. Obviously she had been in the hands of an exacting teacher.

The driver opened the heavy wrought-iron gate leading to the house, waited for the two women to go through, and then closed it firmly behind them. The front door swung open as they climbed the marble steps leading to it, reveal-

ing the dark silhouette of a maid awaiting their return.
Once they were safely inside, the driver climbed back into
the carriage and drove it down a narrow lane at the side of
the house, which Damien assumed led to the stables.

Hidden amidst the shadows, he watched the house from
the opposite side of the street. After a moment a gleam
spilled through the cracks of the curtains in a room on the
second floor. A minute passed, and another curtained window was bathed in a gentle wash of gold, making it appear
that both Celia Reed and her aunt were preparing for bed.
Damien did not know whether Josephine would attempt to
deliver her message tonight or wait until morning. Her
hasty departure from the ball led him to think she intended
to pass on her information immediately. But if that were so,
why had she taken the time to return here? He watched as
the light shining from one room was extinguished. A few
more minutes dragged by. Finally the glow in the window of
the second room was also doused. The glass panes became
black, and the occupants of the house gave the appearance
of being settled in their beds for the night.

Damien was not convinced.

He leaned his shoulder against the trunk of the massive
tree he was using for cover, and continued to watch the
mansion. An hour seeped by, and the street remained silent
and still. He ordered himself to stay alert, but the long, exhausting hours spent in the saddle traveling to Charles
Town waged a formidable battle against his discipline. Just
as he was thinking perhaps it wouldn't hurt to sit down and
close his eyes for a moment, the sound of hooves clopping
slowly against the ground sharpened his senses. A horse
emerged from the narrow lane beside the mansion, bearing
a man clad in a dark coat and breeches. His tricorne hat was
pulled low over his forehead, depriving Damien of a view of
his face. The man carefully guided his horse along the
street, evidently trying to make the least amount of sound.
Once he had neared the end of the avenue, he grew bolder,
permitting his mount to break into a brisk trot.

Damien experienced a flicker of disappointment. It appeared Miss Armstrong had sent someone else to deliver her message.

He wandered over to the lane in which he had hidden his horse and withdrew his pistol from his saddlebag, permitting the distance to grow between himself and the luckless messenger who would lead him to Josephine's fellow spies. He deeply regretted that she would not be there to witness their capture. He shoved his pistol into its saddle holster, then swung up onto his horse and started off after the man.

He would have to be satisfied with her shocked expression when he returned here afterward to arrest her.

The whitewashed mansions and elegant gardens of Bay Street quickly gave way to crumbling, ramshackle buildings and filthy, slop-strewn streets as one approached the wharves along the Cooper River. The reek of sour ale wafted out the windows of the crowded taverns, mixing with the acrid harbor odors of tar, fish, and salt. Rough shacks had been carelessly erected on the sites of buildings that had been burned by British shells during the siege of the city. White and coffee-colored women in various states of undress lounged casually in the doorways, calling brazen invitations to the drunken men and British soldiers staggering out of the taverns. Aunt Hazel had sternly warned Jo of the degeneracy of this area of Charles Town. Perhaps she had feared one day Jo might be forced to come here to deliver information. The elderly woman's counsel had not gone unheeded. Jo pulled her black tricorne hat lower over her forehead and straightened her spine, trying to appear an inch taller. It was safer to be here dressed as a man, but a slightly built man riding alone could be seen as easy prey for thieves.

She steered her horse along the muddy road, ignoring the lewd remarks of the whores who propositioned her as she passed. No one paid much attention to her, perhaps because her clothes were not fine enough to mark her as a gentleman with a fat purse. She kept her horse's pace steady and glanced up only occasionally to read the signs on the buildings, trying to look like someone who knew exactly where he was going. After a while the number of taverns dwindled. The street became darker, flanked on one side by large brick warehouses, and on the other by massive wharves ringed with magnificent, tall-masted ships. They slept peacefully on the black water, groaning gently as they strained against the heavy bonds that moored them to the docks. A few sails flapped languidly in the harbor breeze, making a soft, rustling sound. The air grew rich with the salty-sweet aroma of molasses, rum, and coffee.

Jo continued to move quickly along the street, studying each of the warehouses in the thin moonlight. Finally she came to a dark brick building with a huge wooden sign in the front, identifying it as the company of "Elliott and Sons. John D. Elliott, Proprietor." She halted her horse and looked around. The street was veiled in silent shadows. Suddenly, a howl slashed the air. Jo gasped as a cat burst from an alley and streaked down the road. Her heart pounding, she eased her grip on the reins and ordered herself to get control of her nerves.

She rode her horse a little farther up the street. A narrow lane between two buildings provided a den where she could leave her mount hidden. She secured the reins around a heavy board she propped against the wall, then moved swiftly through the darkness back to the warehouse.

The windows at the front of the building were barricaded with thick wooden shutters. No light spilled from the cracks, but Jo had been told she could come any time of the day or night and someone would be here to receive her information. She moved cautiously along the side of the building, searching for an entrance in the back. She came upon a weed-choked yard, and was forced to pick her way through a trail of broken crates and rotting lengths of burlap. Finally she found a narrow door, framed by a slender beam of orange. Someone was within.

She lifted her fist and knocked tentatively upon the peeling paint, two long knocks immediately followed by three short ones, as she had been instructed. Several moments passed, but no one came. She raised her fist to knock again. The sound of footsteps stopped her from striking the wood. There was the faint scrape of a lock, and the door swung silently open on well-oiled hinges. A thin, balding man with black eyes peered at her suspiciously over the wavering flame of a candle.

"Yes?"

"I have a shipment for your swiftest vessel," Jo said, her voice low.

"Come in."

Jo stepped into the barely lit room, which was a small kitchen. A steaming kettle hung over a low fire, and the room held a lingering smell of fresh coffee, onions, and boiled meat. "I am here to see Mr. Elliott," she whispered urgently.

He frowned in confusion and lifted his candle closer to her face. "You're a woman," he concluded after a few seconds of study.

"It is dangerous for a woman to visit the wharves alone in the middle of the night," Jo explained, adjusting her hat over her powdered wig. "I aroused far less attention dressed like this."

The man nodded appreciatively. "Come this way."

Jo obediently followed him through a narrow corridor. It led into an enormous open room that comprised most of the building. The room was dark save for the glow of the candle her companion used to light their way. From this Jo was able to discern great piles of bulging brown sacks, stacked nearly to the rafters.

"What is in the bags?" she asked, curious.

"Rice," replied her escort shortly. "Waiting to be shipped."

Jo accompanied him through the dim cavern toward the faint gleam rimming the door of another room. Her escort knocked twice, then entered when bid.

"A message," he said to the man seated at the desk within, and motioned for Jo to step forward.

The man at the desk rose to his feet. His face was slack and deeply lined, leading Jo to put his age at well past fifty. He was dressed only in a white shirt and charcoal breeches, which were limp and rumpled. His desk was cluttered with towering stacks of papers and leather-bound ledgers, some of which he had been studying. At one corner rested a tray bearing a steaming coffeepot and an empty mug. The man's exhaustion was evident, yet he also radiated vitality.

"I am John Elliott," he said, and offered her a chair.

Mr. Elliott studied her as she seated herself, his gray brows drawn together in puzzlement.

"He's a woman," announced the other man. "Dressed like that so she wouldn't attract attention coming here."

"Good thinking," commended Mr. Elliott. He pulled his waistcoat off the back of his chair and shrugged into it, evidently deciding his appearance was too disheveled for a lady's company, even if she were dressed as a man. "Thank you, Lucas."

The balding man nodded and disappeared back into the black cave of the shipping room.

"This must be important, for you to risk coming here at this hour," Mr. Elliott observed, taking his seat behind the desk.

"It is. Tonight I learned the redcoats are in the process of concentrating their forces at Camden—"

"We know that," he interrupted. "What else do you have?"

"There is a supply train filled with weapons, ammunition, food, and clothing for the soldiers leaving Charles Town for Camden on Saturday," she continued. "Perhaps the rebels could arrange an ambush as the supplies move north through the countryside."

His eyes grew wide with interest. He leaned back in his chair and steepled his fingers together. "Are you absolutely certain?"

"Yes," Jo assured him. "I heard it from Major Nigel Ferguson, who is assisting General Cornwallis in the administration of Charles Town."

"Any reason to think he may have lied, or that his information is inaccurate?"

She shook her head. "His tongue had been loosened by alcohol. If the information is wrong, he doesn't realize it."

"Which makes it a possibility," pointed out Mr. Elliott.

He drummed his fingers on his desk, considering. "But the prospect of capturing a British supply train is far too tempting to disregard."

He rose from his desk to examine the map hanging on the wall behind it. The chart was a detailed rendering of the southern states, ending at the northern border of Virginia. South and North Carolina were studded with numerous little black boxes, each of which was identified in a margin on the side. Ostensibly the map was to show the various rice plantations with which the company of Elliott and Sons did business. Jo realized it also enabled her contact to study the terrain of the southern states, and make observations about the placement of British posts and the movements of their troops.

"We have brave men leaving their homes to join our ranks every day," he murmured, staring at the map. "My sons among them. One of them, Simon, went north, to fight under General Washington." His voice was resonant with bitter pride. "He was killed at Brandywine," he said softly. "My other son, Joseph, fought right here in Charles Town, under General Benjamin Lincoln. When the city fell, he was taken prisoner. At this moment he sits rotting on one of their stinking prison ships, out there in the harbor. I pray to God he will be able to survive long enough to be traded." He opened a drawer in his desk and pulled out a bottle of amber liquid. He splashed some into his coffee mug and downed it in a single gulp.

"Many of these men come to us with nothing but their bare fists and a burning will to fight," he reflected, filling his mug once again. He took another swallow, then lifted his eyes to her, his brow creased with anger and frustration. "Noble as that is, it will not protect them against a fully armed regiment of bloodthirsty redcoats. We need muskets, shot, clothing, and food. We have families donating what they can. We even have women melting down their pots and pans to make shot for our weapons. But it isn't enough." He seated himself and leaned forward on his desk, his expression filled with mounting determination. "We must get our hands on that supply train. If we capture it, it will help us *and* deal a significant blow against the British troops at the same time."

"A pity you won't have the opportunity to do so," stated a harsh voice.

Jo gasped and twisted around in her chair.

Damien threw her a condemning look as he leveled his pistol at Mr. Elliott. "Miss Armstrong," he drawled, stepping into the room, "I compliment you on your new disguise. It is most convincing, although not nearly as enjoyable as the gown you wore earlier this evening."

No, thought Jo, her stomach coiling with fear. *He cannot be here. He cannot.*

"Colonel Powell," she began, her voice thin and hollow, "this is not—"

"Quiet!" Damien snapped. He had thought he would enjoy the frozen shock on her face. Instead her ashen expression reminded him of the moment he first saw her kneeling before that Indian. He had tried to save her then. Now he would arrest her and see her tried for treason. Which was no more than she deserved, he assured himself bitterly. He wrenched his gaze from her and shifted his attention to her fellow spy. "Forgive the interruption, but it is my duty to place you both under arrest for treason."

Mr. Elliott's stunned eyes moved slowly from Jo to Damien, then back to Jo again. "My God," he whispered as understanding dawned on him, "you *led* him here."

"I didn't know he was following me!" she protested, horrified.

His face contorted with anger. "How could you be so careless!"

"How I found you is hardly relevant," observed Damien. "Step away from the desk, and move over here."

"I've got a better idea, lobsterback," drawled a caustic voice. "Place your pistol on the desk, and turn around to face me, slowly."

Jo watched as the faintest hint of surprise crossed Colonel Powell's face. He was quick to master it, however. Calmly he laid his pistol on the desk and turned to face

Lucas, who stood in the doorway pointing a musket at his chest.

"Well, now, looks like we have a little problem here, don't we, redcoat?" Lucas said scornfully.

"It would appear so," Damien agreed.

Lucas looked at Mr. Elliott. "What do you want me to do with him?"

Mr. Elliott considered barely a moment before answering. "Take him into the back," he instructed. "And kill him."

"You cannot!" exclaimed Jo, appalled.

"What do you expect me to do with him?" he demanded furiously. "Do you think I should let him go if he promises not to come back and arrest us?"

"You don't have to kill him," Jo insisted, trying to control the swell of panic coursing through her. Colonel Powell was her enemy, but she could not stand by and let him be murdered. Not when he had risked his own life so she could live. Not when she had stitched him and bathed him and watched over him, begging God not to let him die.

"You could make him a prisoner," she suggested hopefully, "and exchange him for an officer of equal—"

"Charles Town is a heavily occupied city," interrupted Mr. Elliott. "We cannot just take a British officer prisoner, and then step outside and offer to trade him back to the redcoats patrolling the streets."

He was right, Jo realized with sickening dismay. This was not the countryside, where rebel soldiers could take a redcoat captive and transport him to a rebel prison if they chose. This was a city under British occupation. They could not keep Colonel Powell prisoner here. Even if they could, without the ability to trade him for an American soldier, of what possible advantage would it be for them to keep him alive?

"Take him into the back," repeated Mr. Elliott stiffly, "and finish him."

"No," Jo protested. "You cannot do this! You cannot murder him!"

Mr. Elliott's expression was bleak. It was clear he was not

relishing this unexpected turn of events. "We have no choice," he said grimly.

"Let's go, lobsterback," Lucas ordered, gesturing with his musket.

Terror surged through her as she watched Colonel Powell move toward the door.

"Colonel Powell!"

Damien turned at the desperation in her voice. She was staring at him with those enormous, summer-sky eyes, her face chalky with fear. It was as if she were expecting him to do something, anything, to save himself. In that moment, Damien realized she did not want him to die. In truth, he was not entirely convinced he was about to. Much could happen as he and this rebel made their way in the dark to the back of the warehouse. But Josephine believed he was about to be executed.

And the possibility terrified her.

It was strange, but as he stood there staring down at her, he wanted to reassure her. It was ridiculous of course. This rebel farm girl was his enemy. She had betrayed him to the rebels once before. And yet, as she looked up at him with pleading eyes, he felt a slender thread of warmth puncture the cold fury that had been gnawing at him all these weeks.

The rebels were clearly puzzled by Josephine's incomprehensible anxiety over his fate. Damien realized her fear for him could jeopardize her safety. And so he took a step toward her and regarded her with glacial disdain, a look that spoke nothing of the maelstrom of emotions suddenly churning within him.

"Miss Armstrong," he drawled, his voice dripping contempt, "I am deeply touched by your concern."

She hardly felt the sting of his derision. Instead she stared at him, silently begging him to do something. She was not entirely sure what sort of feat she expected from a disarmed man who was outnumbered and had a loaded musket at his back. She only knew she could not accept the guilt of knowing she had unwittingly led him to his death.

And worse, she could not bear it if he died.

"Colonel Powell," she whispered, "please—"

"That will do," interrupted Mr. Elliott. "We cannot waste any more time. Lucas, you have your orders."

"Let's go, lobsterback," commanded Lucas, shoving his musket into Damien's back.

Damien ignored the man as he looked down at Josephine. Her eyes were wide with terror. Despite his desire that she not be implicated by her concern for him, he found he could not resist giving her a small sign that all was not lost. And so he held her gaze in his and casually remarked, "You know, Miss Armstrong, I believe in the future I would prefer it if you called me Damien."

Jo wondered what on earth he was talking about. If he was trying to give her a signal of some kind, the meaning was completely lost on her. His dark gaze held hers. She desperately tried to understand.

"I said move, redcoat!" snarled Lucas impatiently.

Colonel Powell pulled his gaze from hers and turned.

In that moment Jo panicked.

"Damien!"

Without thinking, she snatched up the pot of coffee and hurled the scalding liquid into Lucas's face. Lucas howled and raised the back of one hand to his eyes. Seizing the moment, Damien drew back his fist and smashed it into Lucas's nose. There was a sickening crunch as the soft bone gave way. Damien hit him again, smearing the blood leaking from his nostrils across his face.

"Redcoat bastard!" roared Lucas, enraged.

He struggled to point his musket at Damien, but they were too close to each other, rendering the weapon useless. Damien thrust his fist into Lucas again, this time aiming for his mouth. The musket fired, rocking the office with a deafening explosion as it blasted a hole in the wall.

Out of the corner of her eye, Jo saw Mr. Elliott reach across his desk for Damien's pistol. Her hand shot out and seized the heavy weapon, which she pointed directly at him.

"What in God's name are you doing?" he demanded, stupefied.

"Don't move," she commanded, lifting the pistol higher.

"You're a Tory spy!" His eyes were filled with fury and disgust.

"No I'm not!" Jo countered fervently. Even as she said it she realized how absurd her denial must seem as she pointed a weapon at a fellow rebel.

In that horrible, impossible moment, nothing made any sense. Not the war, or her mission to spy, or the fact that in order to procure weapons and clothing for American soldiers, Colonel Powell had to die. Everything was spinning out of control, and she could not grasp hold of what was right and what was wrong.

The only thing she knew with absolute certainty was that she could not stand by and let them murder the man who had saved her life.

Lucas was still fighting with powerful fury, but Damien managed to give him a blow to the stomach, causing him to double over. The empty musket fell to the floor. Damien shoved him against the wall and smashed his fist into Lucas's jaw, snapping his head sideways. Lucas grunted softly. Damien could feel the fight draining out of his opponent.

"What the hell is going on here?" bellowed a voice from the doorway.

Jo turned to see two white-wigged redcoats rush into the office, their pistols drawn and ready to fire. It was over, she realized numbly. Colonel Powell was safe.

And now she and Lucas and John Elliott would be arrested.

Slowly she lowered her weapon, her initial sensation of relief degenerating into fresh fear.

"Here," said Damien, grabbing Lucas by the front of his coat and shoving him toward the two soldiers. "Arrest him. And that one as well," he added, gesturing toward Mr. Elliott. "Charge them with conspiracy against His Majesty the King. They have been running a rebel spy operation out of this warehouse."

"What about this one?" demanded one of the soldiers, looking suspiciously at Jo.

Damien did not hesitate. "He is with me."

Jo stared at him, stunned. Damien shot her a warning look, which told her to keep her mouth shut and let him handle this situation.

"Traitorous Tory bitch!" snarled Mr. Elliott. He glared at Jo, his face twisted with loathing. "You redcoat whores sicken me."

"Shut your filthy rebel mouth," ordered one of the soldiers. He gave Jo an uncertain glance, evaluating her masculine attire.

"Get them out of there," Damien commanded.

He went to Josephine and relieved her of his pistol. Her face was pale and her lip was trembling. She looked as if at any moment she might fling herself at the British soldiers and beg them to arrest her, just so she could prove to these rebels that she really was on their side. He wanted everyone out of there before that happened.

"I will need your name, sir, for my report," said one of the soldiers.

"Lieutenant Colonel Damien Powell," replied Damien, keeping his gaze fixed on Josephine.

The young man blinked. "The commander of the Scarlet Legion?" he said, clearly in awe.

"Yes."

"It is an honor to meet you, sir," the soldier said. He lowered his weapon, apparently forgetting he was in the process of making an arrest. "I am Corporal Andrew Dowland, and this is—"

"Corporal, may I remind you that you have a duty to perform?" Damien interrupted.

The young man snapped to attention. "Of course, sir! I trust I can count on you, sir, to file a report that can be used at the trial of these rebel spies?"

Damien saw Josephine blanch. Good, he thought to himself. Maybe the sight of these Patriots being arrested was what she needed to give up being a spy.

"I will file my report with the office of General Cornwallis. If you require any further information after I have left Charles Town, General Cornwallis will know how to reach me."

"Thank you, Colonel Powell," said Corporal Dowland. He gave Damien a small bow before turning his attention to his prisoners. "All right, you stinking rebel scum, let's move!"

Jo watched in misery as Mr. Elliott and Lucas were marched out the office door by the two British soldiers. She dropped her gaze to the floor, unable to look at Damien.

"Come, Miss Armstrong," he said quietly. "Let us leave this place."

She followed him in silence out of the warehouse and onto the street.

Early dawn was filtering across the sky, caressing the black water of the Cooper River with ripples of gold. The street was beginning to stir as the men who worked on the docks appeared, banging open the doors and shutters of the warehouses, preparing to load and unload the sleeping ships.

"Get your horse," Damien ordered in a low voice, "and bring him here."

Without protest, Jo walked blindly to the lane where she had hidden her mount and clumsily untied him. Guilt and fear threatened to choke her. She had turned against her rebel contacts, resulting in their arrest. Once again, she had betrayed her duty to the Patriot cause. What would become of Anne and Samuel and Lucy when Captain Lee learned of this? she wondered frantically. This time she could not expect him to be understanding. She and Anne would be arrested for treason, leaving no one to look after her younger brother and sister. Her heart lurched with fear. How could she make Captain Lee see that she had had no choice?

She led her horse onto the street. Damien had hired a carriage, and was handing the reins of an enormous pearl and gray charger to a young soldier. The animal resembled the one Captain Lee had ridden. Jo wondered vaguely if Damien had stolen the animal during his escape.

"Give me your horse, and get in the carriage," Damien commanded. "And keep that hat low over your face." He was acutely aware of the danger she was in, and wanted as few people as possible to see her. Within the hour this area would be teeming with stories concerning the rebel spies arrested in this warehouse. He did not want anyone to get a good look at the slight young man leaving with him.

Jo obeyed, because she did not know what else to do. She retreated into the dark chamber of the carriage and huddled in a corner, staring miserably out the window. A moment later Damien climbed in and banged the door shut. The carriage lurched into motion, rattling swiftly down the street.

Damien leaned back and contemplated the woman opposite him. Her actions at the warehouse stunned him. Josephine Armstrong was an ardent rebel. Yet she had turned against her own to help him, acting as though she could not bear to see him hurt. Why, then, had she betrayed him by turning him over to the rebels on the farm? Surely she had understood that was a sentence of death. Or had she? He was no longer certain.

Her dark coat and breeches were loose enough to conceal the curves beneath them, and her powdered wig and hat effectively obscured her face. In the charcoal shadows of night, Damien reflected, it was a convincing disguise. But early morning was drifting through the carriage window, painting her in ribbons of gold and peach, and the delicacy of her features was slowly being unveiled. She had washed away the cosmetics worn by Celia Reed, revealing the fresh-scrubbed face of the rebel farm girl. A farm girl who had come to an occupied city and transformed herself into a woman of sophistication and elegance. An exceptionally clever woman, who could spend the evening dancing with her enemies before riding off into the night in breeches to deliver vital information. If she were a man, he might have grudgingly respected her for risking her life for her cause. But she was a woman, and he found her activities reckless, stupid, even selfish. She had a farm to manage, and a family to feed and care for. She had no business participating in treasonous activities that could easily get her arrested.

Or killed.

"What in the name of God are you doing here?" he

snapped, cracking the brittle silence that had fallen between them.

Jo pulled her gaze from the window to look at him. "I should think my reasons for being here are obvious," she replied, her tone hostile.

"Why did you help me, Miss Armstrong?" he asked brusquely.

Jo regarded him in confusion, disconcerted by the intensity of his gaze. His expression was hard and impatient, the look of a commanding officer interrogating a subordinate. He obviously expected a simple, logical response. But she had no logical response to give him. All she knew was the moment Lucas started to take him away, she had been overwhelmed by a terror so immense it had caused her to act without considering the consequences of her actions.

"I could not just stand by and let them murder someone. Even if you are a redcoat," she added contemptuously.

"I see. So you would have thrown scalding coffee and pointed a pistol at your fellow rebels regardless of what redcoat they held captive."

She returned her gaze to the window. "I believe I would have made an exception for Nigel Ferguson."

Damien considered this a moment. "I am deeply flattered, Miss Armstrong," he said finally, "to know you do have some standards."

His tone was slightly milder, perhaps even teasing. Surprised, she turned to look at him.

"Why didn't you let those redcoats arrest me?"

Her summer-sky eyes were openly searching his. Incredibly, Damien found himself longing for a fragment of honesty between them. They were enemies. And yet they had each sacrificed their duty to their country for the other's sake. He could not comprehend why she had been so desperate to save him. He did, however, have some understanding of why he had not been able to turn her over as he had planned.

She had risked herself for him.

In the wake of that unexpected, wholly undeserving gesture, his bitter desire for vengeance had disintegrated. But he could not reveal this to her. She was a rebel spy, and if he did not arrest her, he had to make certain she left this city and returned to her farm. All she could do there was offer food to passing rebels, and perhaps stitch up the odd wound. To let her go was a flagrant breach of his duty, for which he could be arrested. He understood that. But he had to do it. And he did not believe the release of this farm girl would alter the outcome of this war.

"Even my blackened soul would not permit me to toss you to the British army after you went to such lengths to prevent my execution. But understand, Miss Armstrong, I now consider the debt between us paid."

He grasped her chin with his fingers. "Listen well, my little rebel," he said, his voice hard. "The information you tried to pass on is useless, because I am going to ensure that the schedule for that supply train is changed. Since you no longer pose a threat to the operations of the British army, I will deliver you to the home of your supposed 'aunt.' You will leave Charles Town within the hour, and return to your farm, where you will resign from this dangerous game you have chosen to play. There is no safe place for you in this city. Not only will I have you arrested if I find you still here after an hour, but when your rebel friends discover what happened in that warehouse, you can be sure they will want you punished. Since you cannot stay in Charles Town, and since your family needs you at home, you would be extremely foolish to disobey my orders."

His grip on her chin made her wince as she stared into the gray steel of his eyes. Everything he said was true, Jo realized. If the supply schedule was changed, she no longer had a valuable message to give the rebels. And she could not remain in Charles Town. Damien was offering to let her escape. Captain Lee had ordered her to return home if anything went wrong, and that was where she must go. When he came to see her, as he inevitably would, she would try to make him understand the events in the warehouse were not her fault.

"Very well," she said, resisting the impulse to wrench her chin away. "I will leave Charles Town and go home."

Damien stared into her eyes, trying to decide if she was frightened enough to heed him. He saw wariness, and a generous measure of contempt, but nothing akin to the naked fear he had witnessed earlier. Apricot light was streaming through the carriage window and spilling across her pale skin, revealing a coral cast on her cheeks and lips. It was strange, but the natural blush of her lips in the soft morning light seemed far more appealing than the artfully applied stain she had worn last night as Celia Reed. Her breath was shallow, and he was vaguely aware of the scent of jasmine and roses. He let go of her chin to lightly caress the warm silk of her cheek.

"If I ever hear of you spying again, Josephine, I will take great pleasure in punishing you personally. Do you understand?"

A flicker of fear ignited in her eyes. Damien was not sure if it was kindled by his threat or his touch, but he drew perverse satisfaction from it. He wanted her to fear him, just as he wanted her to fear the threat of the British army. Only then would he feel confident that she would obey him and retreat to the relative security of her farm. Seeking to augment that fear, he lowered his head and captured her lips with his.

Jo let out a murmur of protest as Damien's mouth pressed roughly against hers. She threw her hands against him and tried to shove him away, but his arms clamped around her and pulled her close. A myriad of sensations swept through her as she felt the hardness of his chest beneath the palms of her hands, the hot pressure of his mouth sweeping over her lips, the powerful strength of his arms as he imprisoned her against him. His tongue grazed languidly over her and she gasped in shock. He responded by boldly invading her mouth, kissing her deeply, robbing her of breath and thought and even the ability to protest. A hot current of desire began to pour through her, making her flushed and breathless. The masculine clean scent of him filled her nostrils, a smell of brandy and leather and spicy soap, and his body felt hard and heavy, pulsing with strength and vitality and life. She was no longer pushing her hands against him, for somehow they had moved up to his neck and were pulling him closer, so she could feel the sculpted contours of him beneath her fingers. This was the man she had stitched and bathed and cared for, she reflected hazily as she explored the chiseled breadth of his back. This was the man she had risked her life for.

And betrayed her cause for.

Suddenly she remembered the wool grazing her fingers was scarlet, and that she was kissing a redcoat, who was trained to fight and maim and kill. Fine, brave men like her father.

And Elias.

Overwhelmed by shame, she wrenched her mouth from his and shoved against him with all her might. Caught off guard, Damien went flying backward.

"Don't ever touch me again, redcoat," she commanded, her voice trembling, "or I'll blast a hole in you so wide no amount of stitching will stop the blood."

Seeing the hate in her face, Damien could not imagine what had possessed him to kiss her. He was there to fight a war, not dally with rebel farm girls, for Christ's sake.

"Your pardon, gentlemen, but this is the address," announced the coachman curtly through the window, a disapproving look on his face.

Evidently he had looked in the window and thought he had seen two men locked in a passionate embrace. Damien shook his head in irritation and returned his attention to Josephine.

"You have one hour to leave, Miss Armstrong. Not a second longer. The horse you rode to the docks will not be delivered here until this evening, so you will need to find another means of transportation. Judging by the appearance of this house, I would assume your dear 'aunt' keeps an adequate stable."

The mention of her aunt filled Jo with concern. "Mrs. Tucker knew nothing of my activities," she said urgently. "All she did was provide me with a wardrobe and a place to stay. You have nothing to gain if you arrest her."

Damien had no intention of arresting an old woman

whom he suspected was little more than a chaperone for Josephine, but he would gladly exploit her anxiety.

"Then tell your 'aunt' that she is being watched," he replied harshly, "and that she would be extremely foolish to provide accommodation for any more 'distant relatives.' Do I make myself clear, Miss Armstrong?"

"Perfectly." She moved toward the door, anxious to escape the confines of the carriage.

"Josephine."

She halted, her eyes downcast. When he did not immediately speak, she raised her eyes questioningly to his.

He regarded her a long moment, his expression unreadable. "You cannot win this conflict on your own, Josephine," he said finally. His voice was soft, and perhaps even bore a trace of regret. Before she could be sure, he cleared his throat and finished brusquely, "Leave this war to the soldiers."

With that he placed his hand on the latch and pressed down firmly, opening the door and setting her free.

Chapter 7

Silvery dust danced slowly in the sunlight pouring through the open barn door.

Jo watched as it languidly eddied and swirled, her thoughts drifting to a jeweled sea of dancers awash in candlelight, twirling in a Charles Town ballroom. The cow she was milking pressed her massive side against Jo's cheek, making it clear she had not been adequately relieved. Jo gave the animal's rump a firm shove to move her over. Then she wrapped her hands around Molly's soft teats and continued to fill the pail at her feet with warm, rhythmic squirts of foamy white liquid.

"Did all the ladies in Charles Town wear gowns like that?" asked Lucy, fascinated by the picture Jo was painting of life in the city.

"Yes," she replied. "Of course, some gowns were finer than others, and you didn't wear your fanciest one in the middle of the day. But they all had these enormous hoops underneath that made them puff out around you like a giant bell."

Lucy stroked the tiny kitten in her lap as she considered this. "How did you sit down?" she wondered, frowning.

"It wasn't easy," Jo admitted. "The first few times I tried it, I ended up flat on the floor. And when you wanted to go through a doorway or get into a carriage, you always had to think about your gown, and how you were going to make it fit."

"Sounds foolish to me," scoffed Samuel, dropping a huge armful of straw into a stall. "Why would anyone want to wear such a thing?"

"I think it sounds beautiful," countered Lucy defensively. "And someday I shall go to Charles Town and buy a gown like that. And then I will go to a lovely ball and dance all night in tiny, satin-covered slippers, just like Jo did."

Jo smiled. She realized her description of Charles Town was fanciful. Her younger brother and sister knew Captain Lee had sent her there, but Jo had told them she had merely gone to report on how the city was faring under British occupation. Samuel, she suspected, did not entirely accept this explanation. Lucy, however, was far too entranced by Jo's colorful tales of balls and gowns and carriages to associate her absence with the war.

"I'm going to Charles Town one day too," Samuel declared as he carried another armful of straw into the stall. "Except when I go, it will be to help the rebel army kill every last stinking redcoat there."

"The redcoats will be gone long before you are old enough to join the army," Jo told him. "Until then, you'll stay right here and help manage the farm. Benjamin and Abraham will be home in a few months, and they will expect us to have kept everything running just the same as if they were here."

"Really, Jo?" Lucy's blue eyes were wide with anticipation. "You think Benjamin and Abraham will be home that soon?"

"Of course they will. This war has dragged on so long, the redcoats are getting tired. I heard them talking in Charles Town about how the British soldiers aren't accustomed to fighting in the heat and swamps we have here in

South Carolina. Some of them collapse in battle just from being too hot. People were also saying it's costing England a fortune to keep this war going. As soon as they realize we will never stop fighting, the British army will give up and go home."

"Not before I've had the chance to kill a couple of them," Samuel swore fiercely. "One for Father," he growled, thrusting his pitchfork deep into the clean straw, "and one for Elias."

"That will do, Samuel." Jo realized Samuel still agonized over the deaths of his father and brother, as they all did. But she would not tolerate talk about killing redcoats as if it were some kind of sport. And she would not encourage Samuel to think that he would ever join the rebel army. Her little brother, she had decided, was the one Armstrong male who would not be going to war.

"If Benjamin comes home in a few months, he will be able to see his baby when it is still small," Lucy said brightly as she stroked her kitten. "That would make Anne very happy."

Jo smiled at her sister's attempt to divert the conversation. The beam of light shining through the door had turned her pale blond hair to spun gold as she sat on her little stool. Lucy was only eight, but already she showed the attributes of a peacemaker. Jo wondered if this was in response to growing up during war. Lucy's father had been killed when she was barely four. Benjamin had gone to war when she was five. And Abraham and Elias had followed shortly thereafter. It occurred to Jo that this child could probably not remember a time when her family was safe and whole. The realization bit deep into her heart.

"You are right, Lucy," she agreed softly. "I am sure that would make Anne very happy."

A fragile peace descended on the trio as they contemplated this remote possibility. Lucy scooped up another tiny kitten escaping from the empty stall where Missy had decided to give birth, and gently placed it beside the one sleeping in her lap. Samuel continued to idly toss forkfuls of straw around Belle's stall. And Jo kept rhythmically coaxing milk from Molly's udder. The only sounds were the tiny mewling of Missy's kittens, and the gentle cadence of squirting milk. In that quiet, sheltered moment, Jo felt as if she were surrounded by an impregnable wall of contentment.

Until the disturbing memory of what really happened in Charles Town suddenly came back to her.

She was appalled by what she had done. Yet despite the guilt coiled tightly inside her, she knew she could not have stood by and let those rebels kill Damien. He was alive, and she was glad of that.

Even if he was her enemy.

Escaping Charles Town had not been difficult. Once inside Aunt Hazel's home, Jo had swiftly explained that she had to leave the city within the hour. Instantly adopting the manner of a military leader, Hazel announced they would travel together under the guise of taking a trip to her plantation, Redbud Hall, as this was unlikely to arouse suspicion. She ordered Cain to prepare her carriage, and instructed her maids to be ready to leave within the half hour. Scarcely twenty-five minutes later, Jo was changed into a traveling costume and climbing into the carriage beside a perfectly composed Aunt Hazel. Her heart pounded with trepidation as she waited for a band of British soldiers to appear and prevent her from escaping. But no one stopped their carriage as they fled the city that day. After seeing Jo safely delivered to her home, Aunt Hazel continued on to Redbud Hall. In the week since Jo had been back, no redcoats had come to arrest her and return her to Charles Town. Damien had kept his word.

But Jo did not feel completely secure. Because soon she would have to deal with Captain Lee. She tried to convince herself Captain Lee would not hear of her part in the arrest of Mr. Elliott and Lucas. After all, the only people other than Damien who knew what took place in that office were in custody of the British army.

Since witnessing the humiliating occupation of Charles Town, Jo now realized how much she was needed to help the struggling rebel cause. Although she told her family the war could not last much longer, in her heart she feared this was not true. In Charles Town she had seen firsthand the formidable power and resources of the British army. To win this war the rebels needed the help of every person available, and that included her. Before that terrible night in the warehouse, she had proven she could assume a false identity and procure information from the redcoats. Information was vital in war, as vital as a soldier in battle. Jo wanted the chance to continue to fight the redcoats by passing on information. The Armstrong family would not be sending any more men into battle, but Jo knew she could make a significant contribution by spying.

When Captain Lee came to see her, she intended to ask him for another assignment.

The gentle squirts of milk filling the bucket were growing smaller. Jo released her grip on Molly's teats and gave the cow a gentle pat.

"Good girl." She grabbed the bucket and lifted it out of the path of Molly's heavy feet. "Lucy, take those kittens back to Missy. It's time for us to go in for supper."

"Can't I bring them with me?"

"No," replied Jo. "They are probably hungry, and Missy will want to feed them. Samuel, you don't need to keep arranging that straw. Belle is going to spend the night outside anyway."

Holding the rope tied around Molly's neck, Jo walked her out of the barn, with Samuel and Lucy trailing behind. Sunset had arrived in a magnificent explosion of amber. Jo gave Molly a slap on her rump, sending the cow off at an idle pace to join Belle in the fields for the evening. Anne had told Jo of several redcoat attacks in the area while she was gone. Jo decided that if the redcoats came and tried to steal Molly or Belle, they would not find them conveniently locked in the barn. First the soldiers would have to find them, and then they would have to catch them. Molly especially seemed to like this new arrangement, and never gave Jo any trouble when she went to bring her in for milking.

The setting sun was painting the fading blue of the sky in shimmery bands of peach and melon and gold, cascading warm light onto the little white farmhouse. A thin stream of smoke puffed from the chimney, fragrant with the promise of supper. In that moment Jo could almost imagine there was no war, and everything was just as it always had been at the Armstrong home. She closed her eyes and indulged in the fantasy, enjoying the easing heat of the day against her skin, the comfortable weight of the heavy milking bucket in her hand, and the smoky-sweet aroma of the chimney in her nose.

This is as it should be. No war, no fear, no hatred. Just the warmth of the sky and the openness of the land. And the knowledge that this is, and always will be, my home. Where my family lives, happy and safe.

And together.

"Jo—Samuel—Lucy!" called Anne, her musical voice spilling across the yard. "Supper is ready!"

Jo opened her eyes, swallowing down a painful throb of grief. They weren't all together, and they never would be again. Her beloved father and her charming, handsome brother were dead, lying mangled in shallow, unmarked graves below blood-soaked battlefields. And Benjamin and Abraham were away fighting in the north where either, if not both, could be killed at any moment. She hated what this war had done to her family. It had been going on for four endless years, and would continue as long as the British troops remained. Somehow, rebel men and women would have to find the strength to keep on fighting. Because even though they were not winning, each day they resisted sapped the resources of the powerful British army. And brought the Americans one step closer to victory.

She was certain of it.

"Hurry up, you three—aren't you hungry?" called Anne teasingly from the kitchen doorway.

Jo's anguish eased slightly as she looked at her sister-in-law. Anne's body was round and lush with the child sheltered inside her, and Jo found her growing shape more beautiful every day. Her heavy red hair had fallen slightly from its pins, and was turning to fire as she stood in an amber shower of sunlight watching them.

"We're coming, Anne," called Lucy, skipping on ahead.

"Race you, Lucy!" challenged Samuel with rare playfulness, bursting into a run beside her.

Jo did not hurry as she walked toward the flame-haired expectant mother in the little gold house. *Tonight there is no war,* she told herself adamantly. And somehow she found she could almost make herself believe it. Because the countryside she loved so dearly was quiet and peaceful, and in this brief, sunlit moment, the war seemed very far away.

Captain Lee did not wait long to find her.

It was afternoon of the following day. Jo was upstairs in Anne's bedroom helping her to make up the bed with freshly laundered linens.

"Oh my," gasped Anne suddenly, dropping the sheet to clutch her swollen belly.

"What is it?" Jo rushed around the bed to help Anne sit down. "Annie, are you in pain?"

Anne slowly exhaled the breath she had been holding then raised her eyes to Jo's. "Not pain, exactly. More like the baby suddenly decided to kick both feet straight out, and some of my insides got in the way." She gave Jo a shaky smile. "It just took me by surprise. Here." She took Jo's hand and pressed it against her. "I think she is going to do it again."

Jo sat beside Anne and waited, her hand against the firm swell of her belly. After a moment, she felt a sharp kick against her palm. She looked at Anne and laughed. "She's strong, isn't she?"

"Like my Benjamin," agreed Anne, rubbing her hand soothingly over her stomach. "Strong and restless. It wouldn't surprise me at all if she came early."

"Do you think it's a girl, Annie?"

"I am hoping she is a girl," she admitted, "because I don't want to bear a child that will have to go to war someday." Her expression grew pensive. "Do you think that's selfish of me?"

Jo wrapped her arm around Anne's shoulder. "Not at all," she said gently. "No mother could like the thought of her children going to war. But this war is going to be over soon, Annie. I promise. Benjamin and Abraham will come home safe and whole. And this little baby won't know war as anything but a faded story her parents tell her when she is older. You'll see."

Anne leaned her head against Jo's shoulder, trying to absorb some of her confidence and strength. "Of course you're right, Jo," she murmured. "It can't last much longer. I just wish Benjamin would come home. I miss him terribly, and I had hoped he would be home in time to see his first child born."

"Maybe he will get some leave. But if he doesn't, we will write him a long letter telling him all about how wonderful the baby is. And you can be sure when he gets that letter, he will be the proudest father in the world. Even if," she added teasingly, "the baby inherits his nose."

"Jo, how can you say such a thing?" Anne chided. "Benjamin has a perfectly fine nose! Why, it's handsome, and distinguished, and—"

"Really big," finished Jo, laughing.

Anne looked properly exasperated, as any good wife would, before starting to giggle.

Suddenly they heard Samuel calling urgently. "Jo! Jo! Come quick!"

Jo leapt to her feet and rushed toward the stairs. The front door banged open and Samuel tore into the house.

"It's that rebel captain again, with two of his soldiers," he reported breathlessly. "Riding through the yard."

"Where is Lucy?"

"In the barn playing with Missy's kittens."

"Go out the kitchen door and get her. And take her upstairs. *Now.*"

Samuel turned without a word to follow her orders.

Jo straightened and breathed deeply, praying Captain Lee was here because he had learned of her flight from Charles Town. The other possibility was that he had come to tell her Benjamin or Abraham had been killed. She banished the thought from her mind.

At the front door she saw Captain Lee dismounting from a pale brown horse that bore no resemblance to the magnificent pearl and gray charger he had ridden on his last visit here. He had brought two soldiers with him. One was the huge bear man who had taken such cruel pleasure in shooting Damien's horse. The other was a tall, thin boy she did not recognize, who appeared to be no more than sixteen or seventeen.

"Good afternoon, Miss Armstrong."

"Captain Lee," she returned. "Won't you come in and take some refreshment?" She tried to keep her voice light and cordial, the way Aunt Hazel had trained her.

"Thank you, Miss Armstrong. I believe I will." He removed his hat as he stepped heavily up onto the porch.

Captain Lee was not a small man, and Jo had to resist the impulse to shrink back from him as he stared at her, his blue eyes cool and assessing.

"If you could send out a drink for my men, I'd be indebted."

"Why certainly, Captain."

Jo led her guest into the house.

Anne was standing at the top of the stairs regarding them anxiously. Jo asked her to see to the captain's men.

"Of course," replied Anne, her voice taut. She grasped the banister and began to slowly descend the stairs.

"Thank you. This way, Captain Lee." Jo moved down the corridor and pushed open the doors to the parlor. "What can I offer you?"

Captain Lee dropped his hat and gloves on a table. "Do you have any whiskey?"

Jo went to the end of the parlor and began to open the windows to let fresh air into the hot room. "I am afraid not," she lied. She had taken the precaution of removing the whiskey decanter from the parlor. She sensed their discussion would go better if Captain Lee kept a clear head. "Would you care for some water, or perhaps milk?"

"No, thank you," he replied, obviously disappointed. "Well, Miss Armstrong," he began after they had seated themselves. "It seems you had an eventful time in Charles Town."

He knew. Jo fought to remain calm. Perhaps she was rushing to the wrong conclusion. "I hope my work there was of some help. I managed to get out two messages. I was in the process of relaying a third when I was almost captured by the redcoats. Since it was not safe for me to remain in Charles Town, I immediately returned home, as you had instructed."

Captain Lee studied her a moment, weighing her statement. "I understand your contacts down by the Cooper River were not so fortunate."

"No." She decided not to elaborate on the matter. She would wait and see what Captain Lee knew first.

"A pity. Fortunately, we have other spies at work in Charles Town. The loss of two is regrettable, but not overly damaging."

The tightness in her chest eased slightly. It seemed Captain Lee knew nothing of the events that took place in the warehouse. Whatever his reasons for coming here, it was not to arrest her for treason.

"What was the message you were trying to deliver?"

"I wanted to let the rebels know about a supply train that was leaving Charles Town for the British army camp at Camden," she replied. "I thought if we could capture it, we would not only strip the redcoats of their supplies, but it would give us some of the arms and food and clothing our troops so desperately need."

His gray brows rose with interest. "When were the wagons leaving?"

"They were supposed to depart last Saturday. But as I was fleeing Charles Town, I learned the schedule was going to be changed. They could have left anytime this week."

"Perhaps. Which means they might still be on the road. Or maybe they have not left yet." He was silent for a moment, contemplating these possibilities. "I will see that this information is relayed to the appropriate contacts. There is a chance that supply train is still on its way to Camden, in which case we might be able to capture it for ourselves."

He rose from his chair and moved to study the view from the window, his hands clasped behind his back. "And now," he said, his voice low and reflective, "we need to discuss what I am to do with you, Miss Armstrong."

Fear began to churn once more in Jo's stomach. "What do you mean?" she asked cautiously.

"By all accounts you were very effective in Charles Town. Hazel Tucker reported that you were quite remarkable. Apparently you were quickly accepted as a fine lady by the British officers."

He turned and cast her an appraising look, as if trying to imagine this miraculous transformation. Jo was suddenly aware of her faded, much-mended work dress, and the fact that her hair was falling loosely from the hasty arranging she had given it early this morning.

"I have no doubt that had you been able to remain there, you would have become a vital source of information. All you needed was to befriend one senior officer, and we would have had a reliable flow of news from the redcoat side. However, since you were not able to remain in Charles Town long enough to adequately repay your debt to me, I have decided to send you on another assignment." He raised one eyebrow speculatively. "I trust you are still interested in our arrangement?"

"I am anxious to continue working for the rebel cause," Jo said quietly. "Not because of your threat to arrest me. Because I want to help us win this war."

"Really?" he drawled, unconvinced. "Forgive me if I sound cynical, Miss Armstrong, but aren't you going to tell me how much you are needed here on the farm?"

"Anne and the children managed well enough without me while I was in Charles Town," she pointed out. "The women and boys in the area will help them bring in the crops when they are ready. And Anne's baby is not due for another two months or so. If possible, I would like to be home in September, so I can help her when the baby is born. Until then, I am willing to do everything I can to help fight the redcoats, just as my father and three brothers have."

Captain Lee regarded her a long moment, his expression pensive. "In truth, Miss Armstrong, I did not intend to give you a choice. However, I am pleased you are going into this assignment willingly. I trust that will make your work all the more successful."

He returned to his chair, his face grim. "We know the British have been concentrating their forces in and around the town of Camden since the beginning of June, after the fall of Charles Town. Strategically, it makes sense. Camden puts them in an excellent position to make a move into North Carolina, or to attack the Continental Army if it tries to march south."

"How many soldiers are gathered there?" asked Jo.

"We are not certain," he admitted. "New troops are arriving all the time. We estimate somewhere between two and three thousand."

Fear rippled through her. The idea of such an immense British force assembling close to her home was terrifying.

"The new commander of the Southern Department can easily put together an army twice that size," he assured her, sensing her distress. "Any day now, General Horatio Gates will arrive at Coxe's Mill in North Carolina and assume command of the army stationed there. Soon thousands of militia from every southern state will march to join him. Then we'll show these bloody redcoats who controls our destiny." His voice was bitter.

Jo frowned. "If you are so certain we have the numbers to win against them, what do you need me for?"

"We know where they are, and we suspect they are preparing for a major battle. However, we don't where or when they plan to attack," he explained in frustration. "So far every man we have sent to spy for us at Camden has either been discovered and executed, or worse, has elected to desert to the British side. The redcoats offer a generous package to any American soldier willing to desert and provide them with information that will help their military planning. With the war dragging on and army pay months in arrears, some men are easily bought." He shook his head in disgust.

"What would I be expected to learn?"

"At first, we would require detailed reports on the size and condition of the British troops. How many men are

able-bodied and how many are sick? What is the general attitude and morale of the troops? We need to know about
their supply lines, their artillery, their movements. Then,
once you were more accepted and trusted by the soldiers,
you would have to get as close as possible to the officers. The real information lies with them. From documents
in their quarters you can learn about specific military plans,
including numbers, places, dates, and intended maneuvers."

Jo considered this a moment. "But how would I get in?
Under what guise would the British army accept a strange
woman into their midst?"

"All armies require the services of women, Miss Armstrong. You would infiltrate the army camp at Camden by
pretending to be a camp follower—a homeless Loyalist
woman who is willing to offer her services to the British
army in exchange for food and a place to sleep."

"What kind of services?"

"The usual kind," he replied with a shrug. "Cooking,
laundering, assisting with the sick and wounded. Of
course," he allowed hesitantly, "some women elect to perform more, shall we say, intimate services for the soldiers."

Jo looked at him in shock.

Captain Lee had the grace to look mildly embarrassed.
"Your methods for securing information would be left entirely up to you," he hastily assured her. He leaned back in
his chair and pressed the tips of his fingers together,
awaiting her answer.

Jo bit her lip. The prospect of entering a British army
camp and living intimately amongst her enemies was terrifying. In Charles Town she had dealt with the redcoats at
formal social occasions, where strict codes of conduct
reigned. Every evening she had been able to retreat to the
refuge of Aunt Hazel's home. In an army camp there would
be no such sanctuary. She would be living openly amongst
the soldiers. One small slip, and she would be hanged for
spying.

The mission Captain Lee was assigning her was almost as
repugnant as it was dangerous. In her new role, she would
not only be forced to befriend the redcoats, but she

would have to perform personal services for them as well. She would be washing and cooking and nursing for the men who had savagely murdered her father and Elias, and thousands of other brave rebels like them. To perform these duties without revealing her hatred of the redcoats would be almost impossible. But if she *could* do it, she might learn crucial information that could alter the outcome of a battle. And perhaps bring the war closer to an end.

The potential significance of her actions was awesome. And she would unequivocally prove her rebel loyalty to Captain Lee, erasing the shame she had brought to herself and her family by hiding Damien in her barn.

The thought of Damien made her pause. Was there a chance that he and his Scarlet Legion were at Camden?

My men are posted to the British garrison at Ninety-Six, he had told her. *I will be returning there when my business in Charles Town is finished.* Assuming his business in Charles Town had only taken a few days, he was probably back at Ninety-Six by now. But would he stay there?

"Are all the British troops gathering at Camden," she inquired, "or just some of them?"

"Unfortunately, General Cornwallis isn't foolish enough to position his entire army in one place," Captain Lee replied. "He has to make sure Charles Town remains well occupied. The British also have a string of posts that must be kept strongly fortified, so they can control the surrounding areas."

Jo's heart began to beat a little faster. "Does that include Ninety-Six?"

He nodded. "Ninety-Six is one of their most important posts in South Carolina. It gives protection to the Tories in the western countryside, and is used as a communications base for their Indian allies. General Cornwallis cannot afford to call in his troops from there." His drew his gray brows together. "Why do you ask?"

Jo was positive Damien had told her he was returning to Ninety-Six. If it was as important a garrison as Captain Lee claimed, there was no reason to think he and his legion would abandon it to go to Camden.

"I was just wondering," she murmured. Nervous excitement poured through her as she contemplated what she was about to do.

"I accept this mission, Captain Lee. Tell me how I am to get to Camden."

Chapter 8

Near Camden, South Carolina

August 1780

Blistering clouds of fetid steam blasted from the enormous iron kettle, causing rivulets of sweat to pour down her face as Jo stirred the murky soup of bed linens.

She pushed a damp piece of hair off her forehead and examined the fire. The soldiers' uniforms and linens needed to be boiled thoroughly in order to kill the parasitic mites that burrowed into the seams and caused the men to suffer from the "itch." In truth, the idea of British soldiers tormented by this most unpleasant affliction pleased her, for any discomfort they endured would render them less able on the battlefield. But the more than two thousand redcoats gathered around Camden were theoretically required to have their bedding washed once a month. Since that colossal task could not be accomplished with the few camp women and limited facilities provided, Jo did not want any soldiers returning their linens to her and demanding she wash them again. She picked up a few sticks of wood and tossed them onto the fire. The wood hissed and refused to light. Frowning, she poked at it with the heavy pole she used to stir the linens. There was a loud snap as a burning log exploded, sending a brilliant shower of orange embers onto her skirts. With a startled cry, Jo leapt back, shaking the glowing coals onto the ground.

"Gracious, Caroline, are you all right?" demanded Alice anxiously.

"I'm fine," Jo muttered as she examined her skirts for damage. A dozen holes of varying sizes peppered the faded fabric. She sighed. She had only brought one other dress with her to Camden.

"Here, let me take over the pot for a while," offered Alice as she finished folding a threadbare sheet into a neat square.

"No," said Jo shaking her head. "You shouldn't be boiling laundry in your condition."

Alice placed her tiny, work-roughened hands on her swollen stomach and smiled. "And who do you suppose will be boilin' the laundry when me and my James are back in England on our little farm, with this babe born and another on the way? My very own lady-in-waitin'?" She tilted her head back and laughed, the hearty, unaffected sound of a girl who had never had much, and found pleasure in the simplest things.

Jo shrugged her shoulders. "Perhaps James will help you."

Alice's sunburned cheeks puckered into dimples as she let out another squeal of laughter. "Do you hear her, Lily?" she asked the tall, thin girl who was slapping wet sheets over ropes strung between the trees. "Caroline thinks my darlin' Jamie will take over doin' laundry."

"And I'll be leavin' here to marry a duke next week," Lily chuckled. She fished a gray sheet out of her basket and draped it across the narrow front of her faded yellow dress. "The fabric is lovely," she declared, attempting an elegant accent, "but can you make a weddin' gown by Saturday?"

"Oh, certainly, ma'am," returned Alice as she bobbed a playful curtsy. "Whatever you like."

"I can't help what you do once you are back in England, Alice," Jo admitted. "But as long as I am here, you won't be standing over a boiling cauldron in this dreadful heat."

Alice gently put her hand on Jo's arm. "You're very kind, Caroline," she murmured. "None of the other camp women would care if I fainted dead away and fell right into the pot."

Jo looked down at the small, reddened hand resting lightly on her arm. Alice's gesture of friendship made her intensely uncomfortable. She had no desire to like the wife of a British soldier. Even if Alice *was* pleasant and hard-working and amiable. She and Lily had been much nicer to Jo than any of the other camp women when she first arrived, nearly two weeks ago. Food and bedding were in short supply at the British camp, and although there was more than enough work for all, the established women treated newcomers with barely disguised animosity. Their coolness suited Jo fine. After all, she was here to spy, not to make friends. But pretty, dark-haired Alice Clarke was nearly eight months with child, and Jo was appalled at the amount of work the girl was expected to do. She could no more allow this tiny expectant mother to boil laundry in the scorching sun than she could permit Anne to do so, and that was that.

"Lily, be a love and take over for Caroline here, would you?" asked Alice sweetly.

Lily finished arranging a soggy sheet on the line and took the pole from Jo.

"Thank you," said Jo gratefully. Although she was accustomed to hard work, the amount of labor required at the army camp was staggering, and this blistering heat wasn't helping. She walked over to the laundry lines and began the somewhat cooler task of hanging wet linens to dry.

The town of Camden was comprised of only eighty houses, located just forty miles south of the North Carolina border. It served a sparsely settled area of fragrant pine woods, fertile farms, and lush marshes, providing the inhabitants with a saw mill, a grain mill, a brewery, a distillery, a tobacco warehouse, and a dye works. Most of these businesses belonged to a fervent rebel named Joseph Kershaw. When General Cornwallis arrived here with his army, he promptly arrested Kershaw and locked him in the town's jail. Cornwallis then moved into Kershaw's elegant, three-story plantation home, generously permitting his wife and five children to remain, but only in one room. He ordered his soldiers to build an encampment around his new headquarters, and Camden was swiftly transformed from a peaceful market town to a key British post.

Although some redcoats remained in Camden, the majority of them were camped here, north of the town, in anticipation of the arrival of the American army under the command of General Horatio Gates. By casually making conversation with the dozens of men who brought her their filthy uniforms and bed linens to wash, Jo had learned that the British were expecting the arrival of an American force of five to six thousand men. With over eight hundred British soldiers at Camden incapacitated by putrid fever, dysentery, malaria, and heat stroke, that left barely two thousand ablebodied redcoats. Jo assured herself that the hopelessly outnumbered redcoats would not stand a chance.

The thought filled her with bitter pleasure.

"Afternoon, ladies. A real sizzler today, ain't it? I'm so hot I feel like my ballocks are meltin'," announced Tommy Brown.

Alice and Lily shrieked with laughter.

"Tommy!" exclaimed Jo. "What a disgraceful thing to say!"

Tommy seated himself on a rock and placed his wooden drum on the ground beside him. "That's soldier talk." His tone was slightly arrogant. "I heard some of the men sayin' it."

"Soldier talk or not, it is a vulgar expression, and you will not use it in the company of women again, is that clear?"

Tommy shrugged his shoulders. "Lily and Alice don't mind."

Jo cast the giggling women a disapproving look and they sobered their expressions. "They most certainly do mind," Jo assured him, although the difficulty they were having keeping a straight face indicated otherwise. "It is most improper for a gentleman to speak so in the company of ladies. You don't hear any of the officers talking that way, do you?"

Tommy raked his hand through his shaggy brown hair, considering. "No," he admitted.

"Of course not. And you told me you wanted to become an officer one day, didn't you?"

"Yes, ma'am," he agreed, his tone contrite.

"Then you must try to behave like one."

Tommy stared glumly at his mud-caked boots. Jo's heart softened. Tommy was thirteen, the same age as Samuel, but his small, thin frame made him look younger. Jo had been so shocked by his youth when she first met him that she could not help asking how he had joined the British army. Tommy told her he had run away from home because his father was a drunk who often beat him. When he found he could not steal enough on the streets of London to keep his belly full, he decided to join the army as a drummer. That way, he informed her, his voice tinged with pride, he could eat three meals a day and wear a uniform while he saw the world.

But the miserable meals he got here were barely enough to feed a growing boy, Jo thought in disgust, and his ill-fitting uniform was filthy and worn. His coat was buff-colored to match the color of his regiment's lapels, with red facings and cuffs, a red waistcoat, and red breeches. Jo imagined that when he first donned this outfit he must have thought it the most splendid costume in the world, especially when he pulled on his tall bearskin cap and slipped his painted wooden drum over his shoulder. After almost a year in America, however, his coat was badly frayed and torn, his waistcoat was stained, and his breeches were dark with grime and threadbare at the knees. Jo did not want to think about what kind of vermin were residing in the sweat-soaked fabric of his shirt. The day was stifling hot, and Tommy had undone the tarnished buttons of his waistcoat and shirt in a futile attempt to keep cool beneath the torturously heavy layers of wool and canvas.

Perhaps, she allowed ruefully, his ballocks were indeed melting.

"Tommy, why don't you give me your uniform to wash?" she suggested as she slung another sopping sheet over the line.

Tommy looked up at her. "Why?"

"So it will be clean."

He stared in bewilderment at his grimy uniform. Noticing a mud splatter on his breeches, he spat into his hand and tried to rub it away, grinding the dirt into the fibers. "It's clean enough," he informed her with a shrug.

"I am afraid I must disagree with you." Jo walked over to him and eyed him up and down. "You are finished drilling for the day. Why don't you give me your uniform, and I will wash it while you go down to the river and bathe. You'll feel much better afterward, I promise."

"I feel just fine, Caroline," he assured her.

Jo would never tolerate Samuel looking so dirty, and was suddenly determined to see this filthy redcoat boy clean. "After this load of bedclothes I'm going to heat some fresh water, and your uniform will be the first thing we wash. In this sun your shirt and breeches will dry in no time, and your coat will certainly be dry by tomorrow morning. What do you say?"

"Better do as she says, lad," advised Alice, her bow-shaped mouth curved in a gentle smile. "Otherwise, knowin' Caroline, she'll strip the clothes right off you as you sleep, and you'll awaken naked as the day your mother birthed you."

"But I don't want to bathe," protested Tommy.

"But Tom, why ever not? There's nothin' as nice as a man freshly bathed and in a lovely, clean uniform," Lily assured him, her voice teasing and suggestive.

"Lily," Jo said in a warning tone, "we'll have none of that, if you please."

Lily Hawkins was one of the camp women who elected to offer services other than cooking, washing, and nursing to the men. Although Jo did not approve of her behavior, neither did she feel she could judge her. Lily was from North Carolina, where she and her family had been cruelly persecuted for being Loyalists. Her father had been killed and her home burned to the ground, not by any army, but by a mob of drunken rebels who felt it was their patriotic duty. Homeless and alone, Lily had decided to seek the protection of the British army. At twenty-two, she had a body made lean by the deprivations of war, and a smooth-skinned face that was almost pretty when she let down her chestnut hair. She was well liked among the soldiers, and in exchange for her services, they paid her with money, trinkets, or a bit of food or rum. Lily was a well-meaning girl who was trying to survive, and Jo could not condemn her for prostituting herself. Even though she was certain she could never do such a thing. Not even to help her country win the war.

"What about it then, Tommy?" Jo asked. "You go behind these sheets and take everything off, then wrap yourself up and go down to the river. Get cool and clean, and by the time you come back I'll have your uniform looking as bright and smart as an officer's."

"All right," he said with a shrug. He marched between the lines of sheets to shed his clothes.

"This lot's done," announced Lily, fishing the steaming linens out of the kettle.

"Then let's throw out this water and start fresh," suggested Jo.

"My goodness, Caroline, you're so particular." Alice tossed another folded sheet onto her pile. "After you've been with us a few months, you'll not care so much when the water becomes a bit dirty."

I won't be here that long, thought Jo. She and Lily eased the kettle onto its side and watched the black water run onto the sun-scorched grass.

Already she had managed to get out two messages, in which she had reported on the size and condition of the British troops. Whenever she had something to report, she was to go into the town of Camden and make a modest purchase at the general supplies store. Her message was to be written on a tiny scrap of paper, and passed to the store owner as she handed him her money. Like Charles Town, Camden was filled with rebels who appeared to accept the occupation of their town, when in fact they were determined to do whatever they could to undermine the redcoats.

So far, Jo had not been able to learn anything about their strategic plans, either for winning the war or fighting the battle almost at hand. Although the soldiers she came across liked to talk, they did not seem to have any idea of what their leaders were planning. In order to obtain more detailed information, she was going to have to befriend an officer. But the social rules in Camden were far different from those in Charles Town. If a woman flirted with an officer in a ballroom, it was simply a game, a frivolous, choreographed dance of fluttering fans and lowered eyelashes, which went no further than was deemed socially respectable. In an army camp, there was no mistaking a flirting woman's intentions. Many of the women wanted the luxury of sharing an officer's tent, which were private and larger than those used by the soldiers. Being an officer's mistress meant less work, better food, and the certainty that no other soldiers would dare touch you. For Jo, it could also mean access to vital information. However, she did not know how to achieve such a relationship without sleeping with the chosen officer.

"Christ, it's hotter than hell over here, eh, girls?" sneered a short, squat soldier with a greasy-looking mop of red hair. "Just look at that goddamn fire."

"Don't know how you stand it," added another, clearly amused by the thought of their discomfort. He was much taller than his friend, with a skinny frame, receding brown hair, and glassy, bulging eyes set about an inch too far apart. Jo thought he bore an uncanny resemblance to a snake.

"Hey there, Lil, how about you, me, and Sidney get together tonight and have some fun?" suggested the red-haired one. He grabbed Lily's bottom and gave her a hard squeeze.

"You take your filthy hands off me, Harry!" Lily snapped, shoving his hand away. "For your information I'm busy tonight, and every night from here till hell freezes over, if you take my meanin', so don't bother askin' me again." She stalked out of his reach.

The thin line of Sidney's mouth curled downward.

"What the hell is that supposed to mean? Everyone knows you'll lift your skirts for nothin' more than a swig of rum."

"Not for the likes of you two, I won't," Lily returned flatly. "I heard how you treated poor Agnes the other night. Beat her till she was black and blue. You've a cruel streak in you, and I won't have nothin' to do with either of you. And neither will any of the other camp women who might have warmed your bed now and then. So take your sheets and get goin', 'cause it sickens me just to look at you."

Harry walked toward her, cracking his knuckles as he advanced. "Gettin' a bit fine on us, are we, Lil?"

"Too fine for the likes of you."

Harry spat on the ground. "We were just havin' fun with Agnes," he assured her. "No permanent harm done."

Lily fixed him with a hard glare. "Your kind of fun makes me sick. Now get out of here, you spineless dog."

"Spineless dog is it?" Harry snarled, raising his hand. "You goddamn worthless whore—"

Jo shoved her stirring stick into his chest, knocking him flat on his back before he could crack Lily's face.

Harry lay perfectly still for a moment, a look of astonishment on his pudgy face. Then, his expression contorted into a vicious scowl.

"Goddamn bitch!" he roared.

Jo was on him before he could find his feet, the pointed end of her stirring stick positioned at the base of his throat.

"I think we've heard enough from you for one day, Harry," she said tautly. She looked up at Sidney, who was watching her with enraged amazement. "If you came for your sheets, soldier, take them and get out of here, and be glad I don't report both of you to your superior officer."

Alice pulled some clean, folded linens out of her basket and began to waddle toward Sidney. "Here you go," she offered sweetly.

Sidney reached out to take the sheets from her. Suddenly Alice let the clean bundle fall to the ground, into a puddle of dirty wash water.

"Oh my, I'm ever so clumsy," she apologized. Her hand

rested in mock distress against her dimpled cheek. "So sorry. See you next month."

Sidney glared at her. "Why, you little—"

"Keep a civil tongue in your head, or Harry here is going to have an awfully sore throat," Jo warned.

"What the devil is going on here?"

An immaculately uniformed officer was striding toward them. Suddenly concerned about the penalty for knocking a British soldier to the ground with a sharp pole, Jo withdrew her weapon, allowing poor Harry to scramble unceremoniously to his feet.

"You there, Bates, what the hell is happening here?" the officer snapped, his keen brown eyes glaring at Sidney.

"Nothin', Cap'n Dunmore, sir," replied Sidney. "Me and Harry was just gettin' our sheets, is all, when this crazy girl attacked him with that stick."

Captain Dunmore's eyes turned to Jo. He was a handsome enough man, Jo allowed, with a smooth brow that seemed to indicate he was not given to anger or worry. His unpowdered hair was dark brown and tied back in a neat queue, and he had a sturdy, muscular frame that spoke of many hours spent in the saddle.

"Is that so?" Captain Dunmore drawled. His eyes moved from Jo to sweep over the other two women. "And I suppose you and Perkins did nothing to provoke this sudden, unreasonable attack?"

"No, Cap'n," returned Harry, his voice dripping innocence. "Nothin' at all."

Captain Dunmore returned his gaze to Jo. "Anything you'd like to tell me, miss?"

His tone seemed reasonable, despite the fact that he was a redcoat. Jo had the feeling Captain Dunmore was probably a fair man. It occurred to her that someone with authority should know about the plight of poor Agnes, and Harry's attempt to strike Lily. She opened her mouth to speak. Before a word came out, Alice's rough hand clapped around her wrist and gave it a hard squeeze.

" 'Twas just a foolish game we were playin', Captain

Dunmore," Alice offered cheerfully. "No harm meant, and none done."

Captain Dunmore's eyes fastened suspiciously on Jo. "Is that true, miss?"

"Yes," she stammered.

He hesitated a moment, then turned to look at Harry and Sidney.

"You men take your sheets and get away from these women," he ordered. "And don't let me see any more nonsense happening around here."

"Yes sir, Cap'n," Sidney returned.

"Thank you, Cap'n." Harry paused to throw a final scowl at Jo before retreating.

"I fear long months spent living in the open can make some soldiers a bit rough," Captain Dunmore commented dryly. "If you have any more trouble, ladies, please do not hesitate to bring it to my attention." He gave them a small bow, then turned on his heel and left.

"Perkins and Bates are a right nasty pair," remarked Tommy. He stepped out from behind the curtain of sheets with a swath of gray linen wrapped around his skinny waist. "Best to stay away from them."

Jo frowned and turned to Alice, who had resumed folding sheets. "Why didn't you want me to tell Captain Dunmore about them?"

"Because it would only make things worse if you did," Alice explained. "Bein' a soldier's wife, I know the bonds that tie these men together. From the moment they put on that scarlet uniform, they're trained to think of themselves as part of a group. Like a brotherhood of sorts. My Jamie says that's how they learn to fight as a unit, 'stead of every man for himself. When someone attacks one soldier, it's as if they're attackin' the whole regiment. Do you see?"

Jo shook her head.

"If we report Harry and Sidney to Captain Dunmore, all that would happen is he would question them and let them go," said Lily. "The army needs every man who's able to be trainin' and ready for battle, not locked up for beatin' a whore. Besides," she finished with a shrug, "no one can prove what they did."

"But Agnes could tell him what happened," objected Jo.

Lily snorted. "Poor Agnes would never say a word against them. And even if she did, who's goin' to believe her, or even care if they were rough on her? It's just a couple of rum-soaked soldiers havin' some fun."

"But they beat her," persisted Jo, outraged. "And Harry tried to strike you."

"Men beat whores all the time." Lily tossed some more sticks onto the fire. "It's a hazard of the trade. No one thinks anythin' of it."

"Reportin' them would just make all the soldiers angry with us for turnin' in their own," continued Alice. "And that would make life in the camp worse for all of us."

Jo stared at them in disbelief. "So we just accept it and do nothing?"

"No," countered Lily. "What happened to Agnes is common knowledge among the women who lie with the soldiers. You can be sure none of them will be warmin' Harry or Sidney's sheets any time soon."

"Especially since their sheets are so dirty," Alice added with a laugh.

The fact that no woman would sleep with these men hardly seemed sufficient punishment for their abuse of Agnes. However, if Alice and Lily were right, there wasn't any point in taking the matter up with Captain Dunmore.

"Fine," Jo conceded. "But they better not try to hurt you again, Lily," she swore, "or they'll wish I had left them to Captain Dunmore."

Night spread a cool veil of darkness across the sleeping camp, concealing Jo in shadows as she silently made her way toward the river.

It was not easy for the women living amongst the soldiers to find an opportunity to bathe. During the day the river was frequented by hundreds of men who had finished drilling and were attempting to cool off, or were fetching water to make coffee or boil food. Evening was no better, because that was when the soldiers drank their fill of their daily allotment of rum. If any of them saw a woman heading toward the river, their addled senses interpreted this as an obvious invitation to join her. And so Jo had learned to wait until deep into the night, when the camp purred with the low, rhythmic rumble of over two thousand men snoring, before venturing out of her tent to seek the cool haven of the river. Some nights she was too exhausted to stay awake, and just splashed herself with tepid water from a basin before collapsing on the thin blankets she had piled together to serve as her bed. But the endless hours spent stirring the pot of filthy bedclothes left her hot and smelling of smoke, and tonight she was determined to scrub herself free of that odor before facing her task again tomorrow.

She moved quickly through the grove of feathery pines, taking pleasure in the sweet, sharp scent that wrapped around her as her feet pressed a narrow path into the carpet of needles. The darkness of the woods gave way to a brilliant glimmer of moonlight playing over the surface of the water. Searching the shadows, Jo saw nothing but a swath of grass and rock bordering the deliciously cold ribbon of black. She swiftly stripped off her shoes, stockings, dress, and petticoats, leaving herself clad in her chemise. Although she would have preferred to bathe nude, she was not so careless as to think it was impossible for someone to happen by, even in the middle of the night. There were guards posted to keep watch over the camp, and if one of them decided to take a walk by the river, she did not want to be discovered stark naked. She abandoned her clothes on the grassy bank and left her precious sliver of soap on a ledge of rock. Then, with a little sigh of anticipation, she raised her arms over her head and dove into the liquid ripple of moonlight.

The water engulfed her in pure, cooling pleasure, causing her to momentarily relinquish all thought except for the glorious sensation of flying through infinite darkness. When her lungs grew taut she pulled herself to the surface, emerging in the still night air. The moon had slipped behind a dense cloud, leaving the star-flecked sky without a beacon.

Jo lay on her back and kicked her feet, enjoying the feeling of the river pulsing against her as she languidly sailed into the night. After a few moments she dove under again, losing herself in the velvety depths, pulling herself through the water with strong, sure strokes as her aching muscles stretched and her hair swirled softly against her skin. Finally she returned to the rock and went to work with the soap, rubbing it into her hair and skin until she was cloaked in sweet-smelling foam. Once she was sufficiently lathered she stood and dove into the river once more, swimming beneath its surface as the pearly beads of fragrant suds disappeared in her wake.

Eventually her flesh grew chilled. She hoisted herself onto the rock and twisted her hair into a thick rope, causing water to pour from its silken length and splash against the smooth stone surface. Then she wrung out the drenched linen of her chemise, scooped up her wedge of soap, and began to climb up onto the riverbank where she had left her clothes.

Suddenly a strong hand clamped around her wrist and dragged her up. She lost her footing and scraped her bare legs against the rocks jutting out of the earth.

"Well, well," sneered Harry. "Looks like we found ourselves a mermaid."

"Take your filthy hands off me!" ordered Jo, a surge of fury racing through her as Sidney wrenched her arms behind her back.

Harry smiled, revealing a row of brown, rotting teeth, then raised his hand and struck her full force on her cheek. Jo's teeth snapped together as a brilliant streak of pain flashed through her head.

"Shut your goddamn mouth," he spat, "or it'll go much worse for you, you troublemakin' bitch."

Blood seeped onto her tongue. Jo focused on it for a second, trying to clear her head. Then she lifted her eyes and regarded Harry with loathing. "You spineless, gutless pigs," she began, her voice low and even, *"take your filthy hands off me!"*

"Christ, Harry, shut her up before she wakes the whole

goddamn camp!" pleaded Sidney. He tightened his grip, twisting her arms in a painful hold.

Harry yanked a rag out of his jacket and shoved it into Jo's mouth, stuffing it as far back as her throat would allow. She gagged, but it was in too deep for her to dislodge it. Overcome with rage, she began to kick at him, landing heavy blows to his shin and upper thigh before he had the sense to back away from her. She twisted and squirmed in Sidney's grip, but his arms were strong and his hold intensified. Harry's rough hands clawed at her legs, seizing her ankles and hauling her up into the air.

"Let's take her into the woods," he snapped as Jo heaved and bucked against them. "We're too exposed out here."

Jo watched with desperation as the star-flecked sky disappeared, and a canopy of spiky black pine trees closed above her. Harry and Sidney lowered her roughly onto the ground. Sidney jerked her arms up high over her head while Harry knelt and pinned her thrashing legs beneath his knees. He threw her a savage smile as he began to free himself from his breeches.

"You shouldn't have crossed me today," he snarled. "Maybe you'll remember that after tonight."

He wedged his legs between hers, forcing them open as he crawled onto her. Jo flailed beneath his crushing weight, aware that the clean, sharp scent of pine had been obliterated by the nauseating stench of rum and sweat and filth. She struggled to stay focused, but despair flooded through her as she realized she could not possibly match the strength of her tormentors. These were the ignorant, vicious redcoats who carried out raids on the people of the Carolina countryside. They called themselves soldiers, but in truth they were men who were trained to thirst for blood, and to take pleasure in inflicting pain and terror. In that dark, helpless moment, Jo hated every British soldier to the depths of her soul. She hated them for coming to America and making war in her home. And she hated them for trying to break the spirit of her country, just as she hated these two for trying to break her. She felt her chemise being wrenched up to her waist. She lurched and squirmed; a muffled scream rose from the back of her throat, but the rag choked off the sound. Harry grabbed roughly at her breast as he forced himself between her legs. Tears of rage and frustration sprang to Jo's eyes. She closed them and tried desperately to recall the image of Anne standing at the kitchen door in an amber shower of sunlight, seeking to lose herself in the memory. If nothing else, she must survive this barbaric attack with her mind and spirit intact.

A deafening shot roared through the air, shattering the black stillness around them.

"Get off her, you filthy son of a bitch," commanded a low, harsh voice, "before I blow your goddamn brains out."

Harry rolled off her and stumbled to his feet. Sidney released his painful grip on her arms and joined his accomplice, his eyes bulging in terror.

"Caroline." Tommy raced over and knelt beside her. "Are you all right?" He helped her to sit up, then pulled the filthy rag from her mouth.

"Tommy," she rasped, her throat strained. Shaken, she turned her gaze to Harry and Sidney. A man stood in front of them with his back to her. In the darkness, she could barely make out the fact that he was dressed only in his shirt and breeches. He contemplated the two soldiers in silence a moment. Then he stepped toward Harry, grabbed him by the shoulders, and rammed his knee into his groin. Harry shrieked and collapsed, moaning.

"See if that will keep you from using that particular appendage as a weapon for a while, Perkins," the shadowy figure snapped.

He moved to stand in front of Sidney, who was trembling with fear. "It is strange, Bates," remarked the figure sardonically, "but I don't recall training you to attack helpless women in the middle of the night. Did I?"

"No, sir," admitted Bates. He sounded as if he were going to be sick.

"I thought not," agreed the man, his tone thick with contempt. He raised his fist and smashed it hard into Bate's face, then immediately struck him in the stomach. Bates sank to his knees.

Uneasiness began to swell within Jo. There was something disturbingly familiar about this man who wielded such power over her attackers. She adjusted her torn chemise, struggling to control the ripple of anxiety coursing through her.

Finished with the two soldiers, the officer turned and moved toward her, his face still hidden in blackness. Jo crossed her arms protectively over herself. Numbly she took in his towering height, the breadth of his shoulders, the muscled contours of his legs. *It cannot be,* she told herself, her anxiety hardening into fear. Her rescuer's face was shrouded in darkness, but in that moment it did not matter. She could *feel* him. Silver stars pierced the pine roof above them as they stared at each other in silence. Suddenly the moon emerged from its charcoal cocoon, causing a soft wash of light to stream across his face.

It must have cast light over her as well, because Damien's dark eyes grew wide with stunned surprise.

"Jesus Christ," he muttered furiously.

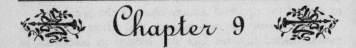

Chapter 9

$\mathscr{A}$nother cloud extinguished the light as quickly as it had come.

Jo sat there, paralyzed with fear. There could be no doubt Damien realized she was there as a spy. She fought to control her panic as she stared up at his shadowed face, waiting for him to expose her and place her under arrest.

For a long, frozen moment, he said nothing.

And then he knelt and wrapped one arm under her knees and the other around her shoulders. Lifting her against the powerful expanse of his chest, he enveloped her in his strength and warmth. Jo knew she should be afraid. She was the enemy, and he had discovered her in the midst of his camp. Damien could not betray his duty to his country and his regiment by letting her go. And yet, for one brief moment, wrapped in his arms, she felt safe.

Her respite did not last long. The harsh sound of men's shouts surrounded them. Jo stiffened, preparing for Damien to turn her over to the approaching soldiers.

"Colonel Powell, sir," called an eager-looking young man, leading a small band of redcoats who held their muskets menacingly in front of them. The soldier scanned the scene and then looked at Damien. "We heard a shot, sir. May we be of assistance?"

Damien hesitated for the barest of seconds.

And then, incredibly, Jo felt his arms tighten around her.

"Arrest that scum," he commanded, indicating Harry and Sidney. "I'll deal with them in the morning."

"Yes, sir!"

Leaving the soldiers to take care of the prisoners, Damien began to walk out of the woods, holding Jo in his arms. Tommy followed closely behind. A cluster of redcoats and camp women were waiting as they emerged, straining to see who Damien carried. He ignored them, striding past the maze of tents and smoldering campfires.

"Caroline!" shrieked a woman's voice. "Oh, dear Lord, Caroline!"

Jo lifted her head to peer over Damien's shoulder. Alice was waddling toward them, her tiny hands shoving the soldiers who got in her way.

"Caroline!" she called, waving her arms.

Damien turned.

"Oh, beg pardon, Colonel Powell, sir," said Alice breathlessly, "but if I can be of any help to Caroline, it would surely be my pleasure."

"You know this woman?"

Alice looked at him, startled by the severity of his tone. "Why, yes."

"Then perhaps you can tell me who she is," he suggested tautly.

Alice raised a reddened hand to her mouth. "Can the poor thing not remember?"

"She has been through an unpleasant ordeal," replied Damien, casting Jo a warning glance. "I would prefer it, Mrs. Clarke, if you would enlighten me."

"Her name is Caroline Skye, and she's been with the camp about two weeks now," Alice told him. "She's been helpin' me and Lily with the laundry, and a harder workin' girl you'll never find."

Damien raised one dark eyebrow as he looked down at Jo. "Is that so?"

"If there's anythin' I can do—"

"Thank you, Mrs. Clarke, but I will attend to Miss Skye myself."

Alice looked stunned. It was not common practice for a senior officer to tend the wounds of a woman. She bobbed him as much of an awkward curtsy as her enormous size would allow. "As you wish, sir."

Damien carried Jo past the main area of the camp and headed toward a large, isolated tent of bleached canvas.

"Anythin' else I can do, Colonel Powell?" asked Tommy as Damien bent to enter the tent.

"That will be all, thank you, Tommy. You performed your duty well by coming to get me."

Tommy looked uncertainly at Jo. "Will you be all right, Caroline?"

"I'll be fine," answered Jo, her tone reflecting considerably more conviction than she felt. "Thank you, Tommy."

The boy nodded, then snapped to attention and gave Damien a respectful bow.

Damien lifted the flap of his tent and carried Jo inside. The airy canvas dwelling seemed enormous compared to the cramped spaces the regular soldiers occupied. It boasted a trestle bed, a small washstand, a chest, a narrow desk strewn with papers, and a single chair neatly draped in his jacket and waistcoat. There was an open bottle of wine and a half-filled crystal goblet sitting on the desk, as well as a five-tiered candelabra which filled the room with a wavering yellow glow.

He carried Jo to the bed and set her down. She eyed him warily as he went to the washstand, where he poured water into a ceramic basin and dropped a cloth into it. Moving a chair in front of her, he seated himself and began to sponge at the blood in the corner of her mouth, causing her to wince.

"Sorry," he muttered, lightening his touch.

Damien continued to dab at the cut until he was certain it was clean, using the simple task to help him gain control of the rage boiling within him. Once the blood was gone, he gently swabbed at the dark smudges on Josephine's face, cursing silently as he saw the purple shadow of a bruise begin to form on her cheek. It was just as well he had not known it was her lying helpless beneath those bastards, he reflected.

Because if he had known, he would have killed them.

When Tommy had come to tell him Bates and Perkins were attacking a camp woman he had been concerned, but he was well acquainted with the fact that many of the women there willingly shared their bodies with the soldiers. It was possible what Tommy had heard or seen in the woods was entirely consensual. But when he came upon them in the darkness and saw the way Bates was brutally holding her down, when he heard those muffled screams filtering through the still summer air, he had been filled with a revulsion so thick he nearly choked on it. He wanted to tear them apart, piece by goddamn piece. It was only the years of relentless control he had practiced since his lashing that prevented him from doing so.

Then moonlight splashed across her and he had discovered it was Josephine they had been hurting. He had seen the blood and dirt on her face, and the fear in her eyes. In that moment he had almost relinquished his control and killed the bastards anyway. It was only when he realized that some of her fear was directed toward him that he decided to push the matter of Perkins and Bates aside for the moment. And allow himself to absorb the fact that Josephine Armstrong, ardent rebel and experienced spy, was here at the British army camp in Camden.

For weeks he had wondered what he would do if they ever crossed paths again. The answer had eluded him, but of all the possibilities, he had never envisioned being thrust into the role of her protector. Especially in the midst of over two thousand fully armed and restless British soldiers. The danger she was in was appalling. At the same time, her presence here posed a significant threat to the safety of the army, and the success of its imminent battle. He thought of the maps and documents spread across his desk, and won-

dered if she had managed to find her way into any other officers' tents during her stay here. Alice Clarke said she had
been in the camp about two weeks. More than enough time
to assess the condition of the army and make a detailed report on its size and artillery.

He rinsed the cloth a final time and placed the basin on
the ground. Then he folded his arms and regarded her with
barely controlled rage.

"What in the name of God are you doing here?"

Jo's mind began to race. What explanation could she
possibly give him that would not condemn her as a spy?

"Be warned, Miss Armstrong, I am in no mood for lies.
Do not expect me to believe you have suddenly switched
your sympathies to the Loyalist cause."

She lifted her chin. "What are you going to do with
me?"

Damien rose from the chair and went to the desk. He
picked up his wine glass and swirled its ruby contents
against the delicate crystal. "I must admit, I find myself
somewhat torn," he drawled. "If I perform my duty and
have you arrested, you will be hanged by your lovely little
rebel neck before the week is out." He paused, perversely
pleased to see some of the color drain from her face. "Yet
if I let you go, you will immediately report on everything
you have learned here, which could cost the lives of hundreds, if not thousands, of men." He took a deep swallow
of wine and contemplated her. "Which do you think is
more important, Josephine? One life, or a thousand?"

She could feel his fury blazing across the small space that
separated them. She fought the sensation with her own anger. All she had done was remain true to her cause. No one
had the right to condemn her for that.

"You cannot blame me for being here, redcoat. I never
said I would stop fighting for my country."

"Fine!" he snapped, his rage cracking through his calm.
"Fight for your precious country! Hide rebels in your barn,
give them food and blankets, send the odd message if you
must." He struggled to keep his voice low. "But for Christ's

sake, don't show up in the middle of the *goddamn British army!*"

"It's too late. I'am already here."

He turned from her in exasperation and swallowed the rest of his wine, fighting to regain some semblance of control. She was right, he reflected. She was here, and arguing about the fact was pointless. In this moment, all that mattered was that the British army was about to meet the rebels in a major battle. A battle which could determine the control not only of South Carolina, but of the entire southern colonies. He could not possibly let Josephine go. Not when she might have vital information that could jeopardize the outcome of that critical engagement. Nor could he stand by and watch her be arrested and executed. She had stitched him and watched over him and forced him to live, when he had been wholly indifferent to the prospect of dying. And in that warehouse in Charles Town, she had risked her life and sacrificed her loyalty to her country when she thought he was going to be killed. He could not repay her by turning her over.

"Get into bed," he snapped.

Jo looked up at him, incredulous. "I beg your pardon?"

"Get into bed," repeated Damien. He set his empty glass down and pulled on the end of his stock, unraveling the black neckcloth.

"Surely you cannot mean to—"

"Don't insult me, Josephine," he interrupted as he unfastened his shirt. "The hour is late, and since I cannot stomach the idea of turning you over as my duty clearly requires, let us get some sleep. We will discuss what I am to do with you in the morning."

Jo watched in confusion as he stripped off his shirt, revealing the magnificent, sun-browned expanse of his chest and stomach. The jagged scar where the musket ball had torn into his side had healed well. Someone had carefully removed the stitches, and the remaining evidence of her handiwork was shrunken and fading. Damien draped his shirt over the waistcoat on the back of the chair, then picked up the basin and threw the stained water out of the tent. Sitting across from her, he pulled off his heavy boots and regarded her with arched brows.

"Are you planning to sit there all night, or do you intend to actually lie down?"

His hair had escaped the confines of its ribbon and was brushing against his shoulders in dark waves. Jo noticed his face bore the shadow of at least a day's growth of beard, perhaps more. The lines of his brow seemed more deeply etched than they had in Charles Town. She found herself recalling the moment she had first studied him at leisure in her barn some two months earlier. At the time she was convinced the creases in his forehead were the marks of anger and cruelty. Tonight she realized she had been wrong. Once again Damien had refused to have her arrested. If anyone found out who she really was, his failure to turn her in would result in his own arrest and execution.

She pushed the thought aside.

He rose from the chair and collected the papers on his desk before blowing out the candles. Shrouded in darkness, Jo lifted the single sheet and crawled under it, moving as close to the edge as the narrow frame would allow.

Damien placed his papers beneath the thin mattress and stretched out on top of the sheet, unwilling to suffer the distraction of Josephine's velvety skin brushing against his. He assured himself he had no desire to touch her. The woman lying beside him was a rebel spy. She was treacherous and deceptive, and her presence at Camden was a threat to him, his men, and the entire British army.

Yet as he lay there listening to the whispered cadence of her breath, his mind drifted back to the moment in the carriage in Charles Town when he took her into his arms and kissed her. She had been all softness and strength and burning life. She had wanted to fight him, but in that stolen, shimmering moment, when she abandoned her resistance and opened herself to his touch, Damien had been flooded with a desire unlike any he had ever experienced. Trapped next to her in the fabric confines of his tent, he found that desire surging through him once more.

Get hold of yourself. You are here to win a war, not to lust after your enemy, for God's sake.

He moved to the edge of the bed, until he was almost in danger of falling out of it. Then he gritted his teeth and forced himself to imagine the sensation of diving into an ice-cold lake.

The cool, gray light of morning was filtering through her eyelids. But in her dreams Jo was back on the farm, spreading a cold lunch in the shade of the oak tree that grew in the yard. Samuel was tossing a ball to Lucy, while Benjamin, Abraham, and Elias came in from the fields, listening to their father tell them how much more rain the corn would need to make the ears crisp and sweet. The kitchen door opened and a very pregnant Anne walked slowly from the house, carrying a pitcher of cold tea. This made no sense at all, because Benjamin hadn't married Anne until after Father was killed, but Jo liked the fact that they were all together so she ignored it. She called to everyone and they looked at her and smiled. *"We're coming, Jo,"* they said, their laughing voices dancing like music on a summer breeze. *"We're coming."* Jo sighed with pleasure and nestled her head into her pillow.

A deafening explosion shattered the air. The images of her family dissipated, leaving her alone and racked with loss. Music filled her ears, but it was the ugly symphony of war. Fife and drums, and the heavy, terrifying rhythm of thousands of boots, mixed with the cries of the drill sergeants as they shouted orders to the various regiments. Another boom of musket fire, and another, coming in steady, deadly waves.

Morning drill had begun, and for the first time since her arrival at the camp, Jo had overslept.

She eased back the sheet and crawled from the bed, her body aching. Someone had brought her clothes and shoes from the riverbank, and put them on the chair. A plate bearing a hard wedge of cheese and a chunk of bread had been left on the desk. She washed and dressed, then sat down to eat, trying to formulate a plan.

Damien's failure to have her arrested indicated he did not

wish to see her hanged, but that did not mean he would let her go. She had defied his orders by not staying on the farm. He must realize that if he released her, she would simply go and spy somewhere else.

But at this moment, the most critical information for the rebels could only be learned here. Jo had heard the soldiers bragging about how once they defeated the rebels in this upcoming battle, the southern states would be at the mercy of the British army. That meant there would be no American forces left in the south to stop them from marching northward, to help General Clinton battle Washington's Continental Army. She thought of Benjamin and Abraham, with little to wear and even less to eat, bravely fighting yet another onslaught of redcoats. Her mind dragged her to the lifeless bodies of her father and Elias, lying alone in their muddy graves, their handsome faces smeared with blood and dirt. Despair surged over her. She inhaled deeply, fighting it with a measure of steely determination.

The American army would arrive soon. If she could remain in the camp another day or two, she might be able to learn something essential about the British army's strategy, which could help the rebels. Perhaps she could even discover something from Damien himself. She scanned the surface of his desk and jerked open the drawers. It was empty save for blank paper, quills, and ink. He had removed his maps and documents before leaving the tent this morning. She moved to the bed and hauled up the mattress, revealing only the bed frame. Then she spied the chest on the ground by the washstand.

A vapor of clean fragrance puffed into the air as she lifted the heavy lid. Arranged in a neat row lay a comb, a razor, a toothbrush, and a hard cake of soap. Rifling beneath them, she discovered three crisply folded shirts, two pairs of white breeches, four pairs of stockings, a second coat and waistcoat, two carefully rolled stocks, and a length of black satin ribbon. As she carefully rearranged the chest's contents, she noticed something shimmery peeking out from under one of the shirts. She lifted the garment up.

Nestled in the crisp linen of the shirt below lay a magnificent gold locket and chain.

The front of the locket was intricately worked, depicting a crescent moon with five tiny diamond stars sparkling around it. On the back was a detailed pattern of waves and swirls. What was Damien doing with such a valuable item hidden amongst his shirts? Unable to control her curiosity, she opened the pendant.

On the right side was a portrait of a beautiful girl, whom Jo guessed to be about seventeen. Her elegantly arranged hair was the color of rosewood, which complemented the liquid brown of her enormous eyes. Her skin was pale and fine, and she had the tiny, perfect features of a porcelain doll. She wore a gown of rose satin, with a ladder of pink and white bows trimming the narrow bodice, and a pink bow tied around the slender column of her throat. Engraved in fine script on the opposite side of the locket were the words, *Forever in my heart, Victoria.*

As Jo stared at this girl, she suddenly realized that she knew nothing about Damien. During the time he had lain injured in her barn, she had shared the story of her father and mother with him, and talked about her brothers and Anne and Lucy. But Damien had revealed nothing of himself to her. Was he married, she wondered. Was this beautiful Victoria his wife, who was anxiously awaiting his return? Did he have children who missed him, and worried he might never come home? Shaken, Jo snapped the locket closed and returned it to its resting place, carefully arranging his clothes over it before lowering the lid of the chest.

Whether or not Colonel Powell had a wife and children was of no interest to her. He was a redcoat, and therefore her enemy. If she could not learn anything from him, staying there would be a waste of time. She had to convince him that she would no longer spy, and it would be safe to allow her to return to her own tent. The second she obtained some information she would escape the camp and deliver it to her contact in Camden. Then she would head home and remain there until after Anne's baby was born. The thought of a new life at the farm soothed the ache that clung to her from the memory of her father and Elias. She must do everything she could to ensure that Anne's baby did not grow up in the shadow of war, as Lucy and Samuel had. That meant she had to help the rebels win this battle.

Fortified with purpose, she lifted the flap of the tent and went outside.

"Good morning, Miss Skye."

Jo stared at the stocky soldier standing outside the tent. Had Damien changed his mind and had her arrested?

"Colonel Powell asked me to keep an eye on you, after that unfortunate incident last night," the soldier explained. He was a man of about forty, with a pleasant face and curly brown hair that he wore tied in the back and lightly powdered. "My name's Charlie Beaton. I'm the one who brought you your clothes, and a bite to eat. Anything else you need, just ask."

"Thank you." So Damien had not had her arrested. Instead he had taken the precaution of assigning a guard to her, under the pretext that she needed protection. "Where is Colonel Powell?"

"He's over on that hill," said Charlie, pointing, "taking his legion through morning drill."

The various redcoat regiments were assembled on the surrounding hills and fields, each being drilled by their respective officers. Jo shielded her eyes with her hand and searched for Damien. The fields were churning with scarlet-coated soldiers, their silver bayonets flashing in the morning sun. Jo had no trouble finding Damien, who sat apart from the others atop his magnificent dappled gray charger, with his unpowdered black hair neatly tied back. From his position on the hill, he watched his troops drill in the field below him. There was another mounted officer beside him, who appeared to be Captain Dunmore. Jo gathered her skirts in her hands and began to hike across the field toward them.

Charlie Beaton followed behind her.

Jo stopped. "You don't need to follow me, Mr. Beaton. I am only going over to the hill to speak with Colonel Powell. I am quite certain I will be all right."

"Colonel Powell said I was to keep my eye on you, and that's what I have to do, Miss Skye. At least until my orders are different."

Jo regarded him in frustration. "Very well, Mr. Beaton." She offered him a stiff smile as she resumed her pace. "We will discuss the matter with Colonel Powell."

"Call me Charlie," he suggested, trailing behind her.

Damien watched his men perform their exercises, making mental notes to speak to his drill sergeant about before the next session. It was his habit to begin the morning drill with a half hour of running, before the day became too hot. The rugged terrain and vast distances that had to be covered in the southern colonies demanded that his men be in top physical condition, although heat, sickness, and lack of proper food often undermined this requirement. Under normal conditions the Scarlet Legion would march at least fifteen miles a day. If they had to move quickly, the objective doubled to thirty miles a day. Damien carefully developed their strength and endurance by making them run. For the first fifteen minutes of drill they ran free of the burden of their muskets, cartridge boxes, balls, bayonets, scabbard, flints, and cleaning materials. Then Damien added these accoutrements, which amounted to some twenty-six pounds of extra weight, and had them run an additional fifteen minutes. By the time they were finished, his men were happy to slow down to a simple march.

Marching was integral to the life of a British soldier. When traveling great distances they used a steady pace of seventy-five steps a minute, and they were further burdened with an additional thirty pounds of gear on top of their weaponry. The men were trained to maintain their formation of a solid line, which enabled them to advance as a single, tightly woven unit. When they were on the offensive in battle or rapidly changing position, their pace increased to one hundred and twenty steps a minute. Many hours were spent drilling them in the complex exercises of reconstructing their positions. A battlefield exploded with noise and smoke and death, and synchronizing the movements of large numbers of men could only be achieved if they learned those maneuvers well in advance, like a perfectly choreographed dance. The repetition of training took the thinking out of a man's actions.

To think was to hesitate, and hesitation in battle was lethal.

After running and marching, the troops went on to practice loading and firing their muskets. The flintlock musket required a complex process of some twelve separate motions to ready the weapon for firing. These had to be performed endlessly in order to develop swiftness and precision. Because the weapon lacked accuracy at a distance beyond eighty yards, the British army depended upon massive, rapid volleys to achieve the desired crippling effect. A well-trained soldier could fire approximately two rounds a minute. But a superbly trained soldier could achieve four rounds a minute, and Damien demanded that his men meet this difficult standard. He watched as his two hundred soldiers split into two lines. They simultaneously half cocked the firelock of their weapons, drew a cartridge from the pouch at their sides and bit off the top. Each man quickly shook powder into the pan, shut it, then charged the barrel with the remaining powder, followed by the paper and ball. Then he withdrew the ramrod, rammed it down the muzzle, and returned it to its position on the musket. The firelock was cocked, the weapon was lifted, the soldier took aim, and two hundred muskets exploded as one, filling the bright morning air with a noxious cloud of smoke. The drill sergeant shouted "Load!" and the soldiers began the procedure again.

As she reached the hill, Jo watched Damien's troops change position while loading their muskets and maintaining their tight formation. Within seconds their weapons were lifted and another explosion screamed into the distance, filling her with fascinated horror. She found herself recalling one of Benjamin's early letters to her, written when he first joined the Continental Army in 1777. In it he described the horrendous problems General Washington faced as he struggled to train his Continental Army. Benjamin wrote that although the men were most anxious to kill redcoats, they were largely arrogant and disorderly, and seemed to think their mere presence in the army with a weapon in their hands was all the training they needed. They knew nothing of fighting as a unit, and had little interest in learning. There was also a general lack of respect for the commanding officers, whom they felt were no better than they. The result was an untrained, undisciplined group of men who often broke ranks in the heat of battle, leaving the soldiers beside them exposed and vulnerable. Desertion was also a major problem, because men joined thinking they would only have to fight for a few weeks and the war would be over. As the war dragged on, the lack of decent food, adequate supplies, and the promised army pay spurred many to simply go home. This left the army thin and dependent on new recruits, who once again were disorderly and untrained.

As Jo looked down at the British soldiers advancing across the fields in a deadly, determined unit, she felt a shiver of fear. The redcoats were professional killers, who knew no life other than the army. These men were not fighting this war because they believed in their cause. Like Damien, they were fighting because it was their job to fight. This life of constant training, harsh discipline, and a stringently enforced hierarchy in which every man knew his place and respected his superior officer, made them a terrifying opponent. In her heart Jo knew the Patriot cause for freedom was right, and that the rebels had to win.

Hopefully when General Gate's army arrived, it would be a formidable match for the redcoats below.

Damien studied Josephine as she stood on the hill. Her wheat-colored hair shimmered in the morning light, wrapping her in a veil of gold. She had looked perfectly at ease as she hiked across the hilly terrain toward him, like a girl born to wander through fields and woods and feel the warmth of the sun upon her skin. He remembered her exquisite, porcelain appearance on the night he had discovered her in that ballroom in Charles Town, and he very nearly laughed aloud. She had fooled them all, he thought with reluctant admiration. She had transformed herself into a delicate flirt, and no one had been able to see that underneath those silly, fragile layers of silk and pearls was an enemy forged of pure steel. He was furious she was here and that he had been put in the impossible position of protecting her. And yet, the sight of her standing on this hill brought him a rush of pleasure, distracting him from his legion, and the war, and anything beyond the simple indulgence of watching her.

"The men are performing well today."

"What?" he mumbled, pulling his gaze from Josephine.

Gil regarded him curiously. "I said the men are performing well."

Damien frowned as he focused his attention back on the field. "Well enough, I suppose. How many are we missing today?"

"Fourteen," replied Gil. "Five are out with dysentery, three have malaria, four are down from the heat, and Perkins and Bates are recovering from their lashing this morning."

"It seems the heat, the food, and the flies of this bloody colony will be more devastating opponents to us than the rebels themselves," Damien cursed.

"The Scarlet Legion has held up better than most. I heard Rawdon left nearly eight hundred sick soldiers behind in Camden when he decided to march the troops north to these new camps."

"All we can hope is that General Gate's army is experiencing similar problems." Damien pulled out his watch. "Tell Campbell to give them five more minutes of slow marching. Then have him announce that this afternoon's drill will be at the river, and the men may come without their jackets and waistcoats. I don't want any more to fall sick from the heat. We will practice shooting at floating targets on the water, and the man with the most consistent aim will win an extra ration of rum tonight."

"That should inspire them," remarked Gil. His eyes fell on Jo as she advanced toward them. "Looks like you have a visitor. Perhaps Miss Skye wishes to thank you for so gallantly rescuing her last night. I'll leave you to accept her sweet words of appreciation alone." With a roguish smile, he kicked his heels into the sides of his horse and galloped down the hill.

Charlie Beaton had stopped at the bottom of the rise and Josephine approached Damien alone. "Miss Skye," he drawled. "I trust you slept well?"

"Not at all. That bed is far too small to accommodate both of us. I lay awake all night."

"Really? How odd. You appeared to be resting comfortably enough when I left the tent this morning."

"Perhaps I fell asleep once you got up, because I finally had enough room to move."

"My apologies for making your stay so uncomfortable," he remarked. "Perhaps tonight will be better."

"I am afraid I cannot share your tent again tonight, Colonel Powell," Jo informed him. "If it is not your intent to allow me to leave Camden, and if I am not under arrest, then you must permit me to return to my own tent."

"And why is that?"

"Because my presence in your tent is entirely inappropriate," she declared, assuming the prim air of the sheltered Celia Reed. "Everyone will think I am your mistress."

"After last night, I believe your reputation here is already in something of a shambles," he pointed out. "Staying with me could not possibly hurt it any more. And since I have no intention of either letting you go or permitting you to return to your own tent, I suggest you resign yourself to the fact that you are my prisoner, and as such, you will stay with me."

"You cannot do that!"

"Actually, I can," he said mildly.

"But surely—"

"Listen to me, *Miss Skye*," he interrupted, his tone suddenly harsh. "I have no doubt that during your two weeks here you have already passed on detailed descriptions of the regiments, including their number, their condition, and the amount of heavy artillery at our disposal. It is also highly possible you found your way into other officers' tents and discovered maps and charts detailing battle strategies and maneuvers, or reports outlining our strengths and weaknesses."

He paused a moment, studying her expression. She remained infuriatingly silent and composed, neither confirming nor denying his suspicions.

"Since I don't know precisely what information you have stored in that insanely reckless head of yours," he continued darkly, "there is no way in hell I am going to release you until after we have defeated the rebel army in this upcoming battle. After that, your information is useless and you can go. Until then, you are my prisoner, and you will do *exactly* as I say, or I will have you arrested for spying, and not give a damn what happens to you. Is that understood?" His voice was low, but there was no mistaking the harsh gravity of his threat.

"You cannot keep me in your tent all day under guard, or everyone will know I am your prisoner," argued Jo.

"I have no intention of permitting you to lie about in my tent all day," Damien replied. "You will continue with your laundry duties, and whatever else it is you do around here to earn the precious food and drink you consume. You will avoid contact with *all* officers except me, and you will cease *any* activities that may compromise the safety of the soldiers here. Charlie Beaton will watch over you, to make sure my orders are obeyed, and see that you don't suddenly wander off when you think no one is looking. And at night you will sleep in my tent, for your own safety and the safety of my men. Is that understood?" He turned from her abruptly and regarded his legion. "I cannot afford to flog all my soldiers."

Jo frowned in confusion. "What are you talking about?"

"Perkins and Bates. The men who attacked you. They were sentenced to be lashed this morning, and their punishment began at dawn. Right now they are lying in their tent on their bellies. They will be useless to me for days."

"How many lashes were they sentenced to?"

"Six hundred lashes each."

"Six hundred lashes!" she gasped.

Damien regarded her, his dark eyes contemptuous. "Not severe enough for you?"

"It is a horrible sentence!" she burst out. "How can any man be expected to survive six hundred lashes?"

Her concern for her attackers surprised him. "Rape is a capital crime in the British army, Josephine. Those men are lucky they were not sentenced to death for what they did to you. Only the fact that the assault had not progressed very far kept me from asking for their execution. As for the lashes, they will not receive them all at once. The punishment is inflicted in increments, over time. An army surgeon will inform me when they have recovered sufficiently to be lashed again. In the meantime, they will have the opportunity to reflect on the price of taking a defenseless woman against her will. I will not tolerate such bestial behavior from my men, drunk or sober. And—" he finished, turning to look at his legion below, "I would never inflict a punishment on my men that I myself could not endure."

She recalled the web of scars on his back. Clearly Damien led his men with an iron discipline. Six hundred lashes was a horrendous punishment that would scar Perkins and Bates for life. But it would neither kill nor cripple them. And perhaps it would deter other soldiers from assaulting women in the future. Frowning, she thought of the story Captain Lee told her about the Scarlet Legion cutting out a rebel woman's baby. She could not imagine Damien permitting his men to commit such an appalling act.

Was it possible he became a different man in battle or a raid?

"Don't you have duties to attend to, Miss Skye?"

"You have made it clear I am your prisoner until the rebels come and defeat you in the next battle," she returned, her tone acid. "Don't expect me to cook and clean for your loathsome army while I wait."

Damien regarded her a long moment as she glared up at him, her arms folded across her chest in defiance. His men could not hear them, but her stance made it obvious to anyone watching that this camp woman was not demonstrating the requisite respect due a senior military officer. He was taking an enormous risk by sheltering Josephine from arrest, and her infuriating lack of gratitude and cooperation effectively extinguished what little remained of his tolerance. He slowly dismounted from his horse and grasped her chin in his gloved hand.

"If you are not willing to earn your keep by assisting the other camp women," he drawled, tipping her head up to meet his gaze, "there is another option I am willing to consider."

Before she could protest, he leaned down and roughly claimed her lips with his. Jo flattened her hands against his chest and tried to shove him away. Damien responded by wrapping his arms firmly around her and pulling her even closer. She murmured a fierce protest and continued to struggle against him. He held her steady, not hurting her, but not releasing her either. His kiss deepened as his hands caressed her back in long, gentle strokes. Despite her desire to stop him, she found herself overwhelmed by his powerful strength. His scent was clean and masculine, and somehow his kiss seemed more like a promise than an assault, a reminder of something that had almost been. The morning sun blazed down on them as he held her tightly in his arms, and her body became flushed with heat and need. His kiss grew deeper and more tender as his touch transformed from menace to something akin to reverence.

Damien was dimly aware that his men were whooping and cheering in the background. He had wanted to mark Josephine as his, so no other man in the camp would dare touch her. Obviously he had succeeded. Strangely pleased with his ability to make her desire him, even in the middle of a field surrounded by an army of redcoats, he withdrew his mouth from hers and regarded her with amusement.

"I see this second option is not entirely unappealing to you."

His mocking tone stripped away the spell that had fallen over her. A hot spring of humiliation bubbled up to her throat as she heard the redcoats below laughing and applauding. Swallowing her shame, she held his gaze as she languidly drew her hand up the length of her body.

And cracked it with all the force she could muster across his smug-looking face.

There was a moment of stunned silence. Damien lifted his hand to his stinging cheek and stared at her in astonishment.

"I would rather spend eternity walking barefoot through the fires of hell, redcoat," Jo hissed, her voice trembling with fury. "Failing that, I will resume my duties as a laundress." Without waiting for him to reply, she spun on her heel and marched away.

Damien turned to see his two hundred soldiers staring at him, their expressions ranging from shock to barely contained amusement. Gil was laughing so hard it looked as if he might fall off his horse.

"What the hell are you men looking at?" he shouted. "All of you about your duties—now!"

"Yes sir, Colonel Powell," several men called out.

Their voices were laden with suppressed laughter. He elected to ignore it. He mounted his horse and thundered down the valley on the opposite side of the hill, feeling an overwhelming need to put some distance between himself and the infuriating Miss Josephine Armstrong.

"Did he touch you?" demanded Alice with a worried frown.

"No," Jo assured her. "We just slept."

"And you say you're to stay with him from now on?"

"That's right. And Charlie over there is going to keep watch during the day." She stabbed her pole into the sheets with murderous vigor.

"Some luck," said Lily. "Stayin' in an officer's tent, and not havin' to do anythin' for him at night. Not that I would mind doing a little somethin' for Colonel Powell," she added with a brazen laugh.

"Well, I won't be doing anything but sleeping in that tent," Jo swore.

"If he tries anythin' with you, Caroline, you tell me." Tommy's expression was serious. "I didn't ask him to stop Harry and Sidney just so he could take their place."

"He's the son of an earl, you know," announced Lily casually as she slapped a dripping sheet over the line.

Jo halted her attack on the linens. "An earl?"

Lily nodded. "Of course, he's the second-born son, so the title didn't go to him. Went to his older brother, whom he hates."

Despite her desire not to care, Jo found herself intrigued. "Why does he hate him?"

Lily shrugged her shoulders. "Don't know. Likely 'cause the brother got everythin' when the father died. He's probably sittin' in some fancy castle countin' his money, while Colonel Powell is crawlin' through marshes and rivers and gettin' shot tryin' to find rebels for a livin'. That would be enough to make me bloody angry," she finished with a snort.

"My James says he's as fine an officer as they come," Alice declared as she dropped another gray sheet into her basket. " 'Course he has a terrible temper, but they say it used to be much worse. When he first joined the army, his temper got him a good lashin'. Since then he's been more careful."

Jo seized this opportunity to ask, "Why was he lashed?"

"Struck a superior officer," Alice replied. "This was before he was a lieutenant colonel, of course. They say the man he attacked deserved it, but that doesn't count for anythin' in the army. After that, he learned to control himself, at least when dealin' with his superiors." She hesitated a moment before adding, "They also say he killed someone."

"I would expect, being in the British army, he has killed lots of people." Jo speared the linens again.

"Not in the army." Alice qualified. "Before he joined, when he was a young man."

Jo looked up from the pot. "Whom did he kill?"

"No one is sure," Alice admitted. "Some say he killed a man in a fight for a lady's heart."

Jo thought of the locket she had found hidden amongst his shirts. *Forever in my heart, Victoria,* the inscription had read. Had Damien loved this Victoria enough to kill for her?

"Others say he killed a man for no reason at all, in a drunken rage," continued Alice. "And others say 'twas a woman he murdered, and that 'twas only because of his noble family he managed to get away with it. That's why he got a commission in the army and left England. To escape the terrible shame he brought on his family."

Jo poked absently at the fabric in the kettle, considering this new information. The idea of Damien killing someone out of rage was frightening. Yet she could not help but think if he did kill someone, he probably had an extremely good reason. Taking a life did not necessarily make someone evil. Her own father had been a convicted murderer, and he was the most honorable, decent man she had ever known.

Her arms froze as she realized she had just supplied an excuse for Damien's actions.

She attacked the boiling linens with renewed vigor. Damien was her enemy, and she was now his prisoner. But somehow the carefully drawn lines between them were deteriorating. Even her growing friendship with Lily and Alice and Tommy was becoming confusing. Any reports she made could only endanger them. She found herself disturbed by that fact, since these three had shown her nothing but kindness and concern.

She would gather one last piece of information and find a way to escape the army camp within the next two days, before she started to think of all of them as people, and not the enemy.

Chapter 10

Evening

August 15, 1780

Damien strode across the rapidly disintegrating camp, grimly contemplating his meeting with General Cornwallis.

Things had not gone well for the British these past two days. Yesterday a Patriot force under the leadership of a rebel named Thomas Sumter had captured the Loyalist-held position on the west side of the river at Camden. Seven soldiers were killed and thirty captured. Even worse, Sumter seized a desperately needed British supply train of some thirty wagons which had been waiting to cross the river on ferry barges, including over three hundred cattle and sheep. Sumter then caught seventy British regulars coming into Camden from the British post at Ninety-Six. This amounted to a total loss of over one hundred men.

This afternoon General Cornwallis ordered every sick man who was not flat on his back to report to his unit and be prepared to march. He then sent Lieutenant Colonel Banastre Tarleton off to gather intelligence from an American patrol. Tarleton rode north and captured three American soldiers who were waiting for the arrival of General

Gates's southern army. From them he learned that Gates was planning to march toward Camden tomorrow morning. On receiving this information, General Cornwallis ordered every unit to be ready to march at ten o'clock tonight. Rather than waiting for the Americans to attack, they would surprise the rebel army at Rugeley's Mills in the morning.

The British forces were very much outnumbered, but they were also some of the finest, most highly trained men the British army had to offer. They included Damien's Scarlet Legion, Tarleton's British Legion, the Royal Welsh Fusiliers, Colonel Webster's Thirty-third Foot, Rawdon's Volunteers of Ireland, and the Royal North Carolina regiment, a well-organized Loyalist unit. By contrast, the majority of General Gates's army was inexperienced militia. The rebel army had also been on the march for over two weeks, through barren, Tory-inhabited territory that could not have yielded much food. If the number of sick soldiers at Camden was any indication, Gates's army was badly weakened. At least that is what they were hoping, Damien thought grimly.

If they were wrong, he was about to lead his men into a slaughter.

The anticipation of battle sharpened his senses as he rapidly gave orders and organized his legion for the fight ahead. He had instructed his men to prepare to move out. In a few minutes soldiers were coming to dismantle his tent. Now he had to find Josephine and tell her to get ready for the upcoming march. He disliked the idea of taking her with the army, but he was not fool enough to think he could trust her if he left her behind. The moment he was gone she would steal a horse and race ahead of them, trying to warn the rebels of their approach. He had no choice but to make her march with them. He would have her watched closely to make sure she did not slip away. And he would see that she remained far behind the lines once the battle began, out of harm's way.

The honeyed glow filtering through the heavy canvas of his tent told him she was inside. The soldier he had assigned to watch over her was positioned a few yards away.

"Good evening, Beaton," Damien called. "Everything all right?"

"Yes, Colonel," Charlie replied. "Miss Skye worked all day doing laundry, and then retired to your tent just before dark. She has not come out since, sir."

"Excellent. You are relieved of your duty here, Beaton. The army is marching out this evening. Go and pack your things."

Damien lifted the flap of his tent after Charlie had left and stepped inside, half expecting to find Josephine rifling through the drawers of his desk, or digging through his chest searching for the documents he had been studying the night before. He had no doubt she searched his tent every day, in the hope of finding some carelessly mislaid document. The candelabra was burning brightly, filling the room with a welcoming haze of apricot light. But Josephine lay stretched upon the bed, fully clothed, and sound asleep. As he gazed at her sun-stained cheek resting against the cool linen of his pillow, he elected not to disturb her for another moment or so. It was obvious she was exhausted from her long hours of boiling laundry in the hot sun. He was suddenly irritated by the prospect of rousing her and making her march into the night. He tossed his hat and gloves onto the desk, then moved his chair closer to the bed and sat down.

She wore a simple dress of faded blue cotton, which she had unbuttoned as far as her modesty would allow, barely exposing the soft swell of her breasts to the warm night air. The hem of the dress was scorched and dotted with burn holes from the fire on which the laundry caldrons boiled. The frock was quite a contrast to the exquisite gown she had worn that night in Charles Town, yet its faded, tattered condition could not mask the beauty of the woman who wore it. There was an unsettling vulnerability to her as she lay there, oblivious to the fact that the army around her was preparing for battle against her countrymen. But Damien knew she was far from the innocent, fragile creature she appeared to be in this moment. He had watched her bury a hatchet deep in the back of an Indian warrior twice her size, and hurl scalding liquid into the face of an armed rebel who easily could have shot her. Josephine Armstrong was as strong and fearless as she was lovely, as she had proven to him again and again.

And as treacherous.

She had turned him over to the rebels after swearing before God that she would not. Then she appeared as a spy in Charles Town, playing the beguiling role of the wealthy and pampered Celia Reed. And after he generously gave her freedom and ordered her to stay out of the war, she turned up to spy in the most crucial British army camp in all of the southern colonies.

Clearly, a passion burned in Josephine Armstrong's heart that drove her to fight this war in her own way. She was determined, and courageous, and convinced of the righteousness of her cause. He found himself strangely jealous of this. Especially since his own motives for fighting this war were not nearly so noble. He had joined the army as a way of escaping the drunken, worthless legacy he had so mindlessly created for himself in England. His devotion to Victoria had ended in her unborn child's death, and extinguished the possibility of other children. In one irrevocable moment, he had killed a child and destroyed the life of the woman he loved. It had driven him out of England and into this brutal, nomadic existence. According to the army, he was doing his duty.

And yet, as he gazed down at the sleeping rebel before him, he suddenly found himself questioning that duty. America was dangerous, and unrefined, and wild. But it was gloriously beautiful in this raw and natural state, with the potential to become a country unlike any other in the world. Because it was filled with men and women like Josephine, who loved their country more than life itself, and who had an incredible ability to fight back, and to survive, despite pain and death and appalling hardship. What right did he have to vanquish a people who lived a world away from Britain, and who only wanted the right to choose their own destiny?

She stirred, and a honey lock of hair fell across her face.

Without thinking, Damien reached over and brushed it away. Josephine opened her eyes and regarded him with sleepy languor. And then she drew the pale arches of her brows into a puzzled frown. Her eyes darted about the tent in confusion. Damien watched in fascination as an array of emotions spilled across her face, from sleepy pleasure to hazy confusion, before hardening into disappointment, and finally, wariness. He sensed the exact moment when she became closed to him, and he experienced a bewildering sense of loss.

"What do you want?" Jo asked sharply as she sat up.

"I have come to tell you we are preparing to march," he replied brusquely. "I need you to pack up whatever belongings you have. Some men will be here in a few moments to take down the tent. You will be going with us."

"March? At this hour?" She glanced over at the desk to see the candelabra burning, confirming it was still night. "Why on earth are you going to march now?" As she spoke the words the answer suddenly became clear. "The American army is upon us!" she exclaimed, her heart pounding with excitement.

"Not exactly upon us," Damien clarified. "But they are near. We are going to find them before they find us." He rose from his chair and began to carelessly toss a few items from his desk into the chest on the ground.

Her excitement degenerated into fear. "A surprise attack?"

Damien nodded. There was no way of keeping it from her. Every soldier in the camp knew exactly what was happening, and as soon as she stepped out of this tent she would as well.

A multitude of thoughts began to race through Jo's head. She must find a way to escape while marching with the soldiers. Then she would move through the woods and work her way ahead of the British line. She had to warn the American soldiers that the British army was coming. The rebels could pick the battlefield, and set up a trap for the redcoats to walk into.

"Do not even consider trying to escape and warn the rebels, Josephine," Damien said harshly, sensing her thoughts. "You will be on foot at the back of the line, and someone will be assigned to watch you at all times. If you try to leave the line for any reason, I will have you flogged first, and ask you for an explanation afterward."

"I expected as much," she replied, her tone caustic.

He closed the distance between them and clamped his hands onto her arms.

"This is a battle, Josephine, not the crowded dance floor of a Charles Town ballroom," he ground out savagely. "The lives of my men and the outcome of this attack take precedence over every other consideration, including your welfare. If you do *anything* to compromise this attack, I will take great pleasure in flaying the skin on your back personally, after which I will reveal you as a spy and demand that you be hanged. Is that clear?" He gave her a hard shake.

"I don't need to warn the rebels you are coming, redcoat," she spat. "The American army will easily crush each and every one of you without any help from me."

He abruptly released her.

"You may be right," he conceded, thinking of the impossible numbers they were facing. He banged the lid of his chest closed and secured the lock. "If so, you will have much to celebrate tomorrow as we drag our bloody, broken bodies off the field. Until then, you will remain at the back of the line with the other camp women, where you will be safe."

He pulled on his gloves and lifted his hat from the desk. He was ready to leave, but he hesitated, turning to look at her. "Grant me one boon, Josephine," he said, his voice suddenly low. "Swear to me you will not try to escape tonight. And I promise you that after tomorrow, regardless of the outcome of the battle, I will let you go free."

She stared at him in confusion. It was her duty to try to warn her countrymen. How could he possibly expect her not to attempt to escape?

Damien sensed her confusion. Strangely enough, he was pleased by it. Instead of lying to him, she was clearly struggling with her answer. Despite the fact that they were enemies, he was not unsympathetic to the impossibility of her situation. When she finally opened her mouth to speak, he raised his hand and stopped her.

"Never mind, Josephine," he said quietly. His voice was rough, but not angry. "Perhaps it was an unfair request. I know you are anxious to do everything within your power to help your country. Therefore I will keep you watched at all times. It will be easier that way."

He tilted his head in a small bow, then lifted the flap of the tent and disappeared.

Jo stared blankly ahead of her. A terrifying helplessness swept over her as she listened to the voices of the soldiers coming to take down the tent.

The redcoats were about to march on the American army.

And she was being forced to march with them, trapped on the wrong side.

Moonlight labored to pierce the silvery quilt of clouds that stretched across the warm night sky. The road they traveled was a narrow ribbon of white sand, flanked by towering pine trees and wide, humid gum swamps. They marched through the eerie silence, the only sound the crush of hooves and boots and wheels against the pearly road. At midnight they had come to Sanders Creek. There the men and horses and wagons had fallen out of formation, grunting and splashing and shoving and pushing as they struggled to wade across its two-hundred-foot width, their muskets and powder lifted high above their heads. Once on the north bank, the soldiers were ordered to gather and remain silent as the sergeants quietly organized them into their respective units again. And then they were marching once more, sopping wet, unable to see, exhausted and uncomfortable.

And entirely uncomplaining.

Damien rode near the front of the enormous column of soldiers. He was flanked by his mounted soldiers, and situated behind the horsemen of the British Legion led by Lieutenant Colonel Tarleton. General Cornwallis was farther back in the column, with his foot soldiers. There was a palpable alertness to the men advancing silently around him. No one knew exactly where the American army was. They might be moving toward the British army at this very moment. Or they might be camped somewhere, sleeping peacefully, in anticipation of starting their march in the morning.

They were ready for anything.

There was a noise from up ahead in the darkness. Colonel Tarleton called out. A voice shouted back, muffled by the unmistakable sound of dozens of muskets being loaded in the distance.

They had found the rebel army.

"Attack!" roared Tarleton, his voice slicing through the warm night air. *"Huzzah! Huzzah!"*

Damien instantly withdrew his sword and kicked the sides of his horse, joining Tarleton as they led a wave of mounted soldiers down the road. Shots exploded like bursting stars. The soldiers surrounding Damien fired back, enabling them to reach the patrol of mounted rebels. Damien raised his sword and crashed it against the silver arc of a rebel's sword, joining the ringing and scraping of steel shattering the stillness of the night. Damien fought with fierce precision, but the rebel he had engaged was neither weak nor afraid, and he expertly parried his thrusts blow for blow. Suddenly more shots were fired from American flanking parties in the woods on either side of them, hemming in the mounted British soldiers.

"Retreat!" bellowed Tarleton, recognizing the precariousness of their position. *"Retreat!"*

Damien and the others pulled back. As the mounted soldiers extricated themselves from the trap and retreated toward the British army column, a hundred and fifty British light infantry surged forward through the woods. Realizing he could fight better on foot, Damien dismounted, jerked his musket from his saddle, and headed into the dark pine forest. For several minutes the sound of musket fire crackled through the air as men on both sides shot blindly at shadows and tree trunks. Eventually the British soldiers gained some ground, pushing the American infantry back. Damien pressed farther into the woods, straining to make out shapes, firing only when he was certain the uniform he saw was blue and not red. Finally the shots grew random. The silhouettes of the American soldiers began to disappear. Damien waited a while, watching the ghostly shadows in front of him retreat. Already the other British soldiers around him were returning to the main column of the army, to await further instruction. For the moment at least, the clash was over. He turned to go back.

A musket ball whizzed through the air beside him, narrowly missing his head.

Damien instantly lifted his musket. A muffled groan filtered through the darkness from the direction of the shot. Cautiously, Damien moved toward the groan.

Through the darkness he saw a rebel soldier lying on the ground, clutching his bloodied thigh in agony. His empty musket was abandoned beside him. As he looked up and saw Damien approaching, his face contorted into a mask of hatred.

"Goddamn lobsterback," he snarled. "Thought I'd get one last shot in, but it looks like I missed. Come to finish me off?" His tone was seething with contempt.

"No," Damien said. He lowered his musket, knelt down and wrapped his arm around the injured rebel's waist. "Let's go."

The man vainly tried to shove him away. "Forget it, redcoat," he grated out, wincing at the pain his movement cost him. "I won't be taken prisoner. Finish me off, or leave me here to bleed to death in peace."

Damien hesitated, so completely did he understand his sentiments. He thought back to when he had been shot on Josephine's farm, and the moment he realized he was at the mercy of a rebel. He had told her he would rather die than be taken prisoner. But she had forced him to live. And even though she had turned him over to the rebels, he had survived. And escaped. Looking back on it now, he was damn glad she hadn't conceded to his wishes and let him bleed to death.

"We have some excellent surgeons, soldier," Damien told

the man. "There is every chance you will live to be traded back for one of our men." He lifted the man to his feet and was surprised to find he weighed far less than his height suggested. He began to escort him out of the woods, bearing as much of his weight as he could. "Then you can rejoin your regiment and take another shot at me," he added dryly.

"Christ Almighty," swore the man through clenched teeth as he struggled to walk. "Don't think I won't, you redcoat bastard."

They staggered together out onto the road, where the front regiments had returned to their formation and were awaiting further orders.

"Powell! Come over here!"

Holding tightly onto his injured prisoner, Damien moved toward General Cornwallis's voice. He found him at the side of the road, surrounded by the other commanding officers. A table had been set up and a lantern lit. A map was spread out on the table.

"General!" Damien called out as he approached. "I have a prisoner."

General Cornwallis looked up at him. "Excellent, Powell. Rawdon, give our guest a chair."

Lord Rawdon pulled a chair from the table and set it out for the injured rebel. Damien seated the man in it. By the pale glow of the lantern, he quickly took in his gaunt cheeks and bony frame. The man looked as if he were half starved.

"What is your name, soldier?" demanded General Cornwallis.

The rebel gave him a malevolent glare. "Joshua Fraser."

"Well, Fraser, perhaps you can tell us exactly what we are facing here. Is this merely an advance patrol we have encountered, or is it the entire rebel army?"

The rebel gave a bitter laugh. "You are facing the whole southern army under the command of General Horatio Gates."

General Cornwallis frowned as he contemplated this. "What time did you set out?" he asked curiously.

"At ten o'clock this evening," reported the soldier. "We

weren't expecting to find you on this road. We were planning to surprise you at your camp at Camden."

Damien stifled a curse. The two armies had coinciden-
tally started to march toward each other at exactly the same
moment on the same road, and had run straight into each
other. And now here they were, in the middle of the night,
with thousands of armed soldiers standing in their columns,
unable to see each other through the darkness.

"What regiments are we facing?" demanded General
Cornwallis.

The soldier sneered. "The first and second Maryland
Brigades, including the Delaware Continentals. Then we've
got General Caswell's North Carolina Militia, General
Stevens's Virginia Militia, Colonel Armand's Legion, and
light infantry. More than enough men," he finished with
scathing certainty, "to beat you redcoats."

"Thank you, Fraser," said General Cornwallis. "I hope
your injury is not overly grave. Wilkes," he called, indicating
one of his aides, "see that this soldier has the immediate attention of a surgeon."

"Yes, sir," said Wilkes. He helped the injured rebel to his
feet and began to slowly guide him down the line of soldiers. Once again Damien was shocked by the sight of his
captive's emaciated frame. Didn't General Gates feed his
men? he wondered angrily.

"Incredible," mused General Cornwallis, returning his attention to the map. "We encountered each other by accident. Tarleton, any of your Tories familiar with where we
are?"

"Sergeant Blake was born and raised on a farm not five
miles from here," Tarleton replied, gesturing to the young
man beside him. "He can tell us about our position."

A boyish-looking soldier with a brilliant shock of red
hair stepped forward and scanned the map on the table.
"We are here," he announced, pressing his forefinger on the
black line that represented the road leading to Rugeley's
Mills. "The area is sandy and mostly flat, with tall pine
woods on either side. The land rises slightly as you go
north."

"Giving those damn rebels the advantage of higher ground," grumbled Tarleton.

"There are gum swamps on either side of the road," continued Sergeant Blake, "here," he said, pointing, "and here."

"So we have swamps on either side of us, and Sanders Creek behind us," mused General Cornwallis. "That rules out retreating to find a better position for battle."

"But the swamps also mean the Americans can't use their superior numbers to get around our flanks," observed Damien. "They will be blocked by them."

"Exactly," General Cornwallis said. "What kind of position are the Americans in?"

Sergeant Blake considered a moment, studying the map. "They have a clear route to retreat. And the distance between the swamps widens as you go north into their position."

Damien nodded with satisfaction. "Which means flanking maneuvers might be possible for us."

"Perhaps this is not such a bad situation for us after all," commented General Cornwallis. "If we fight here, we only have to cover about twelve hundred yards straight ahead to get to the Americans. We are outnumbered, but they cannot move around us without trapping themselves in the swamp. And it is my guess that many of those soldiers are not in much better condition than that poor fellow we just saw. Looked as though he hadn't had a decent meal in weeks."

"The Maryland and Delaware Continentals are fairly experienced troops," remarked Tarleton. "But it is my experience that the rebel militia are undrilled and inexperienced," he added scoffingly. "They will not hold against our men." He smiled, as if in anticipation of proving this on the battlefield.

Damien clenched his jaw and said nothing. Colonel Tarleton was an excellent officer by any standard, and General Cornwallis was extremely pleased with his successes in the southern colonies. But Damien knew Tarleton and his legion were utterly merciless when it came to the enemy, as they had so ruthlessly proven at Waxhaws Creek. In that way he was like Nigel Ferguson, preferring to kill the enemy over accepting their surrender.

General Cornwallis contemplated Colonel Tarleton's statement, then pulled his gaze from the map and regarded his senior officers. "We will hold off the battle until dawn. Let us send some pickets forward to fire at the Americans occasionally, to let General Gates know we will attack if he decides to retreat. It is only a few hours until morning. Until then, gentlemen, order your troops to lie down and get some sleep."

Jo sat on the bed in Damien's tent, which had been set up at the back of the army column. It was in the same area where the surgeons were preparing the hospital tents for the coming battle. She had not seen Damien since the march had come to a halt over an hour earlier. Sketchy information had been passed down the long column of men, revealing that they had walked right into the rebel army, and there had been a brief but bloody clash. A number of soldiers were injured or missing, presumably taken prisoner by the Americans. Evidently Damien had been riding up front and had participated in the skirmish.

No one seemed to know if he had been injured or not.

She assured herself she did not care. It was the rebels she was worried about, not some redcoat officer who had to ride up front so he would be one of the first to be shot when the rebels opened fire. And yet, when the flap of the tent finally lifted and Damien walked in, she was flooded with a wave of intense relief, which served to further agitate her.

"Where have you been?"

Damien arched his brows in surprise. "I have been attending to my duties," he answered quietly.

"You mean you've been trying to murder as many rebels as you can," she said bitterly.

"It is war, Josephine," he pointed out. "In a few hours scores of men will die on the battlefield. British and American. Tory and Patriot. I cannot stop it. I will lead my men, and I will fight to the best of my abilities, because my duty requires me to do so. And some rebels will die by my sword. But I will kill them fairly, in battle. Their deaths will not be murder. Do you understand?" Even as he said it, he felt it was a shallow argument. Perhaps he was trying to convince himself more than her.

"It is still death," she protested. The thought of Damien killing her countrymen made her feel sick.

"Yes," he admitted. "But not murder." He stripped off his gloves and dropped them onto his desk. Then he poured himself a stiff glass of brandy.

Taut silence stretched between them for a moment. And then Jo suddenly whispered, "You could be facing one of my brothers tomorrow."

Damien took a hefty swallow of brandy before turning to face her. "I know that," he replied grimly.

"I shouldn't be here. I should be on the other side, with the rebels. Tomorrow they will need my help. And I will be here, with you redcoats."

Damien finished his brandy and set the glass upon the desk. "I cannot let you go now, Josephine," he said gently. "Even if I decided to look the other way and let you escape, you would never reach the American side safely. The woods are dark, and there are soldiers posted on both sides firing at each other. You would be shot before you ever reached Gates's army. You must stay here until the battle is over."

She knew he was right. She was trapped here, and there was nothing she could do to help the rebels fight this battle.

"I won't help with the injured," she announced, suddenly fearing he might expect her to. She folded her arms across her chest.

Damien looked at her in surprise. He had no intention of asking her to help in the surgical tents.

"I know the other camp women will, but you cannot ask such a thing of me. I am hoping the rebels will kill as many of you redcoats as possible tomorrow, and I won't do a thing to hinder them. Do you hear?"

"Yes," he replied quietly. "I understand."

She raised her eyes to his. They were glittering with tears. "I want the rebels to win tomorrow," she continued, her voice small and desperate. "I want them to have an over-whelming victory, so this war will come to an end and we can get on with the rest of our lives." Her words began to crack as they fell in an anguished stream from her mouth. "And that means I want the rebels to kill as many of you damn redcoats as they possibly can," she finished brokenly.

He knelt before her and reached up to capture the tear leaking down her cheek. It shimmered on his fingertip, a silver drop of pain.

In that moment he hated himself for what he was, for everything his uniform represented.

"Perhaps you will get your wish, Josephine," he murmured, seeking to comfort her. "We are severely outnumbered. The rebels may well crush us tomorrow. And then you can go home."

Her eyes held his for a moment, as if she did not comprehend what he was saying. And then she let out a sob of pure grief, the sound of someone whose heart is being wrenched in two, and who cannot bear the pain of it another moment. She threw her arms around him and clung to him in desperation.

Damien understood then that nothing he could say would ease her suffering. Because she was not only afraid the rebels might lose.

She was also terrified he could die.

He wrapped his arms around her and held her close, trying to absorb some of her torment and fear, and give her his strength and calm. If there had been time, he would have held her and rocked her in his arms, soothing her anguish with gentle caresses and words of reassurance. He would have let her cling to him and weep. But dawn was fast approaching and he had to go to his men, so he could lead them to their battle positions with the first gray wash of light. They had no more time, he and Josephine, he realized with agonizing clarity. He could be killed tomorrow. Or she would leave when the battle was over.

Either way, he would not see her again.

He forced himself to raise his arms behind his neck and

gently break her embrace. Then he pulled away, and regarded her with naked regret.

"I must go now," he said hoarsely. "I want you to stay in
this tent until the battle is over. You will be safe here. Is
that clear?"

She nodded.

He rose and retrieved his gloves from the desk.

"And as soon as it is finished, regardless of who is vic-
torious, I want you to leave," he continued as he pulled
them on. "I want you to go back to your farm. To Anne
and Samuel and Lucy, and those endless fields of green
corn." He looked at her intently, memorizing every magnificent detail of her. "Promise me you will do this, Josephine."

His darkly handsome face was etched with lines of
remorse, and his gray eyes reflected his reluctance to leave
her. Somehow, she drew a fragile scrap of comfort from
that. Comfort from the fact that he seemed loath to leave
her and lead his men into battle against her countrymen.

"I promise," she whispered.

Damien nodded with approval.

And then, realizing there was no time to tell her all the
things he suddenly wanted her to know, he lifted the flap
of the tent and was gone.

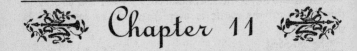

Chapter 11

August 16, 1780

Dawn was sifting through the forest in pearly beams, unveiling the hazy August morning.

The air was heavy with moisture and utterly still, save for the occasional chirping of a bird who sat high atop one of the magnificent pine trees that surrounded the two armies. It was, Damien reflected, the beginning of a glorious summer day. A day perfect for a long ride and an invigorating swim, followed by several hours lying on a bed of sweet grass and contemplating the brilliant azure sky that was promising to appear once this haze burned away. A magnificent day for doing almost anything, except slaughtering thousands of men in the name of England.

You have a battle to fight, he reminded himself harshly. He focused his attention on the twenty-two hundred British soldiers who stood sweating in their torturously hot scarlet wool uniforms. Each was determined to kill as many American soldiers as possible on this fine summer morning. It was his duty to ensure they were successful.

Stay focused.

General Cornwallis had positioned his troops on either

side of the road. On the left, under the command of Lord Rawdon, he had arranged the Volunteers of Ireland, the British Legion infantry, and the Royal North Carolina Regiment. To the right, commanded by Lieutenant Colonel James Webster, were three companies totaling about twelve hundred light infantry. Behind this front line were the North Carolina Tory Militia, Damien's Scarlet Legion infantry under Gil's command, the 71st Highlanders, and both Damien's and Tarleton's cavalry. General Cornwallis had placed himself at the back of his troops, from where he would direct the action of the battle.

The forest was eerily silent as both sides waited to begin.

The deafening roar of a cannon shattered the hazy morning stillness. The Americans had opened fire. From his vantage point Damien could see parties of American militia slowly advancing toward Webster's line on the right, and a line of Continentals marching with steady precision toward Rawdon's troops on the left. General Cornwallis rode up to Webster and gave the command for his troops to move forward. The British infantry began to march toward the American militia. They raised their heavy muskets and fired, releasing a thick cloud of oily black smoke into the windless air. Damien squinted his eyes and strained to see the effect of the firing, but the morning haze trapped the smoke close to the ground. Both armies disappeared behind a charcoal shroud.

When the black fog dissipated, he could see the British soldiers moving forward in a solid, scarlet line, three men deep, their muskets raised and their razor-sharp bayonets glinting like silver spears in the sunlight.

On sight of them, the American militia slowed their advance, as if shaken by the ruthless red wave emerging from the dark smoke.

Damien watched the Americans with increasing alarm, wondering why they hesitated.

Fire, you goddamn rebels. Lift your goddamn muskets and fire.

Instead it was the British infantry who fired. A thunderous, deadly volley exploded through the air toward the rebels, cloaking the redcoats once again in smoke.

The American militia stopped in its tracks.

"Charge!" shouted Lieutenant Colonel Webster, sensing the uncertainty of the inexperienced Americans. *"Charge!"*

The British troops let out a deafening battle roar. Then they lifted their bayonets and charged toward the startled militia, emerging through the veil of smoke as a screaming crimson and steel tide of death.

The American militia stared in shock at the oncoming British attack.

Fire at them, you damn rebels, thought Damien, appalled. *Fire!*

A British bayonet charge was an awesome, terrifying sight, which had effectively paralyzed many of the bravest regiments around the world.

This moment was no exception.

One American soldier suddenly turned and ran. Another followed, and then another, this one throwing down his musket so he could run faster. And then whole groups of men were breaking away from the line and fleeing, many hurling their weapons to the ground so they would not be burdened by their weight. Within minutes the entire right side of the American line had completely disintegrated. The panic-stricken militia disappeared into the trees, many of them running straight into the brigade of Continentals who were moving up from the reserve to reinforce them.

The British infantry continued to march toward the center of the American line, where another militia regiment was positioned.

The rebel soldiers watched the redcoats advance as the regiment beside them rapidly vanished.

And then suddenly these men broke and ran as well, many without firing a single shot.

It was the debilitating panic of untrained men, realized Damien in grim frustration as he watched the American militia surge backward. Not cowardice, but a lack of uncompromising resolve that took endless hours and weeks and months of drilling to cultivate. Only with rigorous training could a man learn to shackle his fear, to shove it to one side so it did not cripple him when he faced his enemy in battle. The fact that these men had joined the rebel militia was proof that they desperately wanted to fight for their country. In Damien's mind, there was no doubt that each of them had the courage to do so.

Unfortunately, no one had taken the time to arm them with the training they needed to face their enemy.

Lieutenant Colonel Webster elected not to follow the fleeing militia. Instead he wheeled his men to the left and attacked the Continentals, who were now surging forward to replace them. The Continentals were fighting with fearless tenacity, unfazed by the fact that nearly two thousand of their army had turned and fled the battle scene. These were obviously well-trained, seasoned fighting men. Already they had succeeded in taking a British cannon, and had also captured a good many prisoners from Rawdon's men.

Strangely, Damien took heart from the sight of those rebel soldiers fighting his own legion with such ability and courage. They were clearly outnumbered by the British troops, and yet they fought with unrelenting conviction. These men had marched all the way from the northern colonies, where they had been led in numerous battles by the American general, George Washington.

Apparently General Washington understood exactly what it took to make a soldier of a man.

"They are fighting with the ferocity of lions," observed General Cornwallis from behind him. His tone bore the esteem of a military man who respects and even enjoys a worthy opponent. "Take your cavalry in there, Powell, and see what assistance you can offer Lord Rawdon."

"Yes, sir," replied Damien. He was anxious to lead his men into the battle, and yet he was also dreading it. *You could be facing one of my brothers tomorrow.* Was one of those brave Continentals out there Josephine's brother? he wondered uneasily. If so, and this brother was killed, how would Damien ever face her again?

"Is there a problem, Colonel Powell?" demanded General Cornwallis impatiently.

"No, sir." Pushing the thought of Josephine and her family aside, he pulled his saber from its sheath. Lifting it high above his head, he turned and gave the signal for his cavalry to advance.

"Scarlet Legion—*charge!*"

He kicked his heels hard into the sides of his horse and galloped forward into the bloody battle, leading his deadly throng of cheering cavalry behind him.

Jo sat on the edge of Damien's bed, trying to block out the terrible sounds of war. Although his tent had been set up at the back of the British army column, nearly a mile from the actual fighting, the distance was not great enough to deafen the thunderous explosions of musket and cannon fire. The roar of the men was muffled as it traveled on the hot summer air, and Jo was profoundly grateful for that. From this distance, she could not tell if the men were cheering with excitement, or screaming in agony.

Probably both, she realized despairingly.

She would not leave the tent until it was over. If she went outside, she would be tempted to move closer to the fighting, so she could see what was happening. Anxious as she was to know how the rebels fared, she could not bear to witness the horrific gore of battle. Men were being shot out there. Beloved fathers, brothers, husbands, and sons. They were being cut to pieces by the thrusts of sabers and bayonets, and blown apart by artillery fire. She was strong, but she did not have the cold, passionless reserve necessary to watch thousands of men openly slaughter each other. No, she would wait here, hidden inside this fabric sanctuary until it was over. Until the rebels won.

And then she would go home.

An hour passed, or perhaps two. She was not sure, because the constant blasts and the muted bellows and screams of the men made every minute seem like an eternity. She lay on the bed and pressed her fingers to her ears. She tried to picture other things. To think of Anne and the beautiful little baby she would have next month. Of how quickly Samuel was growing into a fine young man. Of Lucy sitting on her wooden stool, gently stroking her kittens. Yet amidst these reflections, horrible images forced their way in. Thoughts of her father lying dead and cold on a crowded battlefield in New York. And Elias being hacked to pieces by the gleaming bayonets of the British Legion at Waxhaws Creek. It was possible Benjamin and Abraham were being cut to pieces at this very moment, she realized, tormented by the thought. Perhaps just a mile up the road, beneath the dripping edge of Damien's saber.

She fought to stifle a sob and buried her head under his pillow.

Time passed. The battle continued. Then, just when she was certain she could not bear the ghastly noise a moment longer, the musket and pistol firing became sporadic. In the wake of these dying explosions came another sound. A low, faint din which she did not understand. Her heart pounding, Jo sat up. Long minutes passed. Eventually she could discern the distant crunch of boots and hooves. The redcoats were returning. But the sound they made did not have the confident, rhythmic cadence of an army on the march.

Instead she heard the scraping, dragging, shuffling steps of exhausted, broken men staggering back from battle.

Many of them screaming in agony.

The cries slashed into her heart and soul, so helpless and tortured did they seem. She told herself she did not care. She clenched her jaw and remained on the bed, determined not to be moved by the British soldiers' misery. In her mind these evil, heartless redcoats deserved to suffer and die. Each of their deaths was but a small measure of vengeance for the deaths of her father and brother, and the thousands of other brave American soldiers who had been ruthlessly murdered by them. *It is war, Josephine,* Damien had told her last night. *Some rebels will die by my sword. But I will kill them fairly, in battle. Their deaths will not be murder.* As if that somehow made the killing all right, she mused bitterly. She folded her arms across her chest and tried to steel herself against the screams of the wounded redcoats. The cries grew louder, swelling in intensity as more and more soldiers were dragged and carried to the vicinity of the surgical tents. She could hear men shouting for help with the wounded, and she felt a stab of guilt.

I will not help them, she swore fiercely. *They are my enemy. I hate each and every one of them. And I will not help them.*

"Leave me alone!" screamed a terrified voice. "Just leave me alone!"

The desperate plea sliced into her heart. It was a voice she knew.

She raced out of the tent. Scores of wounded men littered the ground, and more were coming as their comrades dragged them from the battlefield and deposited them close to the tents where the surgeons were working. Their scarlet and cream uniforms were blackened with grime and soaked with blood. Many were cursing and screaming, while others lay quietly, too weak or overcome with pain to make a sound.

"Leave me alone!"

Jo scanned the assemblage, searching for that anguished voice. Finally her eyes fell upon young Tommy, who was struggling to break free of the iron grip of Alice's husband, James Clarke.

"You have to see a surgeon, lad," James was saying forcefully as he tried to drag Tommy toward one of the medical tents. "Unless you plan to bleed to death here and now!"

"No!" screamed Tommy. "Leave me be!"

Jo swiftly made her way through the dozens of injured soldiers sprawled on the ground. Tommy was turned away from her, so she could not see the nature of his injury. He was standing though, and giving James Clarke quite a fight, so how bad could it be?

"Tommy!" she called. "Tommy Brown!"

He turned at the sound of his name.

Horror surged over her as she saw what it was that had James so concerned. At the end of Tommy's left sleeve, where once there had been a slim, boyish, usually less than spotless hand, was a bleeding, mangled pulp of bone and flesh. It was leaking a steady stream of blood down the front of his buff-colored drummer's uniform. The uniform Jo had so carefully washed a few days ago, because she wanted the boy to be clean and comfortable.

"Caroline," Tommy called, his voice small and desperate, "don't let them cut my hand off!"

She inhaled deeply, fighting to compose herself as she walked over to him. She put her hands firmly on his shoulders. "Listen to me, Tommy Brown," she began, her voice calm and authoritative. "Your hand is badly injured. We must have a doctor look at it right away, do you hear? Now show me how brave you are and come with me and James into the surgical tent."

Tommy raised tear-filled, pleading eyes to hers, and Jo felt her resolve weaken. "But they'll cut it off!"

She wrapped her arm around his shoulders, heedless of the blood that dripped onto her dress. "They will only do that if there is no other choice," she assured him. Although she feared cutting the mangled mess off was all that could be done, she knew they would never get this child to a surgeon by telling him that. "Now come with me and let's talk to one of the doctors."

She and James guided him into one of the huge, open tents, where a dozen or more tables had been set up. Horribly injured soldiers were lying everywhere, groaning and cursing as they waited for someone to tend to them. The air in the tent was hot and still, and filled with the fetid, meaty stench of blood. Jo swallowed thickly as she looked around for a surgeon to examine Tommy. Alice was at the back of the tent, wrapping a linen bandage around the bleeding leg of a soldier. Lily was standing beside a young surgeon, holding his tray of instruments as he inspected a soldier's chest. Near the center of the tent, another surgeon was in the hideous process of sawing off the leg of a man.

"For Christ's sake, hold him!" the surgeon barked at the two soldiers who were trying to pin the flailing man to the table. Blood poured in a crimson stream from the table onto the grass floor. The surgeon resumed his sawing. The sound of steel cutting through bone was drowned out by the man's screams.

Bile rose in Jo's throat. She felt Tommy stiffen in shock beside her. She wrapped her arm even harder around the boy and turned him away from the ghastly sight. On the other side of the tent she saw another, much older surgeon at work. His gray head was bent over the body of the soldier lying on the table before him, his hands buried in the injured man's gut. After a moment he pulled his red, wet hand out. He briefly examined something dark between his fingers, then dropped the object with a metallic clang into the basin beside him. His hand disappeared back into the soldier and began to root around once more.

"Caroline——" began Tommy, in a shaken, pleading voice. "I don't think——"

"Shhh——" soothed Jo. "It will be all right, Tommy." In truth she was not certain it was going to be all right at all.

The gray-haired surgeon stood up. With a stifled curse, he reached his bloody fingers up to the soldier's neck and felt for a pulse. Then he lifted his fingers away.

"Get him out of here," he ordered, gesturing to two soldiers standing nearby. "He's dead." Wiping his hands on his liberally bloodstained apron, he turned to another table, where another unconscious soldier lay bleeding.

"Excuse me," said Jo, hurrying over to him before he could begin his examination. "I have an injured boy here who needs your help."

He looked at her with weary frustration. "The army does not provide medical treatment for the children of soldiers."

"He is not the child of a soldier," protested Jo. "He is a soldier himself. A drummer in the Scarlet Legion."

The surgeon looked beyond her at Tommy, quickly assessing the bloody mass at the end of his wrist. "Then step up here, soldier," he ordered. He gestured to the table on which the other man had died, just as the two assisting soldiers lifted up the body.

Tommy took a terrified step back. James put his hands on his shoulders and firmly pressed him toward the surgeon. "Do as the doctor says, lad," he instructed gently. "Let him help you."

Tommy looked questioningly at Jo, and she nodded.

"Let me see," said the surgeon.

Tommy reluctantly held out his arm. The surgeon pushed back the blood-soaked sleeve.

"That will have to come off," he said.

"No!" Tommy choked, snatching his arm back.

He was barely more than a child, thought Jo. How could he deal with such pain?

"Isn't there something you can do to save it?" she asked hopefully.

The surgeon shook his head. "If I try to save it, the flesh will fester and poison the rest of his body. And he will die. It has to come off."

"I'd rather die!" Tommy said fiercely.

"Well, I don't want you to!" Jo snapped. She fought the horror she was experiencing with ice-cold practicality. "That hand is coming off, Tommy Brown. And you are going to heal, and grow up, and live to be an old man, do you hear me?"

He raised frightened, shimmering eyes to hers.

"But I'm a drummer, Caroline," he said, his voice suddenly small and trembling. "How can I be a drummer with only one hand?"

She fought the moisture springing to her own eyes and cleared her throat. "You will just have to learn to do something else," she told him, as if the answer were ridiculously simple. She reached out and tenderly smoothed a brown lock of damp hair off his forehead. "There are lots of things you can learn to do, Tommy Brown," she continued softly. "You have a fine mind, and a brave heart, and that is worth more than two hands and two feet put together. You'll see."

He shook his head as tears began to spill down his cheeks. "But it'll hurt," he whispered.

She nodded. She could not lie to him about that. "Only for a while. But as soon as it is off, your arm will begin to heal. And in a few days you will be feeling much better. I promise."

"Take a few swallows of this, soldier." The surgeon handed Tommy a tin cup filled with rum. "As much as you can get down. It will help with the pain."

Jo looked at the surgeon in shock. "Don't you have anything else to give him?" she demanded. "Something stronger?"

He shook his head. "Usually we give opium for the pain afterward, but it's all gone. We were expecting a supply train to bring us some, but it was captured by the rebels."

Guilt washed through her. Was this the supply train she had told Captain Lee about? she wondered miserably. She tried not to think about it.

Tommy lifted the cup to his lips and took a deep, desperate swallow. And another. And another. It was obvious life in the army had made the boy well accustomed to the taste of rum. Finally the surgeon had to pry the cup away from him.

"That's enough, son," he said. "Any more and you'll be sick."

"Let me help you, lad." James wrapped his enormous arms around the boy and lifted him onto the wooden table. "I'm going to hold you," he told him gently. "All right?"

Tommy nodded. "Caroline," he called, his voice thin and shrill with fear, "will you stay with me?"

Jo hesitated. She did not want to stay. She wanted to pick up her skirts and run from this tent. Away from this terrible heat and blood and death. Away from these tormented screams. And from the unbearable, childish screams that were about to begin. She swallowed down her cowardice. This boy needed her. It was all that mattered.

"Of course I'll stay with you, Tommy."

Tommy lay back down against the table. Jo grasped his right hand and held it firmly. The surgeon took a pair of scissors and began to cut open the fabric of his left coat sleeve. Tommy whimpered with fear. Jo stroked his arm and tried to give him a reassuring smile. Then the surgeon clipped open his shirt sleeve, pushing the fabric out of his way so he could better see his work.

"Hold him down," he instructed James grimly.

James pressed one massive hand heavily against the boy's chest. With the other, he pinned down Tommy's wounded arm.

The surgeon lifted his saw.

The next few seconds were sheer, mind-shattering agony, for both Tommy and Jo.

And then, mercifully, Tommy fainted.

Jo wished she could have done the same.

The surgeon was quick. Jo closed her eyes, unable to watch the gruesome operation. She simply clasped Tommy's other hot, limp hand in her own, and prayed as hard as she could.

Please, God, please don't let him die. He's just a boy. And don't let the pain be too horrible when he wakens. And please, help stop the pain of every wounded man in this tent, she added. *And out of it,* she continued desperately, thinking of all the men lying outside in the dirt waiting to be seen by the surgeons. *I mean rebel and redcoat, God,* she clarified fervently. *Help them all. Because no one should have to endure the agony these men are going through.*

"I'm finished."

Dazed, Jo opened her eyes. The surgeon was tying off the end of a sling which pinned Tommy's neatly bandaged arm against his chest.

"Are you going to look after him?" the surgeon asked Jo.

Jo hesitated. How could she take responsibility for Tommy, when she was leaving the camp? But if she didn't look after him, who would?

It seemed James sensed her hesitation. "My wife Alice and I will take care of him," he said. "Until he can manage for himself."

"He should sleep for quite a while," the surgeon informed them. He wiped his bloodstained hands on an already bloody cloth. "When he wakens, give him rum for the pain. And water too. The sooner he starts eating, the better. His body needs some food in it to help him heal. Leave the arm alone for at least a day, unless it starts to bleed a lot. If it does, bring him back and I'll check the stitches."

"Thank you," James said. He placed his huge arms under Tommy and lifted the boy against his chest as if he weighed nothing.

Jo let go of Tommy's hand and began to follow James out of the tent.

"I need your help here, miss," the surgeon said flatly.

Help to save injured redcoats? Men who had just finished maiming and killing dozens, or even hundreds of her own countrymen? How could she nurse men who had come here to make war on her? Jo hated them. All of them. They had killed her father and Elias. Now they were trying to kill Benjamin and Abraham as they fought to conquer her country.

"The boy needs me," she said hastily.

"The boy will sleep for hours, and I need your assistance here."

"But—"

"Check that soldier over there and make sure he is still alive," he ordered. "If he is, open his clothing so I can see what his injuries are. I'll be there in a moment."

"But—"

"For God's sake, just do it!" he thundered. He turned his back on her and went to examine another man who had a dark, bloody hole where his cheek had once been.

Jo felt suddenly ashamed. How could she plead with God to help these men, and then refuse to do so herself? There was no denying that they were her enemies. But they were also just men. Not monsters. Plain, ordinary, flesh-and-blood men. Fathers and brothers and husbands and sons, just like the rebels. If Abraham or Benjamin lay wounded somewhere, and there was a Loyalist woman near who could ease their pain or help them to live, would Jo not expect her to put her loyalties aside in the name of sheer humanity?

Jo moved toward the soldier the surgeon had indicated. And slowly began to open his bloodied scarlet coat.

For the rest of the day and into the evening, Jo blindly followed the orders of the surgeons who toiled endlessly to stop life from seeping away. She cut off uniforms and did rudimentary assessments of how badly the soldiers were wounded. She handed the surgeons their instruments, choking down her revulsion as she watched them saw off limbs and open flesh, and probe with their fingers for musket balls and pieces of shot. She had thought herself familiar with the sight of blood. She had stitched her share of injuries, and had buried the bodies of four Indians. But nothing in her life had prepared her for the horrendous sights and sounds she was exposed to in that medical tent. At first she thought she would faint. Or vomit. But she did neither. Somehow, somewhere, she found the strength to quell her nausea and her horror, and simply get on with the job of helping these men.

After demonstrating her skill at stitching wounds, she was complimented and told to work faster. The army surgeons were trained to perform with astounding speed and efficiency, as they fought the losing battle to save the wounded soldiers deposited on the dripping wet tables. The hours melted away, and Jo learned to tolerate the terrible sounds and stenches that had initially seemed so overwhelming. At some point during those hours, the soldiers ceased to be redcoats, and became just men. Dozens and dozens of them, who were bleeding and suffering and dying.

"Miss Reed?" murmured a voice in disbelief. "Miss Celia Reed?"

Startled, Jo looked at the face of the soldier she was undressing. Damp, lightly powdered blond hair framed a handsome, black-smudged face with piercing blue eyes. Jo instantly recognized Captain Robert Williams, who had been one of her many admirers in Charles Town. She had laughed and flirted and drunk champagne with this man, she realized with painful surprise. She had done everything she could as Celia Reed to spin a web of enchantment around him, as she had with so many young men in Charles Town. And Captain Williams in turn had been sweetly attentive and even protective of her. One night when a drunken officer had tried to force her onto the dance floor, young Captain Williams had gallantly come to her rescue.

"No," she replied uneasily, shaking her head. She guiltily pulled her gaze from his and returned to the business of unfastening his buttons. "My name is Caroline. Caroline Skye."

Captain Williams frowned in confusion. "Sorry, miss. For a moment you looked like someone I knew." He wearily closed his eyes.

Jo peeled away the fabric of his coat, waistcoat, and shirt, each layer more bloody than the last. When his upper body was exposed, her eyes fell upon not one, but four separate bayonet wounds, each pulsing a little spring of blood that covered his stomach in a warm, red pool.

"Dear God," she murmured, horrified. She looked up and sought out the surgeon who had operated on Tommy. She had since learned he was not just a minimally trained army surgeon, but an actual physician who had left a thriving practice in London to come to America and serve the British army. If anyone could help Captain Williams, it was he.

"Dr. Howard! Come quickly!"

Dr. Howard looked up from the bleeding body he was working on. "What is it, Miss Skye?"

"This man is gravely injured. I do not believe he can wait any longer."

"I'll be there in a moment." His gray head lowered once again to his task.

"Don't you worry, Captain Williams," Jo told the young soldier earnestly. She grabbed a clean rag in each hand and pressed them firmly against his wounds, vainly trying to stanch the flow of blood. "Dr. Howard is one of the finest surgeons in the British army."

The young soldier opened his eyes and regarded her in bewilderment. "How do you know my name?"

"Why—I heard one of the other soldiers say it when they brought you in," she lied.

He looked at her a moment, his blue eyes clouded with pain. And then he closed them again, too exhausted to question her further.

"What are his injuries?" Dr. Howard asked as he approached the table.

"Bayonet stabs," Jo replied. "Four of them." She lifted her rags so Dr. Howard could see.

Dr. Howard gently examined the four slashes, quickly assessing their depth and the organs they pierced. Then he looked at Jo and shook his head.

"Keep him comfortable, Miss Skye," he muttered softly. He began to walk away.

A sickening feeling of loss swirled through her. He was leaving Captain Williams to die, without even trying to save him. She went after him. "You're not going to do anything?"

Dr. Howard turned to face her, his blood-webbed eyes filled with frustration. "There is nothing I can do for him," he said curtly. "And I cannot waste precious time and supplies on a man who is only going to die anyway. Not when there are so many others who might be saved."

"But you have to do something!" Jo had watched countless men die today. Somehow she had endured it and moved on to the next one. But this was different. This was a man she had danced with. A man who had brought her champagne and laughed at her jokes. This was a man she knew. "Please," she added beseechingly.

Dr. Howard shook his head, unmoved. "Keep him comfortable, Miss Skye," he repeated. Then he added with gentle apology, "I am sorry, but there is nothing more that can be done." He turned away and went to another table where another soldier lay moaning.

Jo blinked hard and returned to Captain Williams. The rags she had left on his body were soaking with blood. She tossed them into a basin filled with blood-drenched fabric and snatched up two fresh pieces of linen, which she pressed firmly against his wounds.

"Don't you worry, Captain Williams," she said, her voice artificially bright. "All we have to do is get this bleeding under control, and you will be just fine."

Captain Williams lifted his lids and studied her a moment. Then he smiled. "You were the most beautiful woman I had ever seen, Miss Reed," he murmured reverently. "And you still are."

Jo opened her mouth to deny once again that she was Celia Reed. But she found she could not lie to him. Not when he was dying. In this moment, he deserved the simple dignity of honesty.

"Thank you, Captain Williams," she whispered. She cleared her throat and added with the forced gaiety she had been so accustomed to as Celia Reed, "But I fear you flatter me shamelessly, sir. Now do behave yourself, or I will be compelled to report you to your superior officer."

His pale lips curved into a weak smile. "Remember the night you went off and danced with Colonel Powell?" he said, his voice slightly teasing. "Major Ferguson walked around the room, watching you, his face almost purple with jealousy. We all laughed about it for days afterward. He looked like such an idiot."

"Major Ferguson most certainly *is* an idiot." Jo pressed down harder on his wounds. "I expect he was doing a fine job of looking the part before I came along."

The blood continued to pulse from him and fill the fabric in her hands.

"It is a beautiful city," Captain Williams murmured wistfully. "Charles Town. So white and clean. And filled with flowers. I thought I would live there when the war was over."

"Why, I am certain you still can, Captain," Jo told him. "When you are better." Her eyes glazed with tears as his blood soaked through the cloth and wet her fingers.

Captain Williams closed her eyes. "I don't think so, Miss Reed," he whispered. His voice was barely audible amidst the terrible sounds filling the tent. "I don't think so."

He moaned softly. And then he let out a long, weary sigh, emptying his body of breath as his head dropped to one side.

"Captain Williams," Jo called shakily, still pressing against his wounds. His expression was peaceful, like a man who has fallen into a deep sleep. "Captain Williams!"

He did not stir.

Hot tears trickled down her face. A wave of blinding grief crashed over her, and she flung herself over his body, weeping. She cried for Captain Williams, and for Tommy, and for all the dying, bleeding redcoats around her who were struggling to live. And for the dying rebels a few miles down the road, who were also fighting to survive. And for every man and woman whose life had been devastated by this terrible war. Redcoat and rebel. Loyalist and Patriot. It did not matter. She cried for everyone, until she was sure her heart would break from the agony of it.

Strong hands closed over her shoulders and gently pried her off the body of Captain Williams.

"Shhh—" soothed a low voice with aching gentleness. "It's all right now, Josephine," Damien whispered into her ear. "Come away from here."

Her eyes flooded with tears, she blindly turned toward the comfort of his presence. She was too distraught to speak, her sobs wet and choking.

"Come with me, Josephine," he whispered tenderly.

He wrapped one strong arm around her, and slowly led her out of the tent, away from the suffering and death, and into the silver veil of rain that was starting to wash away the bloodstains on the ground.

He had never thought to find her there.

He had half expected, half dreaded to discover her gone when he finally returned from the long hours spent chasing the retreating militia. After all, he had ordered her to leave. He wanted her away from here. He wanted her home, far from the brutality of war. Then he would know she was safe. And yet, when he entered the darkness of his tent and found her not there, he had experienced a bewildering sense of loss, even a little anger, as if she had abandoned him.

He had left the tent and ordered two of his men to move it far from the screams of the injured soldiers. It was not callousness that instigated this decision, but the necessary practicality of a commanding officer. The medical staff could use the extra space around their overflowing tents, and he needed a few hours of rest before leading his men back to Camden tomorrow.

Then he had gone to check on his injured soldiers. Damien's legion of one hundred and eighty-six had suffered thirty-nine soldiers wounded, eight of whom had died so far. As with every battle, he felt each man's death acutely. Damien had led the Scarlet Legion in America for three long years. With few exceptions, it was comprised of outstanding men he had picked and trained personally. They lived, rode, and fought together as a tightly knit unit, each man understanding his duty to sacrifice everything for the good of the legion. Only in this way could they fight effectively and emerge from battles strong and relatively unscathed.

As they had today.

It was in seeing to his injured men that he learned of Josephine's presence in one of the surgical tents. He had been deeply shaken to learn young Tommy Brown had lost his hand. When he went to see how the boy was faring, James Clarke told him the woman named Caroline had helped him take Tommy into the surgical tent this morning, and had stayed with the boy as they amputated his hand. To Clarke's knowledge, she had not emerged since. Others confirmed this incredible tale, adding that she had stitched them, or bandaged them, or cleansed their wounds and given them words of reassurance as the surgeons did their gory work.

Damien had told himself the soldiers must have Josephine confused with someone else.

"Drink this." He handed her a glass half filled with brandy.

Jo took a deep swallow, then closed her eyes as the liquid spread heat down her throat and into her chest. She took another greedy swallow, wondering how much of the stuff it would take to block out the horror around her.

"Feel better?"

She looked up at Damien. His dark eyes were filled with concern.

"Yes," she murmured tonelessly. She quickly took in the state of his uniform, which was blackened with smoke and grime, and torn in both sleeves. A long gash opened the scarlet fabric across his back. The tears appeared to be the result of bayonet slashes. "Are you hurt?"

"No."

Her gaze moved over him again, just to be certain. And then she accepted it. Damien was here. Alive and unharmed.

Thank you, God.

She looked small and vulnerable as she sat there in her

bloodstained gown. Damien wanted to wrap his arms around her and hold her close. Instead he turned away. He had never expected to find her in the surgical tent, working to save the lives of the very men she so adamantly claimed to hate. And yet there she had been, her gown splattered with their blood, weeping uncontrollably over a man who a few hours earlier had been doing his damnedest to kill her countrymen. It made no sense at all.

And yet, knowing Josephine, it made perfect sense.

Josephine, it was now clear to him, bore an innate, uncompromising reverence for life. It was a reverence Damien had lost years ago. Out of necessity, he had allowed this war to strip it from him. After all, one could hardly be an effective soldier and respect the lives of those you were supposed to kill. The realization that this quality burned so brightly within her made him feel humbled by her presence. Humbled and ashamed.

While he had been out there trying to take life, Josephine had been working feverishly to maintain it.

"I am tired," she whispered.

He moved to the bed and took her empty glass from her hand. "Stand up, Josephine."

He turned her around and swiftly unfastened the back of her gown. Then he drew back the sheets on his bed for her as she stepped out of the bloodied garment, abandoning her petticoats and stockings at the same time. Exhausted beyond measure, she climbed onto the cool sheets he offered, and closed her eyes as he drew a soft layer of linen over her aching form.

"Sleep, Josephine." His voice was as comforting as the patter of the rain on the canvas roof above her. She felt him tenderly brush a wisp of hair off her brow. "Sleep, and think of going home. Think of Anne, and Lucy, and Samuel, and your fields of ripening corn. Think of how blue the sky is there, and how wonderful it feels to waken in your own bed. Feel safe, Josephine," he ordered quietly, "and sleep."

Her mind languid with the images he had created for her, her body limp with exhaustion, she let out a little sigh.

And released herself to the soothing balm of sleep, knowing she was safe while Damien watched over her.

It was still raining when she awakened. The honeyed glow of the candelabra told her morning had not yet arrived. Damien was seated at his desk, toiling over something. His coat, waistcoat, and stock were uncharacteristically tossed on the ground. He worked in his breeches and shirt, the sleeves of which had been rolled up to the elbow. His black hair had fallen free from its ribbon and spilled in a dark, tangled wave across his shoulders. He cursed suddenly and buried his head in his hands. Jo rose from the bed and silently moved across the tent to stand behind him.

The bottle of brandy on the desk was empty, as was the glass that sat beside the letter he was writing.

> *Dear Mrs. Williams,*
>   *It is with deep regret that I must inform you of the death of your son, Captain Robert Williams.*

The letter stopped there. Jo could see it was only one of several letters that Damien had written while she slept. The completed correspondence was sealed in creamy envelopes and lined in a neat row on the edge of his desk. *To Mr. and Mrs. William Gloucester. To Mr. and Mrs. Charles Lynch. To Mrs. Oliver Pembrooke. To Mr. and Mrs. Donald Rutledge. To Mrs. Alexander Fenwick.* Each envelope bearing the news of a son's or husband's death. A death that occurred an ocean away, in a strange country these parents and wives had never seen, and would forever hate from the moment they scanned that first, terrible sentence.

She tentatively placed her hands on his shoulders. He sat up and turned in his chair. His dark eyes were filled with pain, and a distant, haunted quality that revealed something more, something that went far deeper than his torment over the loss of his men. The British army must have suffered a devastating blow today, she realized. She was vaguely aware that she should be glad the rebels had won. But her memory of those men screaming in agony was far too raw for her to find any pleasure in the American victory.

All she wanted in this moment was to ease Damien's suffering. Part of her also longed to escape, to forget the war and lose herself to the strength and safety of Damien's warmth and touch. Her hand reached out and caressed his unshaven cheek. Slowly, she lowered her lips to his, pressing them with infinite tenderness against the brandy-sweet line of his mouth.

He hesitated, then he pulled away, his dark eyes filled with regret.

"You cannot want this, Josephine," he stated hoarsely.

She knelt before him and drew her fingers along the line of his jaw. "Tonight there is no war, Damien," she whispered, desperately wanting to believe it. "There is just you, and me, and nothing else."

She raised herself up to kiss him again.

He accepted the velvety caress of her lips against his. She touched him with nothing but her mouth, yet he was aware of every soft curve beneath the opaque linen of her chemise. There could be no future for them. He understood that. They were enemies, and would be for as long as this cursed war dragged on. Yet somehow a strange kinship had formed between them. Summoning the last vestiges of his self-control, he drew back from her kiss, grasping her wrists as he held her away from him.

"Think, Josephine," he said roughly. "We are enemies. You don't want this. You are distraught over all the terrible things you have seen today. Tomorrow the war will continue, and you will regret what happened between us tonight."

She contemplated his words a moment. And then her carefully constructed composure began to unravel. "I want it to end," she admitted, her voice hushed and taut. "I want the killing to stop, and the dying to stop. I want everyone who was injured today to heal, and everyone who died to live again." Tears began to well in her eyes.

"I want my father and brother back," she continued brokenly. "I want to go home, and have everything the way it was before this revolution began. But I can't have these things, can I?" The question was both a plea and an accusation.

"No," he admitted. He released one wrist to caress her cheek. "You cannot."

She drew a ragged breath. "As I saw those men lying there, screaming and bleeding and dying, I could not think of them as my enemy. I could not." Her tone was despondent, as if she thought this was a failing on her part. "They were just men, Damien. Just like you, and my brothers, and my father." Tears fell in two hot streams down her face.

"Josephine," he murmured thickly, feeling her pain as surely as if it were his own. He guided her up onto his knee. And then he wrapped his arms around her and began to gently rock her.

"Don't cry, my love," he crooned, stroking the silk of her hair.

Were it within his power, he would gladly declare the war over tonight. He would admit defeat, and agree to whatever terms the rebels demanded, just to stop her pain. He didn't give a damn what England wanted. He didn't even care what the Americans wanted. All he longed for in that moment was to ease her torment. But in truth he had nothing to offer her but himself. And so he kissed her hair, her weeping eyes, her silver-streaked cheeks. Tomorrow she would leave him. But tonight she needed him. And much as the realization appalled him, he needed her. Pushing aside all thought of how she would hate him tomorrow, he took her trembling lips in his.

With a little cry of abandon Jo threw her arms around Damien's neck and kissed him desperately, urgently, seeking to lose herself to the strength of his embrace. She wanted to be enfolded by his flesh, to be part of him, strong and warm and pulsing with life, and unafraid of what the future would bring. Her hands moved hungrily over his shoulders, his back, his waist, learning the sculpted contours of him.

He carried her to the bed and set her down, then began to unfasten the buttons of his shirt. His fingers were too slow and clumsy for her so she stood and attended to the task herself, stripping off his shirt with practiced ease. She had undressed dozens of men today, exposing every part of their broken, battered bodies to her view, and the last vestiges of her innocence or feminine modesty were gone.

No sooner had Damien removed his boots than her hands were upon him again, sweeping possessively across his massive shoulders and chest, trailing over the web of scars on his back, assessing, appraising, making certain he was truly uninjured. And then her hands were opening his breeches and peeling them down the muscled length of his legs.

When he finally stood naked before her, all bronzed planes and chiseled curves, whole and strong, filling the confines of the tent with his masculine power and vitality, she felt her breath tighten in her chest. He was, without question, the most beautiful thing she had ever seen. And she wanted him with a desperation that was frightening. She pulled her chemise over her head and dropped it to the ground. Then she pressed herself against him and wrapped her arms around his neck.

Damien groaned as he pressed his mouth against Josephine's and crushed her in his arms. Her urgency was infectious, making him forget everything except this need to drown himself in the sweet softness of her. He eased her back against the bed and began to kiss her cheeks, her throat, the gentle slope of her shoulder, rapidly moving to the lush swell of her breast. His tongue played lightly across the dusky pink tip, already taut with desire, and then he took it in his mouth and suckled. He felt her hands plunge into his hair and hold him there, but there was so much more of her to taste and touch and feel.

Breathing in the sweet, womanly scent of her as he moved across her silky skin, he paused to fasten his lips on the raspberry peak of her other breast and slowly caress her with his tongue. She moaned, a throaty, breathless sound that intensified his desire. His hands moved across her, touching her, claiming her, making her shiver as she clung restlessly to him. His fingers drifted down, and down, learning the lush contours of her stomach, her hips, her thighs, caressing the firm, smooth length of her calves, then trailing lightly up the creamy satin of her inner thigh. Up and up and up, until his fingers slipped inside the heated wetness of her, causing her to gasp with pleasure and kiss him even more deeply. Hot, liquid desire spread across his fingers, driving him mad with the need to be inside her.

He kissed her hard as his fingers moved within her, playing lightly over the delicate, slippery petals of heated flesh, quickly, then slower, teasing her, tormenting her, until finally she was lifting herself against the rhythm of his hand and breathing in shallow, rapid pants. He pulled his mouth from hers and rained kisses down the length of her body, drawing circles with his tongue, tugging at her velvety skin with his lips, laying the roughness of his cheek against the softness of her breasts, her stomach, the tangled curls at the apex of her thighs. There was no part of her he would not lay claim to. He wanted her to be his, and the knowledge that she was not and never would be made him desperate to mark her with his touch. Breathing in the heat of her passion, his tongue flicked lightly inside her. She gasped in surprise and tried to push him away, but he was determined to know every intimate detail of her, and he would not relent. She tasted sweet and hot and womanly, and as his tongue lapped gently at her satiny folds he felt the resistance in her slowly melt, causing her body to grow limp as she gave herself up to the incredible pleasure he was inflicting on her. He pressed two fingers deep inside her, causing a low moan to curl up the back of her throat. Then he began to gently thrust them in and out as he slowly stroked her with his tongue, tasting her and filling her until her breath was coming in tiny, ragged puffs and she was pulsing restlessly against the bed.

Jo felt as if she were on fire, so exquisitely glorious were the sensations that Damien was igniting throughout her. She writhed shamelessly beneath his caresses as he kissed her and stroked her and touched her, filling her with a need that was intensifying with every shallow breath. Damien was like a torch burning brightly against the darkness of war and death, and she wanted to drink in the healing force of his passion and his power until she was whole once again. And perhaps in taking this wonderful gift from him, she would be able to give him something in return. And so she called out his name, begging him to come to her. "Damien," she murmured, her voice a wisp of sound against the pattering of rain on the canvas roof, "please."

He did not hesitate, but raised himself over her, covering her with the heat of his body. He threaded his fingers into her hair and stared down at her, his gray eyes smoldering in the apricot light, filled with passion, and need, and perhaps a hint of despair. "Josephine," he whispered, brushing his lips lightly across her forehead, her cheeks, her nose. She laid hands possessively over his back as she looked up at him, trailing her fingers across the tangled web of scars, memorizing them, burning them forever in her mind so when she remembered this moment she would be able to recall what it was like to wrap her arms around Damien and know that he was hers.

She raised her lips to his and tasted him deeply, moaning softly into his mouth, running her hands over the smooth heat of his shoulders and back and hips, feeling as if she were drowning beneath the power of his body and his soul. She felt him position himself against her and then hesitate, seeking to enter her with care. She raised her hips in encouragement and he moved inside her, slowly, gradually, filling her with velvety hardness. And just as she began to feel whole and complete he withdrew. Desperate longing swept through her, because she knew that tomorrow they would part and these few stolen hours were all they had left. And so she ran her hands along the length of his back, into the gentle slope at the base of his spine, and up over the firm curve of his hips. Then she whispered his name and pulled him down into her, joining their bodies and hearts and souls.

Damien groaned with pleasure as he surrendered himself to the liquid heat of Josephine's embrace. He did not want to move, for fear he could not control the sensations threatening to shatter within him. After a moment he felt the tension in her body seep away, and he began to gently move in and out of her, filling her and emptying her, losing more of himself to her with each deliberate, aching thrust. Her hands swept hungrily over him, urging him to go faster, and he quickened his rhythm to meet her need, feeling his own pleasure intensifying. He wanted her desperately. Not just tonight, but every day and night for the rest of his life, and the knowledge that he could not have her made him drive himself deeper into her, as if to somehow become part of her. Her wheat-colored hair was cascading in golden ripples across the pillow, her head was arched back as she breathed with frantic concentration, exposing the pale column of her throat to his kisses. His hand slipped down to where they were joined and he began to stroke her there, intensifying her pleasure, causing her breathing to come in tiny gasps as she writhed beneath him. He stroked her and kissed her and filled her until she was pulsing rapidly against him, until the heat between them was so intense he was no longer certain where his body stopped and hers began.

"Josephine," he called, his voice low and husky, "look at me."

She opened her eyes, which were dark and shimmering with passion, and looked at him, letting him see into the depths of her soul. And in that moment, he understood.

He loved her.

Her head fell back and her eyes closed, perhaps in ecstasy, or perhaps in anguish at what his expression may have revealed to her. He could not be sure. A soft cry tore from the back of her throat as her body closed around him. He arched his back and drove into her again, and again, his body straining for control as he filled her with his love and his need. When his passion burst with shattering intensity, he cried out, feeling as if he were dying as he poured the essence of himself into her.

Jo wrapped her arms around Damien and held him tightly, acutely aware of the heat of his breath against her shoulder, the weight of his body pressing her into the mattress, the pounding of his heart against hers. She could not let go. And so she clung to him with childlike desperation, absorbing the feel of his powerful body entwined with hers.

Something had changed between them. Perhaps she had known it was happening even before they touched each other tonight. She was not sure. All she knew was a storm of emotions was raging through her, raw and confusing and frightening. She exhaled raggedly and buried her face against Damien's neck.

After a few moments he raised his head and looked down at her. His dark eyes were shadowed with regret, so intense it hurt her to meet his gaze.

"If there were no war," he began, his voice rough with emotion, "I would take you away, Josephine." He stroked the flushed velvet of her cheek with the back of his fingers. "I would keep you safe, Josephine. And I would never, never let you go."

She stared up at him, wrapped in his tender warmth, feeling his heart beating softly against her breast. She wanted the world to stop, she wanted to stay like this forever. But there was a war, and tomorrow she would leave him. The pain was so devastating she did not think she could bear it. She buried a hand into the black thickness of his hair and slowly pulled him down to her. "Pretend there is no war, Damien," she pleaded, her lips a breath away from his. "Please."

He crushed his mouth against hers and kissed her with fierce, hopeless need. And then she felt him stir within her, and her body heated and quickened once more. They began to pulse gently together, soothing each other with caresses and whispers as they fleetingly shut out the darkness of war, and the inevitable coming of morning.

Rain continued to fall, as if the sky were weeping for the lives that had been lost the day before. Clinging to the last hazy threads of sleep, Jo turned and reached for Damien, seeking more of the warm solace he had given her through the night.

At the touch of empty, rumpled sheets against her skin she opened her eyes.

The tent was painted in shadows. Damien was nowhere to be seen. She drew the sheets to her chest and sat up.

Outside, the muffled shouts of soldiers mixed with the drumming of the rain as the remainder of the army prepared to leave this makeshift camp.

Home, she thought, feeling desolate. *Today I am going home.*

She rose from the bed and began to dress. She left her bloodstained gown in a crumpled pool on the ground and put on the only other dress she had brought with her. Then she quickly washed her face and tidied her hair, regarding her ghostly reflection in the small mirror on the washstand with complete disinterest.

Just as she finished, the tent flap lifted and Damien stepped inside, instantly flooding the gloomy space with the warmth of his presence. Rivulets of water poured off his black hat as he removed it and dropped it on his desk. His torn uniform was drenched with rain. Although his hair was neatly tied back, some of the shorter strands in the front had worked their way loose and were curling in the moist air. Jo fought the urge to reach up and gently brush those damp curls off his face.

"Good morning." His tone was strangely formal, as if the intimacy that had kept them twined in each other's arms all night had never happened.

She stared up at his grim expression, focusing on the charcoal darkness of his eyes. Last night they had burned with silver fire as he touched her and kissed her. This morning they were cold and shrouded, revealing nothing of his feelings.

"I have made arrangements for your safe escort back to the proximity of your farm," he announced. "You will leave within the half hour. Charlie Beaton and another of my men, Oliver Yorke, will accompany you. When you are within a mile of your property, they will leave you, assuming it is still daylight. I do not think your family or neighbors would understand your being returned under the guardianship of two British soldiers."

He was making her leave him. Which was what she wanted. Why then did she feel so lost?

"Do I have to go today?"

He looked at her in surprise. "Are you saying you do not want to go?" His dark eyes seemed vaguely hopeful.

She had to turn from him to answer. "No," she admitted, confused. "I—I don't know what I am saying."

Damien felt the flicker of light within him die. She seemed fragile and unhappy to him in this moment, and he had to control the impulse to take her in his arms and ask her to remain with him. The battle was over. The army was moving out. And it was time for her to go home. Much as he wanted her, he could not keep her with him. He understood that. He had always meant to send her away once the battle was finished, when he was certain she would not have any damaging information. But that was not why he had made arrangements for her to leave so quickly. He was sending her home today because he did not want her to be further traumatized by the horrors of war.

And because if she stayed with him another night, he would never let her go.

"There are some friends I must say good-bye to before I leave," Jo said.

Damien looked at her in genuine surprise. "Friends?"

Jo nodded, thinking of Tommy and Alice, James and Lily. They were people she had come to know and like during her stay with the British army. She worried about how Tommy's arm would heal, and how poor Alice would cope with having a baby in an army camp. "I have to tell them I've decided to go home," she explained. "If I just disappear, they are certain to worry about me."

"Then you had best do it now, before my men come for you."

Jo slowly moved toward the entrance of the tent. She wanted to ask if he would be there when she returned, but she feared his answer would be no. Somehow it was better not knowing for certain that this moment was the last time she would see him. Before lifting the flap, she hesitated.

"Perhaps you will think this strange, given my loyalty to the rebel cause," she murmured softly. "But I am sorry the British army suffered such a terrible defeat, Damien."

He looked at her in confusion. "Defeat?" he repeated blankly.

"In yesterday's battle," she clarified. "I am sorry your losses were so severe."

Damien stared at her in disbelief. A cold feeling swept over him as he realized she did not know the outcome of the battle.

"Josephine," he began uneasily, "we were not defeated in yesterday's battle. We won."

Jo frowned. "No you didn't." She tried to remember who told her the redcoats had been defeated. Surely she had heard it from a soldier in the surgical tent. She could not recall. "I saw all those wounded men," she pointed out, as if this were proof the rebels won. "They were everywhere. Hundreds and hundreds of them."

"There were a lot of soldiers wounded," Damien admitted. "But we won all the same."

She shook her head. "You were vastly outnumbered," she persisted.

Damien nodded. "That is true. But the rebel numbers were not nearly as large as we anticipated. And of the regiments we faced, many were untrained militia." His tone was gentle, almost apologetic. "They could not hold against our soldiers."

Untrained militia. Jo thought of the endless hours of drilling the British soldiers did each and every day while ensconced at the camp near Camden. Hour upon hour of practicing their skills. Marching and loading and firing. Performing complex maneuvers. Learning how to run and thrust and parry with their bayonets. Honing their ability to murder.

"Were none of the rebels trained?" she demanded tonelessly.

"There were some regiments of Continentals," Damien said. "And they fought exceptionally bravely and well. It was obvious they were experienced soldiers. But without the support of the militia, they could not defeat us."

Blood began to pound in her ears. "How many did you kill?" Her tone was hollow and strained.

"Josephine—"

"How many?" she snapped fiercely. "How many rebels died yesterday, Damien, while I struggled to save British lives?"

Damien did not want to tell her how devastating the American losses had been. But if he didn't, she would walk out of this tent and ask someone else, and God only knew what wildly exaggerated figures she might receive.

"We are not certain of the numbers," he began quietly, "but we estimate the American casualties to be somewhere between eight hundred and a thousand."

Jo struggled to absorb this. "A thousand?" she repeated, incredulous.

His expression grim, Damien nodded.

"And how many did you take prisoner?" she persisted, dreading the knowledge.

He hesitated before answering. "About a thousand."

The pounding in her ears became a deafening roar. The thought of all those men, broken and bleeding and dying, or being stripped of their weapons and herded into groups to be marched away as prisoners, ripped into her heart. Benjamin or Abraham could be one of those men, she realized helplessly. They could be prisoners. Or their lifeless, mutilated bodies could be lying on the battlefield drenched in rain, waiting for someone to bury them.

"Murderer!" she screamed. She threw herself at him and began to smash her fists against his chest, crazed by the need to lash out at someone, to hold someone personally accountable for all the terrible, needless bloodshed. "Murdering redcoat bastard! I hate you! *I hate all of you!*"

Damien stood there and let her strike him, not flinching beneath the rain of blows. And when he felt her strength begin to weaken, and her fury gave way to painful sobs, he wrapped his arms around her and held her close, trying to ease her torment.

"I did not start this war, Josephine," he remarked quietly, fighting the emptiness and guilt pouring through him. "I came to America because it was my duty as an officer in the British army."

She continued to sob brokenly against his chest. He could not be sure if she heard anything he said. In truth, he did not know if he said it for her benefit or for his own. He wanted her forgiveness, even though he knew he should not need it.

"I hate you," she told him in a tiny voice as she wept into his chest. "I hate you."

He began to gently stroke her back. She did not wrap her arms around him, but she did not try to escape his embrace either. He knew in this moment she probably did hate him, perhaps almost as much as he hated himself. He held her close until her crying finally began to abate. And then, when he sensed she no longer needed the comfort of his touch, he forced himself to release her and moved away.

"Beaton and Yorke will be here in a few minutes to escort you home," he stated in a low voice. He went to the desk and retrieved his hat. Then he turned, indulging in one last look at her. Her hair was slowly falling from its pins, trickling onto her shoulders in honeyed strands. Her freckle-spattered face was flushed, and her summer-sky eyes were sparkling with tears. She seemed small and fragile in this moment, but he knew beneath this momentary weakness was a woman of extraordinary strength. She was, without a doubt, the most glorious woman he had ever known.

"I am sorry, Josephine," he murmured helplessly.

Realizing there was nothing more he could do or say, he lifted the flap and left the tent. He jammed his hat on his head and began to stride across the rain-drenched camp, bitterly wishing he had never joined the British army, and cursing God for once again torturing him with love for a woman who was forever destined to hate him.

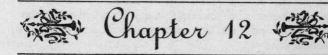

Chapter 12

Sunlight burst through the rain-soaked clouds the following afternoon, making the woods shimmer with color as the scent of damp earth and drying bark permeated the air.

Although Charlie and Oliver made every effort to be pleasant with her, Jo was too consumed with bitterness to speak to them. When she was within two miles of her farm, she informed them she no longer required their protection. The soldiers asked if she was certain, and then turned their horses and headed north. That left Jo to finish her trip with only Belle for company, which seemed appropriate, as the aging mare had been her sole companion when she first set out for Camden nearly three weeks earlier.

She told herself she was glad she had left. She was weary of war and death, and wanted nothing more than to be home, far from both armies. She tried to soothe her spirits with thoughts of Lucy and Samuel and Anne, and the baby that would soon come and fill their little household with new life. But somehow these reflections could not ease the pain tearing at her heart. While her countrymen lay bleeding on a rain-washed battlefield, she had been tending the wounds of her enemies, and weeping over their deaths. And then she had sought comfort in the arms of a redcoat who had slaughtered rebel soldiers that day, an act of such monumental disloyalty and cowardice she could scarcely believe she had done it.

The shame flowing through her was unbearable.

Perhaps worst of all, when the time had come for her to leave, a part of her had been loath to go. Despite everything that had happened, despite all the reasons to hate Damien and everything he represented, some part of her had not wanted to leave him. She had lost something to him, and the loss had left her scarred and empty. From the moment he walked out of the tent, she felt as if she would never be whole again.

The verdant cover of the woods gradually opened to acre upon acre of emerald fields, rolling in gentle waves before her. She halted Belle a moment and studied the green sea, allowing herself a small measure of comfort at the sight of the tall, ripening stalks of corn. At the back of the cornfields grew an orchard of peach and apple trees. Jo could just barely make out the pale globes of unripe fruit dotting the thick foliage. She shielded her eyes with her hand and tried to see the outline of her house, but the fiery brilliance of the sun obliterated the little white building. She urged Belle into a trot. In a few minutes she would be home, and Lucy and Samuel would be running across the yard to greet her.

Her spirits lifted with anticipation.

As the distance to the house shrank, a black, broken skeleton began to emerge through the veil of amber sunlight. Jo kicked her heels hard into Belle's sides, sending the mare into a gallop.

It cannot be, she told herself desperately as she raced toward the dark, lifeless shell. *Please, dear God, don't let this be.*

The black frame grew larger and she slowed Belle's pace, her urgency quelled by shock. She stopped and stared at the charred remains, struggling to accept the hideous sight before her.

A burnt-out square choked with blackened remnants of timber and brick. Crumbling chunks of soot-covered wall. And smoky fragments of shattered glass and china. This was all that remained of her home. She dismounted and walked slowly toward it. She felt strangely void of emotion, as if it were not really her facing the devastation, but someone else. Only this sensation of distance kept her from screaming. It kept her legs from melting beneath her, kept her from dropping to the ground to weep. She stepped toward the house and tentatively laid her hand on a charred timber. It felt cool and damp against her palm. Her eyes scanned the ashes and burned remnants which filled the area between the fallen walls. Everything was wet from the rain of the previous day, but no trace of smoke came from the black rubble. The fire was not recent, she realized. A few days, at least, had passed since this horrible event.

Which meant if Anne and Lucy and Samuel had perished in it, someone had likely removed their bodies from the ashes for burial.

"Miss Armstrong!" a voice called in the distance. "Jo Armstrong!"

She turned at the sound of her name. A man was thundering through the west field on a black horse, his coat flapping behind him as he expertly made his way along a narrow path between the stalks of corn.

"They are safe!" Jacob Heath shouted as he came closer. "They are safe!"

Numbly, she absorbed his words. And then relief flooded through her, forcing her to lean against the black timber for support. She inhaled deeply and closed her eyes.

Thank you, God.

The horse halted in a spray of dirt and her gray-haired neighbor awkwardly dismounted. "Your family is safe," he repeated. He began to limp toward her, favoring the stiff leg he had broken years earlier when his horse lost its footing and rolled onto him.

"Where are they, Mr. Heath?" she asked, her voice hollow. "Are they with you?"

"They stayed with us for about a week after—this." His

weathered face was lined with fury as he gestured at the ashes of her home. "And then Anne took the children and went to stay with her parents on their new farm in Virginia. A rebel officer named Captain Lee arranged for their journey. She was reluctant to leave without getting word to you, but with so many redcoats roaming the countryside, she felt it wasn't safe in South Carolina anymore."

"She did the right thing," murmured Jo.

They are safe, she repeated to herself. She turned to stare at the crumbling grave of her home. Perhaps there was something she could salvage. Her eyes scanned the wreckage, looking for some treasured piece of china or pewter. Some little memento that somehow had managed to escape the fire, that she could take with her. But there was nothing left.

They are alive. My family is alive. That is all that matters.

"Why don't we go to my house?" Jacob suggested. "We can talk there."

Jo lifted her eyes to another black skeleton on the other side of the yard. "They burned the barn too." Her tone was stripped of emotion.

She was vaguely aware of Jacob moving beside her and putting his arm around her shoulder. "Come with me, Jo," he ordered with quiet, almost gruff insistence. "There's nothing more for you to see here."

She swallowed. He was right. It surprised her that she did not rage, or scream, or fall to the ground and cry. But she had seen far too much suffering and death these past few days to shed tears over a pile of burned timbers and crumbling bricks. Her family was safe. In this moment, that was all that mattered.

Turning her back on the blackened ruins, she mounted her horse and began to ride toward Jacob's home. She didn't look back.

There was nothing more for her to see.

"They came early one morning, about a week after you left."

Jo wrapped her fingers around the glass of cider Jacob's

wife poured for her. The acrid smell of ashes permeated her senses, rendering her unable to drink.

"Anne told us they were not British," continued Jacob. "They were a band of troublemaking Loyalists, under the command of a lobsterback called Tarleton."

"The British Legion, they called themselves," Margaret Heath added. "Even though every one of those boys was born and raised here in America."

"I have heard of Lieutenant Colonel Tarleton," Jo said stonily. "He led the massacre at Waxhaws Creek. That's where Elias was killed." Once she had seen the young, arrogant redcoat officer riding in front of his men at the army camp, but she could not tell the Heaths that.

"Then you know of the British Legion's reputation for cruelty," Jacob remarked. "Tarleton and his scum came to the farm and said they were searching for rebels. They have been terrorizing South Carolina all summer. When they attack a farm, they steal what they can and burn the rest." He shook his head in disgust.

"Anne went outside with the children." said Margaret, seating herself at the kitchen table. She was an attractive woman in her mid-forties, with brown hair lightly streaked with gray. Her body was slim but not delicate. The physical demands of raising two sons, combined with years of working alongside her husband in the fields, had given her a strong, hardy appearance that Jo had found lacking amongst the fleshy ladies of Charles Town.

"She told the redcoats there were no men on the farm, and begged them to take what they wanted and go," Margaret continued. "Some of them raided the house. The poor girl said she could hear them turning over furniture and smashing things, for no reason except it amused them. Others dug up everything in the garden, ripe or not. Two of them caught your cow to take with them. The corn was not ready yet, so they satisfied themselves by trampling through it."

Jo's stomach turned at the image of the redcoats tearing apart her farm. Fighting to keep her voice even, she asked quietly, "Did any of them touch Anne?"

"No." Jacob's tone was adamant. "However cruel their actions were, they could see she was far gone with child, and they let her be."

Bitter gratitude pulsed through her. "What about Samuel and Lucy? Were either of them harmed?"

Jacob sighed. "When they began to set the house afire, young Samuel went crazy. I suppose being the man of the house, he felt he should do something to protect the family home. He lunged at one of them, and the redcoat struck him to the ground. Then he reached for his sword, as if he meant to run the boy through. Anne screamed, and the redcoat stopped. He stared at Samuel a moment, as if he were trying to decide what to do. Then he laughed and got on with the business of torching the house."

Jo could picture Samuel wild with the need to do something, just as he had been the day the Indians attacked the farm. He was just a boy, but in his heart he was much older. The war had robbed him of his father and one brother. The other two brothers were away fighting, and Jo had left. Then the redcoats had come and burned his home. Whatever scrap of youthful innocence that might have remained since Elias's death was now gone.

"After the soldiers left, Anne and the children came here," said Margaret. "We told them they could stay with us as long as they liked. Since Adam and David left to join the fight, we have lots of room. But of course, with the baby coming soon, Anne was anxious to go to her mother and father. She said she didn't know when you would be back, but when he arranged for her travel, Captain Lee said he would try to get a message to you."

The mention of Mrs. Heath's sons made Jo think of Damien's comment about the terrible losses in the recent battle near Camden. *Many were untrained militia. They could not hold against our soldiers.* She had known Adam and David since she was a little girl. She wondered if they had been fighting the British that day. She was about to ask when she suddenly realized it was possible Mr. and Mrs. Heath had not yet heard about the battle.

"Which forces did Adam and David join?" she asked cautiously.

Margaret's face beamed. "They are fighting with Lieutenant Colonel Francis Marion, the man they call the Swamp Fox. Of course they cannot write to us—it is too dangerous. But we hear reports of their raids on British outposts and detachments all over the countryside. The redcoats will *never* capture them."

"No one knows the swamp forests and backwoods of South Carolina better than Marion and his men," said Jacob. "They live on sweet potatoes and cornmeal, and fight with sabers hammered out of wood saws, and old hunting muskets. They fight with their hearts.'"

The three were quiet for a moment, each privately worried about the fate of the young men. Jo elected not to tell them about the defeat near Camden, at least not yet. If she shared the devastating news with them, they would want to know how she knew. She silently prayed Francis Marion's men had not taken part in the fighting that day.

Something small and feathery brushed against her ankle. Jo looked down to see a tiny apricot and gray striped kitten absorbed in the pleasure of rubbing its bony back against her leg.

"Oh!" exclaimed Margaret. "That's your kitten!"

Jo regarded her with confusion. "My kitten?"

Margaret nodded. "When the redcoats burned your barn, your cat disappeared with her kittens. The next day we went back to see if there was anything left. This kitten was wandering around the yard, and Lucy said it was one of Missy's."

The scrawny creature meowed insistently as it stared up at Jo. She reached down, grabbed him by the soft fold of skin at the back of his neck, and pulled him up to sit on her lap.

"Why didn't Lucy take the kitten with her when she left?" she asked as she ran her fingers lightly over the animal's narrow back.

"Lucy was very worried about you coming home and finding your house burned and everyone gone," explained

Margaret. "The child insisted we keep the kitten for you until you returned. She said you would be upset and would need him for company."

Jo was deeply touched by her younger sister's concern. She rubbed the kitten's little pink ears, causing him to curl into a striped puff of fur and close his eyes.

"Does he have a name?"

"Lucy called him Ashley," replied Margaret, "because he was covered in ashes when we found him."

Ashley, thought Jo. So something had survived the fire after all. She stroked his back, and Ashley began to purr with volume amazing for a creature so small.

"It was a little early for him to be separated from his mother," Margaret remarked, "but we have been doing our best to get him to eat."

Jo continued to stroke the animal, who seemed content in his new resting place. She was sad that she would not see Anne and the children today as she had hoped, but she was enormously grateful to the Heaths for sheltering them. She was also indebted to Captain Lee for arranging their travel to Anne's parents. "How is it that Captain Lee knew about what happened to Anne and the children?"

"I sent word to him," explained Jacob.

Jo looked at him in surprise. "How do you know Captain Lee?"

Her aged neighbor smiled. "This stiff leg of mine may have kept me from joining the army with your father, but it doesn't keep me from helping the cause of my country. I told my sons when they left that they were to make it known Jacob Heath was willing to do whatever he could. A few weeks later I was approached by some rebels who told me of their need for information to travel quickly. Since then I have been helping to send messages."

Jo could not contain her astonishment. "You have been spying?"

Jacob's face creased into a smile. "Nothing as grand as that," he replied. "I am part of the system that moves information. The rebel network runs deep through the Carolina countryside. This is why the redcoats are trying so hard to break us, by terrorizing our homes and families. They know those of us who did not join the army are fighting this war in our own way. What they don't realize is, with every action they take against our families and friends, they only succeed in deepening our resolve to never give in to them." He leaned forward and banged his sun-browned fist on the table. "Never."

Despite the fact that she agreed with his conviction, Joe could not restrain the enormous yawn that suddenly escaped her. She raised her hand to her mouth and murmured an apology.

"Enough talk of war," stated Margaret firmly. "This poor girl is exhausted. Come, Jo," she said, rising from the table. "Let me show you to your room. Then you can wash and rest before we have our evening meal."

"Thank you." Jo lifted the sleepy kitten into her arms and began to follow Margaret out of the kitchen.

"Jo," called Jacob.

She turned.

"I realize you wish to join Anne and the children in Virginia, but do not feel in any rush to leave. We have lots of room and you are welcome."

Jo was touched by his invitation. These people had been friends to her parents since before she was born. In this moment, Jacob and Margaret Heath were the closest thing she had to family, and it was comforting to know she was welcome. Even though she knew she would not stay with them for long.

"Thank you, Mr. Heath," she replied. "I am not certain what I will do. But it is good to know I have a place to stay. You are most kind."

"Come along, dear," said Margaret. "You don't have to decide now. For the moment, you must sleep."

She hurried away, and Jo followed wearily behind her.

Rain beat heavily against the roof and walls of the farmhouse. The rhythmic sound was reminiscent of the patter on the canvas roof of Damien's tent, and Jo found herself strangely comforted by it. Her mind clouded with sleep, she reached out, searching for the firm heat of his body so she could press against him. Her hand brushed over cool, empty sheets. She stared in confusion at the darkness around her, wondering where she was. The house was silent except for the drumming of the rain.

A soft, mewling cry came from somewhere in the sheets. Raising herself onto her elbow, Jo searched the rumpled shadows of the bed until she found a small, dark form sitting in the crook of her knees. She reached down and scooped up the kitten, placing him on her chest as she settled against her pillow.

"Hello, Ashley," she whispered. "Did we miss dinner?"

Ashley responded with a demanding mew. Jo stroked him from the softness of his head to the end of his tail. He closed his eyes and purred, rubbing his ears against her hand to encourage her attention.

Jo stared into the charcoal of the room. She must have fallen asleep, and the Heaths decided not to disturb her. She was grateful for that, as she had not slept much these past few nights. She was feeling better now, and remarkably alert, considering it was so late. An aching void still bled through her, but she had gained some control over it. Her home was destroyed. Her family was gone. And she had willingly, shamelessly given herself to a redcoat, whom she would never see again.

These were the realities of the revolution.

Her situation was ironic, she reflected. She had come home to escape the war, but it seemed the war had gotten here first. The terror Anne and the children must have suffered made her sick with anger and guilt. She should have been here. She was not foolish enough to believe she could have stopped the redcoats. But she could have helped her family bear the anguish. And taken them away, to a place where they were not in constant danger.

Jo wondered if Virginia was such a place.

She had never been there. Anne's uncle had died last autumn, and left his farm to Anne's father, his only living relative. Since the property was three times the size of the farm Anne's parents owned, her family decided to sell their property and move to Virginia. This imminent relocation was part of the reason Anne and Benjamin married during his leave at Christmas. They had only been courting a few short months before Benjamin went to war. Anne's parents had not supported their daughter's decision to remain in South Carolina and marry a man who could be killed at any moment, regardless of the fact that he was fighting for their country. For Anne to return to her parents with two children from her husband's family and a baby on the way could not have been easy for her. Unfortunately, Jo reflected, she had little choice.

The same, however, was not true for her.

For the first time in her life, she was completely on her own. It was a lonely feeling, but not unbearable. She was secure in the knowledge that Anne would take good care of Samuel and Lucy. That gave her several options as she considered her next move. She could follow Anne and the children to Virginia and wait out the rest of the war there. Which could mean months, or even years. The prospect of being with her family was appealing. She did not know how much fighting was going on in Virginia, but with most of the southern forces concentrated in South Carolina, Virginia might be a kind of haven from the war.

A less enticing possibility was to remain here with the Heaths. Although she was certain Jacob Heath's invitation to stay had been genuine, she had no desire to abuse her neighbors' hospitality by moving in with them. Food was scarce in the countryside, and taking on another mouth to feed was no small burden. Even though she knew she could be of help around the farm, Jo could never be comfortable with the arrangement. Living beside the decaying skeleton of her burned home would only intensify her hatred and bitterness. It could be years before Benjamin and Abraham came home and her family started to rebuild. During that time she would only grow older, and harder, and more bitter.

She had no desire to just sit out the rest of the war anyway. She had fled the army camp, because in that desperate moment she had wanted to escape the revolution. And the hideous shame of turning to a redcoat officer for comfort. She had sought the sanctuary of her home and family, but her home had been destroyed, and her family driven away. Making it brutally clear that the revolution was not something that could be escaped.

The rebels had been badly beaten at Camden. Her country needed her now more than ever. She was only one woman, but if every man, woman, and child who lived this ugly war banded together, they would become an indomitable army.

She did not understand why the redcoats had defeated them so thoroughly at Camden. Damien had spoken about untrained militia. Was that the only factor to blame? Whatever the reasons, she hoped the lessons they acquired from this disaster would make them stronger. Just as the sight of her home burned to ashes had made her stronger. Hatred could bring out uncommon fortitude in the weakest of beings, she reflected bitterly.

In the morning she would send word to Captain Lee that she wished to continue to work for the rebel cause. If she were sent to another camp, perhaps even a British post, she could be an effective spy once more. Her work at Charles Town and Camden had given her a degree of experience and confidence. Perhaps more importantly, she was hardened by her rage at returning to find her family gone and her home burned. Whatever her next mission was, she had no doubt she could perform it with ruthless precision. War was not a time for compassion or weakness.

If she was to go back amongst her enemies, it was vital she remember this.

The rebel network for sending messages was remarkably effective. Just three days later, a gaunt-looking Captain Jackson Lee was seated at the Heaths' kitchen table, relaying the terrible details of the American defeat at Camden. Jo was shocked by how much weight he had lost since she had last seen him. His filthy blue coat and stained waistcoat hung limply on his tall frame, and his face seemed even older than it had before.

"The battle was lost before the first shot was fired," he said grimly.

"Because so many of the soldiers were untrained?" Jo asked.

Captain Lee nodded. "That was a major factor. Most of the boys on that field had never been in battle before. When they saw that line of redcoats running toward them with their bayonets aimed at their bellies, they just didn't know what to do."

"Why weren't they drilled?" she demanded. "Why hadn't they been prepared for battle?"

"Because our so-called hero of Saratoga, General Gates, didn't seem to think it was necessary," he snorted. "He was so anxious to march south and engage the British at Camden, he didn't stop to evaluate the condition of the men he was leading. The troops he took command of at Hillsborough in July were sick and starving. Instead of getting them supplies and allowing them to gain their strength, he immediately ordered them to march. Then he picked a route that went straight through wilderness and swamps, which offered nothing to eat. Most of the men who faced the redcoats that morning had been marching for over two weeks, living on green corn, green peaches, and green apples. Christ almighty," he swore, "some of them were so starved they actually used hair powder to thicken soup made from boiling unripe fruit." He shook his gray head in disgust. "By the time my men and I joined up with them, they were all falling out of line with bellyaches, dysentery, and sheer exhaustion."

"Couldn't General Gates see his army wasn't fit for battle?" demanded Jacob.

"He was convinced he had more than enough men to do the job," Captain Lee replied. "The night before the battle, most of us were ready to drop. Instead of letting us rest, they told us to prepare for a night march. Some meat and cornmeal had been secured for dinner, but there was no rum. So Gates issued a ration of *medicinal* molasses instead, to mix with our cornmeal for dessert."

"Oh, my Lord," gasped Margaret. "He gave you a physic?"

Captain Lee scowled. "He had no idea what the effects would be. We filled ourselves with half-baked bread, undercooked meat, and cornmeal mixed with this molasses. Within a half hour everyone's bowels were exploding. The march began anyway, and men were forced to break ranks to relieve themselves all night."

"And this is what the British army faced the next morning?" blazed Jo. "Starving, exhausted men weakened by bellyaches and diarrhea?"

Captain Lee nodded.

"What happened to General Gates?" she asked furiously. "Was he captured?"

"When the militia turned and ran, Gates fled the battlefield, leaving the rest of us to fight," Captain Lee replied. "He rode sixty miles to Charlotte that day, and continued north the next. I don't know where he is now." His gaunt expression grew savage. "And I don't much give a damn."

"My God," murmured Jacob. "This is a terrible blow for the American cause."

"It's bad," Lee admitted. "Some of us managed to escape. But the destruction of the southern army so soon after the capture of Charles Town is a major defeat. There isn't a rebel in the country who isn't discouraged by the events of these past few days. Which means," he concluded, his gaze falling on Jo, "we have to take more drastic action."

"I think we should leave Captain Lee and Jo alone," Jacob suggested to his wife. "I believe they have things to discuss."

Captain Lee politely rose from his chair as the Heaths left the kitchen. When he was certain they were out of earshot, he turned his attention to Jo.

"Why didn't you get word to your contact that the British army was about to march?" he demanded harshly.

"I didn't know until a few moments before they left," replied Jo, startled by his anger. "The camp was full of talk that the rebel army was coming, but no one knew exactly when."

"The second the order was given for the redcoats to move out, you should have relayed that information to your contact," Captain Lee told her. "Failing that, you should have stolen a horse and ridden ahead of the army, to try to warn us. We could have selected an advantageous site, and initiated a surprise attack. Only you were in a position to convey that critical information. Your failure to do so contributed to our defeat." His eyes were burning with condemnation.

"But I couldn't," Jo protested, experiencing a fresh swell of guilt. "As soon as I learned the army was marching, I was ordered to go with them, on foot. Everyone was immediately placed in position and watched, so there was no opportunity for me to escape the column and try to move ahead. I was trapped," she finished helplessly. Even though it was true, she could not help but feel some responsibility for the rebels' terrible losses. They had desperately needed that information, and she had failed to get it to them.

Captain Lee contemplated her explanation. There was a wariness to his gaze, as if he were not certain whether to accept what she told him. "Why did you leave the camp?"

She could not possibly tell him that Damien had discovered her and forced her to stay in his tent. Captain Lee would conclude she had once again betrayed her cause.

"When the battle was over, I was very upset by the American losses," she confessed. "I wanted nothing more to do with the redcoats. So I told them I had to go home to care for my sister, who was expecting a baby. And they let me go."

"Did you see your friend Colonel Powell at the camp?"

The question caught her off guard. Did he know she had stayed with Damien? Or was he asking because Damien had escaped him and Captain Lee had an interest in his movements? She decided it was better for him not to know about Damien's presence there, as it would only cast suspicion on her.

"No. I did not."

"So you could go back," he concluded "and no one would think it suspicious."

Jo stared at him. "Back? To the army camp at Camden?"

It was unthinkable. Damien knew exactly who and what she was. She could never send any messages with him watching her. And to see him would only intensify her shame, which she already found almost unbearable.

"I cannot go back there."

"The assignment I have in mind requires you to return to the British camp," Captain Lee said. "If you cannot go back there, you are of no use to me."

"Why can't I spy somewhere else?"

He raked his hand through his hair. "The British forces are extremely confident right now," he told her. "First they capture Charles Town, a vital port and the most important city in the southern states. Then they crush us in a significant battle, giving the impression that even with superior numbers, the American army cannot stand against them. General Clinton and General Cornwallis have every reason to think winning this war is not far beyond their reach. We need to undermine their leadership, and throw the British offensive into a state of chaos."

"What are you proposing?"

Captain Lee regarded her a moment, as if debating whether to share his plans with her. Finally, he stated in a low voice, "I am proposing, Miss Armstrong, that you assassinate General Cornwallis."

"What?" she sputtered.

He leaned forward, his expression harsh. "With Cornwallis dead, the southern troops will be thrown into a state of confusion as they wait for another leader to arrive. Their advance into North Carolina will have to be delayed. We need that time, Miss Armstrong. We need to find more men, train them, and prepare ourselves for their offensive."

It was impossible.

It was murder.

"Why me?" she demanded. "You have other spies. Why does it have to be me?"

"We have other spies," he admitted, "but none of them are an exceptionally attractive young woman. It will be easier for you to gain private access to General Cornwallis than it would be for a man. You won't be considered dangerous."

Except by Damien.

"You will do it quietly, at night," he continued. "General Cornwallis uses the residence of Joseph Kershaw for his headquarters at Camden, but he often stays in the army camp with his troops. Find out when he is there. Send him a note saying you have an important message for his ears alone. Tell him you will visit his tent at one o'clock in the morning. Most of the troops are asleep by then. Inform him that due to the sensitivity of the information, he must post his guard no less than ten yards from his tent. That will ensure no one hears what takes place inside. Wear a cloak, so your face is hidden. Once you enter, remove it and allow the general to see how attractive you are."

Jo listened to him in uneasy silence.

"Pretend to be nervous and ask for a glass of wine. Encourage him to have some as well. Then engage him in conversation. All officers enjoy the company of a pretty woman, especially lonely ones who have been in an army camp for weeks. See that he drinks enough wine to make him relax. Then, when the moment is right, take the knife hidden beneath your gown and give him one quick, deep thrust in the heart." He demonstrated the movement with his hand. "Then replace your cloak, walk out calmly, and whisper to his guard that the general does not wish to be disturbed until morning." He leaned back in his chair, the corners of his mouth lifting in a taut smile. "By the time his body is discovered, you will be gone."

Jo reflected on his plan, overwhelmed. "How would I get out of there?"

"The night before you act, send a message to your contact in Camden." He spoke as if she had accepted the mission. "That will give me time to arrange a patrol for you at the edge of Lynches Creek, northeast of the town. Get there, and these men will escort you north. You can go to Virginia if you like. It is unlikely the redcoats will waste much time trying to capture you. After all, they will hold the American army responsible for the assassination, not you."

The mission he was proposing was extraordinarily dangerous. And yet, she sensed it was possible. Since Damien had not exposed her, she could easily return to the camp and resume her role as Caroline Skye. Alice, Lily, and Tommy would welcome her back. The only person who would question her return was Damien, but it was possible he might not be there. The Scarlet Legion was a mobile striking unit, used for lightning attacks on bands of rebels. With the battle at Camden over, it was probable Damien's legion had resumed its practice of going off on missions for weeks at a time. If he was there, she would somehow convince him that she had returned to be with him.

Given the shameful way she had acted during the last night they spent together, he might be willing to believe her.

The prospect of coldly murdering a man revolted her. She had killed two Indians, but it had been an instinctive reaction, born of the need to defend her family and home. Damien said deaths taken in battle were not murder. Perhaps the same argument applied to killing a man who led thousands of troops into battle to slaughter her countrymen. It was still war, she reflected, whether on a field, in a tent, or in a drawing room. By accepting this mission, she was going back into battle for her country.

Perhaps by assassinating General Cornwallis, she could eradicate some of the shame and hatred burning deep within her.

Jackson Lee was almost smiling as he mounted the pale brown horse waiting for him in the yard. The animal served him well enough. But he was nothing like the magnificent gray charger that bastard Powell had stolen from him.

The humiliation of losing his illustrious prisoner *and* his horse still festered in his gut. He had long hoped for an opportunity to either kill Powell or take him prisoner.

This would be a far more satisfying vengeance.

Reports from another source at Camden had alerted him that his female spy was Powell's mistress. Jackson had patiently waited for Miss Armstrong to offer him an explanation. He hoped she would say she slept with Powell so she could use the bloodyback for information. But she didn't mention it. And when he finally asked her if she had seen the bastard, she said no.

The blatant lie condemned her.

She had been an effective spy in Charles Town and Camden, until the army set out on its march. This was approximately the same time that she became Powell's mistress. Her relationship with him was puzzling, given her apparent rebel sentiments. The loss of her farm had obviously devastated her, as had the deaths of her father and brother. Jackson believed her hatred of the redcoats was genuine. Why then would she cavort with a British officer? He sighed. It didn't really matter.

If she was successful in her attempt to kill Cornwallis, it would be a stunning blow to the British army. But even if she tried and failed, his plan would still be a success. Because she would never escape the British troops. The arrest and trial of a beautiful rebel woman for spying would capture the heart of every Patriot across the country. Her actions would serve as an inspiration, rousing men to join the army, and motivating those who were already in it. When she was executed, a flood of rebel fury would pour across the country. Jo Armstrong would become the beautiful rebel martyr that was desperately needed right now.

Beyond that, her arrest would be a sweet form of vengeance. Because when she was questioned, everyone would learn that the esteemed Lieutenant Colonel Damien Powell had been harboring a rebel assassin in his tent.

And for that, Jackson thought with bitter satisfaction, the bastard would be hung for treason.

Chapter 13

*Y*ou're back!"

Alice waddled out from behind the dripping wet sheet she had just slapped over the line and gave Jo as much of a hug as her enormous girth would allow. "Lily, look, our Caroline's come back!"

Lily abandoned the pole she was using to stir the murky stew of linens simmering in the black caldron. "Well now, we didn't think you would be comin' home so soon." She gave Jo a hug. "Did your brother's wife not want you to stay and help her with the new baby?"

"She went to be with her mother and father," explained Jo stiffly, disconcerted by the women's unexpected show of affection. "Since she and the children didn't seem to need me, I decided I could be of more use here. So I came back."

Lily lifted a skeptical eyebrow. "And I suppose missin' Colonel Powell had nothing to do with your return," she teased.

"Of course not," Jo retorted.

"I think maybe he's been missin' you," Alice said. "My Jamie said Colonel Powell was in a terrible temper the day you left. Of course it doesn't help that so many men in the camp are down with fever or recoverin' from their wounds." She shook her head sadly. "A number have died since you left, and—"

"Where is Colonel Powell?" Jo interrupted. She did not want to hear about the sorry condition of the British troops. None of them could possibly be suffering as much as the sick and starving rebels were. She had no intention of feeling pity for them.

Not this time.

"He left nearly a week ago with part of his Scarlet Legion," Alice told her. "General Cornwallis sent them on a mission to track down a band of rebels, leaving Colonel Richmond in charge of the remainder of his legion. My Jamie went with him." She sighed and rubbed her rough hand over the round expanse of her stomach. "I was hopin' he would be able to stay close, with the babe comin' any day now."

"Never you mind, Alice," said Lily brightly. "Now that Caroline is back, we're both here to help you when your time comes. Besides, James will be back soon, and like most men, he'll just be gettin' in the way. Isn't that right, Caroline?"

Jo nodded blankly. She was relieved that Damien wasn't there. It would make her stay far less complicated. Why then did she feel this twinge of disappointment?

"How is Tommy?"

"His wrist is healin' well enough," Alice replied. "I change his bandage every day, and Dr. Howard has checked it a few times to make sure infection isn't settin' in. Of course, it hurts somethin' awful, but Tommy's a brave lad, and he doesn't complain much." She sighed. "It's his spirit that worries me."

Despite her resolution not to care about *any* of the redcoats, Jo could not help but feel a flicker of concern. "What do you mean?"

"The boy thinks he can't do anythin'," Lily explained. "When he was able to play his drum, he felt he was an important part of the army. He hoped someday he would be trained to fight, and then travel the world with the British troops." She shrugged her shoulders. "With that dream gone, there's nothin' left for him to do."

"That is pure foolishness!" Jo said vehemently. "There are all kinds of things he can learn to do."

"I've tried to tell him just that, but he won't listen." Alice shook her head. "He's just a boy, really. Maybe it's too soon to expect him to accept his injury and get on with livin'."

"I'll talk to him, after I've had a chance to rest a while." Jo picked up the two cloth bags she had deposited on the ground. A small mew filtered out of one of them. Ashley poked his head over the edge of the bag and regarded Alice and Lily with sleepy curiosity.

"A kitten!" Lily burst out laughing. She reached out and began to stroke Ashley's tiny striped forehead.

"His name is Ashley. I decided to bring him with me."

"Hello, little love," Alice cooed as she ran her fingers down his neck. She raised her eyes to Jo. "Whatever will Colonel Powell say about him?"

"I don't suppose he'll even notice him," Jo said dismissively. "He's very tiny, and not likely to get in the way, especially in the middle of a camp."

"Oh, certainly," Lily agreed teasingly. "I've never known a kitten to get in the way, have you, Alice?"

The two women giggled.

Jo ignored their amusement. If Damien returned and didn't want Ashley in his tent, then she wouldn't stay there either. It was as simple as that.

"Did Colonel Powell take his tent with him when he left?"

"No," Lily said. "It's where it was before we marched out of here."

The idea that Damien's tent was in exactly the same place it had been before was strangely comforting. "I am going to unpack and have a rest. Then I'll find Tommy and talk with him. And tomorrow," she added, casting her gaze at the enormous piles of filthy linens heaped upon the ground, "I'll be back to help with the laundry. It looks like you two could use some assistance."

Alice gave her arm an affectionate squeeze. "It's ever so good to have you back, Caroline. Things just weren't the same after you left."

Jo looked down at Alice's hand resting on her sleeve. The knuckles were swollen and her skin was cracking from dryness caused by handling rough fabric washed in harsh soap. She knew these hands were an indication of how exhausted the poor girl must be.

"Thank you, Alice," she murmured. She cleared her throat. "As of tomorrow, you will no longer be helping with the laundry. If you insist on working, we will find you something to do where you can sit in the shade. Perhaps some of the officers' uniforms require mending. Regardless, you will not be standing on your feet all day in the blazing sun. Is that clear?"

Alice stared at her in surprise. For a moment it seemed she intended to protest. Then her mouth curved into a radiant smile. "Thank you, Caroline. I must admit, with the baby almost here, I'm findin' it a bit hard to do everythin' I used to. You're a dear friend to be so concerned."

Her words made Jo feel guilty. She awkwardly mumbled something in return, then began to make her way across the camp toward Damien's tent.

To her surprise, many of the soldiers she passed greeted her enthusiastically and told her it was good to see her again. She supposed it was not unusual for the men to readily accept her presence. After all, she was Colonel Powell's mistress. But the way the men smiled and earnestly welcomed her back suggested something more than simple courtesy toward an officer's mistress. Perhaps the story of her working in the surgical tent had spread amongst the soldiers. Or maybe Damien's temper really had been far worse after she left. Whatever the reason, no one seemed to be the least concerned that she had disappeared for a week and was now moving back into Colonel Powell's quarters while he was away.

On entering the tent, Jo found Damien's bed, desk, washstand, and chest arranged in the same positions they had occupied before. Everything was perfectly neat, reflecting

Damien's predilection for order. The result was a calming
sense of familiarity, almost as if she had come home and
found everything exactly as it should be. It was ridiculous,
of course. This tent was not her home. *Your home has been
burned to the ground,* she reminded herself bitterly. She scooped
Ashley out of her bag and put him down so he could
stretch his legs and explore his new surroundings. Then she
lifted the heavy lid of Damien's trunk, thinking to put a few
of her things inside.

A spicy puff of fragrance floated into the air, so clean
and masculine and so like Damien she could not help but
close her eyes and inhale deeply. Somehow the scent of him
was reassuring, making her feel a little less alone. She
opened her eyes and reached into her bag to unpack her
things. She was about to lay a clean gown over his clothes
when she stopped and stared in confusion at the folded garment resting on the top layer of the chest.

She recognized her faded, much-mended dress immediately. This was the gown she had abandoned on that terrible
morning after the battle. It had been horribly stained with
blood at the time. Someone had washed it, but a hint of the
stains remained. Why on earth would Damien want to keep
this? she wondered. The garment was barely fit to be ripped
apart for rags. Yet Damien had evidently ordered it washed,
then carefully folded it and placed it in his chest. As her
fingers wandered over the threadbare cotton, she could only
think of one explanation why he would keep such a thing.

It was all he had to remind him of her.

She swallowed, struggling to suppress the emotions
threatening to erupt within her. She hastily covered the
dress with other garments and closed the lid with a bang.
She could not afford to have her feelings clouded. She was
here because she had a vital mission to carry out. A mission
which would throw the British army into a state of turmoil,
turning the tide of war in favor of the rebels, and perhaps
bringing this war closer to an end. It was her duty to complete her assignment as quickly as possible, and get out of
here. If she could find General Cornwallis and assassinate
him before Damien returned, so much the better. It would

be far easier to stay coldly focused on her task without him around.

She picked up Ashley and deposited him on the bed, then stretched out beside him. Once she had rested, she would go in search of Tommy and have a long talk with him. She would make him see there was far more to life than becoming a soldier and traveling the world in search of people to slaughter. In a strange way, the fact that he had lost his hand might become a good thing, she mused. It might free him to reevaluate his strengths and his goals, and choose a different path in life than he would have before his injury.

She did not know how long she would have to wait before killing General Cornwallis. First she had to find out if he was in Camden or camped here. Once she knew he was here, she would send a message to her contact so Captain Lee could arrange for her escape. Then she would deliver a note to General Cornwallis, asking him to meet her. She would not think about the actual act of killing him. Although it was for the cause of liberty, she had not yet reconciled herself to the deed. She forced the subject from her mind, afraid if she thought about it too much she might lose her resolve. She yawned and turned on her side, feeling herself drift toward the comfort of sleep.

Tomorrow, she reflected hazily, was soon enough to initiate her plan for the general's assassination.

"Caroline! Caroline! Come quick!"

Jo turned and buried her head farther into the pillow, wondering sleepily who Caroline was.

The tent flap tore open and Tommy burst into the soft gray light. "Caroline," he called, his voice sharp with panic, "wake up!"

Her mind instantly cleared. "What is it, Tommy?" She sat bolt upright. "Are you hurt?"

"It's Alice," he panted. "You've got to come right away!"

Jo needed no further information. She leapt off the bed and followed Tommy. Together they rushed through the maze of tents and low-burning campfires on which the soldiers were cooking their suppers. Although Jo had never been to Alice's tent, she knew they were getting close when she heard a woman's screams shattering the air.

Jo gathered her skirts in her hands and began to run.

She wrenched open the tent flap and went inside. The tent was much smaller than Damien's, and the low ceiling prevented Jo from standing straight. There was no furniture inside, except a small wooden chest which served as a table for three thick candles. Alice lay on the ground, writhing atop a straw sleeping mat that was covered with a few blankets. She was screaming hysterically. Lily was kneeling beside her, vainly trying to calm her.

"What's wrong?" Jo demanded. "What has happened to her?"

Lily abandoned her position at Alice's side. "James has been killed," she explained, her voice low and anguished.

Jo was stunned. "How do you know? Has the Scarlet Legion returned?"

Lily shook her head. "A few men in the legion were wounded in a skirmish today. Colonel Powell sent them back to the camp so they wouldn't slow the rest of them down. Two of them came to Alice to tell her James had been killed. She became crazed, and her birthin' pains began soon after."

"My darlin' Jamie, how could you leave me?" Alice wailed pitifully. "Bring him back, please God, bring him back!" She dissolved into another fit of tears, flailing her fists at air and blanket and earth.

Jo moved to her and knelt down. "Listen to me, Alice." She grabbed hold of a wrist and tried to get the distraught girl to look at her. "You must try to calm yourself. You've a baby to birth, and you must think about the life you're about to bring into the world. Do you hear me?"

Alice's dark eyes were wild and flooded with tears. "I don't care," she cried. "I don't care about anythin'—oh, my darlin' Jamie, don't leave me here alone, please God, let me die with him, please, all of you, *just let me die!*" She let out a scream, born half of pain and half of grief.

"I am going to fetch Dr. Howard. Everything is going to

be fine, Alice." She stood as much as the tent allowed and faced Lily. "Try to get her out of her clothes and cover her with a sheet. See if you can calm her. I'll be back with the doctor in a few minutes."

Jo and Tommy raced across the camp to where the surgical tents had been erected.

"Do you need me to go in there with you?" Tommy asked, his voice betraying his fear.

"No. You stay out here. I won't be long."

When she entered the tent, she was assaulted by the fetid stench of raw flesh and warm blood. She swallowed thickly, trying to control the revulsion rising in her throat. All the tables and beds crowding the tent were filled with miserable-looking soldiers. Some had their bandages unwrapped and were waiting for one of the surgeons to look at them. Others were shivering and rolling their heads from side to side, obviously suffering from fever. One gaunt young man was in the process of being bled. His arm was positioned against a small brass basin, which was rapidly filling with crimson liquid from a neat gash in his wrist. Dismay washed through her, undermining her resolve not to care about the suffering of the redcoats. More than a week had passed since the battle, yet the injuries sustained there and the subsequent illness those injuries caused were keeping the surgical tents full. Finally she saw Dr. Howard, standing by a table inspecting the blackened foot of a young soldier.

"Dr. Howard!" she called frantically. "I need you to come with me!"

Dr. Howard looked at her in surprise. "Miss Skye," he murmured, "I heard you had left us."

"I came back." Jo began to thread her way through the tables of injured soldiers to get to him. "Alice Clarke is having her baby. You must come and deliver it."

He wearily shook his head. "I am afraid I cannot do that, Miss Skye." He turned his attention back to the soldier with the black foot. "This will have to come off immediately. You have left it too long as it is."

The soldier's face turned white.

"You don't have to come right this minute," Jo qualified, trying to control her panic. "I am not sure, but I don't think she will have the child for a while. You can finish your work here, and then come."

Dr. Howard signaled for another surgeon in the tent to come over and assist him. "I mean I cannot come at all, Miss Skye," he said. He eased the young man back against the table. "Soldier's wives and children are not entitled to medical attention by army medical staff. Only the soldiers are. The army is extremely stringent on this rule, and I would be severely disciplined were I to disregard it."

Jo stared at him. "You mean you will not come?"

"I cannot. These men need me. I cannot risk being relieved of my duties here, which is precisely what would happen if anyone discovered I abandoned these soldiers to help a woman. But birthing a baby is usually not difficult," he added, seeking to reassure her. "Have you never witnessed a birth before?"

Jo looked at him helplessly. "I was with my mother when she had my little sister," she said. "But I was only twelve. I didn't actually do anything. There were other women there to take care of her."

Dr. Howard nodded, as if this experience more than qualified her for the task ahead. "All you need do is keep Mrs. Clarke as comfortable as possible. Don't let her panic. When the baby comes, hold it upside down and wipe any fluid off its nose and mouth. If it doesn't cry, give it a little tap on its bottom to get it started. Then tie off the cord, cut it, and wrap the child up. The afterbirth should follow soon after. If Mrs. Clarke bleeds, put pressure on the tear, the same as you would any other wound. If she needs stitches, you know how to do that." He wiped his hands on his apron and picked up his saw, evidently finished with his instructions.

"I—I can't do it," Jo stammered, overwhelmed. "Something could happen. You have to come."

Holding his saw in midair, Dr. Howard scowled at her. "For God's sake, look around you, Miss Skye," he blazed impatiently. "I have men dying all around me, day after day!

If they aren't shot and torn wide open in battle, then they come to me burning with smallpox, malaria, dysentery, and putrid fever. We have no medicine, no clean bandages, no equipment, not even any decent food to help them recover their strength. The battle they fought is over, but for weeks afterward I am forced to fight a losing battle to save them. Can you not see these men require my attention more urgently than one woman having a baby?"

She couldn't see it. Not at all. Because Alice was her friend. And nothing must happen to her.

"If you are too busy, perhaps one of the other surgeons could—"

"None of those men know the first goddamn thing about delivering a baby," he said scathingly. "They're not doctors, Miss Skye, they are army surgeons. They apprentice for a few months in a hospital, where they learn the crudest methods on how to root out shot, saw off limbs, and quickly close a gaping wound. They know nothing about the female anatomy, other than what they have learned in the dark from climbing on top of camp whores. They're decent men, but I wouldn't let one of them within a mile of Mrs. Clarke. You will have to manage on your own."

His tone was absolute. She realized there was nothing she could do to change his mind. Shaken and afraid, Jo turned and began to walk away.

"Miss Skye."

She stopped.

"It is a natural act, giving birth to a child," he assured her, his voice milder. "Whether or not the mother or child survives is often entirely up to God. Unlike this," he growled, gesturing with his saw at the misery around him. "War is the work of man. Creating life is the work of God."

Jo considered his words a moment. And then she shook her head. "You're wrong," she informed him tautly. "Creating life is the work of woman, *and* God."

The redcoats were strangely quite as she and Tommy worked their way toward Alice's tent. They were not laughing and joking as they normally did over their evening meal.

Instead the camp was filled with the sound of Alice's cries drifting across the still summer air. It was a mournful, hopeless sound that speared the heart of even the most hardened soldier.

Inside the tent, Lily had succeeded in removing Alice's gown and stockings, leaving her in her chemise. Although she was only covered with a sheet, her face and hair were damp with perspiration and tears, and her brow was heavily creased as she struggled through a wave of pain. Lily was sponging her forehead with a wet cloth, and urging her to be brave. After a moment the pain subsided. Alice began to breathe heavily and whimper something unintelligible about James.

"Is the doctor comin'?" Lily demanded.

Jo shook her head.

Lily's eyes grew wide.

"We'll be fine," Jo said curtly, rolling up her sleeves.

She poked her head out of the tent and gave instructions to Tommy. "I need you to fetch lots of clean linen, and a nice, soft blanket to wrap the baby in when it comes. Also, a basin of warm water, a length of cord, needle and thread, and a pair of sharp scissors that have been thoroughly scrubbed."

"I can't carry all that," Tommy protested, tilting his head in disgust at the bandaged arm strapped across his chest.

"I don't need everything at once. The baby won't come for a while. Take as many trips as you need. And just be thankful you still have one good arm, or I would ask you to carry the items in your mouth."

Tommy regarded her uncertainly, wondering if she was serious.

Alice let out another scream.

"Quick now!" ordered Jo. "Lily and I must stay with Alice, and we desperately need your help!"

A look of surprise crossed his face, which was instantly replaced with an air of self-importance. "I'll get everything you need," he assured her. "Don't worry." He ran off to collect the required items.

Jo knelt down beside Alice, who now seemed oblivious to what was going on.

"Listen to me, Alice," she said, her voice calm but authoritative. "Lily and I are going to help you deliver your baby. But you have to help us as well. Do you hear me, Alice? Look at me, and tell me you understand."

Alice lifted her haunted gaze to Jo. "My Jamie is dead," she whispered desolately.

Jo reached out and stroked her damp brow. "James is in heaven, looking down at you right this minute, Alice," she told her. "And he is smiling, and thinking, that's my lovely Alice, and she is about to have our child. He is sending you his strength and his courage, to help you through this. Can't you feel him, Alice?" she asked gently. "Can't you feel him sharing his strength with you?"

Alice stared at her, mesmerized. Then she shook her head. "No," she whispered brokenly. "I can't."

"Well, I can feel him." She began to rub Alice's shoulders, easing the knots of tension in them. "James has such a strong, wonderful presence. You can't believe that just because God called him, he would desert you." Her hands moved down to massage Alice's sides. "He is here, as surely as I am. Why, his spirit absolutely fills this tent. You can feel him, can't you Lily?"

"Yes," Lily responded earnestly. "I can feel him plain as day."

Alice's shimmering gaze moved across each of their faces, her eyes lit with desperate hope.

"Now, James knows you are upset." Jo eased down the sheet covering Alice and raised her chemise. Then she began to move her hands in soft, rhythmic circles over the hard, pale swell of her stomach. "He knows this has been a terrible day for you, and that you are afraid. But he is here with you, Alice. He will never leave you. And he will share his strength with you, so you have nothing to fear. Nothing to fear at all."

Alice cried out as a fresh wave of pain assaulted her. She gripped Jo's hand with crushing strength. When the contraction finally subsided, Alice released her hand and fell back against the ground, hoarsely panting for air.

"That's very good," Jo praised, flexing her aching fingers. She laid her palms once again on Alice's stomach and resumed her gentle massage. "Every pain you have means the baby is one step closer to being here. Soon you will be able to hold it in your arms. Won't that be wonderful?"

"Yes," murmured Alice. Her voice was thin and ragged.

"Rest now," Jo soothed. "Rest a few minutes, and James and Lily and I will watch over you. All is well, Alice. Just rest."

Alice closed her eyes.

Her labor continued for hours. During that time, Jo and Lily, and perhaps even James, watched over her. They tried to help her endure her pain, and keep her spirits up. They massaged her stomach and shoulders and back, and sponged her with cool water. They praised her constantly, telling her how fine and brave and strong she was, and how proud James was of her. And when at last the dark, wet crown of the baby's head appeared, Jo shouted with excitement.

"It's coming! It's coming! Give us a good push, Alice, your baby is almost here!"

Alice screamed and pushed and strained with every ounce of strength left in her heaving, exhausted body. The black crown became a head, and then shoulders, until finally a dusky gray little person slipped quietly out of her and fell into Jo's hands.

"It's a girl!" Jo cried, her voice ringing with joy. She took a clean, soft cloth and wiped the infant's nose and mouth. The baby took a tiny, strangled gasp of air. And another. Then her little, wrinkled face contorted and she let out a high, tinny cry.

"Oh, Alice, she's absolutely perfect!" Jo exclaimed, enchanted by the wizened creature. She tied a string around the baby's cord, cut it, then wrapped her in a cotton blanket. Cradling her in her arms, she held her close to Alice so she could see. "Look, she's turning pink—isn't she beautiful?"

Alice gazed at her daughter a long, silent moment, her

dark eyes wide and liquid with undiluted love. "She is beautiful," she murmured weakly. "Like my Jamie." She sighed and closed her eyes. "You must always take good care of her, Caroline." Her voice was gentle and pleading.

Jo looked at her in confusion. "Why on earth—"

"She's still bleedin'," Lily interjected tautly. "I don't think—"

"Hold the baby." Jo handed the child to Lily.

The baby's cord had come free from Alice's body, but only a small amount of afterbirth had come with it, which didn't seem right. Jo grabbed a cloth and used it to soak up some of the blood pulsing from Alice, trying to see if it flowed from a tear caused by the birthing of the baby. There was a tear in the flesh, but it was clear that was not the source of the bleeding.

The blood was flowing from somewhere deep within her.

Panic sliced through Jo. She pressed the cloth firmly against Alice, vainly trying to stanch the flow. The cloth was quickly saturated with blood. She replaced it with another. And another.

And another.

Please, God, please don't let her die.

"I can feel him," murmured Alice, her voice soft and laced with wonder. "I can feel my Jamie. He's here, Caroline. He's callin' me."

"Everything is going to be fine, Alice," Jo told her desperately, perhaps more as a way of reassuring herself. "Lily, ask Tommy to run and fetch Dr. Howard immediately. Tell him to tell the doctor he *must* come. He must."

Lily nodded and went to the opening in the tent, where she gave her instructions to Tommy.

Jo bit down hard on her lip and applied more pressure to Alice's body, assuring herself that her efforts were not futile. God was watching.

"Everything is going to be just fine," she repeated, her voice shaking.

"I know," Alice said. She seemed completely tranquil, as if she were at ease with the fact that her life was swiftly seeping away. "You'll take good care of her, Caroline. I know that."

"You're talkin' rubbish, Alice," Lily scolded as she cradled the baby against her. "After a good sleep you'll be feelin' as fit as ever, and you can look after your baby yourself."

Not knowing what else to do, Jo continued to press against the dark stream flowing from Alice's body as she waited long minutes for Dr. Howard to appear.

"I'm tired, Jamie," Alice finally whispered, so faintly Jo could barely make out the words. "I'm tired." A soft sigh escaped her lips as she closed her eyes.

Then her head fell gently to one side, and her body went peacefully limp.

"Alice!" called Lily, her cry choked with tears. "Alice!"

Jo hesitated, unwilling to confirm what she already knew. Finally she wiped her blood-soaked hands on a cloth and reached up to feel for a pulse in Alice's neck. There was none. Numb with shock, she slowly pulled the sheet up to her neck. She could not bring herself to cover her friend's face.

"I'm here!" Dr. Howard called from somewhere outside. He shoved the flap of the tent open and crouched down to enter.

"You're too late," Jo said hoarsely. "She's dead."

Dr. Howard moved toward Alice as if he hadn't heard her. He placed his fingers on either side of her neck. He grasped her wrist. And then he leaned over her and listened for the slightest sound of breath. Finally he raised his eyes to Jo. "I am sorry, Miss Skye," he said gently.

"She just bled and bled," Jo explained, her tone apologetic, as if she felt it was somehow her fault. "I couldn't stop it. I didn't know what to do."

"There was nothing anyone could have done, Miss Skye," he told her. "It was up to God. Not you."

Jo nodded blankly. In her heart she did not believe him. Why would God rob this innocent child of both parents on the same day, leaving her an orphan in the middle of a war? It made no sense at all.

"Who will look after her baby?" She looked at the small bundle sleeping in Lily's arms, then lifted her gaze to Lily.

"I—I can't," Lily stammered. "You know I can't, Caroline. I have nothin'. Lord help me, I work as a whore to get by. I never had any younger brothers or sisters. I know nothin' about raisin' brats. What kind of a mother would I be?" she reached out to touch Jo's arm. "You must do it. You're stronger than I am. You have Colonel Powell to provide for you. And besides, Alice wanted you to care for her."

"That is impossible. I cannot take responsibility for a baby. We will have to find someone else to look after her. Perhaps there is a woman in the camp who already has a child, and wouldn't mind another. Maybe there is even one who is nursing," Jo suggested hopefully.

"There isn't," Lily said. "There's one woman on the other side of the camp who has a boy of about seven, but he always shows the marks of her temper. Even if she were willin' to take the baby, which I doubt, you couldn't possibly leave Alice's child with her." She pressed the baby into Jo's arms, forcing her to take her.

Jo stared at the wrinkled pink face nestled in the crook of her arm. The child's tiny hand was resting solemnly against her cheek, as if she were worrying about what was to become of her. A cloak of protectiveness began to wrap around Jo, filling her with raw, unsteady emotions.

She was not here to care for a baby, she reminded herself helplessly. She was a rebel spy, who was here to assassinate General Cornwallis. But what excuse could she possibly offer Lily and Dr. Howard to make them see she could not care for this child?

And if she didn't take her, who would?

"You must realize, the chances of this infant surviving without its mother are small," said Dr. Howard. "A baby can live on water mixed with a little sugar or honey for a short while, but it will need milk soon."

The responsibility of caring for this child was overwhelming. She could not possibly accept it. A new thought occurred to her.

"This baby is the child of a British soldier who was killed in service to his country," Jo pointed out. "Surely the army bears some obligation toward her welfare, does it not?"

Dr. Howard looked uncertain. Lily shrugged her shoulders.

"I am going to speak with Colonel Richmond immediately," Jo said. "He is the senior officer in charge of the remainder of the Scarlet Legion while Colonel Powell is away. It is up to him to make provisions for this baby."

Cradling the little girl protectively against her chest, she left the tent, taking her away from the mother she would never know, and into the cool darkness of the night air.

Colonel Richmond was far from pleased to be wakened in the middle of the night.

"Just what the devil is it you expect me to do, Miss Skye?" he demanded. He grabbed his gray wig and plunked it over the tangled mess of his own thinning hair in an attempt to improve his disheveled appearance. Clearly he was not accustomed to strange women seeing him out of uniform. "Do you think I should raise the babe myself?"

"This child is the offspring of one of your shoulders," Jo said stubbornly. "Her father was killed fighting for England, and her mother died bringing her into the world. Since she has no relatives here, she is now the responsibility of the British army. It is therefore up to you to assign someone to care for her."

"Fine," he agreed darkly. "I assign you. Will there be anything else?"

Jo shook her head in exasperation. "I cannot look after a baby."

"And neither can any of my soldiers."

"But surely—"

"May I remind you that this is the British army, Miss Skye," he said sardonically, "not a nursery. We do not encourage soldiers to marry and have children, and we certainly don't invite them to bring wives and brats trailing along with them when we go to war."

"No," she retorted caustically, "you just allow a privileged few to come. And then you force them to cook and launder and nurse from morning to night, working them like slaves for nothing, not even the services of an army doctor when they need one!"

"No one forces them to be here," he pointed out. "They work as a way of earning the food and supplies they consume while they are with us. And if they elect to have a child, that is entirely their business, not mine. Have I made myself clear?"

The baby stirred in Jo's arms and let out a tiny whimper. Her sense of protectiveness toward the child intensified. "Perhaps I could look after her for a little while," she allowed, "if someone would make arrangements to unite her with her relatives in England."

Colonel Richmond removed his wig and tossed it onto his desk. "I am wholly unaware of whether the Clarkes have any relatives in England or not. Perhaps Colonel Powell knows. You may ask him when he returns. Until then, the child is yours. Good night, Miss Skye." Having dismissed her, he retreated toward his bed.

Temporarily defeated, Jo turned her attention to a more pressing matter. "I need you to find a cow for me."

He turned and looked at her in open astonishment. "A cow?" he repeated incredulously.

"For milk," Jo explained. "For the baby."

Colonel Richmond seemed to be struggling for control. "This is war, Miss Skye," he began, his voice brittle, "and we happen to be in the middle of rebel territory. I cannot afford to risk the lives of my men so they can go off and try to plunder a cow from hostile rebels, all for the sake of one goddamn baby!"

The bundle in Jo's arms began to cry, filling the tent with the pitiful sound of helplessness.

"Is she to die, then?" Jo asked furiously. "Is that your answer?"

Colonel Richmond stared at Jo a long moment, watching her as she shifted the baby onto her shoulder and stroked her back in an attempt to soothe her. Finally he sighed. "There are men dying all around me. You cannot expect me to stop everything for one baby that probably will not survive anyway. However," he continued, before she could protest, "I have some men going out to search for supplies tomorrow. I will give them instructions that if they come upon a cow, they are to either buy it or confiscate it, providing it does not put them at undue risk to do so. Will that satisfy you enough to leave my tent so I can go back to sleep?"

"Yes," Jo said as she rocked the baby, whose small cry was quickly escalating into something much more demanding. "For the moment."

She left Colonel Richmond's tent. She would like to have further argued the issue of who was to care for the child, but for the moment it seemed to be decided.

She was going to have to look after her, and that meant finding some way of feeding her as swiftly as possible.

It was the deepest point of night, just before the blackness begins to diffuse into the soft charcoal of early dawn. Exhausted, Jo was finally sitting in Damien's chair feeding her small charge.

She had fashioned a feeding bottle out of an empty wine bottle. Into this she had poured some sugar water, which she made by heating clean water and dissolving a little honey in it. Dr. Howard assured her that while this was not ideal, it did have nutritional value, and it was essential to make sure the baby consumed an adequate amount of fluid. Jo washed and rinsed the bottle thoroughly, poured in the water, and then loosely stuffed the neck with a clean scrap of cloth to control the flow of liquid. A search through Damien's chest furnished a fine pair of new, soft leather gloves, crafted with the tiniest stitches Jo had ever seen. She snipped half of the smallest finger off one and pricked the tip a few times with a needle. Then she washed it and tied it tightly over the neck of the bottle. Holding the baby carefully in one arm, she eased the wet leather nipple into her pink crying mouth, and moved it around a little to get her attention. It took determination on Jo's part, but after what seemed an eternity, the hungry infant finally decided to suckle. The air instantly fell silent, and Jo heaved a sigh of relief. Even Ashley, who was perched upon the bed watching her, curled up and closed his eyes with contentment when the crying finally stopped.

Jo had emptied Damien's chest and lined it with a blanket to serve as a cradle. Once the infant had eaten her fill she would hopefully fall asleep, and Jo could put her in it. Then she would strip the top sheet off the bed and tear it into squares to use as napkins. Tomorrow she would get a couple of buckets and set them outside the tent for washing and rinsing the cloths as they became soiled. She would also string up a line to hang them on for drying, so she would be sure not to run out. Fortunately she was well acquainted with the needs of a new baby. Her own mother had died of a fever not long after Lucy was born, and the responsibility of caring for the infant had fallen to Jo. Perhaps, she reflected wearily, that had been God's way of preparing her for this moment.

She was not entirely at ease with the fact that she was caring for a British child. Before her return to the camp she had promised herself she would remain utterly dispassionate toward her enemies, regardless of what happened to them. Yet here she was, feeding and caring for her enemy's baby, worrying over what was to become of her when she had to leave.

The infant's mouth relaxed, releasing its grip on the leather nipple. "Have you had enough?" Jo whispered softly. She put the bottle down, lifted the baby onto her shoulder, and gently rubbed her back. A small amount of water trickled from the infant's mouth onto the cloth Jo had draped over her shoulder. Then she laid her in the chest and adjusted her blanket. Kneeling on the ground, she watched the child sleeping, taking pleasure in the perfection of her little face.

She needed a name, Jo realized. She considered this a few moments. Emily, she finally decided. Emily was a pretty, spirited name, and it seemed to suit the tiny person who slept before her. She reached down and caressed her downy cheek with the back of her finger.

"Hello, little Emily," she whispered. "Welcome."

She stayed like that a long time, watching the little girl sleep. She wondered how Damien would react when he returned to find Jo in his tent and a baby occupying his chest. Somehow she did not think he would be pleased. Well, if he wasn't, that was just too bad, she decided. Emily was staying right where she was until Jo could find someone to take care of her. She had no idea who that person would be. Certainly not that evil woman on the other side of the camp who beat her young son. Jo would have to make certain the person she entrusted Emily with was gentle and kind. This helpless, unwanted child had been thrust into her care, and Jo had accepted the fact that she would have to look after her until a satisfactory guardian could be found.

Until then, her mission to assassinate General Cornwallis would have to wait.

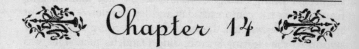

Chapter 14

By early afternoon of the following day, Jo had completely reorganized Damien's tent to suit the demands of caring for a new baby.

With the assistance of Lily and Tommy, Damien's bed was moved to the opposite side of the fabric room. His chest, now Emily's bed, was positioned directly beside it, making it easier for Jo to check on her during the night. This side of the tent was also more shaded in the afternoon, which made it cool for Emily while she slept. Damien's desk was moved to where the washstand had been, and spread with a clean linen to serve as a table for changing Emily's napkins. This meant the washstand had to go where the bed had originally been, and Damien's clothes from the chest were now piled on the ground beside the washstand. Ashley immediately decided the clothes were there for his comfort, and set about kneading them into a bed. Jo placed the chair from Damien's desk in the center of the tent so she could look through the open flap and watch the world outside as she held Emily in her arms.

Once the inside of the tent was organized to her satisfaction, Jo informed Lily and Tommy that she wanted to move the laundry area. Lily could not possibly cope with all the soldiers' washing on her own, and Jo did not want to drag Emily across the camp each day and lay her down in the hot sun while she worked. It made sense to move the laundry station to the clearing surrounding Damien's tent. This was a somewhat greater task, which required her to enlist the aid of her former guard, Charlie Beaton, and Oliver Yorke, the other soldier Damien had assigned to escort her home. Together they moved the iron kettle and the unwashed laundry across the camp to the grass in front of Damien's tent. A roaring fire was built, and Tommy, Charlie, and Oliver carried buckets of water from the river to fill the enormous kettle. As the water heated, they strung a maze of ropes between the trees to serve as drying lines. Then they insisted on helping wash and hang the huge mounds of laundry. By late afternoon the clearing was lined with gently flapping rows of white sheets and scarlet and white uniforms.

"Thank you both so much," said Jo as she rocked Emily, who had just wakened and was fussing. "Lily and I could never have done all this on our own."

"Me and Oliver are glad to be of service, Miss Skye," Charlie assured her. "The men of the Scarlet Legion feel the loss of James Clarke deeply. He was a good man, and as brave a soldier as they come. For him to be killed, and then for his wife to die while birthin' his daughter . . ." He shook his head as he looked at the baby cradled in Jo's arms. "Well, it's a damn bloody shame, and that's all there is to it."

"Here, let me carry that for you," offered Oliver, reaching out to relieve Lily of the basket she was carrying. "You shouldn't be lifting things this heavy."

"Why, thank you, Oliver," replied Lily, sounding flustered. She gazed at the tall, red-haired youth. "That's right gentlemanly of you."

Jo cast an amused glance at the two. She had noticed young Oliver being particularly helpful to Lily today. What was surprising was to see Lily reacting to his gallant attentions like a nervous, inexperienced girl. It was possible, Jo reflected, that Lily had never received attention from a man who didn't expect her to lift her skirts for him before the hour was finished. She sensed Oliver's attraction to Lily was deeper than that, and Lily didn't know how to react to it.

"Good afternoon, ladies," called Colonel Richmond as he approached the little group. His immaculate uniform and perfectly arranged wig gave him a far more commanding presence than his disheveled appearance of the night before. "Men," he added, nodding at Charlie, Oliver, and Tommy.

Jo wondered if Colonel Richmond had come to tell her he had found someone to care for Emily. The prospect should have pleased her, but to her bewilderment, it did not. She instinctively tightened her hold on the baby.

"Did you find a cow?" she asked.

"I am afraid not," the colonel admitted. "The men I sent out this morning were unable to acquire one. Perhaps they will have better luck tomorrow." He shrugged. "I am here to let you know we are having a burial ceremony for Alice Clarke in one hour. She will be buried in the cemetery we have established a half mile west of the camp, beside her husband, James. Colonel Powell's men brought his body with them when they returned yesterday. We buried him last night."

Jo nodded. "Thank you for letting us know," she said quietly. "We will be there."

Colonel Richmond gave her and Lily a polite tilt of his head before taking his leave.

"What are you wantin' a cow for?" asked Oliver.

"Milk for Emily," explained Jo. "She cannot survive on just sugar water, and she is too young to eat anything else."

Charlie stroked his grizzled chin. "Come on then, Oliver. Let's see if we can't steal a nice cow for James's daughter."

"Steal?" repeated Jo. "From where?"

"From one of the farms around here," he replied.

A farm like hers, she thought. Of course, the farm could be Loyalist. But it was more likely to be in the charge of a rebel wife or daughter, who was struggling to maintain it while her husband or father was away fighting.

"You cannot steal it," she said adamantly. "Stealing is a sin."

Charlies raised his eyebrows. "They aren't likely to give it to me, Miss Skye."

Jo considered a moment. "Then you must buy it from them at a fair price."

Charlie shrugged. "Do you have any money?"

"No," she admitted. "Haven't either of you?"

Charlie laughed. "The army pays us the royal sum of eight pence a day. From that they deduct for food, laundry, medical treatment, and replacing our uniform as it wears out. Doesn't leave much, I'm afraid. Certainly not enough to buy a cow. Maybe you've got somethin' to trade for it?"

Jo had not brought anything with her except her clothes and Ashley. But it was possible Damien had something that could be exchanged for a cow. "Perhaps," she allowed. "Let me look."

She entered the tent, and quickly appraised its contents. The candelabra on the desk was silver and exceptionally handsome. It was probably worth five cows, or maybe more. But if she gave it away, she would have no way of lighting the tent at night. Her eyes fell on the porcelain pitcher and basin on the washstand. Although simple in design, they were also of some value. But she needed them for washing herself and bathing Emily. She proceeded to evaluate the worth and essentiality of every other object in the room. The bed. The chest. The washstand. The desk. The chair. Her traveling bags. And Damien's pile of belongings, which Ashley was using as a bed.

Shifting Emily onto one arm, she went to the mound of clothes and lifted Ashley off them. She rifled through the folded layers, searching for the gold locket. Her initial inspection yielded nothing, and she began to fear he had taken the precious object with him. She was far more thorough in her second attack. When she came to the last shirt, the heavy pendant spilled from one of the folds and landed in her lap.

She studied its uncommon beauty and workmanship. Clearly it was worth far more than a cow. She opened it to the portrait of the beautiful young girl with milky skin and rosewood hair. The girl stared placidly back at her, her enormous brown eyes filled with sweet elegance. Aunt Hazel had taught Jo how to pretend she had elegance. Somehow that was not the same as actually having it. She ran the tip of her finger lightly over the fine engraving opposite the portrait. *Forever in my heart, Victoria.*

She snapped the locket shut and took it outside. "Here," she said to Charlie, dropping the gold oval and chain into his outstretched palm. "That should be more than enough to pay for a cow."

Charlie opened the locket, studied the portrait inside, then closed it and put it between his teeth. He looked at her, his eyes questioning. "You're sure you can part with this?"

Jo gave him a level look. "It's the only thing in the tent that serves no purpose. And Emily needs milk. A cow will be more than a fair exchange."

"Very well." He crammed the locket into his coat pocket. "Come on, Oliver." He pulled the young soldier away from exchanging awkward glances with Lily. "Let's go find Miss Skye a cow."

It was deep into the night when Jo stumbled from her bed to feed Emily. Her eyes were clouded with exhaustion as she changed Emily's napkin and settled into the chair to soothe her hunger with sugar water. But the child continued to coo and fuss, so Jo kept her on her lap and sang to her. She tilted her head back and closed her eyes, humming softly, slipping toward the precipice of sleep. A strange, bleating noise jolted her awake. Wondering if she was dreaming, she raised Emily onto her shoulder and lifted the tent flap.

Outside, Charlie hammered a stake into the ground while Oliver struggled to lead a most unaccommodating goat toward the tent. Tommy came from the direction of the river, using his good arm to carry a bucket of fresh water for the animal.

"A goat!" Jo exclaimed.

"That she is." Charlie gave the stake one final crack with

his mallet. "And the woman we bought her from says she's young and healthy, and sure to give you ample clean milk for the babe, with plenty to spare."

"Charlie, you're wonderful! And you too, Oliver," she added.

"Thank you, Miss Skye," returned Oliver, still wrestling with the obstinate goat. "It was nothin'."

Given the amount of trouble he was having just leading the animal to the stake, Jo suspected the feat of bringing the animal here was more trouble than Oliver was admitting. Finally he threw his arms around the animal and tried to drag her bodily to the stake. The nimble creature danced out of his embrace and trotted away, leaving him sprawled on the ground.

"Let me try," offered Tommy.

Oliver shrugged and handed the end of the rope to Tommy. Jo was concerned the goat might charge Tommy and hurt his injured wrist, but he had worked all day helping her, and he was beginning to discover that having one hand did not mean he was useless. If he wanted to try to handle the goat, she would let him.

The goat eyed Tommy warily. Instead of pulling on the rope as Oliver had done, Tommy wrapped the cord around his fist and slowly began to move toward her.

"Hello, girl," he called softly. "How are you?"

The goat lifted her head and eyed him warily.

"I bet you're tired from your long walk," Tommy continued, his voice gentle and sympathetic. "I guess you'd like nothin' more than somethin' to eat and a place to lie down for the night."

Still holding on to the rope, he reached into his coat pocket and pulled out a small, green apple. "Are you hungry, girl?" He took another step toward her, holding the apple just out of reach. "Would you like this?"

The goat arched her neck and pointed her nose in the air, trying to catch the scent of the apple.

"Come and get it," he invited. "It's yours. I brought it here just for you."

The goat took a tentative step toward him, her nostrils flared.

Tommy remained where he was, holding out the small offering. The goat hesitated. And then she abandoned her caution and delicately took the apple from his hand.

"That's a good girl." Tommy stroked her neck as he waited for her to eat. Then he walked her over to the stake, where he secured her rope with just one hand.

"Well, I'll be damned," said Charlie admiringly. "The boy's a goat charmer."

"I should have used an apple," grumbled Oliver.

Charlie laughed. "Come on, Oliver. Let's go find ourselves a drop of rum to celebrate Miss Skye's new goat."

"Tommy, I never knew you were so wonderful with animals," Jo said when the soldiers left.

"I like animals," he admitted, stroking the goat. "Especially horses. I always hoped one day I would learn to ride, so I could be part of Colonel Powell's cavalry. An officer has to be able to ride." His voice cracked slightly.

"If you want to ride, then you will learn to ride."

He shook his head in disgust. "I only have one hand, Caroline. I could never hold on."

"You don't hold on to a horse with your hands," Jo told him, "you hold on with your legs. You certainly don't need two hands to ride a horse. How do you think cavalry soldiers use their swords if they have both hands glued to the reins?"

Tommy frowned. "I never thought about that."

"When Colonel Powell returns, I will speak to him about giving you riding lessons."

He looked at her in amazement. "Colonel Powell? Teach me to ride?" Pure, boyish delight lit his face, making him carefree and handsome, like the boy he had been before his injury. And then he grew sober. "Colonel Powell is a busy senior officer. He would never have time to teach me to ride."

"Nonsense," returned Jo. "He could spare an hour here and there. Of course, in between your lessons, you would have to practice on your own. I would help you."

"You would?"

"It would be my pleasure, Tommy," Jo assured him. "However, there is something you must do for me in return."

"Anything."

"First of all, I am going to need help looking after this goat. I need you to feed her and make sure she always has plenty of clean water. She should have exercise each day, and I would like her kept very clean, especially her underbelly, so no dirt or grass falls into the pail as I am milking her. Can you do all that?"

"Of course I can."

"Good." Jo nodded. "Then there is something else I would like you to do."

"What?"

"With all the work I have to do around here, there is little time for me to read." She sighed. "I would like you to read to me for an hour each day as I work."

He shook his head apologetically. "I can't read, Caroline."

"You can't?" Jo had suspected he couldn't read. How could a boy of thirteen who had run away from an abusive home to join the army have any education? "Then I will teach you. You cannot become an officer without knowing how to read."

"You would teach me to read?" He seemed awed by the thought.

"Yes," she replied. "I will teach you to read, and Colonel Powell will teach you to ride." *And that will be a good beginning toward making a decent life for you.* She had no illusions that she could teach Tommy to read in the short time she would be here. All she hoped to do was create a thirst for knowledge in him. And the realization that he could do almost anything, if he put his mind to it. She would let him think she was helping him to become an officer. In truth, she hoped he would choose a life outside the army. A life that did not revolve around battle and death, however exciting that might seem to a boy of thirteen.

Tommy reached out and laid his hand on her arm. "Thank you, Caroline."

Jo brushed a wayward lock of hair off his forehead. He looked at her in surprise. "Go to bed now, Tommy," she ordered softly. "Tomorrow you will move your tent over here, so you can be closer to your goat. They have a way of getting into trouble, and I have enough to worry about with Emily. Then we will begin your lessons."

"Very well." Suddenly embarrassed by the closeness that had arisen between them, he coughed, using this as an excuse to remove his hand from her arm. "Good night, Caroline."

She watched as he disappeared between the ghostly rows of sheets.

"Good night, Tommy."

Cradling Emily's sleeping form against her chest, she turned and went back into the tent, trying not to think about how betrayed Tommy would feel when she left.

The camp was filled with the low rumble of sleep as Damien made his way toward his tent.

He was exhausted. The Scarlet Legion had been away for eleven days. In that time they had fought pockets of rebels in four separate skirmishes. They had won two of them, but the rebels had fought with the ferocity of men possessed. The legion had suffered severe losses. Twenty-two men killed, and twenty-four horses that were either slain in battle or had to be destroyed afterward.

His illustrious Scarlet Legion was shrinking.

Weary and discouraged, he pushed the thought from his mind. All he wanted to do was collapse on his bed and sleep. He had been lying on the ground for ten nights, and his body was stiff and aching. The idea of stretching out on an actual bed, however thin the mattress, was tantalizing. A few hours of sleep, in which he could escape the ugly business of war. And think of nothing but Josephine. That was how he rewarded himself at night. Rewarded and tortured himself, he mused. At first he had fought the images that flooded his mind the moment he closed his eyes. He had used every fragment of discipline he possessed to will himself not to think of her. But discipline deserted him when it came to Josephine. And so he surrendered to the haunting images, and let them soothe and torment him, finding both pleasure and anguish in the memory of her.

He was a bloody fool to have let his feelings get so out of hand. He had known from the start she was a rebel, and that she had ample reason to despise him. But he had thought himself safe from her. After all, she was nothing but a colonial farm girl, the daughter of a bonded servant and a convicted murderer, for God's sake. How could he possibly have known how glorious she was? But he had known, he reminded himself harshly. He had recognized her strength and courage the moment he first laid eyes on her. She had knelt before the endless blue of this country's incredible sky, her hair burnished by sunlight and her eyes glittering with hatred. And he had realized that he was looking at the most extraordinary woman he had ever seen. Neither the shabbiness of her dress nor the simplicity of her surroundings could hide her magnificence from him.

When he found her again in that ballroom in Charles Town, she confirmed what he already knew: Josephine bore a simple, innate nobility. Not the nobility of genteel manners and refined speech, although she had learned those with a swiftness that astounded him. No, what Josephine Armstrong possessed was a deeply rooted nobility of spirit. It was this quality that made her fight for her beliefs with such resolute passion. It enabled her to risk herself for the cause of liberty. And yet it forced her to sacrifice her duty when her enemy lay broken and bleeding. It was a rare, uncompromising sense of compassion that set her apart from everyone he had ever known.

Even himself, he thought with disgust.

He was not fighting this war for any higher cause. He was fighting it because it was his duty to do so. An integral part of that duty was not to question the righteousness of the kings and politicians who sent his army into battle. But he was finding it increasingly difficult to close his mind to the injustice of this war. The Americans were building a new nation a world away from England. They wanted to do so independently, without answering to power-hungry men on the other side of the ocean. These politicians believed the colonists were wayward children who could not possibly know what was best for them. But the Americans were intelligent, honorable men and women who were carving a new world out of a hostile wilderness. They were creating prosperous farms and towns and cities by sheer force of will and backbreaking effort. It was entirely reasonable they wanted the power to control their destiny in this new land. By what authority did England decide they could not have it?

He shook his head, troubled by these treasonous thoughts. Somehow he had to come to terms with his qualms about the war. Because he led men who depended on him to be certain about what he was doing. At his command they would charge into ruthless battle. A moment's hesitation, a command delayed by a flash of guilt or uncertainty, and their blood was upon his hands.

He cursed, too exhausted to think about the matter anymore.

As he moved away from the lanes of tents and into the clearing where his quarters were, he frowned. Row upon row of sheets, shirts, coats, and breeches were hanging from ropes strung across the clearing. An enormous caldron rested on the charred remains of a fire. He blinked, wondering if he had made a mistake and come to someone else's tent. He and Gil had indulged in a fair quantity of rum during the long ride back. Perhaps the alcohol had affected him more than he realized. He scanned the darkness, confirmed his bearings, and decided these definitely were his quarters. Who the hell had decided to set up the laundry here? He stalked through the lines of fabric, assuring himself someone would have some explaining to do come morning.

As he passed the lines, he noticed a small shelter had been erected about five yards away from his tent.

"What the hell?" His irritation expanded to the brink of anger.

He marched over to the smaller tent with the intention of ordering whoever was in there to get the hell out. The shelter was a tiny affair, made only for sleeping and storing personal effects. The night was warm, so its occupant had left its flaps open, enabling Damien to bend down and scrutinize the miscreant's face. Tommy Brown slept peacefully on a worn blanket, his injured arm free from its sling and draped across his chest. Damien studied him a moment, feeling his irritation dissipate. He had no idea what the boy was doing here, but he could not bring himself to rouse him in the middle of the night. The lad had suffered a grave injury, and needed all the rest he could get.

He sighed and advanced toward his own tent. He would question Tommy about why he had moved here tomorrow. Right now, all he wanted was the blissful comfort of his bed.

Something rammed solidly into his backside, sending him flying through the air to land with a heavy thump on the ground.

Damien blinked and lifted his head in astonishment. A testy-looking goat eyed him warily, ready to butt him again on the least provocation.

"What the devil is going on around here?" he growled.

The goat was tied to a stake by a long rope. Uncertain how far the rope reached, Damien decided to get himself into his tent posthaste. Whatever goddamn idiot had decided to tether the animal here would regret their decision come morning.

The inside of the tent was bathed in black. Too exhausted to light a candle, he began to strip off his uniform. He clumsily walked into a chair, which for some unfathomable reason had been left in the middle of the room. Cursing, he moved around the object and headed toward his bed, dropping his coat and waistcoat as he went.

He collided with the washstand.

"Bloody hell," he muttered, wondering what on earth was the matter with him. Had the rum addled his senses so much he did not know his way around his own tent? He stripped off his shirt as he moved tentatively across the room.

"Meeoowwrrrrr!"

"Jesus Christ!" He backed away from the enraged sound, only to have his shin bang into something.

A high, tinny wailing pierced the room.

"What in the name of God is going on around here?" he roared, confounded by all the noises and objects filling his tent.

"Damien?"

His heart froze.

It can't be, he told himself, unwilling to allow his mind to play such a foul trick on him. *She cannot be here. It is the alcohol that makes you think she is.*

"Damien?" the voice repeated, sounding worried this time. "Is that you?"

It was impossible. It was inconceivable. Yet he would have known the sound of her voice anywhere. There was no mistaking it.

"Josephine."

She was there. In his tent. Guarded joy spread through him as he struggled to absorb this simple, incontrovertible fact.

"What in the name of God are you doing here?"

He watched her dark silhouette move from the bed and bend to lift something.

"Shhh," she soothed, her voice gentle as she rocked the squalling form in her arms. "You have wakened Emily."

"Where the hell are the candles?" he demanded.

"On the desk," said Jo. "Hush, darling," she cooed, "it's all right."

Her words were like a balm over his rattled composure. Even when he realized she was talking to the baby.

He went to the desk and fumbled with a match, passing its yellow flame over the candles in the candelabra. A warm glow filled the tent. Damien studied the light for a moment.

And then he turned to look at her.

She had seated herself in the chair and was trying to get the wailing child in her arms to drink something from a wine bottle. After a moment the tent fell silent, except for a tiny, gurgling sound. Josephine was dressed in a chemise which was so opaque Damien could see the flush of her skin beneath it. Her honey-gold hair was falling in careless, tangled waves across her shoulders and down her arms. She absently brushed a heavy lock of it behind her shoulder, so it would not interfere with her tending the child.

His heart swelled at the portrait of gentle beauty before him. He was afraid to do anything to rupture the moment. Josephine was there, in his tent, with a baby. The state of his tent indicated she had been here a while. Moving things around. Setting up the laundry. Caring for this child.

Waiting for him to return.

None of it made any sense, of course. Yet he was reluctant to question it. Because in that warm, apricot-washed moment, he only cared about one thing.

She had come back to him.

"What are you doing here, Josephine?"

She lifted her head, surprised by the gentleness of his tone. She had expected him to be infuriated by her return. To rage and curse, and tell her she had no business being in the army camp of her enemy, and worse still, with a baby. His apparent calm disarmed her.

"I—I came back," she stammered.

She made it sound hopelessly simple. But it was not simple, regardless of how much he would like it to be. If Josephine had come back, it must be to spy again. The baby made a gurgling sound, distracting him.

"Whose baby is that?"

"Alice and James Clarke's," she replied. "Some of your men returned to camp a few days ago and told Alice that James had been killed. She became hysterical. Her grief brought on her labor, and Emily was born."

He still didn't understand. "Then why isn't the child in Alice's tent instead of mine?"

She lowered her gaze to Emily's tiny, perfect face. "Alice did not survive the birth."

Her despondence was obvious. Despite her determination to have no bonds with the people in this camp, Damien knew Alice Clarke had been her friend.

"I am deeply sorry, Josephine."

He seemed so strong and caring as he stood there watching her. His presence filled the tent with light and warmth. Until this moment, she had not realized how afraid and uncertain she had been since Emily was born. But now Damien had returned, and she felt as if a burden had been lifted from her.

"I was unable to get Dr. Howard to help. He said the army does not provide medical assistance to soldiers' wives or their children. Also," she allowed, "he was very busy. So I had to birth her." Her gaze dropped to Emily. "I am afraid I did a poor job of it," she concluded in a painful whisper.

Damien closed the distance between them and knelt before her. "It seems to me you did a fine job," he murmured gently.

She raised her eyes to his. "Thank you."

A quiet peace drifted over them. Damien was so damn happy she had come back, he almost didn't care why. But he was an officer of the British army, and it was his duty to care. And so, reluctantly, he asked, "What are you doing here, Josephine?"

"I want to be with you."

He silently absorbed this statement. It could not possibly be true. Her hatred of the British army was absolute. Josephine would never have returned unless she felt there was an opportunity for her to help the rebels. Yet something deep within him wanted everything to stop. He wanted to ask no more questions, just accept her statement and take her to bed and thank God for returning her to him, beautiful as ever, and safe. For the past eleven days he had been tortured by fear for her. The British army was trying to destroy the morale of the rebels. Damien knew they had been attacking homes all over the South Carolina countryside. Homes had been burned. Men had been killed. And women had been beaten and raped. He refused to participate in this rampage of brutality, but he was well aware it went on. Only by sheer force of will had he been able to refrain from going after Josephine and dragging her back to the camp.

He suddenly feared her farm had fallen victim to one of these raids, and that was the reason she had returned.

"Is everything well at home?" he asked.

"Yes," she lied. She could not let Damien think she had come here out of hatred. She had a vital mission to carry out. "Everyone is fine."

Emily had fallen asleep. Jo rose from the chair and placed her in the chest. She kept her back to Damien as she arranged a sheet over her, uncertain what to say next.

Damien had no idea what the hell he was going to do with her. Battle and march were no place for a woman. But neither was a war-torn countryside where families were in constant danger of attack. At least here he could keep her safe. No man would dare touch her knowing she was his mistress. As long as she remained far from the battlefield, nothing could happen to her. If he sent her home, she would turn up in another British camp, where she would be in danger of discovery and arrest. If she remained with him, he could watch over her. He tried to convince himself that his decision was based on logic. But he knew logic had nothing to do with it.

He simply needed her with him.

"Swear something to me, Josephine," he said, his voice low and taut. "I will let you stay here. I will let you keep that child. I will make certain no harm comes to either of you. But in return, you *must* swear something to me."

She did not turn to face him. "What is it?"

"Swear to me you will not spy or attempt to pass information to the rebels while you are here. Swear it to me, Josephine," he said roughly, "and we will not speak of it again."

For a long moment, a battle raged in her heart. If she swore this oath, it would not be a lie, she told herself fervently. Because she was not here to spy or pass information. She was here to assassinate General Cornwallis. Damien had not asked her about that.

"I swear."

He wanted to believe she was telling him the truth. He wanted to believe it so desperately, he suppressed the uneasiness gnawing in his gut. He even ignored simple logic, which told him she could not be trusted. He needed to have her with him. It was weak and foolish, but there it was. She would probably betray him. He understood that. But somehow he clung to the possibility that perhaps she would not.

He opened his arms to her.

With a cry she went running to him. He wrapped his arms around her and pulled her against him, drinking in the wonder of her touch, her scent, her being. He crushed his lips against hers and tasted her with savage possessiveness, his hands wandering boldly over the soft curves shrouded in the cool linen of her chemise. Her need rivaled his, for she began to grasp at the layers of his uniform with rough impatience. He gladly assisted her, and when he stood naked before her, he pulled off her chemise and tossed it carelessly to the ground. Then he closed his arms around her and slid his tongue deep into her mouth, tasting the warm sweetness of her as he lowered her onto the bed.

He pulled his mouth from her lips to trail hot kisses across her silky cheek, her pale throat, the smooth curve of her shoulder, caressing and stroking and worshiping every inch of her skin. His tongue danced lightly over the velvety peak of her breast, causing it to tighten into a dusky coral bud. He drew her into his mouth and suckled, and Josephine moaned, threading her hands in his hair, holding him to her breast as he pleasured her with his lips and tongue. He pulled away to give equal treatment to her other breast, gently suckling and tugging upon the lush orb before continuing his journey across the soft valley of her stomach, along the rounded curve of her hip, down the creamy length of her thighs. A hushed moan spilled from the back of her throat as he rained feathery kisses on her exquisite body, branding her with his mouth, marking her forever as his as he slowly moved across the warm, silky flesh, until he hovered a breath away from her satin-slick heat.

Jo shivered with dark pleasure as Damien's tongue flicked teasingly inside her. He tasted her lightly, then harder, rapidly, then with utter languor, arousing her and tormenting her until she felt her body and soul would shatter from the magnificent agony of it. She spread herself shamelessly for him, focused on the honey-sweet pleasure washing through her, deeply aroused by his desire to caress her so intimately. Her hands grew restless, her fingers gripped the linen sheets as her breathing grew shallow and ragged, until the sensations flooding through her started to stretch and surge and swell. She writhed against him as tiny, desperate gasps escaped her throat.

"Please, Damien," she whispered.

Her impatience relieved him, for he was not sure how much longer he could control himself. He moved across the warm softness of her body, enveloping her in his strength and heat and need, and kissed her deeply as he positioned himself against her wetness. She sighed into his mouth, her hands moving over his shoulders, across the ripple of scars on his back, into the contour of his spine. She splayed her fingers possessively over the taut curves of his hips, and pressed down in one swift, deliberate motion. A wave of pleasure crashed over him as he felt himself sheathed by her wet fire. He groaned and buried his face in the silky veil of hair lying against her neck. He could not move, so exquisite were the sensations tearing through him. Josephine had come back. And now he lay joined to her, encompassed by her softness and heat and life, so much a part of her he could feel the steady beating of her heart against his chest. He was suspended between ecstasy and torture, and he wanted this moment to last forever.

Undiluted pleasure surged through Jo as she absorbed the wonder of Damien filling her and holding her. She lay peacefully a moment, feeling his strength and warmth permeate her being, making her feel alive and whole. And then her contentment was displaced by a gradual restlessness, an increasingly aching need that caused her to raise her hips and pulse slowly against him, caressing the powerful curves of his back and hips as she kissed the smooth, sun-bronzed skin on his shoulder and neck. He lifted his head and gazed at her a moment, then thrust deeply into her, and withdrew, then pressed himself into her again, becoming more a part of her with each penetration. There was a deep, burning intensity in his gaze, which seemed to strip away her defenses and pierce her very soul. It was unbearable to have him look at her so as he tenderly joined his body to hers. It made her feel completely exposed, as if he could see into her mind and her heart. In that moment she feared he knew she would betray him. Unable to bear his scrutiny, she lowered her lids, but she knew the action was telling. She plunged her hands into the blackness of his hair, and pulled him down so she could press her mouth against his, her lips trembling with passion and desperate, anguished apology.

Damien told himself he was mistaken. He had imagined that flash of despair, that pleading look that unveiled the fact that he could never trust her. He could not lose her, not now, not when she had the power to wash away the bitter guilt of his past, and make him feel that something good could still come of his life. He wanted to forget about Victoria, and their child, and the war, and simply drown himself in Josephine's softness, her courage, her unrelenting ability to fight for what she believed in. She would not betray him, he assured himself as he thrust powerfully inside her, claiming her, filling her with his passion and need and love. He kissed her deeply as he moved within her, his hand caressing her shoulder, her breast, her hip, trying to bring her closer to his heart, to bind her to him in a way that would keep her from ever leaving him. His hand moved down to where they were joined and he began to caress her there, his fingers stroking her slippery heat, touching her and kissing her until her breathing was a rapid stream of shallow, frantic gasps, until he felt her soft body flexing desperately against him, rising to meet each thrust. She began to tremble in taut ecstasy, drinking tiny sips of air as she clung to him with blinding need. A pleading cry tore from the back of her throat as she tightened around him, gripping him with hot, velvety power, holding him hard inside her. It was a cry of joy and despair, and he understood it with agonizing clarity. He ground his mouth against hers as he arched his back and thrust deeply into her, his body rigid and straining. Again and again he drove into her, his mouth plundering hers with feverish longing, his arms holding her in a desperate embrace. He buried himself in her over and over, each time feeling as if he were losing more of himself to her, and somehow not giving a damn. A fire of pleasure poured over him in unrelenting waves, causing him to groan. He was being consumed by flames, and then suddenly he shattered into a thousand fragments, releasing the essence of his desire deep inside her. He pushed himself into her, trying to prolong the sensation, to make her part of him forever. But his body was sated, and he collapsed against her, breathing in the sweet fragrance of meadows and streams as he buried his face in the golden silk of her hair.

They lay together a moment, breathing deeply, clinging to each other with desperation. Damien was reluctant to stir, for fear it would break the fragile bonds that had wrapped around them. Finally, concerned he might be crushing her with his weight, he gathered her into his arms and rolled onto his side, taking her with him.

Jo lay wrapped in the power of Damien's embrace, her cheek pressed against his beating heart, trembling with raw emotion. She had not sought this, she told herself helplessly. She had known if Damien returned they would share the same bed. But she had never imagined the terrifying feelings that would surge from the depths of her soul, claiming her heart with such cruel totality. She should never have come here. But it was too late. She had a mission to carry out. Nothing could compromise her duty to her country. But when she completed her assignment, Damien would despise her. She would have used him and betrayed him, and he would never forgive her.

She closed her eyes and drew a shaky breath, unable to stop the tears that began to leak across her face.

He sensed her despair even before he felt the wetness on his chest. He tenderly laid his palm on her cheek, then raised her head so she was forced to look at him.

"I cannot end this war," he told her quietly. "But one day it will be over, Josephine. It cannot last forever." He caressed her cheek with the back of his fingers, spreading the trickle of tears over her skin.

She nodded bleakly. And then she raised herself over him and pressed her lips to his, seeking to drown herself once more in the power of his touch. He groaned and wrapped his arms tightly around her, then rolled her onto her back and began to cover her with fiercely possessive kisses.

It cannot last forever. But before it was over, she would betray the man she had come to love.

And he would hate her with a virulence she could not bear to contemplate.

Chapter 15

For the next few days, Jo tried to pretend the war didn't exist.

For someone living in an army camp, this was somewhat challenging. But once she threw herself into the endless demands of caring for Emily, helping Lily with the laundry, and teaching Tommy to read, write, and ride, she had little time to contemplate the war. Every day she managed to find a reason why she could not carry out her mission. She had not found anyone to care for Emily, and she couldn't possibly leave until arrangements had been made for the child. There was also the fact that Damien was there, and she did not want to attempt her assignment until he was away from the camp, in case he tried to stop her. Then there was Tommy, who was proving to be a quick learner, but still lacked enough of a grasp of reading for her to feel comfortable abandoning him to someone else's tutelage. And of course poor Lily could not possibly cope with the endless mountains of laundry that were brought to them each day. The excuses piled one on top of the other, allowing her to banish the mission from her mind.

The days melded one into the other, and in a strange way, she was content. Each night Damien loved her with fierce possessiveness, as if he wanted to make her a part of him so she would never be able to leave. When they were finally spent, he wrapped his arms around her and bound her tightly against him, holding her so close she could feel the steady pounding of his heart against her back. As she lay curled in the crook of his body, encompassed by his strength and warmth, her mind would lull her with thoughts of a farm and children, of long, sun-filled days, and dark, starry nights spent wrapped in each other's arms. There was no war, no hatred, no lies. But just as the warm waters of sleep were closing over her, she would remember that she was a rebel, and she was here to murder General Cornwallis.

And she would turn in Damien's arms and cling to him, feeling lost and afraid, and hopelessly alone.

"Good evening, Caroline."

Jo was sitting outside where it was cooler, and had just finished feeding Emily, who was on the edge of sleep. Now that Jo was formally ensconced as Damien's mistress, Gil had taken to calling her by her first name.

"Good evening, Gil," she replied, her voice hushed. "I'm afraid Damien isn't here. I believe he had a meeting with General Cornwallis."

"Actually, it's you I came to see," he said. "I was riding in the woods today, and caught my arm on a branch." He looked slightly embarrassed. "I hate the idea of going to the surgical tent for something so small. Since I hear you're handy at stitching wounds, I was wondering if you would close it up for me."

"Of course," she said, rising to put Emily in her chest. "Wait here while I get my things."

She returned a moment later with a basin of water, a clean cloth, needle and thread, and a length of linen for bandaging. Gil had removed his jacket and rolled up his torn sleeve, exposing a bloody gash along the side of his arm.

"Sit down," she said, gesturing to the chair.

He seated himself and held out his arm so Jo could better examine it. "The cut is deep, but the edges are clean, so I think it will heal nicely." She dipped her cloth in the basin and began to gently dab at the wound, washing away the blood and dirt.

"You are truly an angel of mercy," Gil said. "No wonder the men are so glad you returned."

Jo looked at him in confusion. "Because of the laundry?"

"No, not because of the laundry," he replied, smiling. "Because they respect you. You work hard. You were willing to take James Clarke's daughter when the army was ready to just let her die. Young Tommy shows marked improvement in both his health and attitude since you started teaching him to read, and got Damien to give him riding lessons. And no one has forgotten how helpful you were after that bloody clash with the rebel army."

His praise made her uncomfortable. She lowered her eyes to her task.

"The other reason, of course, is Damien," he continued, oblivious to her discomfort. "It has not escaped anyone's notice that Colonel Powell is far more even-tempered when you're around."

Feigning only casual interest, she asked, "Why? Does he normally have a terrible temper?"

Gil laughed. "He fights hard to control it, but it's always there. The marks on his back are a constant reminder that he has to keep it on a tight rein."

The scars of his lashing. Alice had told her he received them in punishment for striking a superior officer. She said his lashing was credited with teaching him to control his temper. Jo threaded her needle as she considered this. If Damien had this dreadful temper everyone spoke of, was it possible the appalling stories Captain Lee told her about his attacks on rebels were true? Everything she knew about Damien indicated they were not.

"You know," she began hesitantly, "they say he and his Scarlet Legion have committed terrible atrocities." She pierced her needle through his flesh.

Gil frowned. "What atrocities?"

She pulled her needle through his skin and drew the thread taut, wondering if she dared elaborate. She was terrified he might confirm the hideous story. Trying to keep her tone indifferent, she continued, "They say he attacked a rebel plantation, in which a pregnant woman was murdered." Her voice grew hollow as she finished Captain Lee's ghastly accusation. "Her unborn child was cut out—"

"That wasn't Damien," interjected Gil harshly. "You can trust me on this, Caroline. Damien and I have been friends since we were boys. We joined the army together, and I have ridden with him since we came to the colonies three years ago. He would never sanction such bestial behavior. Never." His voice was rough with anger.

"The atrocity you are describing took place under the command of Major Nigel Ferguson. The Scarlet Legion came to that plantation *after* the attack had occurred. When Damien saw what had taken place, he nearly wept with outrage. And made it his business to report the abominable incident to General Cornwallis, which led to Major Ferguson being relieved of his command and assigned to administrative work in Charles Town."

Relief poured through her as she absorbed this information. Of course Damien hadn't done it. Nigel Ferguson had. She shivered, recalling the night Major Ferguson tried to force himself on her in that garden in Charles Town. No wonder the contempt raging between Damien and Nigel had been so acute when they faced each other in the ballroom. She had never believed Damien was capable of such brutality. Duty forced him to kill armed soldiers in battle, but that did not mean he slaughtered innocent people in their homes. If he had been there, he would have done everything in his power to stop Nigel and his men from their savagery. Just as he had risked himself to save her and her family. From the moment he came into her life, Damien had demonstrated again and again that he was a man of integrity and compassion. She had just been unable to accept this, because of the uniform he wore.

Which meant the tale about him murdering someone in England was probably also false.

"Why did Damien have to leave England?"

Gil regarded her with one brow cocked, evidently uncertain how to answer. Suddenly embarrassed by her forthrightness, Jo fastened her eyes on her stitching.

A moment passed. And then he gently stated, "You're in love with him, aren't you?"

His question took her by surprise. She swiftly lifted her head, ready to deny it. But his eyes met hers with calm conviction, and she knew he would never believe her.

She dropped her gaze in utter misery.

They were both silent for a moment. Finally Gil quietly offered, "Her name was Victoria."

Her eyes flew up in horror. "He murdered Victoria?" she gasped, thinking of the girl in the locket.

"Good God, no," Gil hastily assured her, sounding astonished. "Where on earth did you get the idea that he murdered someone?"

"I heard it in the camp," she said, embarrassed.

His expression grew dark. "It never ceases to amaze me how fool gossip can cling to a man forever."

"You are right," she agreed contritely. "I should know better than to listen to it."

Gil hesitated, evidently debating how much to tell her. And then he sighed.

"Damien was hopelessly in love with Victoria from the time he was a young man," he began. "She was a pretty thing, the only child of Viscount Lytton, who spoiled her endlessly, and sheltered her as much as humanly possible. When Victoria turned eighteen and Damien was twenty-six, they decided to marry. But when Damien went to her father to ask for her hand, he was tersely informed that Victoria's future was already arranged. Her father had just agreed to a marriage with Damien's brother, Frederick, the Earl of Strathmore. This was a far more satisfactory arrangement in the viscount's eyes, because Damien's brother had inherited the title and holdings, while Damien only received a small annual allowance."

"That doesn't seem fair," Jo said. "Why did his father leave him so little?"

"His father never cared much for him," explained Gil. "He was the second-born son, and in the earl's eyes, that made him of lesser value. All through his life Frederick received constant coddling, while Damien was left to do whatever he pleased. From an early age it was made clear he was not expected to amount to anything. And for a long time," he observed candidly, "he didn't."

"What about his mother?" Jo asked. "Did she also favor his brother?"

"No, his mother adored him. But she died when Damien was barely eleven, leaving him alone with his brother and father."

Jo was silent as she absorbed this. Her own mother had died when she was twelve, and she had been heartbroken. But she still had a father who loved her, and three older brothers who showered her with caring and attention. Then there were Samuel and Lucy who needed her. The Armstrong family had openly shared its love and grief during that terrible time. Although she missed her mother deeply, she could not recall a single moment when she felt alone.

"What did Victoria do when her father rejected Damien?"

"Victoria didn't want to marry Frederick, but ultimately she felt she had little choice," Gil said. "She had never defied her father's authority, and unfortunately, she was not made of the stuff that might have enabled her to run away with Damien and lead a simpler life. Victoria was raised amidst luxury and grandeur. Marriage to Frederick would not only preserve her customary way of life, it had the added benefit of making her a countess. These were things Damien could not offer her. And so she accepted her father's decision, and married Frederick."

The knowledge that this girl openly spurned Damien's love in exchange for wealth and a title made Jo's stomach clench. "And was she happy?" she demanded, sincerely hoping she was not.

Gil shook his head. "From the moment the vows were spoken, Frederick treated his new wife with appalling cruelty. It was as if he were punishing her for having loved his brother," he reflected. "Or perhaps he took pleasure in showing Damien that once again he possessed what Damien wanted so badly, and now could do whatever he damn well pleased with it. Damien was horrified by the abuse, but he felt helpless to stop it. Each time he tried to intervene, Victoria was made to suffer. Perhaps in an effort to escape the situation, Damien began to drink and gamble heavily. And," he added hesitantly, "he indulged in numerous other women.

"A year passed, and Victoria failed to conceive, which had the disastrous effect of making Frederick abuse her even more. Frederick was desperate for a son, and Victoria was determined to give him one, hoping that if she produced a child, her husband would treat her better. Finally she wrote to Damien, begging him to help her. And Damien, against his better judgment, agreed."

Jo paused in her stitching and looked up. "I don't understand. How could Damien help Victoria conceive?"

Gil shifted uncomfortably in his seat.

Understanding suddenly dawned on Jo. "You mean—"

Gil nodded. "A few months later, Victoria found herself miraculously with child."

Jo shook her head, struggling to accept what he was telling her. Damien had a child. In England. With this woman in the locket named Victoria. Who was married to his brother. *Forever in my heart, Victoria.* Suddenly everything was very clear. Damien was still in love with this woman. This woman who had rejected him, then asked him to give her a child so she could please his brother. The emotions roiling inside her were almost unbearable. She had known Damien could never belong to her. They were enemies, and had no hope of a future together.

"Is that why he left?" she asked tautly. "Because he could not bear to watch his brother raise his own son?"

Gil shook his head, his expression grim. "Even after Victoria conceived, Frederick continued to beat her. One night, after a particularly violent episode, she sent a message to Damien, begging him to come to her. Damien had been out with me that night, and was frightfully drunk. But when he received the message, he immediately set out for his brother's home. He found Victoria with her face swollen and bruised, and went into a rage. He informed Frederick that Victoria was carrying his child, and that he was taking her away from him." He paused.

"Go on," urged Jo quietly.

He sighed. "A savage fight ensued between the two brothers. I think they were both furious enough to kill each other. It probably looked that way, anyway, at least to Victoria. And so she made the ghastly mistake of trying to intervene, but it was Damien she went to. Frederick became enraged, and raced toward her, brandishing a brass poker. Damien, fearing for Victoria, shoved her out of the way. But his drunkenness affected his judgment, and he threw her far harder than he intended." He cleared his throat before quietly stating, "She lost her child. A boy. He lived for a few moments, but it was too soon for him to be born. The birth was very difficult, and destroyed any possibility of Victoria ever having another child."

"Oh God," breathed Jo, horrified.

"Victoria hated him after that. She blamed Damien entirely for the death of their son. She accused him of killing the baby on purpose, so his brother would never love her and she would be forced to live the life of a pauper with him. Her accusations were madness, of course, but in her mind they were the truth. Instead of blaming the man who had abused her for nearly two years, she condemned Damien, who loved her more than anything. She told him she never wanted to see him again, and of course, neither did Frederick, who could never have the heir he so desperately wanted. And so Damien left England," Gil finished. "There was nothing left for him there except hatred and pain. Of course there was a scandal, although no one beyond the family ever knew what really happened."

"And you went with him?"

He smiled. "I hated the idea of him going off and seeing the world without me. When he bought his commission, I decided to sign up as well. I rather thought I'd wear the uniform and stay out of trouble." He shook his head. "But from the moment we arrived, Damien volunteered for every assignment, then carried them out with utter recklessness. I wondered if he was trying to get himself killed, as a way of punishing himself for what happened to Victoria and their child. When I saw the appalling chances he took, I realized I was right. Damien is a consummate soldier, because he has no fear. And he has no fear," he concluded, "because he really doesn't give a damn what happens to him."

Jo continued to stitch in silence. Damien had not joined the army because he wanted to make a profession of killing. He had joined because he needed to escape, and to punish himself. The army had taken him away from his past, and provided him with harsh discipline. It had instilled in him a sense of duty and purpose, and enabled him to prove that he was fit for more than a life of drinking and gambling and womanizing. He had performed his duty well and earned his men's respect.

She wondered if he had succeeded in earning his own respect.

"I hate to interfere, but I really think you've put in enough stitches, Caroline," suggested Gil, interrupting her thoughts.

Startled, Jo looked down. Gil's wound was sewn neatly shut. "So I have," she admitted with an embarrassed smile. "All you need is a bandage, and you will be as good as new." She quickly wrapped a clean length of linen around his arm and tied it.

"Thank you," said Gil, rolling down his sleeve. "I am indebted to you for your kindness." He rose and pulled on his jacket. Then he hesitated, as if there were something more he needed to say.

"You know, when I said Damien is in a better temper while you are near, that isn't exactly what I meant. What I really mean is, I think you are good for Damien." He coughed slightly, perhaps uncomfortable with this confession. "Thank you again, Caroline. You are truly an angel."

He gave her a low bow and kissed her hand before disappearing between the flapping gray lines of sheets.

His disclosure caused her more anguish than pleasure. Because in that moment it seemed a thinly veiled plea, asking her to stay with Damien. And help him heal from the wounds of his past. Which, of course, she could not do.

Instead she was going to add to the pain and betrayal he had already been forced to endure.

"You are certain the Scarlet Legion is up to this?" demanded General Cornwallis.

"Yes, sir," replied Damien. "Only half my men accompanied me on the last mission. The others remained here, resting and training. Those are the men I will take with me."

"I hate to send you out again so soon, Colonel Powell. But Tarleton is still away, and if the reports about this band of rebels harassing our supply lines are accurate, they must be stopped immediately. We cannot afford to lose any more wagons. Those supplies are necessary to sustain us on our march into North Carolina."

"Yes, sir."

"It won't be much longer, anyway," General Cornwallis assured him. "These rebels know nothing about warfare. Their numbers are shrinking, and their supplies are almost nonexistent. God in heaven, the prisoners we have taken are little more than walking skeletons. Once we have possession of North Carolina, the poor fools will realize they haven't a hope of winning. You and I will be home by Christmas, Colonel, possibly sooner. Away from this cursed heat," he finished grumpily.

"I am not sure it will be that fast."

General Cornwallis looked mildly outraged. "What are you talking about, Powell?"

"The rebels are incredibly tenacious, sir," Damien observed. "Each time we think we have crushed them, they manage to rise again. General Washington has kept them fighting in the northern colonies for years, despite the fact that they have no supplies, are hopelessly outnumbered, and suffer appallingly brutal winters."

"The rebels in the north are General Clinton's problem," declared General Cornwallis dismissively. "For the moment, I am only interested in the enemy we face here. Since our arrival in February, we have captured Charles Town, and handily defeated the rebels in numerous engagements, the most important of which was the battle north of Camden. Not a bad record for six months' work."

"But the rebels have won their share of battles too, sir," Damien pointed out. "They beat us at Ramsur's Mill, Williamson's Plantation, Thickety Fort, and Musgrove Mills. They perform well in smaller engagements, away from the open battlefield. They harass our posts and supply lines constantly, and make surprise attacks on detachments of soldiers. They appear and disappear with ease, because they are familiar with these thick swamps and woods. It is as if they were part of the land," he remarked with guarded admiration. "They know the terrain, which enables them to use less conventional forms of warfare."

"I don't give a damn what kind of warfare they use," General Cornwallis drawled impatiently. "They are merely delaying the inevitable. They are fighting the finest army in the world, and they haven't a prayer of defeating us. We have right on our side, Colonel Powell. Right, and the power of the British army. What more do we need?"

Damien did not answer. He could not expect to make the British commander see what he was beginning to realize. The Americans would never give up their fight for freedom, no matter how hard the British army fought. And just because England decided she was right, did not necessarily make it so.

The longer he stayed there, the more difficult it was to know what was right.

General Cornwallis lowered his head to sift through some papers on his desk. "A letter for you, Colonel Powell." He waved a creamy, wrinkled envelope at him. "Arrived early this morning."

"Thank you, sir," said Damien, reaching out to accept it.

The handwriting was elegant and distinctively feminine in style. A crumbling scarlet seal had been fixed to the back of the envelope. Despite its deteriorated condition, there was no mistaking the waxen impression of the Strathmore crest. A coil of apprehension unfurled in his belly.

The letter was from Victoria.

"Will there be anything else, sir?" he asked, controlling his impulse to rip the missive open then and there.

"No. Just track down that irksome band of rebels and extinguish it. Kill them, or take them all prisoner. I don't want them cropping up again a month from now. I am leaving for Charles Town within the hour. A few administrative matters to see to before we begin our movement north. I expect to be back within nine days. See that you have returned before then, and prepared your men to march. Is that clear?"

"Yes, sir," Damien replied, distracted. He gave the general a small bow before turning and leaving his tent.

He strode purposefully across the camp, heading for the paddock. He wanted privacy to read this letter, and he would not find it in his tent. His horse trotted toward him as he approached, anxious to be freed from the enclosure. He had jokingly given Captain Lee's horse the name of Liberty, thinking it ironic that a rebel horse had helped to free a redcoat. But Liberty suited the powerful, spirited animal, and now he used the name with respect rather than amusement. Damien quickly saddled him, then guided him out of the camp before urging the animal into a gallop. They tore across the open fields, widening the distance between them and the busy military community. Finally Damien dismounted by an enormous live oak tree, leaving Liberty to graze as he impatiently tore open the letter.

May 14, 1780

My darling Damien,

No doubt you will think my endearment inappropriate, given all that has passed between us. But as I write this letter to you, I feel so blessedly free, I am tempted to shout as loud as I can, so the world may finally know how I truly feel. I am like a woman who has suffered a long and torturous imprisonment, who has just been released and is seeing the sun for the first time in years. My dearest, my darling, my beloved Damien. All these endearments I wish to use when I speak to you, and more. Because they are not just words, my love. They are the song of my soul, and finally I am able to sing it.

No doubt you are wondering if I have gone mad. Let me ease your fears by telling you that rather than being mad, I have suddenly become sane. And for that wondrous miracle, there can only be one explanation. Your dear brother, my tender husband, Frederick, is dead. He was thrown from a horse who refused to endure any more of his cruel handling, and after lingering a few days in a troubled sleep, finally died. Perhaps you feel I should be demonstrating a modicum of sorrow. In public I play the role of the grieving widow only too well. But you, my darling, know any bereavement I claimed to endure could only be a lie, and I refuse to have lies between us, my love. Frederick is dead. I am suddenly free from the man who took such evil pleasure in trying to destroy me. And everything you ever wanted, is finally yours.

You are now the Earl of Strathmore, my dearest. I never could have another child after ours, so the title with all its privileges and holdings falls to you. Magnificent Waverley, which you loved so dearly, is once again your home. And I, my darling, am ready and willing to become your wife, if you will have me. The gossips will talk. Let them. We have endured too much, you and I, to be concerned with the idle chatter of those who could not possibly understand.

I beg you, resign your commission and return to England immediately. I realize it may be months before this letter reaches you, and even longer for you to return. The waiting is unbearable. I have never stopped loving you, Damien. I want you here, now, so we can begin our new life together. At last you will have everything you ever wanted. We can bury the pain of our past, and look forward to the pleasures of the future.

This is our time, my love. Finally, we have everything.

Forever in my heart,
Victoria

Icy shock poured through Damien as he absorbed the contents of the letter. Frederick was dead. He was now the Earl of Strathmore. That ancient, august title, which the dictates of the nobility had reserved solely for Frederick, and which his brother had so contemptuously flaunted before him, was now his. And so was Waverley, that magnificent structure of dove-gray stone which he had loved with a passion Frederick could not begin to comprehend from the time he was a child. In one swift, shattering moment, he had gone from being a man with nothing save a meager army salary and a piddling allowance, to being an earl with an estate, properties, servants, horses, and investments to manage. All the accoutrements he had lacked, which immediately reduced him in the eyes of other men, and kept him from marrying the woman who once claimed to love him above all else, were suddenly his.

And she was finally ready to marry him.

It was everything he had ever wanted, presented in one dazzling package. He could ride back to camp, resign his commission, and head to Charles Town to board the first ship leaving for England. He could be sailing home within the week, and if the weather was fair, he would set foot on English soil in less than two months. He could be home, at Waverley, warming himself before an evening fire, with Victoria beside him and a life of grandeur and respectability stretching endlessly before him.

The prospect left him oddly cold.

The sky was sprinkled with brilliant flakes of silvery light as he walked toward his tent. The canvas was luminescent against the soft darkness, telling him Josephine had lit the candles and was waiting for him. A familiar warmth flooded through him, mixed with the relief he experienced each time he returned to find her still there. Tommy had tied Emily's goat farther away from the tent, so the irritating animal could not ram into Damien every time he appeared. She eyed him wistfully as he walked past, undoubtedly wishing she was not tethered so she could take a good run at him.

He entered the tent to find Josephine sleeping on the bed, fully clothed, her head resting against her arm. Ashley was curled in a ball beside her, enjoying the treat of sharing the bed. No doubt Josephine had thought to lie down just for a moment, and sheer exhaustion had drawn her into a deep slumber. Damien placed the chair beside the bed and seated himself, indulging in the pleasure of watching her as she slept. Her wheat-colored hair was spilling over her shoulders and across the pillow like a shimmering river of honey. Her skin was tanned from countless hours spent toiling in the hot sun, and the sprinkling of freckles across her nose and cheeks had grown darker as a result. The faded cotton gown she wore was unfastened just to the swell of her breasts, and clung to the curves of her in a way that was more alluring than the finest of silks.

She had a natural, unaffected beauty to her, Damien reflected as he studied her, and something else, a lean, wild quality that somehow tied her to the land she loved so completely. He found himself comparing her to Victoria, who had managed to enslave his heart for so many years. He was astounded to realize there was no comparison. Josephine was as lean and strong and rugged as Victoria was soft and pale and delicate. Josephine had been born to a convicted murderer and a bonded servant, while Victoria's noble pedigree spanned centuries of carefully contrived breeding. Yet Josephine knew more about honor, courage, and conviction than Victoria could ever hope to understand. By the standards of the British aristocracy, Josephine Armstrong was a criminal's daughter, a farm girl, and a rebel, all of which made her beneath contempt. Yet in this quiet, candlelit moment, the newly titled Earl of Strathmore felt hopelessly unworthy of her.

Emily began to fuss, her face contorting into what Damien had learned were the early signs of a good cry. Not wanting Josephine to be wakened, he bent down and awkwardly lifted the infant into his arms.

"Hello, little one," he whispered. He had heard Josephine speaking to the child at length, and had deduced that while Emily could not possibly understand what was being said, she found the sound of a voice soothing. "Did you have enough sleep?" he asked softly.

Emily instantly ceased her fussing and regarded him with dark, sapphire eyes.

He held her a moment, uncertain what to do next. "Perhaps you are hungry," he suggested. He gazed about for the wine bottle Josephine used to feed her. He saw it sitting on the ground in a bucket of cool water, evidently prepared for Emily's next feeding. Carefully holding the baby in one arm, he rose from the chair, retrieved the bottle, dried it against his breeches, then seated himself again. He tried to get her to take the leather nipple, but Emily would have none of it. She wriggled and squirmed, and her face twisted into an ominous pucker, warning Damien a wail was not far off.

"Very well, we will forget the milk," he quickly assured her, putting the bottle down. A new thought occurred to him. "Are you wet?" he demanded suspiciously. He opened her blanket and tentatively touched the linen wrapped around her hips and waist. It was sopping wet.

For a moment, he was tempted to wake Josephine. But she looked so exhausted as she lay there, he could not bring himself to be so cowardly. He had fought countless battles, and witnessed all manner of blood and gore. Surely he could find the fortitude needed to change an infant's napkin.

He carried Emily to his desk, which was covered with a folded sheet, and carefully laid her down upon it. Then he removed his jacket and rolled up his sleeves, preparing for the task ahead. Taking off her wet linen was simple enough, but he was less certain how to put another one on her. Josephine had left a neat stack of clean squares piled in the corner, along with a small basin and a cloth. Not quite knowing what was expected of him, he poured some water into the basin, then lifted Emily up and dipped her in it. She didn't seem to mind this in the least, so Damien splashed a little water over her, just to be certain she was clean. He then lifted her out of the basin, dried her off, and deposited her in the middle of one of the linen squares. He experimented with it a few times before he was finally satisfied with its arrangement on her, and Emily was remark-

ably tolerant of his ineptitude. Then he wrapped her back
up in her blanket and carried her to the chair.

He offered her the bottle once more, and to his delight
she accepted. She was a remarkably pretty child, he decided
as he fed her. He found himself increasingly enchanted by
her tiny nose, her bow-shaped lips, the delicate little point
of her chin. After a while her lips grew slack and her eyes
closed. Damien removed the bottle and watched her sleep,
gently stroking the downy tuft of black hair that covered the
crown of her head.

If not for Josephine, this child would be dead, he mused,
infuriated by the thought. No one else had been willing to
care for her, and so Josephine had taken charge. She was not
afraid of responsibility. And she was ready to fight for all
that fell under her keeping. Victoria could not begin to
compare to a woman of such honor. Despite Victoria's im-
passioned letter, he could not help but be repelled by her
calculating manner. Her husband's body was barely cold,
and she was already arranging her next marriage. Her assurances of love and need seemed quite a contrast to the hate
she had harbored toward Damien for so many years. He had
wanted to take her away from Frederick after that terrible
accident, but her hatred of him was so great, she elected to
stay with his brother. Yet now that Frederick was dead, she
claimed to have always wanted him.

Perhaps, he reflected disdainfully, what she really wanted
was the Earl of Strathmore, and all that went with him.

He felt a sudden urge to look at Victoria's miniature, to
contemplate her face and see if he was judging her too
harshly. He carefully laid Emily in her chest, then went to
the pile of his garments Josephine had heaped upon the
ground. He searched through the folded clothes twice, decided he was looking too quickly, and began once more, this
time with greater deliberation.

"It isn't there."

He looked up to find that Josephine was regarding him
warily. There was no question she knew exactly what he was
looking for.

"Where is it?" he asked.

Her expression grew guarded, as if she were afraid to tell him.

"Tell me, Josephine," he said gently. He disliked the idea that she feared his response.

"I—I gave it away," she confessed. Realizing he deserved a little more explanation, she hastily continued. "I had no money, so I had to give it to Charlie and Oliver to trade for the goat." She waited for his fury to explode.

He did not look angry. Instead, the look he gave her was one of pure astonishment, as if he could not possibly have understood her correctly.

"You traded a solid gold locket with five diamonds and a detailed portrait for that surly old goat?"

"She is not old," Jo countered. "And a goat is far more valuable to us than a piece of jewelry. Emily needed milk, and now she has it. Without the goat, she would have died. Since the locket was the only thing in the tent we didn't need, it made sense to trade it."

He could not fault her for her logic. Even so, it was a shock to realize the locket he had carried for so many years was gone. Victoria had given it to him when their love was tender and new, long before he went to her father to ask for her hand. He had brought it with him as a way of remembering what had once been. And perhaps to torture himself over that terrible, drunken push that ended in the death of his son.

"Since we got the goat, Emily has been doing very well," Jo pointed out. "I think we made a good trade."

She was right, he realized. Emily's need for milk far outweighed his desire to torture himself with a useless pendant. Josephine had made a very good trade. The fact that she was referring to them as "we," as if they were a family, caused a flame of warmth to ignite in his chest. But the warmth was tempered by a cool draft of foreboding.

In a few hours he would be leaving on his mission. General Cornwallis had given him the assignment before Damien realized he was an earl, so he had decided the mission took precedence over his resignation. He could not tell Josephine he was leaving, for fear she might attempt to warn her rebel contacts. She had sworn she would not spy, but he knew better than to trust her. He was reluctant to leave without making her swear to him that she would not do anything foolish in his absence. But he could not do so without revealing he was going away, and he did not want her to know until he and his legion were long gone. And so he tried to convince himself it would be all right. She had Emily to care for, and Tommy to tutor, and Lily to help. With all those responsibilities, she would not have time to get into trouble, he assured himself.

He sat on the bed and wrapped his arms around her slim, strong form, pulling her tight against him. She smelled sweet and warm, like a meadow drenched in afternoon sunlight. "I think," he murmured huskily, his lips grazing the silky skin at the side of her neck, "now that I know how much that miserable old goat cost, I am going to demand she treat me with more respect."

He began to kiss her throat, using his tongue to draw slow circles down the tender flesh, across her collarbone, and over the soft swell of her breasts, teasing the taut nipples through the worn fabric of her gown. Josephine sighed. He was not angry with her, she realized with relief. He understood. She knew the locket had meant a great deal to him. And yet he was accepting its loss, because Emily needed milk. Pleased beyond measure with his reaction, she threaded her fingers into the black length of his hair and pulled him up to press her mouth against his.

Damien kissed Josephine deeply as he eased her back against the mattress. Tomorrow, he reflected, he must leave her, at least for a few days.

Tonight, he would cloak her in love, so she would stay until he returned.

Lemony petals of warm light were scattered across the tent, wavering slightly as the shivering leaves outside diffused the morning sun into dancing patterns. Jo opened her eyes and regarded the frolicking medallions with sleepy contentment. She had slept far later than usual, but since Damien had made love to her for most of the night, she decided she was entitled to this small indulgence. She yawned, then leaned over the bed and peered at Emily. The child was sound asleep. This was unusual, since it was her habit to waken with hunger by half past five. Jo gazed at her in sleepy confusion, trying to remember if she had fed her during the night. She could not recall doing so, but she had been up with her so many nights, it was difficult to distinguish one feeding from another.

She stretched her arms above her chest and yawned again, feeling deliciously rested and languid. Then, realizing the morning was slipping away and there was much work to be done, she tossed back the sheet and headed toward the washstand.

She stopped when she saw the flowers.

They burst from the pitcher on the washstand in a riot of lavender and yellow, crimson and white, pale pink and azure. But it was not their wild, exuberant beauty that caused her breath to catch in her chest. It was the ivory envelope leaning against the shiny smooth porcelain of the pitcher. Hesitantly, she approached the washstand and picked up the letter, her heart beating with trepidation. There was no name scripted across the front, yet she knew it had to be for her. With trembling fingers, she opened the envelope and pulled out the folded sheet inside.

Josephine,

I must leave you for a while. Please refrain from doing anything foolish while I am gone. If I have not returned within ten days, take Emily and go home. She deserves better than to live amidst constant battle and death.

And so do you.

Damien

Dizziness swept over her. Damien was gone. Numbly, she scanned the note again. He wanted her to wait for him. For ten days. If he did not return by then, she would know he had been captured.

Or killed.

Fear burst through her, leaving her trembling and nauseated. She took a deep breath, fighting to regain the ice-cold conviction she had felt when she decided to return here. This was the moment she had been waiting for. She was now free to carry out her mission. She could ask Lily to take care of Emily, and then she could find General Cornwallis and kill him. Then she would escape the camp, and never see Damien or Emily or Tommy or Lily again.

The anguish tearing through her was unbearable.

Chapter 16

$\mathcal{D}$amien watched with tightly controlled patience as the rebels edged closer to his trap.

He had been tracking this troublesome band for four endless days. They were an elusive prey, always managing to stay just beyond his reach, frustrating his desire for a surprise attack. Damien did not think they knew they were being hunted. But the rebel soldiers were inordinately cautious, avoiding the open road and fields for the thick, dark cover of the woods and swamps. They preferred to travel during the blackest hours of the night and in the hottest hours of midday, realizing this was when the British troops were most likely to rest. After some consideration, he rejected the idea of matching their movements. He did not know the dense wilderness surrounding him well enough to lead his regiment through it in the dead of night. And although the eighty-four men he had brought with him were in good physical condition, he had no desire to sap their strength by forcing them to march during the brutal heat of early afternoon.

The best way to find the rebels, he decided, was to lay a trap, and wait for them to come to him.

He sent his men to confiscate two heavy wagons from nearby farms. No harassment of the inhabitants or looting was permitted. The soldiers were to mention the vehicles were needed to transport a load of muskets, bayonets, shot, and cannons currently on its way to Camden. The original wagon had overturned while traveling up a hill and was beyond repair.

Damien had no doubt this story would streak through the rebel network like summer lightning, alerting them that there was a prize to be caught.

Once the wagons were procured, he ordered his men to fill them with rocks, branches, small trees, it didn't matter, as long as an impressive mound was achieved for each. The soldiers draped blankets over the contents and secured them with ropes. A dozen men were assigned to be the wagons' escort. Damien selected a strategic site along the road that cut through a dark stretch of forest, and had the men halt their horses and make a great show of something being wrong with one of the vehicles. A wheel was removed, and four soldiers set to work on the problem, while the remainder of the men hung about looking hot and irritable. The rest of the Scarlet Legion was scattered amidst the thick forest, on foot and on horse, waiting for the rebels.

For over two hours there was no sign of them. But Damien knew the most brilliant of strategies was nothing without patience. He waited, keeping his senses alert by evaluating the variables of the attack and the position of each of his men. Finally, as the third hour dragged to an end, he saw a flash of movement. He stared at the area that had seized his attention and waited. A moment passed. He began to think he had been mistaken. Just as he was about to look away, he saw a glimpse of a blue uniform. A rebel soldier darted from one tree to another. Damien signaled to Gil, who was hidden a few yards away from him. Gil passed the signal to the soldier next to him, who motioned to the next man. A few more minutes passed, in which Damien detected the movement of more than a dozen rebels, all on foot. This was just the first line, he realized. There were more right behind them, and mounted soldiers positioned farther down the road, ready to thunder out of the woods. The foot soldiers were silently edging toward the wagon, ready to initiate a surprise attack.

Damien could not help but admire the speed and silence with which the soldiers moved. They advanced with guarded confidence, slipping in and out from behind trees and fallen trunks, like wild animals who knew exactly how many steps they must take before they could charge their quarry. As the minutes passed their numbers grew. Some of the men were dressed in filthy rebel uniforms which hung limp on their half-starved bodies. Others were dressed in fringed hunting shirts and buckskin trousers, their outfits blending with the surrounding forest. And others wore only simple shirts and trousers that had been dyed dark brown or blue, so they would not be mistaken for the scarlet and white of the British uniform. They were a motley group, but Damien did not think for a moment this was an indication of lesser ability. If anything, he suspected this band of irregulars was far more dangerous than any group of rebels he had faced before.

These are Josephine's countrymen. They are fighting for their freedom. They are a part of this land in a way that I am not. And I am about to slaughter them over two wagons filled with rocks and trees.

A stab of self-loathing cut deep into his chest.

What the hell was the matter with him? He was under orders to eradicate this group of rebels. At this moment, he was responsible for the lives of eighty-four British soldiers who would follow any command he gave them, regardless of the danger to their lives. This was hardly the time for doubt or guilt.

Stay focused. Or you and your men could end up dead.

He glanced at Gil, who was watching him with impatient curiosity. It was obvious Gil could see the moment to attack had arrived, and was wondering why he hesitated. Damien knew he should raise his sword and give the order to charge. But for the first time in his military career, he was paralyzed by dread.

He did not want to fight these men, he realized with sudden, numbing clarity. He did not want to kill them. Despite the fact that it was his sworn duty to do so.

He wondered if Josephine would understand when she learned what he had done.

Gil's expression was now openly quizzical, as were the expressions of some of the other men surrounding him. The rebels were nearly at the road. Any moment they would aim their weapons and fire at his soldiers, who were playing out their charade around the wagons. They could not know of the rebels' approach. His men were in danger, and he was doing the worst thing a military leader could possibly do.

He was hesitating. He was compromising their safety because of his inability to act.

Blood pounded in his ears. *You are Lieutenant Colonel Damien Powell, commander of the Scarlet Legion. It is your sworn duty before God and your king to attack these rebels and crush them. Your personal reservations on the matter are entirely irrelevant. So get the hell on with it. Now.*

He felt strangely disembodied, as if all trace of conscience were suddenly stripped from his soul. It was the result of three years of the harshest discipline and training a man could endure. It robbed him of his ability to think, leaving him only with the capacity to fulfill his duty and fight.

In that terrible, soul-wrenching moment, not thinking was the only available course of action.

He lifted his saber, silently begging God to forgive him.

"Charge!"

The hazy silence of the forest was shattered by the resounding roar of soldiers, rebel and redcoat. It was a grisly sound, born both of the desire to terrify and the desperate need to bury one's fear in the face of death. The verdant woods were suddenly swarming with men consumed with a hunger for blood. Musket fire cracked through the air in deafening waves. Pounding hooves churned the earth as the mounted soldiers thundered into the fray. Steel blades flashed in silvery arcs through the dark green, scraping and ringing against each other as men fought to make the softer noise of metal slashing flesh. The brutal cries of aggression melded with screams of agony.

Damien fought with mindless, expert precision, as he had been trained to do. He did not see the faces of the men he struck down with his saber. Not for more than an instant, anyway. That was not long enough to contemplate the fact that they were fathers and sons, husbands and brothers. He guided his horse through the maze of trees and rebels, ordering himself not to think. His saber lifted and fell, parried and thrusted, slicing fabric and flesh, drawing blood and curses and screams until he thought he would be sick. A few moments earlier the woods had been quiet and green and beautiful. Now they were choked with smoke and hatred. In a single, irrevocable moment, the forest had been transformed from a place of life into an arena of death.

And he was responsible.

A rebel charged with murderous fury at his horse, causing Liberty to move backward. A heavy branch slammed into Damien's back, knocking the wind out of him as he was cleared off his mount. He hit the ground with a helpless grunt, struggling to lift his saber. The rebel towered over him and pointed his musket at Damien's head. A shot tore through the air. Damien jerked in reaction. He let out a strangled gasp as the rebel's body fell heavily against him.

"Get up, Damien," shouted Gil, recharging his musket. "You're not dead yet."

Damien shoved the body to one side and scrambled to his feet, strangely unnerved. "Thanks, Gil," he called to his friend. But Gil had already turned his horse to fire at another rebel.

Liberty had moved some two dozen yards away from where Damien had fallen, just beyond the chaos of the battle. He now stood sheltered amidst the trees, waiting for his master to claim him. Light was filtering through the branches and flickering on his slate-dappled coat, giving him the aura of a mythical creature. As Damien rushed toward him, a small, thin soldier wearing a dark blue shirt and trousers burst from the trees ahead and raced toward Liberty. Damien reached into his waist belt and jerked his pistol free. Within seconds it was loaded and pointed at the narrow, homespun-covered back. He was about to pull the trigger when a crippling streak of unease turned his hand to stone. Sensing he was in mortal danger, the rebel spun around, wielding his musket in front of him. The unease pouring through Damien's veins transformed into horror.

He stood face-to-face with Josephine's younger brother, Samuel.

The boy's face contorted into a mask of loathing. *"You!"*

Damien swallowed thickly as he felt the emotionless state he had fought so hard to maintain shatter. He could not kill this boy. He did not even think he could defend himself, should Samuel decide to shoot. Samuel was part of Josephine's world. And there was no cause noble enough, or threat dire enough, to make him perform his duty and murder this boy.

"I will not shoot you, Samuel," he said. "So turn around and run as fast as you can out of this battle. And don't stop running until you are back home, where you belong."

Samuel's boyish, freckled face twisted into a malevolent expression of hatred. His musket remained trained on Damien's belly.

"I have no home, you miserable redcoat bastard." His youthful voice cracked with emotion. "Your friends burned everything to the ground a month ago. That's why I joined this rebel outfit. So I could kill murdering, thieving lobster-backs like you!"

Damien stared at him in shock. "They burned the farm?"

His chest tightened. He had come to think of the farm as an oasis from the war, a place where Josephine could go and be safe. But it was gone. She could not take Emily there after all. A month ago Josephine had been staying at the camp. And then she went home, after the battle at Camden. To find it was no longer there.

"Was anyone hurt?" he demanded.

Samuel laughed, a bitter, derisive sound. "Don't pretend you care, redcoat."

But he *did* care. He was terrified by the possibility that

Anne or Lucy had been harmed. What had Josephine gone home to, that sent her back to the camp so quickly?

"Answer me," he commanded sharply. Then, realizing Samuel had no reason to obey him, he added, "Please."

Samuel hesitated, confused by Damien's concern.

"Anne and Lucy are fine," he finally spat. "They went to Virginia to stay with Anne's parents. And I ran away to join the fight." He raised his musket a little higher, aiming for Damien's chest. The weapon shook, betraying his uncertainty. "Now get ready to die, redcoat."

Damien lowered his pistol. "I will not shoot you, Samuel."

Samuel's blue eyes flashed with anger and frustration, reminding Damien of Josephine. "I hate you!" he screamed.

"Why?" demanded Damien. "Because of my uniform? I didn't burn your farm, Samuel. I saved your life. That day the Indians attacked, I saved all your lives. Remember?"

Samuel's lower lip began to tremble. He bit down on it. "You're still my enemy," he informed Damien bitterly. "I turned you in because you were a redcoat, and today I'll shoot you because you are a redcoat."

"Your sister turned me in," Damien countered.

Samuel shook his head. "Jo tried to stop me. She wanted to protect you. But they told us Elias was dead. I hated you. So I told that rebel captain you were in the barn."

Damien stared at him in shock. All this time he had believed Josephine betrayed him to the rebels. At first he had hated her for it. Eventually he had accepted her betrayal as a consequence of war. But she hadn't betrayed him after all. She had tried to protect him.

Just as he must now protect Samuel.

"Kill me if it makes you feel better, Samuel," Damien offered. He held his arms out in a gesture of submission. "I won't try to stop you. But promise me that after you have done so, you will leave this unit and join Anne in Virginia."

Samuel looked at him as if he were insane. "I don't have to promise you anything." He lifted his sagging musket and clenched his jaw. "Now defend yourself, redcoat."

Damien shook his head. He watched as Samuel's hatred battled his innate sense of right and wrong.

A rustling sound distracted him. He turned to see Gil step out from behind a tree, his musket primed and aimed at Samuel.

"Noooo!" roared Damien. He lunged toward Gil, his arms outstretched to knock the musket from his hands.

Gil looked at Damien in confusion.

Samuel, stricken with panic, pointed his musket at Gil. And fired.

Gil's body jerked, but he remained standing. His eyes grew round with shock. A crimson stain began to form on the scarlet of his coat.

"Jesus Christ, Damien," he murmured, "what the hell did you do that for?"

And then he collapsed heavily onto the ground.

Samuel stared at Gil in horror. All traces of hatred had left his expression, leaving only boyish fear and anguish. He threw down his musket and ran, disappearing into the green and gold light of the forest.

Damien dropped to his knees. "I'm sorry," he managed, his voice raw.

He pulled his friend's head and shoulders into his lap and wrapped one arm around him. Then he opened Gil's jacket. A bright red stain was growing on the snowy fabric of his waistcoat.

"My God, Gil," he whispered, "I am so bloody sorry."

The crack of musket fire mingled with the sickening roar of men fighting and dying around him. Damien tried to block it out as he cradled his bleeding friend.

In that moment, he no longer knew what was right and what was wrong. He no longer knew what his duty was, or to whom he owed that duty. All he knew for certain was that this war was a brutal exercise in futility.

And that he had failed, both as an officer and a friend.

Chapter 17

A warm, blossom-kissed breeze blew softly against her skin, causing wisps of her hair to pull free from its pins and dance in strands of gold against her bare shoulders.

Jo gripped the cool iron balustrade of the balcony and gazed desolately upon the shadowed city of Charles Town. Her corset was squeezing unmercifully into her sides and ribs, and the voluminous layers of her gown, underskirts, hooped petticoat, and underpetticoat made her feel as if she were being buried alive. She tried to quell the nausea that had plagued her these past four days. But the tang of salt and spice mixed with the fetid stench of slops and rotting garbage was revolting. She retreated from the balcony in a swish of silk and raced toward the washstand. Breathing deeply, she poured cool water into the porcelain basin and splashed it on her heated cheeks. The nausea gradually eased, and finally she staggered to a chair and pressed a damp cloth to her forehead.

She did not know how she would make it through the evening.

She was determined to complete her mission tonight. The day Damien had left, she made inquiries about General Cornwallis's whereabouts in the camp, and had been dismayed to learn he had departed for Charles Town the previous evening. That left Jo no choice but to follow him. She had actually been relieved that she would not have to assassinate him at the camp. She didn't think she could bear to see the shocked, condemning faces of Tommy and Lily, Charlie and Oliver, and all the others she had come to think of as friends, if they were to discover what she had done.

The person who would despise her most after tonight was Damien. She wrote him a letter before she left, in a wholly inadequate attempt to beg his forgiveness. She tried to explain why she had to fight for her country, why she could not just sit back and leave the battles to others. She asked him to try to forgive her for all her lies and deceit. And she shamelessly pleaded with him to find it somewhere in his heart to take care of Emily and watch over Tommy.

She had left Emily and Ashley with Lily, pretending it would only be for a few days while she went to visit her family. Jo had no doubt that Lily would take good care of Emily for a short while. But the war could drag on for years, and Emily deserved more than being raised in a tent amidst deprivation and death. Damien had said so himself in his letter. He had the power to send Emily somewhere safe, where she could be cared for, and well fed, and given proper schooling. And when he returned to England, he could take her with him, and see that she had all the things the ward of an earl's son ought to have. She prayed he would be able to put aside his hatred of her for the sake of an innocent child.

She swallowed thickly, gripped with an unbearable sense of loss.

She had arrived at Aunt Hazel's last evening. The elderly woman was surprised to see her, but welcomed her with her usual pragmatism. Jo asked her if it would be safe to resume her role as Celia Reed. According to Aunt Hazel, although there was plenty of talk in the city about rebel spies and their network, nothing had cast a shadow of misgiving on the charming Miss Celia Reed. The clothes Jo had left behind were still there, and her room was untouched.

She could step back into the role she had perfected as if she had never left it.

All she had needed was an invitation to a function where General Cornwallis would be present. As it turned out, the general himself obliged her. After weeks spent at the army camp at Camden, Cornwallis was making the most of his brief sojourn in Charles Town. He was staying at Drayton Hall, a magnificent Palladian home on the banks of the Ashley River, and this evening he was throwing a party for approximately one hundred and fifty guests. As a respected Loyalist matriarch of Charles Town society, Mrs. Hazel Tucker was among the invited, and she was most welcome to bring her lovely niece, Miss Celia Reed, as her guest.

Everything was rapidly falling into place.

Jo planned to wait until the hour had grown late, then draw the general away from the party with the word that she had important information for him concerning the rebel positions in North Carolina. That would whet his curiosity.

The moment they were alone, she would take the knife she had stolen from Hazel's kitchen and bury it in the British general's chest.

She inhaled a deep breath, steeling herself against the fear and guilt that threatened to incapacitate her.

The prospect of brutally stabbing an unsuspecting man chilled her very soul. It would not be murder, she told herself desperately. This was war, and conventional rules of right and wrong could not be applied. With their leader dead, the British troops would be forced to postpone their march into North Carolina. That would enable the rebels to prepare for the British advance. By killing General Cornwallis, hundreds, perhaps thousands, of rebel soldiers might be saved.

And maybe it would be the first step toward bringing this loathsome war to an end.

Once General Cornwallis was dead, she would calmly return to Aunt Hazel's side. Then she would surround herself with a flock of drunken officers who would not have any accurate memory of time. Of course, an investigation would follow. But tomorrow Celia Reed would leave Charles Town for good. Aunt Hazel had no inkling of what Jo intended to do, and she did not believe the redcoats would arrest an elderly, deaf Loyalist woman. If and when they ever deduced that the woman known as Celia Reed had committed the murder, Jo Armstrong would be far away.

The prospect of leaving South Carolina filled her with pain. But her home was gone, and she could never return to the army camp. Fleeing to Virginia to be with Anne and the children, though tempting, was far too dangerous. Once she was out of Charles Town, she would change her appearance and make her way north, toward Washington's Continental Army in New York. If General Cornwallis's assassination did not bring the war to a rapid end, she would join an American army camp, and help the rebels continue their fight against the redcoats.

"Celia dear, are you ready?" called Aunt Hazel from the main floor, her deafness causing her to roar the question as if Jo were a mile away. "The carriage is waiting."

"I'll be right down."

She retrieved her fan from the dresser and gave herself a final, disinterested glance in the mirror. Her gown was an exquisite affair of sapphire silk, intricately embroidered with gold thread. Three layers of creamy lace cascaded from the elbow-length sleeves, and rippling lengths of gold brocade flowed across the overskirt and visible underskirt. The narrow stomacher was decorated with a ladder of soft gold bows, drawing the viewers' attention up and up, leading their eye across the expanse of her bosom to a final delicate bow tied around her throat. Letty had arranged her hair into a mass of curls, in which she had pinned a half-dozen tiny white roses.

It was the same lavish way Celia Reed had dressed when she had been in Charles Town at the beginning of the summer. Yet Jo knew she looked different. Her features had not changed, but there was a hopelessness to her expression that had never been there before.

She turned abruptly from the mirror.

• • •

"Drink this."

Gil lifted his head and swallowed deeply from the flask. Then he groaned and lay back against the ground. "Jesus, that hurts."

"Good," Damien said. "As long as you are in pain, I know you're still alive."

Gil groaned. "A mixed blessing, at this particular moment, I assure you."

"Not to me."

The corners of Gil's mouth lifted in a weak smile. "You can't get rid of me that easily, my friend. I just wish you had told me you weren't in danger. That way I could have spared myself the supreme indignity of being shot by a thirteen-year-old boy. Christ," he muttered irritably, "there's a story I can impress the ladies with."

"You should be glad he was so young," countered Damien. "If he had been older, his aim might have been more accurate."

"Thank you," drawled Gil sourly. "That makes me feel much better."

The ball released from Samuel's musket had struck Gil in the side, carving a deep groove along the base of his rib cage, and removing a portion of bone in the process. But it had not pierced any organs or lodged in his body. He had bled a lot, and was in considerable pain, but he did not appear to be in imminent danger of dying. For this, Damien had repeatedly given God his sincerest thanks. Since there was no surgeon traveling with the Scarlet Legion, Damien had done his best to clean the wound and bandage it tightly so the bleeding would stop. His severely battered legion was now slowly making its way back to the camp, where his wounded men could be properly tended.

The rebels had fought ruthlessly. Ultimately, neither side emerged the victor. A few rebels got close to the wagons to tear the blankets off, thinking to appropriate the weapons. When they realized they were fighting over a pile of rocks and branches, they quickly disappeared back into the forest, collecting their wounded as they went. Both sides suffered heavy casualties, but the skirmish had accomplished nothing. Damien had no doubt within a few days the rebel band would be sufficiently recovered to begin harassing the British troops once again. He had failed in his mission to extinguish them. Realizing his Scarlet Legion was in no condition to go after the rebels, he had ordered his men to bury their dead and head back toward Camden. At this point they were only two hours away, but many of his soldiers were too exhausted to continue. Reluctantly, he had decided to stop for the night.

He glanced at Gil, and saw he had fallen asleep, as had much of the rest of his legion, except those posted to guard duty. He should probably try to do the same, at least for an hour or two. He rose to his feet and moved silently into the woods to relieve himself.

The idea that Josephine was so close was unbearable. From the moment he learned from Samuel that her farm had been burned by British soldiers, unease had been gnawing at his gut. She had lied to him. She had told him everything was well at home, when in fact her home had been destroyed and her family had fled to Virginia. She could have gone after them. But instead she had returned to the camp, to live amongst her enemy, saying she wanted to be with him. Even as she said it he had known it could not be true. But he had accepted it, because he needed her with him. He had watched her settle with apparent contentment into camp life, caring for Emily and tutoring Tommy. He had felt her grow heated and wild in his arms every night, enveloping him in her life and strength and passion. And he had told himself it would be all right. That she would not do anything foolish. That maybe, just maybe, she really was there because she needed him, almost as much as he had come to need her.

He had been a fool.

He believed she had forgone her spying while he was there. But with him gone, there was nothing to stop her from passing information to the rebels about the upcoming invasion of North Carolina, and anything else she thought they might find of interest. In truth, her spying was not what concerned him, although it was treasonous to admit that, even to himself.

What he feared most was that she would be caught.

Something rustled in the woods. He raked the darkness with his gaze, searching for a silhouette amidst the black columns of trees. He saw nothing. He stood a moment, listening. It was probably just an animal, he told himself. He turned to go back to the camp.

Then he heard it again.

Cautiously he began to thread his way deeper into the woods, following the sound. The rustling was soft and persistent, drawing him farther into the darkness, yet not revealing its source. Finally, deciding he was being a complete idiot, he turned to go back.

"Leaving so soon, Colonel Powell?" asked a harsh voice.

His body instantly tensed. Feigning casual indifference, he slowly turned toward the dark figure that had stepped out from behind a tree. "Why, Captain Lee," he said pleasantly, "what an unexpected surprise."

"I'll bet it is," agreed Jackson, his musket leveled on Damien's chest. "Throw down your pistol and saber, redcoat. Now."

Damien did as he was told.

Jackson kicked the weapons out of the way. "You disappoint me, Colonel. I would have thought a senior redcoat officer like you would have more brains than to go off into the woods alone."

"Perhaps I am not alone."

"Oh, but you are. I've been watching your camp for nearly two hours. I know where every guard is posted. The rest of your men are too dead tired to be wandering around looking for you."

He was right, Damien realized, infuriated by his own stupidity. None of his soldiers had any idea where he was at this moment.

"Of course, you could call for help," Jackson allowed. "But you must realize the minute you open your mouth, I'll blast a hole right through you."

Damien suspected Captain Lee intended to do that anyway, regardless of whether he called for help or not. He needed to gain a little time in which the rebel officer grew more relaxed. Then he could find an opportunity to overcome him. "How did you find us?"

An arrogant smile flashed through the darkness. "My men and I have joined up temporarily with Lieutenant Colonel Francis Marion and his men. We are the ones that have been causing you lobsterbacks so much trouble in this area. I see by your attempt to trap us today that we are starting to get under your redcoat skin."

"You have been rather a nuisance," Damien agreed mildly.

"Oh, I'd say we've been more than that," Jackson retorted. "I guessed it was your legion we were fighting today, even though I didn't actually see you. So when Colonel Marion gave the orders for us to withdraw, I decided to separate from them for a while and follow you." He adjusted his musket. "I'm afraid I don't take kindly to prisoners escaping while they are in my custody. It makes me mad."

"Forgive me," Damien said dryly. "I had no idea your temper was so easily pricked. Are you here to arrest me again?"

Jackson shook his head. "I have no desire to have your Scarlet Legion chasing after us. This time, Colonel Powell, I'm afraid I am just going to have to kill you. It's a pity this had to happen now," he mused, sounding almost wistful. "I wanted you to see what your rebel whore has been up to."

Damien kept his expression neutral. "Am I supposed to know whom you are referring to?"

A bitter, knowing laugh sliced the air. "Skip the pretense, Powell. It may disappoint you to learn that Jo Armstrong has been working for me since the day I found you in her barn." He paused, waiting for some kind of reaction. When Damien didn't give him one, he went on, "At first I gave her no choice. It was either spy for me, or be arrested along with her sister-in-law for concealing a redcoat. But later, she agreed to spy voluntarily. And after her farm was burned, she was ready to do anything to help us win this war against you British bastards."

"Really?" Damien remarked. His tone was bland, as if Captain Lee had been relaying a detailed account of the weather. "How perfectly fascinating."

Jackson's eyes narrowed. "I'm glad you think so, Powell," he drawled. "Because that's when I gave her the mission of assassinating your friend General Cornwallis."

His air of indifference disintegrated. "You're lying," he snapped. "She never would accept an assignment like that."

"Oh, but she did," Jackson said, drawing pleasure from Damien's evident anxiety. "Why else do you think she returned to the camp at Camden? Because of you?" He snorted. "Perhaps your bed held some appeal," he admitted. "She shared your tent, yet she never mentioned you in her reports. When I asked her about you, she lied and said she never saw you. But I had sources that told me different." Contempt deepened the lines of his gaunt face. "This war has no room for divided loyalties."

Ice-cold fear poured through Damien's veins. "What have you done to her?" he demanded, his voice low and harsh.

"I haven't done anything. I just told her I would have some men there to help her once she left the camp. However, since she lied to me about you, I realized she didn't deserve any help. After she kills Cornwallis, your redcoat friends will arrest her, and she will be executed. Her death will make her a martyr to the rebel cause. I was hoping you could be there to witness it. Of course, you would have been accused of treason, for harboring a rebel assassin. They would have hanged you, and your illustrious reputation as a daring British officer would have been destroyed. That would have been far more rewarding than just shooting you in the woods. Failing that, I would have preferred to kill you in battle, with lots of witnesses." He adjusted the aim of his musket. "I shall just have to be satisfied with the knowledge that I did it, and forgo the glory of recognition."

"The second you fire, my men will be swarming these woods looking for you."

Jackson gave him an amused look. "You forget this is my home, Powell. These woods are thick and dark. A man could easily lose himself in them. I have the advantage of knowing exactly where I am going, while your redcoats will be stumbling around like blind buffoons, wondering where the hell they are."

"I think they might be rather insulted to hear you say that," Damien remarked.

"I know I'm insulted," declared Charlie loudly. "How about you, Oliver?"

"Bloody outraged," agreed Oliver.

Even in the charcoal light of the forest, Damien could see Captain Lee's expression of triumph vanish. He looked around in helpless fury as a dozen armed soldiers stepped out from the surrounding trees, each aiming his musket directly at him.

"I am sorry to spoil this moment for you," said Damien.

"Not nearly as sorry as I am," Jackson snapped. He tossed his musket to the ground.

Damien bent to retrieve the weapon. "Forgive me, Captain Lee." He motioned to Charlie.

Jackson looked at him warily. "For what?"

Charlie slammed the butt of his musket into the back of Captain Lee's head. The rebel soldier crumpled silently to the ground.

"For that," said Damien.

"What shall we do with him, sir?" asked Charlie. "Take him back with us?"

Damien considered a moment. If they took Captain Lee to the camp, he would derive great pleasure from denouncing Josephine as a spy, and revealing that Damien had always known she was a rebel. Damien could not permit that. He was already concerned that the soldiers who had come to his assistance overheard their conversation. His men were unfailingly loyal to him, but that did not mean they would tolerate the threat of a rebel spy.

Or an assassin.

"Leave him here," Damien ordered, picking up his saber

and pistol. "He isn't worth the risk he poses if we take him with us. We don't want that band of rebels chasing after us because we have one of their officers."

"Yes, sir," said Charlie.

Damien turned and began to quickly head toward the clearing where they were camped. "How did you find me, Beaton?"

"Oliver and I were patrolling the edge of the clearing," Charlie explained. "We saw you go off into the woods. When you didn't return after a few minutes, we wondered what happened to you. So we rounded up a few men and went looking for you."

"Lucky for me that you did.".

"Yes, sir."

Damien was silent for a moment. Then, in a low voice, he asked: "How much of our conversation did you hear?"

Charlie regarded him seriously. "I have been in the Scarlet Legion for three years, Colonel Powell. In that time, I have never known you to do anything that compromised your duty to your men, your army, or your king. Whatever you and that rebel captain were talking about, I'm sure you have the situation well under control. And I believe I speak for all the men, sir."

Damien nodded, moved by his men's loyalty. At this moment he was not certain he was worthy of it.

"Thank you, Beaton." He took a few more steps before adding, "Tell the men to break camp. We are leaving for Camden in ten minutes."

Charlie did not look surprised. "Yes, sir, Colonel."

Damien moved toward Gil to wake him and help him onto his horse. Despite Charlie's assurances, he did not believe he had the situation under control at all. Thank God General Cornwallis was in Charles Town at this moment, he reflected. Whatever Josephine was doing, at least she was not in the process of assassinating the man. In two hours she would be in his arms, and he would know she was safe.

Nevertheless, there was a knot of fear in his belly.

• • •

The air was heavy with the cloying scent of oleander blossoms and sweet perfume, thickened with the fetor of smoky candles and overheated bodies.

It was well after midnight, and a hot supper had been laid out for General Cornwallis's guests. Having been too queasy to eat before she left Aunt Hazel's house, Jo went to the tables to fetch herself a plate of food. The silver serving dishes and porcelain platters were piled high with stewed crabs and scalloped oysters, smothered veal and roasted duck, shrimp pie and rice bread. Her stomach lurched in reaction to the rich, spicy fare and she hurried past, her plate empty. A table of sweets offered teacakes of every variety, jumbles, rusks and macaroons, jellies, tarts, and flavored creams, pies, puddings, and heavy custards, as well as a colorful arrangement of sliced fruits and nuts. She helped herself to a thin slice of orange and moved away.

It was only through the force of will that she had managed to conceal her physical distress for most of the evening. She was performing the role of Celia Reed as if she had been born to it, drawing a circle of smitten officers around her from the moment she arrived. Tonight the Loyalist beauty was at her most captivating, fluttering her fan and batting her lashes, tilting her head back to expose the softness of her throat and breasts, pretending to be appropriately delighted and shocked by every pretentious, witless, inane comment or story the officers inflicted on her.

When the subject turned to war, her self-control was truly magnificent. Especially when the soldiers arrogantly boasted of crushing the rebels and showing them who their masters were. Although not one of her pompous, red-coated admirers had left the pleasures of Charles Town since the beginning of the summer, they congratulated themselves on their overwhelming victory at Camden as if they had led the first assault, and dismissed the rebels' successes at Wateree Ferry and Musgrove Mills as nothing more than luck. When their wine-slurred swaggering became explicit, they would suddenly beg Jo's pardon, assuring her that the horrors of war were not fitting for a lady's ears.

I was there, you driveling idiots, Jo thought acidly, as she fluttered her fan and smiled. *While you were here gorging yourselves on food and women, I was up to my elbows in suffering and blood and death. None of you know the first thing about the horrors of this war.*

And then she would look appropriately distressed and say prettily, "My, how perfectly frightful it all sounds!"

General Cornwallis was an affable host, moving his way around the ballroom and speaking with as many of his guests as possible. He was introduced to Miss Celia Reed by one of her admirers, and Jo immediately claimed a dance with him. At first she feared he might recognize her from the camp. Although she had never met the general before, she had seen him on occasion riding or walking through as he made his way to the tent he occupied when he didn't stay in the town of Camden itself. But General Cornwallis showed not the slightest hint of recognition, and after a moment she relaxed. Even if he had seen her, the elegantly gowned woman dancing gracefully in his arms bore no resemblance to Caroline Skye, camp woman and officer's mistress. After a few minutes of idle banter, Jo leaned closer and whispered that she had urgent information concerning the rebels, which could only be relayed in private. She asked him to meet her alone in the study on the second floor at one o'clock. The general raised a gray eyebrow, studied her a moment, then nodded. The dance came to an end, and Miss Celia Reed was delivered back to her flock of waiting admirers.

It was now a quarter to one, and Jo knew she could not stand the oppressive heat of this crowded room a moment longer. After finishing her dance with Captain Laurence Sterns, the handsome young officer who had introduced Damien to her the last time she was in Charles Town, she excused herself and slipped out of the ballroom. She quickly made her way down the corridor, searching for a place where she could sit and rest a moment before going upstairs to meet General Cornwallis. The door to the library at the end of the hall was slightly ajar. She paused beside it, listening for voices. Hearing none, she cautiously pushed it open and went inside, closing the door behind her.

The air in the darkly paneled library was considerably

cooler than the ballroom, and she breathed deeply as she made her way to the rosewood and silk sofa. She sank down upon it, leaned over her lap and closed her eyes, struggling to overcome the fear churning her stomach. *Just a few more minutes*, she told herself desperately. A few more minutes before she went upstairs and killed the man responsible for leading the redcoats on their brutal rampage through the southern states. The man who commanded butchers like Lieutenant Colonel Banastre Tarleton and Major Nigel Ferguson, and all the other lobsterbacks who had killed her father and Elias and burned her home. She tried not to include Damien among them. Or James Clarke. Or Gil. Or Charlie, or Oliver, or Tommy. They were redcoats, but somehow they were not the same. Or did she not include them simply because she had come to know and like them? She gave herself a mental shake, struggling to remain focused.

One quick, deep thrust of the knife hidden in the layers of her petticoats, and her mission was complete. She could turn around and leave this house, disappearing into the night before anyone knew what had happened. One clean, deep thrust. It would not be murder, she reminded herself fiercely. It was self-defense.

"Well, if it isn't the charming Miss Celia Reed," someone said mockingly.

Jo gasped. Nigel Ferguson stood before her, his thin mouth curled in a predatory smile. He sported a different wig than the one he had worn the night he tried to force himself on her in the garden. This one was far more elaborate, with three rows of fat sausage curls on either side, and two thick plaits at the back. The wig was dressed high, adding at least three inches to his already considerable height, and was thickly powdered to a pasty white. Some of the powder had sifted onto the scarlet cloth of his coat, giving the unpleasant impression that he suffered from a flaking scalp.

This was the man who had led the savage attack on that rebel plantation, she realized, thinking back to her conversation with Gil. The man who had allowed a baby to be cut from its womb because the woman was a rebel.

Horror and loathing flooded through her.

"Major Ferguson," she said frigidly. She recovered enough to snap open her fan and flutter it impatiently over her bosom, making it clear his presence was unwelcome.

"I hope I am not disturbing you," he remarked, his tone dry. "I notice you have been away from Charles Town for some time."

"I went home for a while," Jo replied tersely. "I have only just returned."

He lifted a skeptical brow. "Really? How pleasant for your family. Where is your home located?"

"Bellewood is some distance north of here, Major," she answered coolly, "on the banks of the Pee Dee River."

"Is that so?" He appeared to contemplate this for a moment and then shook his head. "Isn't that strange. I have ridden extensively through that particular area of this colony, and I am not familiar with your plantation."

"South Carolina has many beautiful homes. No one could be expected to be acquainted with all of them." She began to rise. "If you will excuse me—"

"Tell me, Miss Reed, is it your habit to work in the fields when you are home?"

His question caught her off guard. "I beg your pardon?"

"I could not help but notice you are rather darkly tanned." His gaze raked over her. "Your face, your shoulders, why, even your arms. Rather unfashionable for a lady of society, isn't it?"

He was right, she realized. The long hours of working outdoors at Camden had turned her skin a golden brown, which was decidedly unacceptable for a lady of wealth.

"When I am at Bellewood, I am a devoted gardener," she said crisply. "And unlike the ladies of Charles Town, I enjoy the sun. Good evening, Major Ferguson." She headed toward the door.

"How is your gallant friend, Colonel Powell?"

She stopped abruptly and turned to face him. His accusing tone was making her uneasy, but she could not afford to let him see that. "I have no idea. I have not seen Colonel Powell since the night we met at the Manchesters' ball."

His brows lifted in mock surprise. "Is that so?"

He knew something, Jo realized. She struggled to keep her expression entirely bland. "Yes."

Nigel casually seated himself on the sofa. "My duties in Charles Town permit me to peruse all reports of arrests. Back in July, a Corporal Andrew Dowland arrested two rebel spies at a warehouse on the wharves along the Cooper River. His report indicated that Lieutenant Colonel Damien Powell was actually responsible for the capture of the rebels. Interestingly, the report also mentioned there was a rather effeminate young man in Colonel Powell's company. A man of small stature, with smooth skin and striking blue eyes."

Jo managed a light, thoroughly amused laugh. "Are you insinuating that I was wandering about the wharves in a coat and breeches, helping Colonel Powell arrest rebels?" She fluttered her fan over her bosom and laughed again, as if she had never heard anything so outrageous.

"Well, I must admit, my curiosity was piqued. As you may know, Colonel Powell and I have a rather unfortunate history. Consequently, I find myself somewhat fascinated by any reports that concern him. So I went down to the Exchange building, where these rebel prisoners were being kept, and I had a little talk with them. A Mr. Elliott . . ."—he paused, as if searching his memory—"and a man by the name of Lucas."

Fear surged within her.

"They told me an interesting story," Nigel went on. "They told me the young man who was there was actually a woman, and a rebel spy. But it seems her loyalty became confused when it appeared Colonel Powell was about to be killed. This had the unfortunate effect of causing Powell to fail to arrest her, which was, of course, a blatant disregard of his duty." His brown eyes narrowed into slits. "Fascinating, don't you think?"

The clock on the mantel struck one. Her heart lurched. It was time for her to meet General Cornwallis.

She pretended to stifle a ladylike yawn behind her fan.

"Forgive me, Major Ferguson. I am certain this story is of interest to you, but since I barely know Colonel Powell, I am afraid I do not find it nearly so intriguing. Good night." She turned and made her way toward the door with a loud rustle of her skirts.

He knows, she thought desperately as she hurried along the corridor. Just how much he knew, she wasn't certain. Obviously not enough to arrest her. But enough to make him extremely suspicious. Which meant when General Cornwallis's body was found, Nigel would be the first to point an accusatory finger at her. She should not go through with her mission. But she had no choice, she realized helplessly as she lifted the hem of her skirts and mounted the stairs. Everything was in place. If she canceled her plans tonight, she might never have the opportunity to be alone with General Cornwallis again. She must complete her mission now, or abandon it completely. And she could not abandon it. Not when her beloved country was in such pain. Not when this war was killing so many, and she could do something to help bring it to an end. She reached down and rifled through the layers of her gown, searching for the knife. She extracted the blade from the fabric sheath she had stitched into one of her petticoats. Then she inhaled a deep, determined breath and rapped softly on the study door.

"Come in."

Concealing the knife in the silk folds of her skirts, she entered the room. General Cornwallis stood with his back to her, contemplating the ink wash of the night sky through a window. He was a man of considerable stature, his girth betraying an exceptional fondness for food.

He looked at her briefly before returning his stare to the charcoal depths of the window. "Do you think the party is a success, Miss Reed?" he asked quietly.

His tentative question surprised her. He seemed uncertain of his abilities as a host.

"Why, yes, my lord. Everyone appears to be having a wonderful time."

He was silent a moment, considering this. "I am afraid I

have little taste for these formal affairs. When I first became earl, I felt bound to attend the balls and masquerades of my neighbors. But when I married, my wife and I found we preferred the peace and quiet of our home in the country to tearing about attending noisy, crowded social affairs with people we barely knew and often didn't care for."

Jo felt the cool handle of the knife grow warm in her palm. The idea that General Cornwallis felt the same way about these parties as she did was strangely disconcerting. She tightened her grip and tried to think of something to say.

"Is your wife at home in England?" *While you are here making war in my country*, she thought bitterly.

"She passed away last year." His voice was excessively gruff, perhaps to mask his pain.

Her acrimony toward him instantly lessened. "I am sorry," she murmured softly.

He continued to stare out the window, apparently absorbed in melancholy thought. "Jemima," he offered, seeking to fill the silence. "That was her name."

Now was the moment to do it, Jo realized. His back was to her. He was entirely unsuspecting. She could close the space between them and have her knife buried deep in his back before he knew what was happening. Then she would slip out of the house. She could not return to the ballroom, not with Nigel Ferguson ready to accuse her in front of everyone. Instead she would flee out the door, down the steps, into the garden. Then she would steal a horse from the stables. She would be far away before anyone realized General Cornwallis was missing. Before they discovered him lying in a pool of blood with a knife protruding from his back.

Why, then, did she hesitate?

"She left me two young children," General Cornwallis continued. "A boy and a girl. When their mother fell ill, I resigned my command in the colonies and went home. I thought I could nurse her back to health. But it was too late." He shook his head, as if condemning himself for his failure to save his wife.

"After she died, I could not stay in England. I could not

bear to be in my own home without her. And so I returned here."

She did not want to hear this. Why was he so intent on telling her? she wondered frantically. Now he was no longer simply a military leader in charge of war and death, he was also a grieving husband and father, for whom the war was a form of escape. As it had been to Damien. It was a cold refuge of military planning and strategy and battle. Of late nights and early mornings, and long days packed with drilling, and marching, and leading men who depended upon their leadership. Only this kind of relentless, exhausting activity, combined with the awesome responsibility of deciding when and where to risk men's lives, could distract a man from the agony of losing his beloved wife.

She did not feel sorry for him, she reminded herself harshly. She hated him. She forced herself to think of the horrendous atrocities the redcoats had committed. She thought of the battles and raids, and of the deaths of her father and Elias. She thought of her beautiful farm, reduced to a pitiful black grave of ashes. She thought of the cherished homes looted and destroyed, the brave men maimed and killed, the helpless women terrorized and raped. Most of all, she thought of all the wasted years spent fighting and killing and hating, and of all the years still to come. *It has to end*, she told herself numbly as she moved toward him.

General Cornwallis continued to stare out the window, oblivious to her approach. She didn't hate him, she realized miserably. She hated the war. Her bloodless fingers gripped the knife with helpless desperation.

Somehow, someone has to bring this horrible war to an end.

Her throat closed with revulsion, and tears stung her eyes.

And the rebels must win. There can be no other outcome.

She raised her trembling arm.

"That's far enough, Miss Reed," said a sneering voice from the doorway. "Or should I say, Miss Skye?"

Jo gasped and spun around, the knife still clutched in her hand. Nigel stepped into the room, brandishing a pistol.

His thin lips were split in an ugly smile, revealing his delight at finding her in this situation.

"Drop your weapon," he ordered.

The knife clattered loudly against the polished wood surface of the floor.

"My God, you really intended to do it, didn't you?" General Cornwallis exclaimed, looking at the silver blade in astonishment. "Major Ferguson told me you were not to be trusted. He warned me there was evidence you were working for the rebels. That was why I told him of our arranged meeting, and asked him to stay near. But my God, I never dreamed you actually meant to *kill* me."

"This is war, my lord," Jo said stonily, fighting to control the emotions raging through her. "We are fighting to win. Killing you is part of the battle. Nothing more."

General Cornwallis looked outraged. "This it not a battlefield, young woman. This is my study, *in my house!*" His face was nearly purple with fury.

"It is *not* your house," Jo flung back. "This is Drayton Hall. You *stole* this property. Your house is in England, where your two children are. And if I sailed across the sea and attacked England, and killed your father and brother, and terrorized your children, and burned your home to the ground and drove you off the land on which you had been born, *you might well want to put a knife in me!*" She was shouting with rage and hatred, exacerbated by an unbearable sense of failure.

General Cornwallis stared at her in slack-jawed amazement. Jo glared back at him, unwilling to feel guilty for fighting for her country. Nevertheless, she had to bite down hard on her lower lip to keep it from trembling.

"You are right," he admitted finally, sounding weary and somewhat sad. "You are absolutely right."

His gentle agreement made her want to cry. She clenched down hard on her jaw and stared at the silver shimmer of the knife instead.

"I am afraid I have to arrest you." His tone was soft, almost apologetic. "I really have no choice in the matter."

Jo nodded. She did not trust herself to speak for fear of betraying her desolation.

"Where shall I take her?" Nigel demanded. "To the prison below the Exchange?"

"God, no," General Cornwallis replied quickly. "Her presence there would incite a riot." He thought for a moment. "We must keep her here until a trial can be arranged. She can stay in one of the bedrooms. Post two guards to her door, two at the base of the staircase, and two outside the front and back doors. She is to be given everything she needs, but can have no visitors without my direct authority."

"Very good, sir," said Nigel. "I will see to it personally." He cast Jo a perversely satisfied smile. It was obvious he was enjoying this moment to the utmost. "After you, Miss Reed," he drawled sarcastically. He gestured with his pistol toward the door.

Calling upon every shred of her swiftly crumbling composure, Jo straightened and began to walk toward the door.

"Miss Reed," called General Cornwallis.

She stopped and turned to look at him.

The general's face was lined with dread. "Are you the same woman the soldiers at Camden know as Caroline Skye?"

It appeared Nigel had done his research on Damien. She nodded stiffly. "I am."

His expression grew haunted. "Did Colonel Powell know of your rebel activities?"

"No," she said emphatically. "He believed I was a Loyalist. He had no idea whatsoever. I fooled him, just like I fooled everyone else."

"I see." His relief was obvious. Then he looked puzzled. "What is your real name?"

She lifted her chin. "My name is Jo Armstrong. My father was John Armstrong, who fought with the Continental Army. He died in the Battle of Brooklyn Heights in seventy-six. My brother Elias fought with the Continental cavalry. He was killed at Waxhaws Creek in May of this year. And right now my brothers Abraham and Benjamin are fighting under the command of General George Washington. We are all fighters, General Cornwallis," she declared with solemn dignity. "And we are going to win."

General Cornwallis regarded her with respect and regret shadowing his features. He gave a little bow. "I am honored to meet you, Miss Armstrong. Deeply honored."

Jo looked at him in surprise.

And then she turned away, before revealing to the general that she was not nearly as strong as she pretended to be.

Chapter 18

His fingers clumsy with impatience and dread, Damien tore open the letter Josephine had left for him in his tent.

Damien,

When you discover what I have done, you will hate me with a passion I cannot bear to contemplate. You will think I lied to you, and used you, and betrayed you.

And you will be right.

Please try to understand. This war has robbed me of my father, my brother, and my home, and it is long from being over. I cannot sit back and leave the battles to others. My life is being destroyed as my country bleeds, and I must do everything I can to fight back. Perhaps, in this terrible, enraged moment, as you condemn me for betraying you, you cannot understand this. I pray that one day you will.

All I ask is that you find it somewhere in your heart to care for Emily. I know this is an enormous request, which I do not have the right to make. But she has no one, and you yourself said she deserves more than a life of battle and death. You have the

power to keep her safe, and give her a life filled with hope. Please,
Damien, please don't abandon her. She is a tiny, helpless flame
against the darkness of war, and she must be protected. I also ask
that you look after Tommy. His respect for you knows no bounds.
Please teach him to read and write and ride, and show him that
a man with one hand is of no lesser value than a man with two.

You and I are enemies. That has always been clear. And yet,
somehow you have become a part of me, and I cannot hurt you
without suffering myself. I know you will never be able to forgive
me for what I am about to do. It is your pain and loathing, more
than anything, that shatters my heart.

I leave you now to perform my duty. If I am caught, it is
certain I will be executed. It does not matter.

I died today, the moment I was forced to choose between my
country, and you.

Josephine

Fear, black, paralyzing, and unbearable, tore through him as
Damien absorbed the meaning of the letter. Not anger or
loathing or rage, as Josephine had so despairingly anticipated. Not even a sense of betrayal. All that consumed him
in this moment was the gut-wrenching torment of knowing
she was in danger, and that he was too far away to protect
her. Charles Town. That was where she had gone. She had
discovered General Cornwallis was there, and she had followed him. To kill him. A miserable, horrified laugh escaped his throat. Josephine had never been lacking in sheer
audacity, he reflected grimly. Or blind courage. It was these
qualities that had first drawn him to her.

And now they would get her killed.

He jammed the letter in his pocket, burning with the
need to take action. Charles Town was over seventy-five
miles from here. It was the middle of the night. By starting
out now, pacing his horse well, and stopping only when he
had to, he should be able to get there in a day and a half.
If he reached her in time all he had to do was get her the
hell out of there. If she had attempted her mission and escaped, he would find her. Then he would send her far away,
somewhere safe. He would ship her all the way to goddamn

England if necessary, and hide her at Waverley until this bloody war was over.

He would not consider the possibility that she had been caught.

"Colonel Powell? Are you in there?"

Lily's voice jolted him from his thoughts. "Come in."

She entered the tent, carrying Emily in one arm. Tommy moved in behind her, looking grave.

"We're sorry to bother you, sir," Lily began hesitantly. "It's just that—" She paused, searching for the right words. Finally she blurted out, "Well, sir, we were wonderin' if you would tell us what has happened to our Caroline."

Our Caroline, thought Damien. Josephine had made friends among her enemies, despite herself.

"We know she is in trouble, sir," Tommy said anxiously. "That story she gave us about goin' home, well, we knew she was lyin'. She would never have left Emily unless she had to. Never." He gave Damien a searching look. "We figure you must know what happened to her."

Damien regarded their expectant faces with uncertainty. What the hell could he tell them? That they had become friends with a rebel spy, who was currently in the process of trying to murder the commander of the entire British southern army?

"The thing is, Colonel Powell, sir," continued Lily, "if she is in trouble, me and Tommy want to help her. It doesn't matter to us what kind of trouble she is in, sir, if you take my meanin'." The inference in her voice was unmistakable. "We don't really care. We will do anything to see she doesn't come to harm."

"Anything," Tommy said fiercely.

Damien was surprised and humbled by their devotion to Josephine. For both Lily and Tommy, the army was their home and family. Yet here they were, risking everything in their desire to help Josephine. Despite their opposing loyalties and interests, a bond had formed between them that was infinitely stronger and more enduring than the allegiances of war. It was a bond of friendship, and respect, and caring.

And perhaps even love.

"You will tell us, sir, won't you?" Tommy asked uneasily.

Damien considered a long moment. If Josephine had not yet attempted her assassination, then it was useless to drag Lily and Tommy all the way to Charles Town. But if she had been arrested, and imprisoned, breaking her free was going to be almost impossible.

Little Emily began to cry. Damien stared at the child as Lily tried in vain to soothe her. The baby's tiny face grew pinched and red, and he found it impossible to think as her high-pitched screaming filled the tent.

Suddenly an idea occurred to him, and he smiled.

"She is to be tried the day after tomorrow."

It was the afternoon of the following day. Damien was standing in General Cornwallis's study, covered in dust and grime from hours spent in the saddle. He had not bothered to wash or change before coming here. As soon as he reached his customary residence on Bay Street, he had been informed by Captain Laurence Sterns of Charles Town's latest shocking news. The charming and vivacious Miss Celia Reed was actually a rebel spy named Jo Armstrong, who had tried to assassinate General Cornwallis the night of his party.

"You cannot hang her for being a spy," Damien informed his commander tautly. "The inhabitants of Charles Town will riot if you do. You must grant her clemency."

"Have you lost your mind, Colonel Powell?" General Cornwallis sputtered. "I realize you had a relationship with this woman, but for God's sake, she tried to murder a general in the British army!"

"You weren't hurt," Damien observed.

"That is entirely beside the point," General Cornwallis replied sharply. He sighed. "Perhaps she won't be sentenced to death," he allowed. "I don't particularly relish the outcry if we execute a woman, rebel assassin or not. I could arrange to have her imprisoned instead. Maybe in England, where she won't be seen as a martyr."

Damien tried to imagine Josephine torn from the land

she loved and locked in a dark, foul cell for years on end. Trapped in a tiny room where she would never see the sun, or sky, or endless miles of open green countryside around her.

They might as well kill her and be done with it.

"I am sorry you are involved in this, Colonel Powell," General Cornwallis said. "Miss Armstrong has assured me that you knew nothing of her association with the rebels, and I have decided to take her at her word. Normally an investigation would follow, but given your stellar record and your numerous successes with the Scarlet Legion, I have decided to forgo it. Besides, I need you to return with me to Camden immediately. Our invasion into North Carolina cannot be delayed by this most unfortunate event."

"I won't be going with you to North Carolina, sir."

General Cornwallis frowned. "What nonsense is this?"

"I have decided to submit my resignation, sir. I have recently learned that my brother is dead, and the title of Earl of Strathmore is now mine. I wish to go home and assume my responsibilities there."

"I am afraid that is impossible, Colonel Powell," General Cornwallis returned flatly. "You are one of my finest officers, and at this moment, you are needed here. Perhaps a special leave can be arranged once we have secured North Carolina. Is there anything else?"

Damien nodded. He had not expected General Cornwallis to accept his resignation, but it was important to him that he offer it all the same. Somehow the gesture of resigning his command slightly mitigated the supreme act of treason he was about to commit.

"I wish permission to see Miss Armstrong, sir. I have brought two of her friends from the camp with me, and the child she cared for. They wish to say good-bye."

"Permission granted."

"Thank you, sir." He gave the general a stiff bow before turning to leave.

"Colonel Powell."

Damien turned. "Sir?"

"I can see why you were so captivated by her," General

Cornwallis said. "She is obviously a woman of remarkable courage and determination, to say nothing of her beauty." He shook his head regretfully. "But this is war, Colonel. And in war, ugly decisions have to be made. Decisions that go against one's moral sense of right and wrong."

"I know," Damien replied quietly. "And I am weary of it."

He bowed once again and quit the room, feeling strangely detached as he left the last three years of his life behind him.

Jo pressed her hand against the windowpane and watched Damien ride away.

She wanted to cry out to him, to beg him to come back. She wanted to plead with him to forgive her. Most of all, in that agonizing moment, she wanted to feel his arms around her one last time, before she was sentenced to death. Instead she watched him in wretched silence. And when his scarlet-coated form disappeared behind a curtain of trees, she leaned her head against the smooth sheet of glass and ordered herself not to cry.

He had obviously come to confirm that she had indeed tried to kill General Cornwallis. And then, overwhelmed with fury and revulsion, he had chosen to not even see her, but simply to ride away. What else could she have expected? she wondered bitterly.

Hot tears welled in her eyes as she drew a shaky, strangled breath. She had been wrong, she realized. She thought she had died the day she left the camp.

She had not known what death truly was until this moment.

Rain drops covered the windowpanes like shimmering black jewels. Damien leaned back in his chair and took a hefty swallow of brandy as he contemplated the wet squares of glass.

In his mind he was on a ship sailing across the ocean, away from this war-torn country, back to the peaceful serenity of Waverley. It was his home now. He pictured himself wandering through the endless dark-paneled hallways and vast, magnificent rooms, playing the role of Lord Strathmore. Josephine's arm was linked with his as he proudly led her through her new home. The charming new Countess of Strathmore was suitably awed and delighted by the grandeur and ostentation, the exquisite furniture and paintings and sculptures, the priceless silver and china and crystal. She was outfitted in the very latest of fashions, which she had developed quite a passion for, and was covered in a tasteful array of glittering jewels. Like most women, his frivolous new wife was hopelessly addicted to diamonds.

He laughed aloud, nearly spilling his drink.

She would die if he took her there, he reflected soberly. Not all at once, but by slow, agonizing degrees as she struggled to adjust to the suffocating life she would be expected to lead. A life of rules and propriety and worrying about ridiculous, meaningless things. Surreptitiously scorned by a rigid society that would never forgive her for being a colonist, a farm girl, and worst of all, a rebel. She would be examined for her pedigree, and found horribly lacking. The daughter of a convicted murderer and a penniless bonded servant. And all this before they eventually unearthed the fact that she was the spy who had attempted to kill General Cornwallis.

Even if her past was never revealed, she could never be happy in England, he realized. Josephine was too wild and free, too strong and independent and true to herself to ever be able to conform to the stifling life of a countess. More than that, she was inextricably bound to the land she was fighting so hard for. To its rugged beauty, its freedom, its vast open spaces and uncharted future. Then of course there was her family, whom she loved beyond life itself and would never consider leaving. America was part of Josephine's blood and bone and soul. He could never take her away from here. Never.

He took another swallow of brandy.

Waverley was all he had ever wanted. Waverley and Victoria. And now he suddenly had both, God help him. And he was going to give them up. The loss of Victoria didn't bother him a whit. But the knowledge that he would never see his beloved home again slashed deep into his heart. After tomorrow, he would lose everything. By rescuing Josephine, he was openly betraying his duty to his king and country. Treason was a crime considered more heinous than murder. His brilliant military career as an officer of the British army, which he had labored so hard to build, would lie in shameful ruins. This time tomorrow evening, the eminent Lieutenant Colonel Damien Powell would be a traitor to his men, his army, and his country. And a wanted criminal in the eyes of British law. He would never be able to return to England and assume his fortune and privileges as the Earl of Strathmore. He would never see his magnificent home again. He would spend the rest of his days under another identity, hunted and despised and disgraced.

And alone.

That by far was the wound that cut the deepest. Because he would gladly give up a thousand earldoms if it meant he could spend the rest of his life with Josephine. But she would never be his. The lines between them were distinctly drawn, and there was nothing he could do to change that. *We are enemies*, she had written in her letter. He was British, he was a redcoat, and worst of all, he was the officer who had led the Scarlet Legion into countless battles and raids against her countrymen. The blood of her fellow Patriots was on his hands. It did not matter that he was heartily sick of it, and would never lift his sword against a rebel again. Josephine hated everything he represented. There was no doubt a bond between them existed. But in the years to come, she would never be able to forgive him for killing her countrymen. Men like her father and brother. How could she absolve him of that? And if a choice had to be made, she would always choose her country. She had made that clear in her letter. She would fight this war until the Americans won, or die in the effort. And although Damien was about to commit a monumental act of treason, he could not change sides and fight his own men. Regardless of his increasing sympathies for the American cause, he would not be a turncoat.

He would simply bow out of this war altogether.

He took another swallow of brandy and stared into the black, rain-drenched world outside. Josephine once risked her life to care for him so he would live. Now he would sacrifice everything he had for her. He was betraying his king, his country, and his men to save her, and let her go. It did not matter.

He would be betraying his heart and his soul if he did not.

Chapter 19

Darkness drifted across her room in gloomy shadows, bringing her another day closer to her trial.

Jo lay back against the bed and stared vacantly at the foamy swirl of netting frothing above her. She hoped tomorrow she would be sentenced to death, so she would not be forced to endure the pain of Damien's hatred a moment longer. If they put her in prison, she would never escape the terrible guilt gnawing away at her, and she knew she could not bear that. She was strong, but nothing had prepared her for the emotions churning through her, stripping her of her ability to remain composed as she awaited her fate.

For the first time in her life, she truly wanted to die.

She realized her feelings were cowardly and weak. But somehow she didn't care. Ever since she could remember, someone had relied upon her to be strong. From the moment her mother died, she had carried the welfare of others on her shoulders. First there had been Lucy and Samuel to care for, and her father and other brothers to worry about. And then, one by one, the men of the Armstrong family abandoned her as they went to fight in this wretched war.

Each one instructing her as they left to look after the family. Benjamin had only added to her worries by bringing Anne home to live with her, and getting her with child before he left. The poor girl had been so weak with sickness and dizziness those first few months, she could barely rise from her bed, forcing Jo to assume the duty of nursemaid on top of everything else.

A wave of nausea swept over her, illustrating what Anne had been forced to endure with dizzying accuracy. Jo pinned her gaze on the crown of netting above her and inhaled deeply as she struggled to overcome it. After a few moments it finally passed, leaving her limp and exhausted.

Her erratic physical condition was keeping her from being strong. That was why she constantly felt like weeping. If she were feeling better, she would be able to carry herself with the same hardened contempt she had always felt toward the redcoats. Instead she felt strangely fragile and weak, like a small child who needed to be cared for and consoled. Hardly the stuff of which a dangerous rebel spy was made, she thought bleakly.

She hoped she would not disgrace herself with tears at her trial tomorrow.

Her greatest concern was for everyone she had left behind. Anne, Lucy and Samuel were with Anne's family in Virginia, safe only until General Cornwallis's army moved north. Benjamin and Abraham were still fighting in the north. She realized they could be dead, but somehow she believed they were not. Emily was being cared for by Lily, but living in an army camp was no life for an infant. Tommy's battered spirits had been healing while Jo was at the camp, but she feared when he learned she was a rebel spy, he would feel so betrayed he would give up his lessons and his riding.

Then there was Damien. She took heart in the fact that General Cornwallis seemed to believe her assurances that Damien had not known she was a rebel spy. Damien was one of the general's favorite officers, and obviously Cornwallis wanted to believe her. She could see it in his haunted expression. She was not nearly so certain, however, that

Nigel Ferguson believed her. Nigel loathed Damien for exposing his despicable methods of warfare. She feared he would do whatever he could to destroy Damien's career, in an attempt to exonerate himself and have his vengeance on Damien.

Beyond that, she was tortured by the thought that Damien would carry his hatred of her with him for the rest of his life. She had used him and flung his love back in his face for the sake of her country. She could not blame him for hating her.

The muffled beat of footsteps sounded against the carpet in the hallway, growing louder as they approached her door. She drew back the netting and rose from the bed, hastily straightening the wrinkled folds of her sapphire and gold gown. Hazel Tucker had played the role of the thoroughly duped aunt well, claiming she had not laid eyes upon her niece since she was a child, and had no reason to think the woman claiming to be Miss Celia Reed was an impostor. After a lengthy questioning, her story was accepted, partly because the redcoats could not believe such a deaf and dotty old woman could be seriously involved in a rebel plot to kill General Cornwallis. The good woman had kindly sent Jo a nightshift and some fresh stockings, but had not thought to send her a day outfit. Consequently, Jo was forced to wear the elegant gown she had put on for the ball.

A key scraped in the lock and the door swung open, spilling a wash of amber light into the shadowed room.

"You have visitors, Miss Armstrong," announced the guard. He stepped to one side, revealing a trio of figures in the doorway. He ushered them in, then went to retrieve a candle from the hall.

Jo felt her heart swell with an unbearable mixture of elation and despair. Standing in the soft, charcoal light, staring at her with grave calm, were Tommy, Lily, and Damien. A silent bundle was wrapped in Lily's arms, which Jo knew had to be Emily. They had come to see her. To condemn her or forgive her, she did not know. All she knew was her heart was torn in two at the sight of them. She wanted to race across the room and wrap her arms around them all, to hold them close and feel their warmth and friendship for the last time.

The fear they would reject her kept her rooted to the spot.

The guard finished lighting the candelabra on the writing desk. "Just knock on the door when you want to leave," he instructed Damien. The door closed, and the key turned the lock once more.

Jo stared at them numbly. She needed to beg their forgiveness. That much was clear. But the words and explanations that came to mind seemed wholly inadequate in this hushed, expectant moment.

"I am sorry," she finally managed. Her eyes lifted to Damien, wide and pleading. "I tried, Damien." The force of his hatred was overwhelming now that he was in the room with her. "I tried to leave the war to the soldiers. But I hated the redcoats for what they did to my family. And I had to do something, *anything*, to help bring it to an end." She drew a deep, shaky breath.

"You imprisoned me," she told him in a raw whisper. "Every time you touched me. Until finally I could not bear it anymore. Not when I knew it was so wrong. Not when I knew we were enemies, and always would be." Tears began to trickle down her face. She angrily brushed at them with her hands, not wanting to appear weak as she faced the man she had betrayed.

"You despise me now. I know that. But I beg you to find it in your heart to take care of Emily. Take her away from all this fighting and death. It doesn't matter what happens to me." She regarded him with naked despair. "Nothing they do can hurt me any more than the agony of having you hate me." She wrapped her arms around herself and sank to her knees in a crumpled cloud of sapphire silk. Then she began to rock back and forth, her head bent, weeping openly.

Damien stepped forward and knelt down in front of her. He gently took her chin in his hand, tilting her head up until she was forced to look at him. Her sky-blue eyes were shimmering with pain. Suddenly he saw what she had not allowed him to see before. She loved him. It no longer mattered to her that they were enemies. She had forgiven him for the color of his uniform. A raw, exhilarating burst of joy exploded within him, so overwhelming he wanted to weep.

"Promise me something, Josephine," he demanded, his voice low and ragged. She stared at him, mesmerized, as he caressed her shimmering cheek with the back of his fingers. "Promise me that after I get you out of here, you will *never* leave me again. Because if I ever find myself condemned to live the rest of my life without you," he continued roughly, bending his head until his lips hovered barely a breath over hers, "I will surely die."

He crushed her in his arms as he ground his mouth against hers, kissing her with desperate possessiveness. Jo wrapped her arms around his neck, clinging to him in joy as he pulled her from the vortex of her despair. Finally, realizing that time was quickly seeping away, Damien broke the kiss.

"Listen to me, Josephine," he said urgently. "We are going to get you out of here. But you must do exactly as I say—do you understand? Take off your gown and give it to Lily," he ordered, pulling her to her feet. "Lily, give Emily to Tommy while you exchange clothes with Josephine. Tommy, wake Emily and see that she starts to cry. Everybody *move*."

His voice bore the calm authority of years of commanding men in the heat of battle. Lily immediately began to undress, and Jo began to remove her gown. Her hands were awkward and fumbling. Suddenly she felt Damien's fingers working expertly on the tiny fastenings. Within three minutes she was wearing Lily's plain gray work dress and heavy brown cloak, while Lily was lost somewhere within the sapphire folds of her enormous evening gown. Meanwhile, Tommy had given Emily a little pinch, waking her up and making her begin to squall.

"Tie this scarf around your head." Damien handed Jo a length of gray cotton that Lily had been wearing. "Hide your hair, then pull up the hood of the cloak so it shadows your face."

Jo did as she was told while Damien went over to assist Lily with her hooks.

"Sweet Lord, Colonel, you're killin' me!" gasped Lily as Damien firmly closed her tight-fitting bodice.

"Pull in your stomach and take tiny breaths," advised Jo, coming over to assist.

"With all the fabric that's in this skirt, you'd think they could have been a little more generous with the top," Lily grumbled.

"What about her hair?" Jo asked, looking worriedly at Lily's chestnut length.

"It won't matter in the dark," Damien assured her. "If anyone comes in here with a light, they will quickly discover she isn't you. Tommy, have you got the rope?"

"Right here." Tommy handed Emily to Jo so he could fish the ropes out of his coat pocket.

"Hush, my darling," she cooed, rocking Emily gently against her. "It's all right."

"Don't soothe her," Damien ordered curtly. "I want her screaming as loud as she can."

Sensing his anger, Emily began to scream even louder.

"All right, Lily, get on the bed and I'll tie your wrists and ankles," Damien said.

Hindered by the suffocating constraints of her elegant gown, Lily began to awkwardly move toward the bed, taking tiny, cautious breaths.

"Lily," Jo called.

Jo went to her friend, wrapped one arm tightly around her, and tenderly kissed her cheek. "Thank you."

Lily sniffed loudly. "I'll never forget you, Josephine Armstrong," she promised fervently. "I don't care what side of the war you're on. You were always a true friend to me and Alice. You watched out for me, and worried about me. And this bloody war has nothin' to do with our friendship."

"What will happen when they discover you aren't me?" Jo asked, worried.

"Why, I'll just tell them the truth," Lily replied with an innocent smile. "I'll tell them how Colonel Powell asked me to come to Charles Town with the baby so you could see the poor little thing one last time. And how when we got in here, the colonel pointed his pistol at me and forced me to change clothes with you. And then he bound me and gagged me, and left me helpless on the bed while you made your escape."

"Just in case they aren't convinced, I am leaving a letter here accepting full responsibility for the escape," Damien said, withdrawing an envelope from his coat pocket. "In which I confirm that neither Lily nor Tommy had any knowledge of my intentions before coming here. I can assure you, they will be far more interested in finding us than trying to blame poor Lily, who will be seen by all of Charles Town as a helpless victim." He tossed the note onto the desk. "Are you ready, Lily?"

Lily climbed awkwardly onto the bed, and Damien bound her wrists and ankles.

"I'm expecting you to find me when the war is over," Lily remarked cheerfully. "I just might be Mrs. Oliver Yorke by then." She gave Jo a wink.

"I will," Jo promised.

Damien gently stuffed a clean handkerchief in Lily's mouth. Then he turned her over so that she was facing the wall, and covered her with a sheet. "Make your story convincing, Lily," he ordered as he drew the mosquito netting around her. "I don't want to have to come back and rescue you as well."

Lily mumbled something unintelligible in return.

"Ready?" demanded Damien, looking at Tommy and Jo. They nodded.

"Then keep Emily crying." He doused all but one candle on the writing desk, plunging the room into near darkness. Then he strode across the room and banged on the door.

The key turned in the lock. Emily had begun to settle, so Jo gave her a little pinch, sending her back into a high-pitched wail.

"God save me from screaming infants," Damien growled as the door swung open. "We are ready to leave," he informed the guards, his voice raised to compete with Emily's crying.

The guard who had let them in grimaced at the shrieking coming from Emily. He looked beyond Damien into the darkness of the room. "Is Miss Armstrong sick, sir?" he asked, gesturing toward the figure lying in the shadows on the bed.

"You could say she is rather distraught," yelled Damien directly into his ear, trying to be heard above Emily's frantic screams. "Wouldn't you be?"

The guard retreated a step and covered his ears. "Yes, sir," he yelled back.

Emily began to scream even more piercingly.

"For Christ's sake, can't you quiet that child!" Damien bellowed.

Jo tilted her cloaked head over Emily's wailing form as if trying to comfort her. It helped to hide her face from the guards as she walked into the candlelit hallway.

"It was like this all the way from bloody Camden, and it's going to be like this all the goddamn way back," Damien complained. "I expect to be completely deaf by the time the journey is over. Come on then, let's go. We've wasted enough time here as it is." He stepped aside, letting Jo and Tommy walk ahead of him. "Good night, men," he yelled at the guards.

"Good night, Colonel Powell, sir," they shouted in unison. Their voices were tinged with relief.

Jo made certain Emily continued to screech hysterically as they marched along the elegant hall and down the enormous staircase. The two guards at the base of the stairs fell silent, wincing, as the baby's screams echoed in the hall.

"Didn't you bring something to give her?" Damien complained loudly as they walked through the front door. He gave the soldiers outside a pained look. "Maybe a shot of rum?" He rolled his eyes and sighed dramatically.

The soldiers laughed.

A small carriage pulled by two horses awaited them at the front of the house. The redcoat in the driver's seat hopped down as they approached and opened the door for them.

"Watch your step, Miss Hawkins," Oliver said politely. He winked at Jo as he helped her into the carriage.

Tommy got in beside her, and then Damien climbed in and slammed the door, prompting Emily to shriek with renewed vigor. Damien cast the guards at the front another long-suffering look, which seemed to say he would rather be flayed alive than forced to travel in this damned carriage with this howling child. The guards chuckled as the vehicle lurched into motion and headed down the drive leading from Drayton Hall.

Her heart beating rapidly, Jo clutched Emily tightly against her and began to soothe her with soft hushes. After a moment the little girl quieted. Jo continued to rock her, using the rhythmic movement to help calm herself. Finally, Emily settled into an exhausted sleep, her little cheeks pinkened and wet with tears.

"It worked," Tommy said, elated. "Just like you said it would, Colonel Powell. It actually worked!"

Damien looked at Josephine and smiled. "Most of the soldiers in the British army have never married or had children, and so they are unaccustomed to a baby's cries. I was counting on Emily's screaming to be so painfully annoying, the guards would want nothing more than for us to get the hell away from them."

"Where are we going?" asked Jo.

Damien pushed her hood back slightly, and the pale glow of the carriage lamp spilled across her face. He lightly caressed her cheek with the back of his fingers, still marveling at the realization of her love for him. He had gone from losing everything, to gaining the only thing that truly mattered to him.

Josephine loved him.

And he would never let her go.

"Rest a while, Josephine," he said softly, still stroking her cheek. "Do not worry about anything. Just rest."

Jo sighed and leaned back against the plush seat, holding Emily close. She had no idea where they were headed, how they would get there, or what was going to happen now that Damien had committed this monumental act of treason. If the redcoats found him, he would be hanged. He had sacrificed everything for her. The realization left her shocked and humbled. The carriage rattled swiftly through the darkness, and she closed her eyes, contemplating the enormity of what he had done.

She dozed a while, awakening to find the carriage slowly grinding to a halt.

"What is it?" Damien called to Oliver.

"It's a British officer, sir," Oliver replied. "He's forcin' us to stop."

Damien cursed softly, loaded his pistol, and opened the door to the carriage. "Pull your hood down to cover your face," he instructed Jo. "Both of you stay in here."

The mounted officer had a pistol trained on Oliver. He had already made him toss his musket to the ground, leaving the soldier unarmed.

"Keep your hands on those reins," the officer snapped, waving his pistol menacingly. On seeing Damien, he dismounted and slowly stepped into the soft glow of the carriage lanterns.

"Hello, Nigel," Damien said calmly. "Out for an evening ride?"

"Colonel Powell," Nigel drawled, his voice dripping with contempt. "I should have known you would be unable to stay in Camden once your rebel whore was arrested. Actually, I am just on my way to see her." His thin lips curled in an ugly sneer. "Did you give the little bitch one last screw?"

Damien smiled blandly. "As always, Nigel, your manners when it comes to women are thoroughly charming."

Nigel snorted. "I don't need manners when it comes to rebel sluts. As your little farm whore discovered last night. Or didn't she tell you?" he taunted.

Damien's breath froze in his chest. *Don't listen. He is just trying to goad you into a fight.* His jaw clenched as he fought to restrain his emotions.

Emily began to cry.

Nigel frowned. "Who is with you?"

"Not that it's any of your business, Ferguson," Damien

pointed out, "but if you must know, I am traveling with two members of the camp at Camden. I obtained permission from General Cornwallis for them to say good-bye to Miss Armstrong. We have done so, and are now heading back to Camden. So, if you don't mind—"

Nigel flashed him a malevolent smile. His eyes piercing the darkness, he moved around the carriage to the side on which Jo sat, and regarded her intently. "What's your name?"

Jo kept her head bent forward, so that her hood shadowed her face. "Lily Hawkins," she replied, attempting to disguise her voice.

"And I'm Tommy Brown," offered Tommy cheerfully. He leaned forward to peer out the window, trying to divert Major Ferguson's attention. "Tommy Brown of Lieutenant Colonel Powell's Scarlet Legion, sir. I'm a drummer."

Nigel ignored the boy, his gaze fastened on Josephine. "Rather a warm night for such a heavy cloak, Miss Hawkins?" he remarked softly. "Isn't it?"

Before she could answer, he reached inside and wrenched her hood down. Josephine gasped and tried to pull it back up, but it was too late. Her kerchief had come loose, freeing the pale blond of her hair.

"Well, well," sneered Nigel. "What have we here? Really, Powell, you should know better than to go traipsing about at night with escaped rebel spies." He pointed his pistol directly in Jo's face. "Get out of the carriage."

He swung the door open. Jo descended from the carriage, cradling Emily against her. Tommy followed, stepping protectively in front of her. The top of his head barely reached her shoulders.

"How touching," Nigel drawled. "The boy seems to have turned rebel as well. What he doesn't realize is that I don't mind killing him first. As for you, rebel slut, I don't intend to kill you right away."

"Drop your weapon, Nigel," Damien ordered quietly, "before I blow your goddamn head off."

Nigel laughed. "Really, Powell, do you think I'm a fool? If you come one step closer, I am going to shoot your whore," he assured him, pressing his pistol against Jo's temple. "You know I will, don't you?" He sensed Damien's hesitation and laughed again. "Yes, of course you do. And I will be a hero for doing it. I will have captured the rebel spy, Josephine Armstrong, as she attempted to escape with the traitorous Lieutenant Colonel Powell, fallen hero of the Scarlet Legion. My record will be wiped clean. I will finally be able to get out of Charles Town and back to my favorite sport. Raiding rebel homes. So *you* drop *your* goddamn weapon, Powell," he snarled, "or I'll blow *her* head off here and now."

"Josephine," Damien said calmly, apparently unfazed by Nigel's threat, "other than that night in Charles Town, did Major Ferguson touch you?"

With the cold steel of a pistol pressing hard against her temple, Jo could not understand why Damien cared about something that seemed so irrelevant. "No."

"I see," Damien said thoughtfully.

"Well, you can be damn sure I'm going to have her," Nigel said savagely. "And when I do I'll make certain—"

A shot blasted through the air, cutting short whatever vile details he had been about to share with them. A pulpy splash of scarlet gouged Nigel's forehead. He instantly fell back, dropping his pistol as he went.

"Jesus Christ!" Tommy exclaimed, staring in shock at Nigel's body. He raised his awestruck eyes to Damien. "What a shot!"

"Oh God," whimpered Jo. Emily was screaming once again. Jo tried to soothe her as she stared in horror at Major Ferguson's bleeding body. She was not sorry he was dead. But Damien had committed another act of treason. He had murdered a British officer.

She lifted her eyes to his in despair.

"He would have killed you, Josephine," he told her, sensing her distress. He went to her and put his arms around her and Emily. "He would have raped you, and killed you." He rested his chin on her head a moment and stroked her back, trying to calm her. "Besides," he added with an irreverent shrug, "if I am caught, they can only hang me once."

She gave a tiny, choked laugh, feeling on the verge of hysteria.

"You and Tommy get in the carriage," Damien said. "Oliver and I will move Ferguson's body off the road. It is entirely possible no one knew he was going to Drayton Hall tonight. Therefore he will not be missed until morning."

After a few moments Damien joined them in the carriage, and the vehicle lurched into motion once again. When Emily quieted, Jo looked through the darkness at Damien.

"Why did you ask if Nigel had touched me?" she asked softly.

He hesitated a moment before answering. "Because if he had," he finally replied, his voice taut, "I would have made him suffer before he died."

She absorbed this for a moment. And then she said, "You can never go back to England now, can you?"

"No. I cannot."

She thought she heard a trace of bitterness in his voice, and it ripped into her heart. "But your brother is an earl," she pointed out. She knew she was terribly ignorant in these matters, but perhaps his brother could use his influence to help Damien. "Surely he could—"

"My brother is dead," Damien interrupted. "I am the Earl of Strathmore now. But treason is treason, Josephine. I cannot go back."

Because of her, she realized, the thought flooding her with misery. If not for her, Damien would have returned to England a respected officer and hero. He would have been an earl, with a magnificent home, and servants, and wealth. Perhaps he could have even gone back to Victoria. He could have had everything he ever wanted. But now he was disgraced and ruined. A traitor to his country. Stripped of everything.

She had destroyed him. And her love for him would never be enough to compensate for all that he had lost.

Chapter 20

It was deep into the night when Jo finally opened her eyes.

The carriage had stopped. Emily was safely tucked onto the seat across from her, sleeping peacefully. Joe felt her to make sure she was neither too cool nor too warm, adjusted her blanket, and then left the carriage to see where Damien, Tommy, and Oliver had gone. She found them standing at the side of the road, talking in low, serious voices with two other men. The distance was too great for her to see their faces, but there was no mistaking the scarlet and white of their coats and breeches.

Fear ignited within her.

"Good evening, Caroline!" called a cheerful voice. "Or may I call you Josephine now?"

"Gil!" she exclaimed, her fear melting into relief.

She picked up her skirts and hurried toward the little group. By the faint wash of moonlight she made out the faces of Gil and Charlie, who were standing with Damien, Tommy, and Oliver.

"We thought we'd come and see you off," Gil explained

brightly, as if the fact that Damien and Jo were fleeing the British army was nothing more than a grand adventure.

"I asked them to meet us here with a cart and supplies," Damien told her. "And that ornery old goat," he added with a sigh.

Down the road was a simple farm cart, pulled by two horses, one of which was Liberty. Emily's goat was standing in the back of the cart, casually gnawing on the wooden side boards.

"There are new clothes for both of you," Gil said as he walked over to the cart and rooted through the bags in the back. "Nothing fancy, mind you, just good, plain farmer's wear. There is also a tent, blankets, food, water, a musket and shot, and a few other things I thought might come in handy. Oh, yes," he continued as an afterthought, "I also suspected you might want this." He reached into one of the bags and pulled out a furry form, which let out a meow of protest at having been wakened.

"Ashley!"

Gil deposited the sleepy kitten in Jo's arms. "There now. I think that's just about everything." He reached into his coat pocket and withdrew a thick envelope which he gave to Damien. "Here is some money to get you started. Once you have settled somewhere, you can send word to me, either through my solicitor in Charles Town or in London. They are very discreet, but use another name anyway, just to be safe. I have forwarded your letter to London. As soon as the sale of Waverley and its contents is completed, you can let me know how much you need and where to send it. The rest I will keep invested, as we discussed."

Jo lifted her brows, confused. "What is Waverley?"

"Damien's ancestral home," Gil said.

A feeling of loss swept through her. Damien was selling his home and everything in it. She could not bear the thought. She turned to look at him, her chest tight with despair. "How long has it been in your family?"

"The original house was built nearly four hundred years ago," Damien answered.

She was silent as she contemplated this. Four hundred

years. Her own home had been nothing more than a simple farmhouse, which had been in her family barely twenty-five years. Yet she had been devastated when it was taken from her. She could not imagine the pain of giving up a majestic home that had been in his family for generations.

"No," she said, her voice trembling but adamant. "You cannot do that, Damien. You must not sell your home."

He regarded her steadily. "Why?"

Because you will hate me if you do. Because you will always blame me for the loss of the thing you loved the most. And I cannot bear to have you hate me. "You cannot," she repeated, swallowing the tears choking the back of her throat.

"Would you men excuse us?" said Damien quietly, never taking his eyes off Josephine.

Tommy and the men moved silently away, leaving the two of them alone at the side of the road.

"What is troubling you, Josephine?" Damien demanded, his voice soft.

"I—I do not want you to sell your home."

"I understand that. The questions is, why?" A startling thought occurred to him. "Were you thinking you might like to live there?"

"No," she hastily assured him.

She looked away, down the road at the rough-hewn cart and Emily's goat. Gil had brought him farmer's clothes to wear, she thought miserably. Farmer's wear, for the handsome, elegant, always immaculate Lieutenant Colonel Damien Powell. Who should have been the Earl of Strathmore, living amidst luxury and grandeur in an ancestral home across the sea called Waverley.

"Because you will hate me," she whispered. Tears began to leak from her eyes. "You have lost everything because of me. To become what?" A wretched, bitter laugh escaped the back of her throat. "A poor farmer in America? Married to a farm girl who was born to a convicted murderer and a bonded servant?" Her tears were flowing faster now. "Maybe you won't hate me tomorrow, or next year. But one day you will. And I won't be able to bear it." She was drowning in tears, rendering the words nearly incomprehensible.

Damien gently took her hand, turned it over, and kissed her palm. Then he lifted it to his chest and pressed it firmly against his heart.

"You are wrong, Josephine. You think I have lost everything, that somehow you have taken it all away. You *gave* me everything," he said fiercely. "I had nothing before I met you. Nothing but anger and bitterness and guilt. And the need to punish myself for the sins of my past. I was fighting a war for no reason other than to escape. I didn't give a damn about England's cause, or America's cause. I didn't give a damn about anything." He caressed her glistening cheek. "I love you," he stated tenderly. "And I would gladly give up everything in the world for the privilege of loving you, and holding you in my arms each night, and waking to see your beautiful face every morning. Do you hear me?"

She wept helplessly and shook her head. But she allowed him to draw her closer, her hand still pressed against his heart. His arms closed protectively around her.

"I swear to you, Josephine, that I will spend every minute of the rest of my life showering you and Emily with love. I don't give a damn if we are rich or poor. I don't give a damn where we live. I don't give a damn whether your parents were convicted murderers or heirs to the bloody throne. And I *certainly* don't give a damn whether I am called an earl or a farmer."

Jo continued to weep noisily against him, whether from happiness or misery she was no longer certain.

"Besides," he continued as he soothingly stroked her back, "who says we are going to be poor?" His voice was faintly teasing.

She lifted her head and hiccoughed.

"At the risk of sounding insulted, I would like to point out that I am not entirely without money or ability. Otherwise, what kind of husband would I make?" He pulled a handkerchief from his coat pocket and began to dry her tears. "And I believe America has a brilliant future ahead, Josephine," he continued, his tone more serious. "The rebels are going to win this war. And when they do, the potential rewards for those who are willing to take risks and work hard to help build this country are going to be enormous." He kissed the top of her head and pressed the handkerchief into her hand. "Now blow your nose and change into the clothes Gil has brought for you. We still have a long way to go."

She blew her nose into the snowy linen square and lifted her eyes to his. "Where are we going?"

"For the moment we will head southwest, out of South Carolina and away from the arena of fighting. For us, the war is over, Josephine," he told her firmly. "All I want is to find a place where we can live in peace. But I know how much you love your family. So when the war is over, we will return to South Carolina and make our home here. Would you like that?"

She wrapped her arms around his neck and kissed him fiercely. "Yes," she breathed after a moment. "Yes."

He looked down at her and smiled. "Good. Now go and change."

Feeling a guarded measure of joy, she went to the cart and began to search through the bags. Gil had packed four plain but serviceable dresses for her, as well as a finer gown, evidently thinking she might have occasion to wear it. There was also an ample supply of petticoats, chemises, and stockings, as well as a pair of sturdy shoes and a pair of leather boots. Jo selected a modest gown of deep green muslin, and disappeared into the woods to change.

When she reappeared Damien had also changed. Gone forever was the elegant scarlet and white uniform with its shiny gold buttons and braided epaulettes. He now wore a common outfit of dark breeches and a loose-fitting white cotton shirt, which he had rolled up at the sleeves, exposing the tanned skin of his thickly muscled forearms. Despite the simplicity of his new clothes, he still exuded a commanding air of barely leashed masculine power.

Tommy hesitantly walked toward them. There was an uncertainty to his expression, shadowed with regret.

"What's wrong, Tommy?" asked Jo.

He shrugged. Then he became preoccupied with drawing a line in the dirt with the toe of his boot. "I was just wonderin'," he began offhandedly, "if you were sure you could handle that goat on your own. I mean, seein' as how you already have Emily to look after and everything."

She opened her mouth to assure him she would have no problems with the goat whatsoever. And then she snapped it shut. Tommy had no home other than the army, and a young boy with one hand was hardly considered a valuable military asset. When the war was over, where would he go? Back to stealing on the streets of London? Who would give him the care and guidance he needed, so he could leave his scarred youth behind and become the fine, honorable, self-supporting man she knew he could be?

She raised her eyes questioningly to Damien.

He nodded.

She gave him a radiant smile. Damien found himself smiling as well. In the midst of a war, with both of them running from the British army, she had just taken on the responsibility of another child. But Josephine did not see it as a burden, he realized. She saw it as a gift.

"There is something I would like to ask you. Tommy," she began. "I realize you had your heart set on a life in the army. But I was wondering if you might consider coming with me and Colonel Powell. We could really use your help," she assured him.

Tommy stopped digging his boot in the dirt and looked up. "You could?"

"That miserable old goat absolutely hates me," Damien muttered in exasperation. "I would appreciate it if you would come along and look after her. And when we find a place to live, it's going to take a lot of work to get a farm going. With three of us, we will be able to get settled much faster."

Tommy frowned. "You mean I could live with you?" He seemed awed by the thought.

"Well, of course," Jo replied swiftly. "We would be a family."

Tommy dropped his gaze to the ground, intently studying the lines he had drawn with his boot. And then he rubbed his fist in his eye, as if he had something in it.

"Well," he said after a long moment, "since you need my help so much, I guess I could go along."

Relief flowed through her. "Thank you. Now go into the bags on the cart and see if you can find something to wear other than that uniform."

"I think you had best get moving," Gil said. "There are only a few more hours of darkness, and you want to put as much distance between you and General Cornwallis's men as possible."

"I'll just fetch Emily," Jo said, moving toward the carriage.

Damien grasped Gil by the shoulders. "My friend," he began, his voice taut with emotion, "I have so much to thank you for, I hardly know where to begin."

"Begin by being happy, Damien," Gil replied quietly. His expression brightened. "And then, make your new home enormous and utterly grand, on a lovely piece of property where I can come for long, lazy visits. You know, I find myself becoming increasingly attached to this country. I may well decide to stay here myself. Perhaps I will even buy some land near yours." He turned and winked at Jo as she approached. Then he scooped up Ashley and handed him to Tommy, now changed into oversized breeches and an enormous shirt.

"Safe journey, Josephine," Oliver said. He hugged her.

"Thank you, Oliver. You will look after Lily, won't you?" He gave her a shy grin. "If she'll have me."

"If you need anythin', you just send word," instructed Charlie.

"Thank you, Charlie. Wherever we are, you will all be welcome."

Damien helped Jo to her seat, handed Emily to her, then climbed up beside her. Tommy scrambled into the back. Damien paused to give one last nod to Gil, Charlie, and Oliver.

And then he snapped the reins and set the rugged little cart in motion.

• • •

Golden threads of early morning light were sifting through the leafy canopy of trees above them. A small stream bubbled ahead, beckoning with the promise of clean, cold water.

Josephine grabbed Damien's arm.

He pulled on the reins and looked at her in confusion. Her skin was milky pale, and a look of utter panic had taken hold of her face.

"What's the matter, Josephine?" he demanded. "Are you—"

She thrust Emily into his arms and bolted from the cart, holding her hand to her mouth. She disappeared as far as she could into the woods before falling to her knees and retching on the soft carpet of pine needles. For several long moments she knelt there. Then, gradually, her nausea passed, leaving her weakened but feeling considerably better.

She rose and went to the stream to splash cool water on her face and rinse her mouth. What on earth was the matter with her? she wondered miserably. For days now she had been suffering this mysterious illness. At first she had thought it was nerves. Then she had suspected sickness, contracted from one of the ill soldiers at Camden. But when she wasn't nauseated, she felt perfectly well, which made no sense at all. It reminded her of Anne and her mother, she thought vaguely as she scooped up a handful of water, when they were in the early months of pregnancy.

Her hand froze, allowing the cold water to drain through her fingers.

Of course, she thought, astounded. *I am going to have a baby.*

A honey-sweet warmth poured through her veins. A tiny life was growing inside her. A child. Hers and Damien's. But she didn't want to tell anyone. She would wait until they were far away from General Cornwallis's soldiers, until they were safe. And then she would tell them.

She splashed water on her face once more, and raked her fingers through her hair, which had fallen from its pins and was spilling loosely over her shoulders. Then she brushed the leaves and pine needles from her gown and hurried back toward the cart, humming softly.

"I'm all right," she called cheerfully as she moved through the trees. "I just—"

"Good morning, Miss Armstrong," called out a familiar voice. "Come and join us."

No, she thought, her joy disintegrating beneath an onslaught of fear. *Please, God, no.*

She burst from the woods to see Damien standing on the ground, facing Captain Lee, who was mounted on his horse with his musket pointed directly at him. Damien in turn had his pistol aimed with deadly determination at Captain Lee. Neither man showed the slightest intention of dropping his weapon. Tommy was seated in the cart, protectively holding Emily.

"Captain Lee," Jo said, her mind racing.

"Miss Armstrong." He gave her a sardonic tilt of his gray head. "I heard through the rebel network that you failed in your mission, and had been arrested in Charles Town. And yet," he observed aridly, "it seems you have miraculously escaped."

"He was sacrificing you, Josephine," Damien told her, his apparent calm masking a savage fury. "He sent you into that camp on a lethal mission, knowing full well that even if you succeeded in killing Cornwallis, you would never be able to escape."

"Your escape was not necessary," Jackson admitted. "Whether you killed Cornwallis or not, the arrest and trial of a beautiful Patriot woman would inspire and enrage rebels throughout the country, particularly if you were hanged. Since our defeat at Camden, the rebels have lost faith in their ability to beat these redcoat bastards. Men are deserting, or refusing to join the fight. We needed something to inflame our determination. Of course," he continued, his voice heavy with contempt, "the arrest of Colonel Powell's whore had the added benefit of condemning the illustrious leader of the Scarlet Legion as a traitor as well. I thought that a fitting payment for all the trouble he has caused me." His gaze narrowed on Damien. "I told you before, I don't take kindly to my prisoners escaping."

Jo stared at him, dumbfounded. "You didn't care whether I killed General Cornwallis or not?"

"It would have pleased me if you had," Jackson said. "But the most important thing was that you be arrested and hanged. You would have been a martyr to the rebel cause, which would have aroused the hatred and determination of Americans across the country."

Jo felt something within her shrivel and die. She had trusted Captain Lee as a fellow rebel, a selfless Patriot hero who believed in the freedom of their country and would help her do what she could to fight for that freedom. Instead he had used her. Used her, and betrayed her.

"You told me you would have men at Lynches Creek waiting to help me escape," she reminded him bitterly. "You lied."

"And from the moment we met you have lied to me, Miss Armstrong," Jackson replied. "You neglected to mention you were nursing a redcoat in your barn. You seemed to forget that you joined up with Colonel Powell in Charles Town, and helped him escape your rebel contacts there, resulting in their arrest. Oh, yes," he drawled, "and when I asked if you had seen Colonel Powell in the army camp at Camden, you assured me you had not, when in fact you were openly living with him as his whore. You don't seem to be able to make up your mind which side of this war you are on, Miss Armstrong. And we rebels have no sympathy for traitors."

"I am *not* a traitor," Jo cried. "I spied for you in Charles Town and in Camden. I followed your orders and tried to assassinate General Cornwallis. I risked myself again and again for the rebel cause. I admit I nursed Colonel Powell in my barn instead of letting him die. I also refused to stand by and watch him be murdered in that warehouse. And I didn't tell you I was sharing his tent because I knew you would condemn me for it. But no matter what happened between Colonel Powell and me, I *never* stopped fighting for my country."

"She is telling you the truth," Damien said, his pistol still trained on Captain Lee. "Regardless of how much you despise me, you cannot accuse Josephine of betraying her country. She continuously put herself in jeopardy in her fight for liberty. Why else do you think she followed Cornwallis to Charles Town and tried to lodge a dagger in his back?"

Jackson contemplated this a moment. "It doesn't matter," he finally growled. "You are all under arrest. A court can decide whether or not she hangs for her crimes. As for you, Colonel," he added, a satisfied smile curving his mouth, "I believe your lack of a uniform has already decided your fate."

He was right, Jo realized, her heart wrenching. Damien had once told her he could never be arrested without his uniform, because he would immediately be convicted of spying. Captured in plain farmer's clothes, the rebels would certainly execute him.

Because of her.

"Captain Lee," she began, her voice imploring, "I beg you to let us go. You know the fact that Colonel Powell doesn't wear his uniform does not mean he is a spy. He has risked everything to save me. By doing so he has become a traitor to the British army. He is no longer the commander of the Scarlet Legion, and he was not responsible for the atrocities of which you accused him. The war is over for us. If you have any compassion in your heart, I beg you to let us go."

Emily began to cry.

"It's all right, Emily," Tommy murmured, shifting her onto his shoulder.

Jackson frowned. "Who are those children?"

"They are part of my family now," Jo answered. "And we are going to raise them as our own. As Americans. Do you plan to arrest them as well?"

He was silent for a long, strained moment. And then he shook his head. "I have no choice, Miss Armstrong." His tone was gruff, but the words were shaded with regret. "It is my duty to arrest all of you. An army court will decide what is to happen to you." He adjusted his grip on his musket. "Drop your weapon, Colonel Powell."

Damien realized he was going to have to kill him. Strangely enough, he disliked the thought. But he could not permit any harm to come to Josephine, and Captain Lee was determined to have her tried as a traitor. She would be executed by the very people she had fought so hard to protect. Executed or imprisoned. Either way, they would destroy her.

He could not allow that to happen.

"I won't let you arrest us, Lee." He raised his pistol.

"No, Damien!" Jo cried. She knew he would do it. The swiftness with which he had shot Nigel Ferguson left no doubt he would do the same to Captain Lee if necessary. Damien would blast a gaping hole in his forehead before Captain Lee had time to squeeze the trigger of his musket. "You must not kill him."

Damien's gaze remained locked on the man who stood between freedom and death. "Why?"

"There has been enough killing," she told him desperately. Tears sprang to her eyes. "I have seen enough death these past months to haunt me for a lifetime. Death, and suffering, and hatred. We cannot begin our new life together by killing a man who is fighting for the same things I believe in." Her throat constricted with emotion as she finished in a tiny, fragile whisper, "We cannot."

She was right, Damien realized in frustration. Captain Lee was merely a man who was trying to do his duty. He was honoring his obligation to his country by arresting those he deemed to be a threat. But he and Josephine were not a threat. This wild, untamed land was his new home, and he would never do anything to harm it again.

And that included killing a man who was fighting for his new country's freedom.

He sighed and slowly lowered his pistol.

"I will not shoot you, Lee," he told him. "But I won't go with you either. So you can kill me and be done with it, or lower your musket and let me and my family continue on our way."

Jackson looked at him in astonishment. "What are you

talking about? You're all under arrest." He menacingly adjusted his aim. "Now throw your pistol on the ground."

Damien regarded him calmly as he shoved his weapon into the waistband of his breeches. "I have given you your choice, Captain. Which is it to be?"

"I'm not afraid to kill you, Powell."

"I am sure you are not. But sometimes it takes far more courage to let a man live, than it does to squeeze a trigger and snuff out his life like the flame of a candle."

Jo watched in terrified anticipation as a myriad of emotions played over Captain Lee's face. It was clear he was struggling with his profound sense of duty. Once he would have had no trouble making his decision. He would have shot Damien dead without a moment's hesitation.

As Damien once would have shot him.

Captain Lee kept his musket trained on Damien. Damien steadily returned his gaze. Emily's cries pierced the still morning air, unaffected by Tommy's attempts to soothe her. Jo's heart pounded against the wall of her chest.

Please, God, please don't let Damien die. I can bear almost anything. But I could not bear losing him. Please.

For an endless moment, no one moved.

And then, slowly, Captain Lee lowered his musket.

Chapter 21

Jo leaned over the wooden side of the cart and stared down in wonderment at Emily's perfect little sleeping face, thinking of the tiny new person sleeping deep inside her. It was far too soon for her to feel anything, yet she was very aware of the precious life she sheltered. She smiled and glanced across the cart at Tommy. He was lying with his injured arm flung casually across his chest, sleeping peacefully, with Ashley curled up in a striped ball beside him.

Her little family was safe.

After they had stopped for the night, Tommy had worked tirelessly alongside Damien, helping to set up the camp. Not once had the boy protested he could not do something because he only had one hand. If anything, he seemed eager to prove to both Damien and Jo that there wasn't anything he couldn't do. Tomorrow night she would set aside some time after they stopped to continue with his lessons. Mastering reading, writing, and arithmetic was going to be just as important as mastering physical tasks, she decided. By the time Tommy had grown to manhood, he would be secure in the knowledge that he could do anything he chose to put his mind to. She and Damien would make certain each of their children faced the world with that vital, empowering gift.

She adjusted Emily's blanket a final time, then moved across the warm darkness to Damien. He was seated on the ground a few yards away from the wagon, staring up at the glittering ocean of black.

"Do they have skies like this in England?" she asked softly.

He pulled his gaze down to look at her. "None that I ever noticed."

She knelt down beside him and regarded the sky in silence a moment. And then she hesitantly whispered, "You're certain you can never go back?"

"I'm certain." His voice was strangely void of emotion.

She thought again of how he had given up everything so she could live. Everything. And in this hushed, starlit moment, as they sat on the brink of their new life together, she wanted to give him something in return.

"There is something I wish to tell you."

She cleared her throat, feeling all at once shy and uncertain.

Damien reached out and took her hand in his. "Let me say this first. Nothing I have given up can compare to the wonder of sharing my life with you." He regarded her intently, then pulled her closer so he could wrap his arms around her. "I have betrayed my army, my king, and my country, and for that I will always be condemned a traitor," he stated, his chin resting on top of her head. "But I stayed true to my integrity and my soul. And ultimately that is far more important than oaths of loyalty or a blind sense of duty."

"I know," said Josephine quietly. She placed her cheek against his chest, and was soothed by the strong, steady beat of his heart pulsing against her. "I felt the same way when I nursed you in my barn and tried to hide you from Captain Lee. It was something I had to do."

"Just staring at this magnificent sky," Damien said, "and

knowing we have long years of happiness ahead, gives me the most wonderful sense of fulfillment I have ever known. We will build our own home, Josephine, and it will be as simple or as spectacular as we choose to make it. Although," he mused with a grin, "Gil has made it clear he is expecting something rather lavish."

Jo laughed softly.

"So do not torture yourself with thoughts of what you believe I have given up," he continued, his voice rough with tenderness. "America is my new home, with all its wild beauty, its dauntless spirit, and its radiant future. Our children will grow up free. And given the love I intend to shower upon each of them, I have no doubt they will make us proud."

His mouth captured hers with fierce possessiveness, sweeping away her fears and uncertainty. She sighed and kissed him deeply, feeling his love pour over her in liquid flames. Her hands threaded into the black length of his hair as she pulled him down, until she lay against the sweet-scented grass and he was stretched over her, his powerful, masculine form etched in starlight.

"You are right," she said breathlessly as his lips left hers to hungrily kiss her cheeks, her eyes, her throat. His fingers began to release the fastenings of her gown, his mouth kissing her inch by heated inch as the green fabric unveiled the transparent linen of her chemise. He pushed the pale linen down and caressed her breast with gentle reverence before lowering his lips to the aching peak. A hot surge of pleasure raced through her as she whispered, "All three will make us proud."

Damien lifted his head, his eyes questioning.

She gave him a shy smile. "In the spring," she murmured softly.

A wash of pleasure lit his face, as brilliantly as if the sun had suddenly burst through the silver-black curtain of night.

"Dear God," he breathed, his emotions rendering him incapable of any other speech.

A child. He and Josephine were going to have a child. A little girl, with hair the color of wheat, like her mother. Or perhaps a boy, who would tag along after him and Tommy, driving him mad with endless questions. Another child. Part rebel, part redcoat. A helpless, wobbly grin spread across his face. His new family, it seemed, was growing by the hour. He raised himself up over Josephine and laughed.

"I love you, Josephine Armstrong," he stated tenderly. He gently stroked her sun-kissed cheek with the back of his fingers. "And this marvelous piece of news has made me realize two things."

Jo wrapped her arms around his neck. "Which are?"

"First of all, we must find someone to marry us," he announced. "Tomorrow, if possible."

She smiled and began to run her hands possessively across the taut muscles of his back. "And the other?"

"The other," he murmured, his lips grazing her cheek, "is that we had better build an enormous home with lots of bedrooms."

"Why?"

"Because, my little rebel," he whispered, lowering his lips to hers, "I have a feeling we're going to need them."

He kissed her deeply. They laughed again, their happiness spilling through the silvery darkness in waves of glorious light.

Author's Note

The city of Charleston was originally called Charles Towne when it was first settled in 1670. By the 1680's, "Charles Town" had become the most popular spelling. When the British army finally left Charles Town at the end of the American Revolution in 1783, the city was incorporated as the City of Charleston.

The events described in this book surrounding the Battle of Camden are historically accurate. However, I have taken a small liberty concerning the movements of General Cornwallis by sending him back to Charles Town for a brief period in early September. In fact, General Cornwallis remained at Camden, where he prepared his troops for their march into North Carolina, which began on September 8, 1780.

About the Author

Karyn Monk has been writing since she was a girl. In university she discovered a love for history. After several years working in the highly charged world of advertising, she turned to writing historical romance. She is married to a wonderfully romantic husband, Philip, whom she allows to believe is the model for her heroes.

DON'T MISS THESE FABULOUS
BANTAM WOMEN'S FICTION TITLES

On Sale in May

From Jane Feather, nationally bestselling author of
Violet *and* Vanity, *comes a sinful new romance*

VICE

Juliana drew the line at becoming a harlot. After all, she had already begun the week as a bride, and ended it as a murderess. But now she's at the mercy of a powerful, handsome Duke . . . and in no position to bargain.   ___57249-0 $5.99/$7.99 in Canada

THE ENGAGEMENT
by beguiling bestseller Suzanne Robinson

An enticing Victorian tale of passion and intrigue that pits the daughter of a duke against a handsome stranger—a man who's part cowboy, part hero, and part thief . . . but altogether irresistible.   ___56346-7 $5.50/$7.50

NIGHT MOVES
by award-winning Sandra Canfield
"A master storyteller of stunning intensity." —Romantic Times

With a spellbinding mixture of passion and suspense, past lovers struggle to find a daughter who has been kidnapped . . . and the courage to reclaim love.   ___57433-7 $5.99/$7.99

SWEET LOVE, SURVIVE
by Susan Johnson
"A queen of erotic romance." —Romantic Times

In this powerful finale to the bestselling Kuzan Dynasty series begun in *Seized by Love* and *Love Storm*, a man and a woman find themselves in a desperate and passionate liaison, while the fires of a nation in revolution burn around them.   ___56329-7 $5.99/$7.99

Ask for these books at your local bookstore or use this page to order.

Please send me the books I have checked above. I am enclosing $____ (add $2.50 to cover postage and handling). Send check or money order, no cash or C.O.D.'s, please.

Name _____

Address _____

City/State/Zip _____

Send order to: Bantam Books, Dept. FN159, 2451 S. Wolf Rd., Des Plaines, IL 60018
Allow four to six weeks for delivery.

Prices and availability subject to change without notice.   FN 159 5/96

If you loved THE REBEL AND THE REDCOAT,
don't miss Karyn Monk's
sensuous and enthralling debut

SURRENDER TO A STRANGER

When a stranger risks everything to rescue
a proud beauty, she owes him her life,
her heart . . . and her soul.

Sentenced to death, Jacqueline never expected to be rescued from her filthy cell by an unlikely visitor—a man whose disguise hid a devastatingly handsome British agent. Now the two were on the run—and for as long as he was there to protect her, she felt strangely safe . . .

They called him the Black Prince, and to save the unjustly condemned he took hair-raising risks, slipping in and out of courtrooms and prisons, brazenly defying the threat of capture and death. The reckless spy tried to tell himself that Jacqueline was just another prisoner to be spirited away to safety. Yet there was something about her fierce dignity, her unrelenting sense of honor, her unbreakable spirit that made him never want to let her go . . .   ___57421-3 $5.99/$7.99 in Canada

"What a riveting and passionate story! Karyn Monk is
a remarkable new voice in historical romance."
—National bestseller Jane Feather